CHILDREN *of* PAPER

CHILDREN *of* PAPER

MARTHA BLUM

COTEAU BOOKS
WWW.COTEAUBOOKS.COM

© Martha Blum, 2002. First US edition, 2003.

Edited by Geoffrey Ursell.
Cover and book design by Duncan Campbell.
Cover photo, "Groupe d'enfants dans le quartier juif, 1900," by Roger Viollet.
Getty One images/Halston archives.
Author photo by Hans Dommasch.
Printed and bound in Canada at Marc Veilleux Imprimeur Inc.

National Library of Canada Cataloguing in Publication

Blum, Martha, 1913-
Children of paper / Martha Blum.

ISBN 1-55050-208-5

I. TITLE.
PS8553.L858C44 2002   C813'.54   C2002-911209-5
PR9199.3.B5566C44 2002

1   2   3   4   5   6   7   8   9   10

COTEAU BOOKS

401-2206 Dewdney Ave.
Regina, Saskatchewan
Canada   S4R 1H3

available in the US from:
Fitzhenry and Whiteside
195 Allstate Parkway
Markham, Ontario
Canada   L3R 4T8

The publisher gratefully acknowledges the financial assistance of the Saskatchewan Arts Board, the Canada Council for the Arts, the Government of Canada through the Book Publishing Industry Development Program (BPIDP), the Government of Saskatchewan, through the Cultural Industries Development Fund, and the City of Regina Arts Commission, for its publishing program.

To Irene.

And to the memory of the Patriarch Selig,
and his three sons, Harry, Abraham, and Solomon.

All streams flow into the sea
Yet the sea is never full
— ECCLESIASTES 1:7

TABLE OF CONTENTS

Song Out of Air

Fools in Suczorno. All living from what the good Lord gives us for free. The clearest, most delicious air to breathe.

Bimbule, no ordinary fool, is much cleverer than all the other fools who make a living from *Luft* – meaning air. And luckier.

Imagine a town of *Luftmenschen* – men living off air. What else is there? No industry, no property, no piece of land, no title to any in all of Suczorno. A title to land is exceedingly funny. Who can own a title? And what is one to do with it? One can't eat it when one is hungry, can one?

Fortunately, Suczorno has an abundance of fools. No jesters to a king, of whom they have heard in distant lands; no magicians, who cut ladies in two and put them together again; no clowns for children, with red apples on noses; no jugglers, catching as well as throwing ten balls at the same time; no fire-eaters, sword-swallowers, or any such market entertainment. No, this is Suczorno, where people have their own home-grown *narrishers*, who pull magic out of air, as they do for their sustenance, all of it, body and soul.

Yes, there is a tsar in Moscovy, but may the Lord save us from his justice.

A piece of bread is hard to come by, but somehow, come Friday night, there is even a carp with carrots and greens, cooked, centre table, and a glass of wine for the blessing. Well, the Lord cannot – as we all know – do without a braided *Challah* bread white as snow, a glass of wine, red as a dark rose for the *Kiddush*. And it seems that He – blessed be His name and may we never take that Name in vain – has to have His carp. And not just any fish.

So He provides for our Friday night dinner, with some left over for the Shabbat. Well, He has to provide, so we'll sing to Him. He knows very well that when all the fools of Suczorno are hungry, the most they can do is tell the wildest stories. But sing they cannot – song and praise being one and the same thing.

And the story goes that without the carp, the wine, and the white, braided, beautiful *Challah* on Friday night, set on a piece of starched linen, no Jew, fool or wise man, would be alive in Suczorno. And it just may be true. Who knows?

Because the rest of the week does not matter: one deals, one works, one goes to the next village, one scratches the ground or maybe puts a seed in it, which grows or does not grow, or is picked by the hens – not geese. Sorry, no geese. They're for the rich in the next village, or the rich in Lemberg.

Fed and gorged on corn pressed down their long unhappy throats, poor things, geese have a suffering life to feed man's appetite for liver: rich, fat, goose liver. A commerce, so to speak, in Suczorno; for the women only. No man would be caught doing it, they are above goose liver; not above eating it. Let's say they are above the commerce and the stuffing of the lovely long-suffering goose.

But not getting it either. How would a poor Jew get goose liver, when one needed to sell it? Not to become a millionaire, mind you, or buy silk blouses for their wives. But just to get the pennies, the little cash for salt and matches – a monopoly of the state – to be purchased for money only. No barter and no promises to bring a goose liver tomorrow.

Oh, yes, for heating oil also. Well, not heating really, who could think of that? Just lighting of the lamps, kerosene maybe, or a bit of petroleum.

So, of course, to lift one's soul there is prayer, but one cannot pray all the time.

So Suczorno is lucky, exceedingly lucky for having an array of fools to be proud of. There is no other town like it: breathing the air they're made of, and catching whatever that *Luft* has to offer.

As I said, Suczorno is lucky: they have the most ingenious catchers, trappers, inhalers of past and future demons, *dybbuks,* fanciful spirits, ghosts invented as if real. A *Luft* so rich in stories that, if not fed by bread and chicken fat, the breathing alone will keep you alive.

Well, bread and chicken fat, with garlic rubbed into it or a slice of onion on top – who could ask for more? This is what one dreams about; but if not that, a dish of buckwheat cooked and not burned will do, with or without the goat's milk. Cows are very rare, unfortunately. We tend them for the rich so they can have rice with real milk – oh, let's not talk about it, because envy makes the bile spill over and then everything is bitter. Even sweet talk tastes bitter and you quarrel with your wife and, God forbid! with the Almighty.

And He – blessed be He – does not seem to favour harangues, tirades of envy and hate; what He wants is praise. He wants adulation and song. He loves us to sing in Suczorno.

But it's hard to sing on burnt kasha – burnt because either the kindling is too wet to burn well, and then of course the kasha is raw, or, when the fire is going well, then it becomes a roaring flame, which is too hot for kasha.

You see, the poor do not have it easy. But the good Lord does not like complaining. He likes praise and song, He loves the beautiful sound of David's psalms.

What are we poor fools to do?

So we catch stories out of that Suczorno air, wild or funny. And sometimes we earn a few rubles, carrying wood or splitting it. Not so easy either. Because *Luftmenschen* have not exercised their bodies, so they find the splitting or any wielding of an axe exceedingly hard. But what will a man not do, when Friday night is close and he has no candles for his wife's table? I am asking you!

Oh yes, let me not forget our clever fool, called Bimbule, the one I mentioned in the beginning. Why would you imagine Bimbule to be cleverer than the rest of us *schnorrers?* It is because of the way he "bribes" the Almighty. Well, how can one outdo the all-seeing, all-knowing essence of life? Oh dear, *bribe* is truly too harsh a term. Let's say Bimbule knows his master and he knows, like all servants – and aren't we just that? – his master's strengths.

But, am I to say – may no misfortune befall my people – or may I be allowed to say, that he knows his master's weaknesses also? Well, he does. Bimbule knows God's weaknesses – may He forgive me! – and because he has this intimate, close friendship, we could almost call it love, he can talk to God and call Him to task.

So Bimbule would – on the day when all of Suczorno was pillaged and some poor huts put to the torch at Easter time, when the peasants called all our pious men Christ killers, and when our blood ran in the gutter between the wooden sidewalks – Bimbule would raise his voice to Him like a prophet of old and cry out: "You have let us down! We serve you with the last of our strength! And where is the King of the Universe, where is Your outstretched arm to hold over your people? Where is it?" And God would be silent, as He had not spoken since Job.

Yet when Easter was over, men and women would become human again, forgetting their Easter-fury. And when we had started rebuilding our houses from scratch, then the cleverest of all fools, our Bimbule, would extend his "bribe" – oh, let's call it that and not be so frightened always! – yes, Bimbule would sing to Him, and not just the *Smiroth* – biblical songs of praise, or the *Shirhashirim* – the Solomonic songs of songs. Bimbule would sing with a voice of heralds of His greatness, that He the Just and Gracious master had "chosen" Suczorno and his people to be rescued, elevated from the multitude "chosen" to prosper and live.

That's his bribe. A beautiful story or song out of air about the right to wake to another day to find nourishment for soul and body, by thinking of Him. And this alone can be sufficient: the sharing in His greatness, *almost* as partners.

I have to say *almost,* because after the pogrom, we have to sit *Shivah* and say *Kaddish.* But at least He has given us one to say. Taught us. Could you imagine the emptiness of soul, had we not the gift of the divine word? This a Jew cannot imagine. Worse than death.

And that is the way we live in Suczorno. In a strange partnership. It limps a little in our disfavour. But just imagine us without it!

SECTION ONE

ELIJAH'S MANTLE

Sarah

"OPEN THE DOOR, MY CHILD, ELIJAH WAITS OUTSIDE TO partake in our Passover celebrations. He is anxious to be with you, my beloved children."

The moment has come. We have been told He is at every door. We have looked. We have looked before the reading starts, have run out in between to check. No sign of the prophet. But when my father stops, takes breath, and says, "Open the door, my child —" I am out there. The youngest of five, I have asked the famous four questions to get an evening worth of answers in Hebrew. Carried by the familiar sung words, whose meaning is in the tune, I half listen, but stung by the "Open the door" – I am out there.

As the door flings open, I hold it for Him, and for the break of a second I feel the air move, a cool breeze touch my cheek as He fleetingly passes me. I go fast, following in His footsteps, careful not to step on His moving cloak. Small as I am, I nearly touch it when He bends over the Passover table to lift the ceremonial glass prepared for Him. I see Him take a sip of the red wine, then He turns, His right hand resting on my head before He vanishes.

All the children rush to look at His wine glass. To measure it.

9

How much did He drink? They all think wine is missing; doubt and measure anew against the small mark my clever brother has made – spurning the rules – after the wine was poured into it.

Did He or did He not? Maybe He just took a drop, wetting His lips to honour us. After all, He'd be drunk, taking full glasses of wine at all the Jewish tables. A drop could not be weighed or measured!

Let them doubt. I know. I have felt His hand, the weight of His benediction.

AND IT STAYS WITH ME. When the ice floats down the creek in Suczorno, driven by a northwest wind, it runs faster over its ancient stones at the approach of Passover. Suczorno Creek, towards which all windows turn on both sides of its banks, unites us at the breakup of its ice. It thunders down the unseen slope, reminding you of the God of Israel. Unpredictable, He holds our precarious lives, so we tremble and look across to the other side.

We are rich. We are the high bank, where houses have roofs with shingles and eavestroughs; front entrances have thresholds and steps of hewn stone. We do not need the poor on the low bank below. They need us. But when the breakup comes, Suczorno Creek rumbles and the voice of God is powerful. It reminds you of your birth and the end of days and you look across to the poor: not all houses are standing up; a fire has swept through. On the one corner, only Noah's outhouse stands untouched; Noah, whose father was Suczorno's pride and joy – a builder. He had worked, before his death, on my father's house, on window frames, door frames, and honed slate.

I do not know that my father owes him money. What does a

child know? She plays her days away, but when God speaks, she hears her father and mother tremble and she hears them whisper to each other.

"Moishe," Mother says. "Go pay your debts, the ice is breaking, Passover is near, there are no *Matzoth* for Passover over there." And father goes into the shed – a proper shed in the back of the house – mouseproof, with a stone floor, and all cracks filled with mortar for protection. He goes into the shed and takes a sack of not-yet-milled grain from an upper shelf. It is a cotton bag, well bleached and sewn by my mother, with a number written on it, in Hebrew: Aleph for one or Beth for two and so forth. It is a ten-kilogram bag, and I watch my father heave it down with an "Oy-vey" moan.

I have run after him. I love that shed. It smells of cinnamon, and before Passover it has been swept clean, the floor rinsed three times as the law demands, and leavened bread – the *Chumetz* – removed, and prayers said.

It is such a splendid time. Wonderful, strange dishes come out of cupboards for those seven, eight days of *Pesach,* white with a blue rim and a touch of gold. They are all out now to be used on the Passover story telling night, when strangers are to sit at your table.

My heart goes out to my father, but Mother says he has not paid Noah's father on the other side of the creek. And now what will my father do?

The ice has broken into boulders, spring is in the air, and people recount their sins. It seems to me that only the rich sin. Because the voice of God is louder on the high bank. So one week before *Pesach* – Passover – there is a flurry of activity, the women bringing their used winter clothes, bags of dry prunes, bags of rye and wheat, and we children look on. Their faces are flushed with their own goodness, but they do it as if it were a natural, normal, or every day occurrence to go across the three wooden-board bridges to the lower side of the creek carrying gifts. We like it, though, we children, we feel it is good to be good. But why did Father not pay?

It is too late now. Noah's father has died in the fire. It is too late. And I'm sad, but it does not last. It is a magic time and I have pretty clothes, hang on my grandmother's hand, who whispers into my ear, "When you, my sweet Sarah, will open the door for the prophet Elijah, see if you can catch his cloak! Just touch it, for the break of a moment –" I dream about it all night before the first night of *Pesach*. We in the *Galluth*, in the dispersal, we always celebrate two nights in a row. In the land of Israel, when the Messiah has come, once is enough, I'm told. To me, only the first night is important, the second is boring, too long a story, I fall asleep, and I'm not sure Elijah can come twice. How can He? To every Jewish home on earth, twice? But now that the other side of the Suczorno Creek has had a fire, we are not that many – so maybe He can? Well, it does not matter.

But before nightfall, I run out in my new clothes, sit on the high bank, careful of my flowery dress, and watch the other side. Comings and goings. Little Srul I favour. He struts about in shoes that do not fit him. Rushes towards me across the small bridge, stumbles, nearly falls into the creek, blushes with shame and anger, and I run towards him and say, "Srul, how beautiful your shoes are and your jacket is new, too."

"Yes," he says, and runs away as we hear his mother shouting. All candles are lit across the creek, and all candles are being lit on the high bank.

"Sarah!"

I run. The time has come.

This is the night when His cloak has touched me. It has floated by. The air has moved. My head is light as a feather and I forget my name. A brown-grey cloak perhaps, covering Him from head to toe. I cannot see his face. No crown, no jewel. But a soft touch of wind, a *parfum* from the East that I breathe in deeply, fills me with wonder. Oh, the greatness of God!

I will not rush around for the *Afikomen* – the hidden piece of *Matzoth* – without which no *Passover Seder* can be finished, and I do not play the game of "bargaining" with Father. Let the other children do it and get their penny.

I have touched the Cloak of Elijah.

Little Srul Contemplates the World

"WHY DO THEY HAVE FENCES on the higher bank of the river? What for?"

My mother says, "They need fences because they're rich and have to watch out for thieves and burglars. We just have weeds no one wants, so we are safe, besides, Elijah does not have to open a gate and He'll come to the poor first."

Pesach. Everyone is busy, no one cares for me. They give me a scratchy-starchy shirt that feels like a board of wood on the skin and they say, "Wash your hands, Srul. Do not sit on the stones of the creek, you're ruining your suit, it's new." Well, it's not new, it is just newly changed, made smaller from the Herschel children across the creek. I know who wore it, three boys of the rich in a row, until it ended up two weeks ago in my mother's hands. And she had to say thank you, thank you. I hate her for it. Then she had to sit until one o'clock in the morning, to trim the worn spots, shorten the sleeves, which were in tatters anyway, turn the collar around, which shone green; and I heard her say, "Look at this, it's perfect on the inside."

I hate her. I do not want to wear my rich cousins' rags. And she said thank you and she put potato starch into the wash of my old shirts and bleached them with vinegar. No one can get vinegar out of shirts. "Do not sit on the stones of the creek, the ice is breaking. Come in Srul, father is ready."

But as I hated her all week, so I love her now. Her face is radiant, flushed with joy. Her mother has died long ago, but always at our table there will be a widow, a lonely bachelor, a stranger. It is a commandment. We cannot break and bless the unleavened bread for ourselves only. Tonight the widow at our table is a sweet woman who had to be carried in by my father, so frail she is. Her silver hair shines through black lace like a thousand crescent moons, and Mother pushes her chair to sit next to the two-year-old-little devil to keep her in order!

The table is set at the centre with the ceremonial plate, greens, a lamb thigh bone and hard-boiled eggs – there are hard-boiled eggs in salt water in a dish apart – and wine-apple-cinnamon mortar, signifying the mortar the children of Israel had mixed for the building of the Pharaoh's temples. How can you eat mortar? Well you can, when father blesses it and it smells of nuts and cinnamon. The tablecloth is as starched as the collar on my shirt is, and it lies like a white board stiffly under all the wine glasses. I shall go to the kitchen shelf where mother keeps the potato starch and throw it into the creek. Oh well, I won't.

All the plagues God sent to the Egyptians are counted out with everyone's little finger dipping into their wineglass to take a drop and discard it on a plate. Not all Egyptians were bad, I'm sure. How could God do that? Some must have been good. All these terrible things: locusts for instance. I shudder. What is "pestilence"? All these words.

Yet, I love the *Seder* night, the questions I the youngest am allowed to ask in Hebrew. Questions by a good, a bad, and a wise boy, but the "one that does not know how to ask" I like best. Because he is like me. The question has to be well asked, put into the right context, because it is more important than the answer. Of course, I have many questions. They crowd my mind. But until I've found the way to ask – correctly, so the adult understands – it's hard. And when the reading starts on locusts, my whole body itches. I sweat and I put my little fingers into my ears to silence their swarming. "Dip your little finger into the wine –" I hear them say. "No, I won't," I say, and I moan.

But it feels good being "chosen" by God. I'm His. A little boy chosen by God. It's quite wonderful. Slowly the lilting Hebrew songs, familiar from the cradle, make me sleepily happy. *Matzoth* with bitter herbs – just parsley, celery, and horseradish – wakes me a little, when pushed onto my tongue. I should recall the labour, the heavy work, and the beatings by the overseers, which the children of Israel had to endure in slavery; it shakes me out of my musings a little, but I do not feel it bitter and cannot cry over their sorrows. I am by now looking forward to His visit: the coming of Elijah. And what a coming it is!

"Srul" – this is all I need. I know the moment by the singsong, and I am out there to open the door, which creaks, and I hope He won't mind. I also decided today to look across the creek to the rich brothers and cousins with the fences around their courts in front of their houses to see if Elijah...wouldn't it be wonderful if He came first to us, the poor. If He came to honour us instead of them over there, who have honours galore, sitting in the first seats in Synagogue, facing the ark and giving gifts of silver and gold to crown the *Torah* rolls. What an honour to be able to give such gifts – I will one day.

I look across with one single glance and I realize they, over there, are not near the coming and indeed He is here. I feel a caress, a breeze touching my hot cheek. Overjoyed, that He is first here, before everyone else, I run in to check the wineglass, to measure how much he has taken from it. Yes, He was here first. It's a greater hon-our than having the best seat on Friday night or *Rosh Hashanah,* which can be bought with money. We're honoured because we're good, because my father does not steal, works with his hands, and my mother mends clothes until – who knows? – the early hours of the morning. We fall asleep to the hum of her "Singer" and wake to her smile to have our faces washed to go to the neighbour's *Shulhan,* the table with all the sleepy little faces having to learn the Aleph-Beth. Good people on this side of the creek who work for others and sometimes do not get paid and have to endure their gifts of worn clothes before *Pesach* or *Rosh Hashanah* – the Jewish New Year. And this is why He comes to us first.

"Srul – go search for the *Afikomen.*" I have nearly forgotten the best part is still to come: the search for the hidden last piece of *Matzoth* and the bargaining for the penny, of course only if I can find it.

Sarah

No one believes me. Just no one. Chaim makes fun of me, saying, "Sarah always sees, touches what no one else can see or touch. She's got imagination – Oh, yes, we know, you have talked to Elijah!"

"No, I haven't talked to Elijah. I said only that his garment touched my cheek."

Oh, no one believes me, I might as well stop talking to anyone, except perhaps to little Srul. I happen to glance across the creek and catch him staring this way when he opens the door, just before I do. It is too dark to tell by his face what he feels. But I am surprised to see him at the door before we are. Does He come first to the other side?

I love Srul. I'm a girl, so I'm not in his class and I do not have to prepare for a *Bar Mitzvah*. We do not count, not when it comes to *Torah* reading, but I learn by myself. Holy Books are around. I know all the letters and I'll beat the boys any day. Srul will believe me. He is the only one to know that one does not have to see or touch with your hands to know. My brothers may mock me, but I think they are afraid deep within themselves that I felt something wonderful they could only dream of. Yes, I tell stories, some truly wicked. They like to hear these; the more wicked, the better. But not strange, holy ones. They tremble.

I have four brothers. That is a lot of brothers for a little girl – the youngest to boot – to fight with. But not always, they protect me, put a woollen shawl at night across my bed, or a heated-in-the-oven brick inside it to warm my feet. Winter is harsh, and they go out with father to cut the wood, and I sit by the burning logs, look into the flames, and feel so loved. Then good stories flood into my head, but wicked ones do also. These are the ones they love.

The eldest is sixteen and rarely home, he is always with father. On weekdays he is out there, with horse and wagon or going away on business for weeks on end. On his return – well, he can tell tales, I must say, taller tales than mine, because my stories are of feelings. Of the unseen, living among us, ghosts perhaps, making us do things we did not intend to do.

Well, his – well, they're about Christians – so different, so hard to understand. The stories my brother tells! Who can believe such things? But he says Christians are people just like us, children crying when they're hungry and mothers holding them close, just like our own. But have you ever seen a Jew drunk?

Nathan, my big brother, tells me they drink their money away – all the peasants around us. I shudder, thinking of my good mother. How lucky we are to be Jews, to have the Law to live by. But Nathan says their girls are prettier than ours, much prettier, taller with big...well I do not have any yet, why should I think about it? Nathan brought a tablecloth home from Lemberg-Lvov, a present for mother, and she said she does not know how to make these stitches. They are called *"ajour"* and go all around the hemmed edge in a fine, long seam. But enough of Nathan. He upsets me.

Brothers are hard on little girls: "Come here, go there, carry this out to the shed, go and see if there are any eggs in the henhouse!" But this I like. We have the nicest henhouse, because we are rich. True, it was built by Srul's father from across the creek and not by my father, who says he has better things to do with his time than build henhouses. Srul told me we owe him money and we better pay up before Passover. But father said that Srul's father Mordechai hadn't finished the ladder to the third tier and hadn't set the wire grate securely enough, so all the hens fled one day and it took the neighbours hours to collect them. Some are still missing, and who can tell one hen from the other? There was a beautiful pearly-grey hen on the uppermost tier, which disappeared.

My mother says she saw the hen with her own eyes at Esther's place, the one before the last home on our side of the creek. Esther says she has one just like it and it isn't ours. The two women have an argument. Esther comes over, shouts abuse – God knows what she said! – recalling things from the time they....I put my two fingers into my ears not to hear her high pitched voice. But I am curious and take my finger out just for a little and hear Esther accuse my mother of terrible things.

"We know you, Leah, you like to look over every man in Suczorno when your husband is on his trips – God knows where he is – to cheat the Gentiles, and that is where all your riches come from, and not paying the Jews for their work. As for your trying your tricks on my husband, that didn't work. He is too good a man. True to me." And she reaches into her big linen bag and throws the slaughtered pearly chicken onto the kitchen table.

Yes, it is our pearly chicken. I know her well because she was blind in one eye, and when my brothers brought dry kernels of corn out to spread them on the ground and opened the coop, all the strong ones rushed to pick the corn, but not "Pearly." She did not see well enough, having one eye fully grown over with a grey skinlet. So I came to her rescue and chased the hungry lot away to give her a chance. She was my favourite. I think she knew me too, was grateful, looked at me with her only eye, as if to say thank you. And sometimes I think Pearly made it a point to wait for me, did not try to go out on her own. Either she remembered having been pushed around by all the others, or she loved me and waited. I loved her too. For her beauty and timidity. For all the designs on her feathered body: grey-white-brown in circles, and when she spread her wings and showed her armpits, she looked

like a princess transformed by magic, waiting for the day of return
to her maiden form.

Unfortunately, Jews have no kingdoms, except the kingdom of
God, and for that we have to wait for the coming of the Messiah.
No king, no queen, no princess. Just rabbis. And they are good
men, but – well, they are not the kings with crowns that I read
about in Russian books. I always find loose pages my brothers
bring home from their trips, so I have taught myself to read.
Often by candlelight, when all are asleep. Of course, they work
hard, so they sleep heavily; not like me, a little girl who is allowed
to dream.

"You have better things to do than read Russian. Godless
books, telling you of their Messiah; you haven't done your
Hebrew lesson yet!"

I let them shout. They mean well and love me, but I know that
there is a world out there, wide, unknown, with churches, songs,
and books. I have to know – oh, it's hard to be young.

Anyway, I am heartbroken. There is my sweet Pearly, lying on
the table like any other dead chicken. But it isn't the same.

"I hope that wicked, wicked Esther had it slaughtered properly
by the *Shoichet,* the ritual slaughterer. Properly, ritually. Or perhaps, to spite us, has simply done it herself, which would be a terrible sin to commit! Especially when given to others to eat, "And
who knows," my mother continues, "who knows when she did
it?" All such worries. Still, it should not go to waste, so they cook
it.

I won't even look in its direction. Chicken soup of my Pearl! I
will be sick to my stomach, and I am on that Friday night when
the terrine is steaming centre table. I am. I hurt all over. Mother
lights the Shabbat candles, thanks God that He in his benevolence

has allowed us to reach the Shabbat, and praises Him for having commanded us, His people, to celebrate the seventh day. Then they sit down to their carp in vegetable juice and Pearl's soup, with her neck, feet, and bony parts inside. Visible. Carrots and noodles. The meat remaining for a little later.

They all sit down, after a cup of blessed wine for Father, Mother, and the two older boys. I cry myself to sleep about the ways of the world.

Shimon: The Jew's Trap

EVERY YEAR SHE GREW, Sarah felt His presence stronger at Passover time. But differently; she felt addressed. When ten years old, or was it eleven, she had waited all day, prepared herself. Washed and dressed carefully, giggled at her own wiggling image in the creek, saying, "What is this? Are you getting married to Elijah? It's dark, He won't look at you, He has no time." But something had changed. In expectation, and silent all day, she hardly registered the *Haggadah* readings.

"She is in her private never-never-land, no one can enter there," said Shimon, the one next to her in age.

"No, I'm not, I'm right here. Where are we?"

Shimon bent over to show her the place in the readings, and she whispered into his ear not to run behind her, to let her open the door for Elijah by herself.

"It will cost you the penny from the *Afikomen,*" he said. "It's a deal." They shook on it under the table.

Shimon was always good to her. He was almost a girl. Slower than the other boys were, inclined to listen. Just a year and a half older, he was shorter than she was; a head shorter, and very slow to walk. He had to wear all his brothers' shoes, all their clothes that had come down to him. He looked funny, awkward, and Sarah loved him. For his stutter, for his peeing his pants, for all his inadequacies, and for his brilliance in *Torah.* He knew which section had to be read on which day in the year and asked impossible questions no one could answer.

Preparing for his *Bar Mitzvah,* for instance, he read the book of Ruth ahead of every other little scholar, and asked at five o'clock in the morning, when the boys and their *Melamed* – their teacher – had just assembled: "How is it that we are strictly forbidden to marry out of our faith when our forefathers could marry Ruth and Orpah who were Moabite women? So it says in the Book of Ruth. Oh yes, and is it because they were not of the tribe of Israel that we do not use their names? Have you met anyone called Ruth or Orpah?"

"No," said Haskel, the *Melamed.* "No, not here, maybe somewhere else. No, not in Suczorno we have not had anyone – and you, Shimon, you always come in the morning with the stupidest questions. What do you dream at night, Moabite women?" Sniggering. "Keep to your task or everyone will have his *Bar Mitzvah* work done but you!"

To say such a thing to Shimon, who read the books on his own and thought about them! Sarah was indignant when he told her.

"Well, don't talk to them, talk to me."

"But Haskel will be a rabbi soon, he is preparing and studying hard."

"Yes, but he is stupid. It is not enough to repeat the holy words. We're not parrots. We should think, like you and I do. Think."

"But Sarah, if it's written in the books it is true, and when it says the women were Moabite, they were Moabite. So I do as you do, I think. But it gets me into trouble."

"Talk to me, not to idiots, talk to me," she said. But sometimes Sarah was impatient with Shimon. Impatient and a little mean: "Stop peeing your pants, you won't grow up, you're already shorter than I am and you're older. It's because you pee your pants. Have you ever seen adults do it? So, you stop it!"

"But I get lost in thought, it happens before I realize it, and then it's too late. You, Sarah, you tell me to think, and I do —"

"Grow up, you can think but rush out when it is absolutely necessary, or you'll stand at the pulpit before the ark, the *Bimah*, on your *Bar Mitzvah* to read from the scrolls and you'll be the laughing stock of the whole Synagogue. Grow up, I say!"

Shimon refused. He did not want to grow up. To be like his brothers, looking after horses, carrying grain for other people to the mill, having to deal with Christians, who owned the mill, and having to travel hours by horse and wagon. And he did not want to be like his second brother, who apprenticed at a cobbler on the other side of Suczorno Creek, where most of the tradesmen, the tailors, the carpenters, and furriers were crowded on the lower bank. So Isaac had to cross every day after prayer bread and milk to sweep the miserable shed of the shoemaker's, for at least a year or two, before even having glanced at a mended sole, let alone look at a piece of leather.

No, Shimon thinks. No, not for me. I hate that woman anyway, she beats my brother Isaac with the broom he sweeps her house with. But Isaac does not seem to mind. He likes his master, who often still has his *Tefillin* on in the morning when Isaac knocks at the door — leather strips wound around your arm and the Law on the forehead. This is the life of a Jew from the thirteenth birthday until his last breath. The law, "Thou shalt not –" from rising in the dark to nightfall.

Isaac told me that his master sings, *Smirim* – songs – of all sorts. Wearing a shiny leather apron and sitting on his low, leather-capped stool in front of his last, he chooses the hide, contemplates the broken seams, the worn heels of a little shoe that has seen generations of tiny scholars get up at the break of dawn to do their duty. "Until a sole ends up in my shop, it has rubbed many a stone," he sings. And this is what Isaac loves. The master's singing. His reciting, and not just holy books, but poetry. Ukrainian, Polish, Russian. "Isaac," he calls. "Come here for a little while. It's enough. Let the women do the rest, it is time for you to see a piece of leather, how it moves in my hand, how it shines in the morning sun, warms in my palm." And Isaac touches it and feels the love of God, love of all things if you have eyes to see them. And the master, having spread his piece of hide on a special table, cuts – standing in front at a crooked angle – with a small but piercing knife, slices with one grand movement the sole-shape out of the hide for the little shoe. And then he sits down, to fit, to scrape the fine edges –

Oh, Isaac tells all these wonders to Shimon, who thinks: But they are not for me. What is so wonderful about a piece of leather, the tiny wooden nails, and the hammering? The singing of the master – but Russian poetry, that is a different story. That I like. But no, I won't be a cobbler, to see all the lives of my neighbours in a shoe. What do I need their lives for? The poor worry about bread and the rich about silk sashes around their fat middles. I do not want their lives – I want the written word. Think about it: are there hidden meanings in the letter?

We have a fool in Suczorno who says there are. God tells you what was, what has always been, and this holds what will be. Spelled out, he says. It's our own Bimbule, whose name already sounds like all his stories. He lives with the bees in the fields in the summertime, and knows things no one else does and everyone is afraid of. So they call him the *narrisher*. I for one, I Shimon, I believe him and I also am the only one who believes my sister Sarah, who consorts with Elijah. She says Srul from the poor side of town believes her also. It may well be. The poor look at things and divine them a little differently than we do on this side of the creek.

A funny word, divine: it has something to do with God. So I am using it. It says other things — when I say "divine" I mean it shows something of the heart of God. A hidden thing. Something we, His people, have to find in order to learn His will, even if it's the "Last Judgment" they all talk about. I am still a boy, so I do not worry about facing Him, but what worries me is to know His will. Is it truly in the letter? Sarah gives me all sorts of ridiculous or contradictory messages. She says, "Think," and then she says, "stop thinking." It's enough already.

A GOOD DAY. Shimon has helped his mother carry wood and arrange it in patterns against the back wall of the shed. The older boys have cut it, as woodcutters do, drawing an enormous saw across a log.

We have learned it from the Ukrainian peasants, he thinks. They know so many "real things" which we pick up from them. And we should stop calling them stupid. They're not stupid. They just do not read or write — which a Jew cannot comprehend: how

do they live without it? Well, their priests do, and maybe it's sufficient for them because they work so hard. Very hard. Toil. Break
the dry ground, know how to loosen it, make it as fine as sand and
seed. We would learn it too, but we are not allowed to own land
and so we do what we can. The good of it is, we have more time
to read the holy books. But they are not stupid – perhaps when it
comes to drink. Now, that's stupid. Not to stop drinking until one
lies flat under the table and snores or hears wife's curses.

One day, I went with the big boys to the mill. When we
arrived to pick up the sacks of grain that were to be carried to the
mill, we heard a moan from the kitchen and my eye caught the
poor lady's face. It was green and blue. She moaned and she cried.
We, "the Jewish boys," we did not see anything, did not hear anything or ask any questions. We just packed the sacks of grain high
up unto the wagon; silently, lest we'll be called "interfering, meddling Yids," and we left, beating our horses harder than they
deserved.

On the way home, a little less comfortable this time because I
had to squeeze in between the sacks – or lie on top, which was
better – I was sad, truly sad for the first time, thinking about the
ways of the world.

I love a ride in the countryside, especially at harvest time,
when August days are long and lazy. My brothers let me stretch
out in our ladder-wagon and I look upwards to the passing
clouds; there is such peace in heaven that fills your soul, and
nothing bothers me, neither the bumpy, uneven road nor the
pangs of hunger. I always beg to go along. Besides, it is time for
me to be a little more like my older brothers. A young man.

AND SHIMON STOPPED TALKING to his sister Sarah, though he would much rather do it than have the sullen company of the boys who dismissed him with one single-handed movement of disdain – but he had to grow up.

Sarah said it all the time to him. And he tried now. His peeing stopped, during the day, of course, more so than at night, when on his own and in his thoughts – but he had to be a man. And he tried. And there was a chance to show his mettle to the older boys. It was not an enjoyable or everyday occasion and it had a price, but he could show his brothers he was as good as they were. It happened on one of their trips.

Jews did not own either the mill or the grain, but to be a *furman* was a respected profession: to ferry the grain back and forth, the grain to the mill and the flour back to the peasant, for a fee. And Jews always had horses and treated them well. Horses were your family, they worked for you like a father, and you could play with them as if they were children. Shimon thought them beautiful.

Why don't we have any dogs? he wondered. Oh, yes, there are a few on the other side of the creek and people get into shouting matches over them. Cats, that's different. They're for the mice. But not in the house, of course.

It happened on one of these "furman" trips. They had to go south this time, to a village that lay in a lovely valley. It was surrounded by wooded hills, and Shimon loved the countryside. The beauty of it. A monastery built – God knows when – sprawling in a cove, was of stone and wood, pictures of saints all around it.

Why do we not decorate our Synagogues or houses, Shimon always asked himself, as Christians would? It is so much better to live with a little colour around, to beautify your walls. But naturally, he knew that Jews "Shall not make carved or painted images of themselves." And that might be the explanation. But to live so differently from one another, if there is one God only for us all — well, there were no answers. One just lived within one's law and tried to please God. So, no pictures. There were worse things, such as what happened on the way down south to the beautiful valley.

In the beginning it was prairie land, as in Suczorno, then the earth heaved gently, fell unexpectedly, groves of stunted spruce intermingled with poplar and birch, and the air was spicier, with something that smelled of garlic, was easier to breathe, as if it held the finest water drops. Shimon loved this land, begged to go along. But the brothers resisted.

"People are rough there, they do not like Jews in any shape or form, and we do not need you, Shimon, to give us one more headache."

"I'm no headache to you, I'll help carry. I'm stronger now, I'm twelve. I'll soon be *Bar Mitzvah,* you'll have to take me then."

"All right, move, we're ready to go."

And it was on one of those trips, going south, on a day when one thinks of the glory of God and the beauty of His creation. Shimon loved the moment when, after an hour's trip in the open wagon with a blazing sun above, the wagon entered a deep furrow towards the valley. Shadows thickened in trees on both sides, sometimes touching above their heads like a green roof speckled with blue, and formed a darkened alleyway. Such comfort after a borderless land, a land where the earth was lifted by steady winds and a yellow sun dried your skin. Such comfort to breathe humid air, perfumed by herbs, which Shimon knew and brought home, be it mint or rosemary, to the despair of his mother, who thought they did not fit Jewish dishes.

"Mother," Shimon would reply, "God does not grow Jewish

herbs or Christian herbs. It's good for everybody."

And she: "It may be poisonous. Jews do not eat what they do not know or what is forbidden in Deuteronomy."

So there was no way to talk to her, Shimon thought.

It was on one such day, when all seemed benevolent. Coming into the sheltered furrow, the horses had to work hard to find their way, the wagon rattled and shook on its axles, but Shimon was happy or even jubilant, if one was allowed to use such exalted words, meant for the praise of God only. But that was what he felt. To live and have eyes to see such beauty! Yes, to be conscious of it and oneself.

And he wanted to shout or sing, when the sound was suddenly stilled in his throat by the rearing up of the horses, the wagon backing up, screeching on its axles, nearly tipped to the side. Attacking them right and left were a number of peasants, whom the boys had seen before, armed with sticks and shouting, "Dirty Yids, get off the wagon."

Blood was spurting from Nathan's face as he lay on the ground, and Israel, trying to revive him, was beaten and kicked until he lay across his brother's body. Enormous boulders on the narrowest part of the furrowed road, and a fallen tree trunk barring it, had frightened the faithful horses.

Shimon, bending over his brothers, disentangled them to see their faces and know they were alive.

Some of the peasants had occupied the driver's seat, and a few of them seated themselves inside, as others tried to remove boulders and the fallen trunk. They sang, vodka passing hands, shouting insults in Romanian-Ukrainian-Yiddish – it did not matter. Shimon saw them drive off with his father's horses and wagon in a cloud of flying mud, axles creaking and the cracking of the whip.

What to do with his poor brothers and how to face their parents? Following the wagon and horses with his eyes until foliage or a turn in the road hid them, he heard only now Israel call out to him, "Shimon, help me. I think my leg is broken." Which brought him back to his task. He turned to his brothers, pulled Israel off Nathan's body to place him as comfortably as possible on his back. He then realized that Nathan had not moved, lay face down in the mud. Shimon, frightened, kicked Nathan a little too hard, heard his moan and thanked God for it, but when he had turned him unto his back, he was shaken to the core. An unrecognizable face, a bludgeoned face, earth-encrusted, an eye protruding – or so it seemed to him.

Shimon put a stone under Nathan's head, ripped a piece of linen off his own shirt, and ran to a small pool of water, which he had noticed almost without registering it. Dipped the linen into it, ran back, and gently, tenderly, cleaned Nathan's face. No, the eye wasn't out of its hollow, just so big and swollen.

"I'm fine," Nathan said, "Shimon, go home, speak to father and bring help. We'll be fine until you come. The peasants won't be back, they have what they came for."

It was a long trek home. Shimon felt nothing. No fear of his father's face or his mother's silent despair; nor of the stones in his shoe or the dust on his brow – he felt nothing except the task. How many hours it took he could not tell, but it was night when he knocked at his father's house. At the entrance to the village, he had dipped his hands into Suczorno Creek, to wash his hands and wipe his forehead, but did not take the time to do so.

Moishe, his father, was at the door. He was dressed, had not expected them back until the day after, but had sat up to read and pray. With a burning candle now in his hand, he looked at his son.

Shimon said, "They have taken the horses and wagon but have left us with our lives."

The father said *"Baruch Ha Shem,* Thanks be to God," called into the house that he'd be back, not to wait for him, and rushed out to the neighbours three houses apart to borrow their horses and wagon. Shimon sat down on the high bank of the creek to wait for his father, his heart filled to overflowing with the same "Thanks be to God, Blessed be His name" he had heard his father utter. And what a magnificent father! Just "Thanks be to God." For the lives of his children; that one is still able to help oneself; and that it is "for God to judge the measure of burden He puts unto our shoulders." Life matters. A wagon doesn't. Horses, of course, do.

But they will not slaughter them, they'll feed them and use them. Peasants know the worth of horses, Shimon thought. I'm not worried. Just that they are mine; I talk to them. They are people to me; they like a carrot pulled from the earth, the green on top, or an extra piece of sugar; they're family. So, they'll be back if God decides and if not – we'll have to accept His ways.

When Moishe appeared with Samuel's wagon and horses, all harnessed and ready to go, Shimon seated himself this time in the driver's seat next to his father. Shimon had not paid attention to the road going out of town when travelling with his brothers, he had hung his thoughts onto the passing clouds and, cradled by the bumpy road, he was a happy child. Now, stars were in the sky, the road was unclear, he felt he could not help his father and started to say, "The road looks different at night –" when his father took one hand from the reins and said – "Not to worry, Shimon, my son, I've gone this way all my life, day and night. I know every stone, every turn in the road at all seasons – do not worry.

"You will have to show me only where your brothers are. I

suspect it to be the thicket in the furrowed pathway, before reaching the open fields. We used to call it the 'Jew's Trap,' because it is not the first time they have attacked us. But nothing has happened in a long, long time. The peasants did well, the harvests were good. Everybody flourished and we had enough to eat. The priests were friendly, came around sometimes to talk religion. Some friendships sprang up between us. They started calling us 'the people of the book' and other nice names, and this is always a good sign.

"But this was a hard summer. Little rain. The earth broke, some lay fallow – what can you expect? They'll soon think it's our fault. The grain is in and it's not plentiful. Not bad, but not good enough for us."

Then they were silent. Both in their thoughts. And Shimon saw his father in a entirely different light: I have always thought him irascible, intemperate, inclined to be the master, raise his voice, pound the table with his fist. Awe was always mixed with the fear of having crossed or misunderstood him. How different tonight! And something one could call love, crept into his heart as he sat next to his father, observing him closely: how expertly, how gently he guided the horses, which weren't even his.

There were hours of silence until: "How hurt are they?" And Shimon told the whole story now and his father let him cry. Fortunately, in the August moon the cove of trees appeared as if painted black. Clusters of black spots descending into the furrow and Father said, "This must be the path."

"Yes," said Shimon. "It is not too far from here, but – we should maybe bring the boys up here, because the road is so narrow, it will be difficult to turn around."

"You're right, Shimon, but these are not my horses. I cannot order them to stay and wait for me. You must have noticed that I gave you the reins at a certain moment to let them feel another hand. And you did well. These two are such stubborn animals – perhaps not stubborn, only unwilling to work at night and for a stranger." But Father succeeded this time very well in bringing the horses to a stop and it was indeed at the "Jew's Trap," exactly at the narrow spot where they had fallen upon the brothers.

Nathan could help now. His face was bludgeoned, but he was strong and unhurt and he alone lifted his brother Israel from the ground to bed him in the hay. Father knew the spot well, he knew where and how to turn, and they were soon in the open moonlit prairie again.

Silent, all of them. Hours to feel the grandeur of God. The inimitable. The sky so close to be touched, and the father humming a *Nigun* – a liturgical melody – Shimon could not identify. Perhaps something you sang or said when a threat to your lives had been overcome. And Shimon listened again, to remember the tune, for there might come a time when he'd have to sing it with all his heart.

Taken out of the carriage, carried into the house and carefully bedded down by his brother, with his mother at his side and his sister, Sarah, serving him steaming tea, Israel smiled. He looked at Shimon and said, "You're the hero of the day," and no one had to tell Shimon to grow up.

Sarah: I'll Marry Srul

"I'll marry Srul," Sarah said unasked and out of an unbroken silence.

She had helped all morning to cut onions into fine cubes by

slicing across the onion top and then through it until well-formed cubes fell into the pot. She hated doing the *Cholent* – the *Shabbat* meal prepared on Friday and kept warm in the oven – all those root vegetables to be washed and cut. She would not touch the raw pieces of beef that went into the pot after salting, and that still had to be done. All those rules. She did not mind the salting, but when her mother had spread every piece of meat on a sieve of braided willow-branches, then Sarah had taken the coarse salt and sprinkled it all over to let the juices run so every last drop of blood would be drained. But she refused to lift it from the sieve or touch its sticky surface. So, there was silence between mother and her only daughter.

Sarah, fifteen now, almost sixteen, had heard rumours, whisperings between Father and Mother before his last trip to Lemberg, or Lvov as the Poles called it: there were as many names to a city as were masters to conquer it. But to Jews it did not matter much whose city it was. Hands and names changed, but the lot of the Jews remained the same.

The Poles fight with the Russians, Sarah thought, and the Jew is caught in between. They are all Christians, but that does not seem to have any importance. The Polish priests write Latin, the Russian priests write Cyrillic, and the people – poor things, they murder each other.

Not always. They could be friendly. And Sarah thought of the many times Ukrainian women from the nearby village had returned a goat that had gone astray or had given a glass of tea and piece of bread to the village's roving fiddlers. And Bimbule, the village idiot, who was not an idiot without brains, perhaps a fool, slept in their fields in the summertime, and they let him be, thinking him good and God-fearing. In the wintertime, one,

Vasselena by name, let him crawl into the stable at night and fed him goat's milk and "Christian butter," which he should not have accepted but, since he suspected no evil, did not hurt him. Of course, he ran from her husband and sons. They could be dangerous.

All the stories Bimbule told them – so the Christians were good. *Just like Jews,* as Bimbule put it. Oh, dear it's all so complicated, Sarah thought, while cutting up the vegetables and the hated garlic, which stole itself under your nails, not to be dislodged for days past the Shabbat day.

But it is good to be a woman, she thought, not to be so bound to the Lord at every moment of the day. We do not have to go to the services. We can always pretend this or that and the service does not depend on us being there. And we are powerful in the family circle. Women hold the reins, the pocketbook. It's good to be a Sarah, the mother of the tribe. A true Sarah.

But she woke at night with the strangest desires: to jump, dress and run. Simply away, from the dailiness of things, from brothers, cleaning up, bringing water from the well, seeing other girls' fancy clothes and recently the fear of the whisperings. Father going to Lemberg. She feared his return. He had done this before and returned with the picture of a young *Yeshiva-bucher.* A young face, perhaps her age, which she perceived sideways, refusing to look.

"I'll marry Srul," she'd said to her mother today after a night of sleepless hours, knowing her father would be back before evening prayers with another picture. "I'll marry Srul," she said to her mother again in the morning. To which she got no reply, just a staring. Sarah knew her mother did not want that whole family from across the creek. They were poor. Learned – which counts –

but poor; a hand-to-mouth existence, like most of them across the river.

"What river?" her mother objected. "What river? A miserable creek. The Lord has not given a drop of rain, the stones are showing. They are hot. You could *kasher* – make *kosher* – your cutlery if you put them into a pot of water; it would boil instantly. No river, a creek, just as miserable as my cousins on the lower bank. There is work to be done, Sarah! No Srul."

FATHER DID NOT COME HOME that Friday night. If a father did not come home, after five days of absence, for the Friday night meal, the family worried. Anything could have happened to him. He could have fallen ill, his wagon, horses and merchandise stolen; outside of Suczorno everything was possible. If a man did not come home for the Friday night service and the *Shabbat* meal, there must have been something truly wrong. And it spread like wildfire, to both sides of the creek. Rich or poor, it did not matter, because all envy, arguments, and even bitter hatred were put aside in Suczorno if a man had not come home on Friday night and had been expected to do so. Sometimes he would stay away for two, three weeks, having business as far away as Odessa, but then, his duties at the Synagogue were filled, the family knew, and the village would not worry.

Father came back a day late and all Sarah's fears seemed justified. After hugs and relieved *ahs* and *ohs* and "Where have you been?" and "Heavens," the dreaded picture lay on the kitchen table.

"Sarah – you've got a bridegroom!" the boys shouted, knowing full well how to annoy her.

And she fled. Out the door, digging roots in the garden, tears flowing.

"I'm not going anywhere, I don't want to be rich and wear a diamond brooch and rings on my fingers. I despise rich Jews, they're cruel, they don't give anything to anyone they're not forced to give. They make holy faces and betray their wives. I won't be one of them. If I can't have Srul, I'll be an old maid."

And she dug around the few tulips that had sprung up from their bulbs, separated them and talked to them. "The best people of Suczorno live on the other side of the river – or creek as my mother calls it – just to dishonour the lower bank. Why the poor river? What has she got against it? Oh, one can't reason around here."

Sarah reentered the house, went straight to the kitchen table, and in an act of defiance picked the picture from the table and tore it into small pieces, cried and shouted: "Thou shalt not make images of thyself!" She had used the law to protect herself. And they all fell silent and Father shook his head, dismissing her with an ungracious, impatient movement of his hand.

And Sarah ran out the front door across the bridge. The bridge was no bridge, just a few nailed-together boards that had to be straightened every day, and the river was no river. But today it was more that, more than it ever had been. It had rained at night. Heavily. It moved swiftly, and from the higher bank the opposite side was lush with green. Sarah ran across the wobbling boards, which were a few houses down, glad to avoid her own windows. She ran, but had to be careful not to fall into the water. She wickedly thought it would serve them right – to even consider sending her away, far away to Lemberg, perhaps never to see her again in a lifetime. She moved up a few houses, because Srul's father's *atelier* was straight across from her own house. Knocked at the door and entered the unlocked door to seat herself across Srul's mother, wordlessly.

Sarah had always liked her. A woman of few words, slow movements, but when she rose from the wooden stool to her full height, she could wear a crown. Her lustrous brown hair she wore for all to see and was shunned by some who, when at the fountain or up-village washing in the creek, implied *they* were the God-fearing ones. Showing one's hair, God's gift to a woman, would tempt the devil, or a demon passing by unseen, they proclaimed, and they would call her a slut. Her name was Naomi. A Hebrew name full of vowels and sound.

Sarah, entering the kitchen, said, "Good day Náomi. Or is it Naómi? Perhaps Naomí. It's a beautiful name. So easy to sing. Easier than Rachel or Rebecca."

"Yes," Naomi said, "it's a beautiful name, but not everyone in Suczorno will like it."

"Why not?" Sarah wondered.

"Well, hard to say. Perhaps the rich, shaven women, with their expensive *perruques* or wigs, are envious of my courage, and I heard them say that Naomi – the Biblical Naomi, a Jewish woman, who followed her husband to the Moabite land – had allowed both her sons to marry Moabite women. She loved those daughter-in-laws, and they loved her so deeply, that when the two young men died they followed Naomi back to Judea. At least Ruth did. If Orpah – I do not remember. Read it in the Book of Ruth. In the opinion of my fellow Jews – of some, not all," she added, seeing Sarah's dismissive hand movement, "yes, some – Naomi was tolerant of foreign women, and so would I be, bearing her name. In fact, I admire Naomi for her love of Ruth and

Orpah, for her intelligence in returning to her tribe after her husband's death, and the permission she gave Ruth to remarry. A powerful mother of all of us."

Sarah loved it when Naomi spoke. The whole Bible was there, she thought. Almost self-taught, a double orphan after the fire, all of Suczorno had brought her up. Naomi did kindling for the *Shabbat* fire, did a small commerce in an abandoned shed selling live carp. They were hard to get, and God knows from where she succeeded in bringing some into Suczorno, reviving them in water from the creek. She had collected an array of old chipped and bent pails, and the fish swam lustily. Quiet like her fish in the pail, Naomi lived by an inner happiness in accord with all living. There was an acceptance of what was ordained, as the fiery death of all her folk, and that God gave her life and took the others. There must be a reason, she thought, He is a father, He should know.

Everyone in Suczorno knew Naomi. She had eaten at everyone's table during the week for her services to the women: bringing water from the river, peeling potatoes, and cleaning the kitchens of the rich. Real kitchens, with work benches and ceramic ovens. She worked for all of them. And on *Shabbat,* she wore their daughters' discarded clothes. Finding pleasure in her own looks, which might have been sinful in the eyes of some, she did not mind an old but colourful silk skirt. And they all saw her beauty. Tall, queenly. She had asked permission to use a sewing machine in order to fix two skirts into a shift, so tall she was. The envy of all women of Suczorno. Men looked and women refused her work, lest their husbands succumb to her beauty and – God knows what a man could think of – not sleeping at night. Why did God not take her, if He took – His name be praised – all of her people? To tempt, perhaps – God's ways may be strange, some thought, and they hated her.

There was a general sigh of relief when Naomi accepted the other "odd-man-out" in an offer of marriage and Suczorno got busy to give her a dowry. Not of the best or the newest, of course, these things were for their own daughters, but pots and pans, forks and spoons, a few good knives with sharpenable edges, *Shabbat*-dinner tablecloths, lovely linen with *ajour* around, and above all, two candlesticks to celebrate her first *Shabbat* at her own married table. It was a fine wedding, with honey cake, herring marinated or salted, cakes filled with prune jam, wine for the blessing, and a good Kümmel-Schnapps for the men.

But Suczorno was stunned when, with the connivance of her bridegroom, she refused to cut her hair, and the old story emerged again. Naomi, like her Biblical namesake who liked her daughters-in-law of the Moabite tribe, would tempt the devil even. "She'll bring demons into Suczorno, who will lurk at our doors, change into women's clothes, and come into the house at night."

And when there was a terrible flood in Suczorno one summer and the creek went out of its banks, flooding the lower bank, of course, the women broke her windows, blaming her, she who wore her hair for all to see. And the rich from the higher bank, untouched by the water, said: "Serves them right, to tolerate someone like Naomi in their midst."

But in the absence of flood or drought, Naomi's gentle ways, tolerance of others, good works, and her open door for all in need, made a truce possible. And when she bore her son Srul, everyone came to the *Brith,* with gifts of money and a silver *Kiddush*-cup from the rabbi, as usual. Of course, there was not just one rabbi. Every Jew a rabbi. If he was learned enough, he could hold a service, marry a couple, or celebrate the birth of a son. Still, one was in charge of the Synagogue, a true official of the town, respected if not revered.

There was great joy at his birth. But Srul remained the only son, and the town started thinking again. What could it be? Why is she barren? Well, not barren – but year after year she kept her youthful figure, while other women lost their beauty with child-birth after childbirth, growing fat around the middle. But when in good time a new baby was born, Suczorno women made their peace with her presence, as you do with things that can't be helped.

Sarah loved Naomi. Her regal crown of hair, her bearing, the beauty of her bending, even when picking up a spool of yarn, her silence, her speaking eyes, her light smile. Sarah had always fled from her own noisy-men household to this shelter of serenity, untold friendship, and the love of Srul who understood her. Or perhaps, if not understood, believed that Elijah had spoken to her, Sarah, a little girl. In godly, silent ways of course. Who needs words! There were other ways to know than words.

She simply knew that Elijah had passed her lovingly, had touched her cheek with His cloak, and that she was allowed to feel chosen. Like all her people. Jews felt chosen. It did not mat-ter what others said, believed, or thought. Jews knew that they were chosen. It said in the books, in the covenants with Noah, Abraham, and later Moses; but all of that was not enough. It was that a Jew had an inner certainty of God. A presence and a bond.

Srul was the only one to whom she could speak. "It is true, Srul, that when I opened the door Elijah came by me and said without words that He knows I am Sarah and he'll always be with me."

"I know," Srul said. "I know." And that was all she needed when she was seven or eight. But now, it was different. Now she talked to Naomi, and avoided Srul more and more. Avoided him intentionally on the outside, but longed for him at night, defied her parents by ripping the picture of the Lemberg-boy and shouting she'd be an old maid. But to say she'd marry Srul was what truly frightened her parents and why her father went near and far to find a bridegroom for her. It was that Srul was Naomi's son and no one in Suczorno would want her as a *Machteineste* – an in-law.

There were other women in the village who kept their own hair as married women, but Naomi was different. She had been caught with her future husband and father of Srul kissing in the bushes: a sign he could not resist her. A clever young man, good in his trade, who might have married a girl from the other side of the creek with money, but could not resist Jezebel or the snake. The women had seen them, lying on the ground in a cool cove down the river, had chased them out and shouted *shame.* When he married her, they thought him honourable. But when she refused to cut her hair, walking through the town without a kerchief on summer days, the village knew: "One can't make a respectable woman out of Naomi."

Still, one got accustomed to all sorts of things. And she did bring up her son to study the law and attend services with his father, and she kept the house *kasher.* They did not exactly know, because no one really ate at her table, but the women just visiting saw the two separate work tables, the separate cupboards to keep milk out of meat, and her shining tablecloths, and it silenced their suspicions. Their vocal ones only.

SARAH'S MOTHER LEAH would sometimes look across the creek; she could almost follow Naomi's comings and goings, her walking up the creek as far as the well, and envied her contained, measured elegance. What purpose could one read into God's design? Leah mused. Why take all her people and leave Naomi, a child of seven or so, for us all to care for and to be a danger to all our men? But it did not concern or worry her too much. It was only that Sarah loved her better than she did her own mother, went over there more often than was suitable for a young lady, a bride-to-be in not too distant a time.

What do they talk about? Leah worried. Sarah is over there again. Every time we argue or teach or guide her to find the right way in life, Leah thought, she is over there seeking solace. I know they sit in the kitchen, I've followed her one day unseen and, hidden behind an open door of the neighbour's house, I could see them. I could not tell if Naomi was sewing or embroidering or if Srul was there.

I'll have to go to the rabbi to talk, she decided. To my own. The wonderful singing rabbi, who knows all the answers without looking into the books. He has come from far away. A wandering, learned man, who sings his prayers so beautifully that when we women go out of his courtyard, we have a feeling of God deep within us, without Synagogue, where we are welcomed but ignored. At his small, derelict, one-room "prayer-house" we are received with open arms. We can tell him if our husbands have avoided us, looked the other way, though we had removed the small partition in our marriage bed to indicate our "clean" time. We can tell him if we worry about our sons not studying or going into the villages and, God forbid, not returning for nights on end.

Thank God it did not happen to me, Leah said silently to herself, but I do worry about Naomi's seduction of Sarah and I must ask our *Baal-Shem* – well, he is not the real one, but has inherited his soul, I'm sure of it. Not the Messiah, I know that, but a messenger perhaps. God always sends messengers, we just have to recognize them. For the Messiah, we'll have to wait –

And so Leah went down the creek, crossed on the last bridge to the lower bank. The day was hot and dusty, no cloud in the sky, but a heavy, burdening weight of things to come – well, who could predict God's intentions? It just felt as if the stretch was unbearably long. Her shoes were through at the soles, but she did not go to the cobbler's house to fix them, not before seeing the godlike face of her own *Baal-Shem* to fortify her. She knew the cobbler to be a good, proper man, but then it was Naomi's house, and she'd rather hurt with all the pebbles on the road than show her face there.

Dust covered the sky so fast that all seemed dark. Leah had not noticed the winds rising from the south carrying what they could find, whirling it around until she was hit by a flying stone just before pushing in the unlocked door of the derelict barn. It stood within a naked land. There was nothing to diminish its singleness; as if to show man's courage and his trust in God. No bush, no tree, no window to look in.

But it withstood the storm. The rabbi, doing wondrous things, calming the fury of the wind and the wild lashings of rain, talked with a tongue of honey to calm her fears. She had left a braided *Challah,* salt, and a bottle of *Shabbat* wine at the entrance barrel when coming in, and the miracle-rabbi in his torn gabardine, fur hat on his brow, had stood up from his only chair next to the wooden table, spreading his arms wide, raising his eyes to the Lord and singing a welcome.

"A mother has come," he sang. "A mother with her womb

hurting. Her children still residing there, not being able to give birth. The Lord be praised. He is by the side of all women bearing the weight of their children within themselves."

They stood and they sang a familiar *Nigun,* though she could not place it. She could not tell from which of the five books of Moses nor from which service. But it felt good. He knew the mothers' faces when they came to his door. He could read their hurt, he did not have to start: "My daughter, tell me –" So he had looked at Leah's face, had greeted her with the love of the wise, and when she opened the door to leave – for it was not proper, she a woman, to be alone with a man – he'd said, "May the Lord show you His countenance and give you peace."

It was strange that she had found him alone in his shabby abode. But she saw his *Chasidim* – disciples of the charismatic rabbi – approach when she opened the door to leave. They had come with him from Poland and she knew they would not stay. Messages that "Good times are near" had to be spread by these pure souls.

The air had cooled. Grasses and weeds stood upright, holding the blessing of water, wetting her broken shoe. She left with a soul full of song. He knew everything. He knew, it was about her child, and what it was, and he told her "Trust in God." The *Chasidim* greeted Leah in passing, and she replied with a nod of her head. He had restored her peace, her love of God, with a song, for the price of her courage in facing him, a *Challah,* salt, and wine.

Why then, she wondered, would the village, why would Suczorno be up in arms against him? The men had nearly burnt his barn down one night, suspecting evil doings, or interference with their marriage problems. The Suczorno rabbi and his sons, a dynasty for centuries, did not preach against the *Chasidim* – these wandering wonder workers, but everyone was aware of their feelings.

Leah wondered, why not tolerate, why not love, such wonderful men, who live to serve the love of the Almighty for the price of a bread and shelter in a barn? I'm afraid they'll chase them out of town. Her heart, full of gratitude, was light. She walked fast, to avoid the coming night. No stone on the road could bother her, and she sang the *Nigun* he had sung with her.

Crossing the bridge boards of the creek, she saw faces in the windows, recording her return. Women knowing women. They knew where she had been, for they also had taken this trek at one time or another and would not betray her. But the men will chase the *Chasidim* out of town, with curses or sticks if necessary, she thought sadly.

And one day they did. But with a calculated reasoning: that there was too much discord in town and that the town needed the barn. Leah had trembled with fear, watching the town's richer citizens taking the road across the upper river bridge. She had followed them with her eyes until they were out of sight, sat down on her kitchen chair, where all women sit when waiting for an unpredictable outcome. In Suczorno it was the kitchen – if there is one – as it would be in the surrounding villages, where the women sit to sew, to cut up potatoes, or to worry about their men. And there was a great deal about men to worry about. Their violence. Not the *goyish* kind, when brawling, drinking, sleeping it out made an end to it. Leah almost longed for this kind of behaviour – because it would be over. In Suczorno men did not drink or shout openly, but Leah knew and so did all her neighbours, that there was an inner violence, a sudden raising of the voice that made the walls tremble. To want to be right always, or having lost a profitable business, men changed colour and the women know the sequence of silence and outburst, the pounding of a man's full fist upon the table while jumping to his feet.

The wandering Messiahs, who turned up in Suczorno from time to time, had annoyed the men. "They live off our work, they spread superstition, they're liars and parasites, and they are not learned enough; they sing and talk, and mainly to our women. They disturb the peace." So the men said. But they often waited. A Jew had to be kind and welcoming to another Jew, open his door, feed the stranger if he was hungry. So the men waited and watched the passers-through. Sometimes they'd leave after a few days of respite. But Suczorno had a good name in the countryside for hospitality and respect for its own deviants. Not this time. To set up rival rabbinical wisdom, with young men teaching to hear the new wandering Messiah, and — God forbid — enchanted by him, would leave house-hearth and father-mother, to follow him. It had happened before and it had to be prevented.

So the men felt. A solid number of four, which had a special significance in the Bible — starting with the fourth day of creation or the four questions on the Passover night. So the four respectable citizens, Leah's husband Moishe in lead, decided to go over the little bridge, one by one, in the direction of the barn.

Leah, hands folded into her apron, heart beating like a drum, would not move. She let her work wait, did not worry about Sarah's visits to Naomi or the tornado that had destroyed her hen-house. She just sat, ears attuned to footsteps, did not go to the window, where she could have sat on her small upholstered and embroidered footstool to comfortably watch the happenings. She wouldn't now. Not this time. She knew what their faces would look like, and she couldn't bear the thoughts that would assault her from the moment she saw the four men appear on the bridge within her field of vision. So she sat on the kitchen chair. A real chair with a good back, built by the master woodworker from the other side of the creek.

"Have we paid our bills, God of all the Universe, I can't remember. Moishe is slow, sometimes fears to be cheated, or the sum is too high, so he holds some money back – one can so easily forget." But she sat on her favourite chair upright and let thoughts come and go, without pursuing them, felt the heartbeat slow down, time passing unnoticed and breathing becoming easier. Still, her ears were on the metal handles of the entrance door, and she jumped to her feet when she heard them turn, and facing her husband, she heard him say: "They, the *Chasidim,* were packing their few belongings when we entered – after knocking, of course, saying *Shalom Alechem,* peace be with us all, and wishes of good health – and assessing the situation I, the spokesman said: 'Revered rabbi, we have come to wish you well, to you and your learned disciples. God's speed, and may the Almighty in His great goodness bind you to Him in service and honour, like all of us.' And I put my hands in the pocket, to hand them a *chazerl* – the little Russian pig – a small gold coin to pay for their help with some of our citizens who had come to see them in their need."

And Leah fell upon the neck of her husband and cried, "My wise, my just, my wonderful husband, to whom I have given my life. I cannot thank you enough."

And Moishe stroked his beard and also thought he had done well, according to the law, not to be harsh with strangers.

Moishe's Chair

SUCZORNO WAS AT PEACE with itself this summer. Rains had come and gone, sunny days had made travel easy, and Moishe thought of harnessing his horses. He had almost given up his fight with Sarah; he knew her kind. She was his child, she was wilful and stubborn, and let the Lord's will guide her. He did not think that using his paternal power and authority would persuade her and he would not force her. Neither could his father have imposed his will on him. Moishe was restless as a young man to travel, see the world outside Suczorno. He did not want to sit in his father's tanning shop, with yellow fingers, yellow teeth, hides hanging to dry, one day following the other with the rising at five in the morning and the going to sleep when the sun set to save on candles. It was not for him. There was a world out there. To sit in his father's tanning shop, inhaling acidy fumes, stretching the hides, nailing them to prepared boards, drying them in the shade in the summertime and controlling the heat in the winter for fear they'd shrink just a little too much, was not for him. Moishe loved the books and was good in *Cheder,* but past *Bar Mitzvah,* there was no holding him. He packed his bags.

"What will you do, my son? Where do you go to? Who will welcome you and how will you eat?"

"I'll trade," he'd said.

"What trade?"

"Little things, first ribbons, thread of all colours, needles, women's needs."

"Wait," his father had said, "wait a week. I'll make you a wooden trading tray with a lid and lock, leather straps to support it wide enough not to hurt your back."

And his father, the tanner, made for Moishe, his eldest son, one of these wonders with different sized compartments, small ones for needles, thread, and thimbles, and bigger ones for scissors and files. Leather pouches with strings threaded through for closing-opening and the holding of glass pearls, long divisions for strips of leather that come in handy when finishing men's sheepskin jackets, those short, embroidered inside-out, hip-hugging jackets for Sunday wear a peasant loves so much. So with a heavy heart his father put his son on the road.

Not having learned a trade, equipped only with a peddler's trunk, a few assembled goods, and a gold coin for saving his life, Moishe had kissed his father goodbye with everyone standing at the door to see him leave. And this was the last picture in his mind: one brother, two sisters standing in the frame of the door, father and mother in front of the house. A last picture. It can't be erased. As much as Moishe has often hoped it would be. It was branded into the brain, stamped with his father's fiery sheepskin branding irons. It was there in moments of longing for their love, or within the aching muscles after a dusty day on the road. It was there when he returned and did not find them anymore.

Moishe was in Odessa, when by the Jewish grapevine, ear-to-ear rumour post, he heard of the great fire which swept the lower bank of the Suczorno Creek. And Moishe feared the worst. He had been born on that side of the creek, where all traders were, the tailors, carpenters, furriers, and his father, the tanner. Craftsmen, but poor. The rich were on the other side. All misfortune, it seemed, befell the poor. Perhaps the land, being lower, was more open to assault of marauding gangs, or Christians at Easter time with their priests leading the hayfork-carrying peasants. Always the lower bank. The rich would come after every disaster and show they were also Jews. Because disaster could strike them too, if not as often. And Moishe had said to his father one day – being still a little boy, while sorting leather bits and pieces, that had been cut off and littered the floor – "When I'm grown up, I'll own a house on the upper bank of the creek. I'll be rich, so you and mother can have a room of your own when you're old." It was not to be. And no fire, however intense, could erase the last picture at the back of his eye.

So, this was the best summer in years. Suczorno Creek had green banks instead of brown, its water transparent down to the last stone. The lilacs behind the houses, fading by now, left the air tangy, retaining their memory. Jews liked to praise the Lord for every day they were allowed to rise and see the sun. Fathers and mothers looked less worried about their children and work was slower. A good summer day. A carp swimming happily in a tub. Not in every house. But there was more sharing, or intentionally leaving some of the head, tail, or the bones perhaps to be sucked by a wandering fiddler. There was a mood of giving, of deep joy; the women stepping outside their doors, humming, glad to see the others.

Houses huddling so close, Suczorno was fortunate to have the river run through it, to separate its people, create a space between them to breathe easier and to remind them that every life flows like its water and only God's law remains steady and forever. In the law there is no yesterday, no tomorrow, no seasons, as summer or winter would be. It is a pivot. A shield: to sing on a summer day and to cry when the days grow dark, or shout and quarrel with the Lord as Job had done. But on such a day as this one, there was peace.

On the fourth day in the week – what did God do this day? –

with two days still to go until *Shabbat* – one did not worry. God would provide. It was far yet, and they gathered at the well, men on one side and women on the other. After prayers. For chat and family news. But in spite of the glory of an unequaled day, a pensive mood had taken hold of the men. They walked in pairs and talked. Bitter news was prevailing. It was not about themselves, but – as the desert-old saying goes: "If you shear the sheep, the lambs will tremble" – it was about their brothers in the next village. So instead of rejoicing, having been granted a day of plenty, of the best water in the well anyone would wish for, Joseph, old now and like his Biblical namesake a reader of man's soul, said to Moishe, with whom he was walking: "I feel like my ancestor Joseph – thrown into the pit, he hears or divines his brothers' evil intentions. Fortunately greed prevailed and they sold him into slavery to a passing caravan of Midianites."

"You're seeing too dark, Joseph. Maybe we'll live by the grace of the Egyptians, but Moses is still far."

And so it was in Suczorno, the past was the present. Everyone was Jacob or his son Joseph. And God worked his purpose through them. What this purpose was, He alone would know, for it was not penetrable. But that there was purpose was not debated. How could one live without this certainty? Had He not elevated His people, had He not given them His law? And not just the celebration of the seventh day, when He looked at His labour and found it good, but the great commandments of ten, and six hundred and thirteen lesser ones to live through a day? Had He not done that? So the spirit rose and Joseph too went home to his midday meal of kasha and goat's milk, or cow's milk on better days.

But Moishe, Sarah's father, went home to the golden porridge of corn. He did not cherish the buckwheat, though roasted on an open fire it would make a good meal, Moishe preferred the Romanian golden corn, milled to perfection, which he sometimes brought home from his southern travels. Boiled to a mush, with fresh or soured milk, there was nothing better in heaven or earth. So he went home in hope of his preferred midday-meal on this beautiful summer day.

Joseph had worried him and he was longing for solace, when he saw his wife, in front of their home, coming to meet him: Sarah had not been seen since six o'clock in the morning and the sun was high, perhaps one hour past noon. And Moishe refused to worry. He had had enough, he wanted to say his prayers, eat, and rest for a quarter hour. But Leah insisted. The low tones in which she spoke and the specific ominous ring in the voice of his wife made him listen. He hated her conspiratorial behaviour, which he thought a woman's weapon: knowing things before they happened, always fearing the worst for their children, and the reading of disaster-omens. "Sarah was sullen all the day yesterday, and I thought something was up or about to happen, and sure enough —" and so forth. Moishe thought himself rational, but he could not help but think that predictions make things happen. So he hated her for interpreting events by calling on them almost. But he would not acknowledge this reasoning. He just looked at Leah with disapproving eyes, annoyed and impatient.

"Stop calling the demons, Leah, I'm tired of it. Sarah is as she is, and she always comes back, even if she bangs the door in anger."

"This is just it. She did not bang the door in anger. She just left quietly. This is what worries me," she said.

"With you, Leah, it's always danger; if it's not one thing it's another. God will guide her, I said. I want to eat and rest."

And he did not let her say what truly worried her, namely, that Naomi had crossed the bridge, knocked at her door, and had respectfully asked if she, Leah, had seen Srul anywhere; not necessarily in her house, but anywhere, passing by, or anywhere at all, because Srul has not slept in his bed all night. Some news! And now Moishe was angry, not to be talked to. Leah served him his golden *mamaliga,* which was all ready and simmering in the pot. Just before sitting down to the meal, she would turn the pot upside down, so a crown of yellow gold would fall upon the plate, steaming hot. To be cooled down with the milk, soured in earthen pots.

Moishe had slumped into his chair wearily. Slept for a little, woke, and Leah served him his meal in silence. She let him be and waited. You couldn't overwhelm a man. She knew her place, her measure, and nothing could be achieved by breaking a man. So she thought. Busied herself with little duties around herself. A drawer with cutlery she pulled out. Saw the knives needed sharpening. Went outside to find a flat stone, wetted it with a drop of water from the rain barrel. Suczorno was "world famous" for its barrels. One wealthy man at the end of the village, who still did his trade the good-old-fashioned way, selected, steamed, bent the finest wood to perfection, let it dry, shaped, and held it with an iron band which never rusted. Leah looked with pride on her lovely barrel. Covered it again, but just half, for the rainwater "to breathe." Everything has to breathe to live, and she smiled a little, relieved for a moment of having to face Moishe.

So she wetted her stone, seated herself on the backdoor threshold, pulling the knife from the handle to the top across the humid stone, several times until, tested against her thumb, it felt sharp.

Then she sat silently to collect her wits until she heard the familiar screech of the chair against the slate floor. She could be anywhere around the home or outside, and Leah would recognize this particular sound of Moishe rising from his chair. There he rested after a meal, never to lie down, as young men like to do. No. After a meal and many hours of work, he'd pull his snuff box from his coat pocket, put a little – with pinched thumb and index finger – into his nose. Then he sneezed, breathed deeply, and closed his eyes.

Leah had watched him all her life. From the day he came back to Suczorno to find himself an orphan, he had lodged with her own parents. They were well-to-do Suczorno-ers – no one ever knew how her father earned a living. He had inherited their two-room house and did not work with his dainty hands, wearing knitted gloves that left only the fingertips free, summer and winter. He wrote beautifully in Cyrillic, Latin, and Hebrew and was a "lawyer," whatever that meant in Suczorno. No one ever saw any diplomas. And who needed them? If one knew the state law and law of Israel, as Leah's father did, people from Suczorno would come for advice. Even Ukrainians and Poles came, because he was so famous, knew how to write an application properly with all the "Your humble, faithful servants" at the end of an application. Yes, she thought, her genteel father never touched a child in anger!

But of course, her mother did not have an easy life. Which woman does? Where? Suddenly the money would run out. So she would take in a boarder or two into the second room. A traveler perhaps, a merchant, a fiddler coming through. A non-Jew, rarely. But for a night or two – what would it matter to everyone else around? But the people of Suczorno, of course, looked out for one another or, to find a less charitable term, watched the lives of one another closely. It was good if you needed help fast, which a Jew in Suczorno often did, but was very bad if you needed to make a ruble, a leu, or a zloty on the side against the unwritten rules. Yes, women stretched the limits of the law to feed the family or just to get by.

That was the case when Moishe, around twenty-four or five, returned to total disaster. He was not poor, he had money in his pockets and merchandise in his trunk. But what was money, what was it worth, if you returned to find the lives of your own extinguished like a light? Yes, you could rent a room for a night or two, get a meal, put some distance between your pain and the acceptance of God's ways. Yes, you could do that. So Moishe came and stayed.

He was very handsome, worldly; and Leah, listening to fine conversations between her father and the young, widely travelled man, fell in love. She was fifteen.

"Wait a year," her mother had advised. "Don't jump into the fire, wait for the embers to settle – wait a year and we'll see."

But it was hardly a year and they stood under the *Chuppah,* the wedding canopy, drank from the blessed wine, and heard the glass crack under Moishe's foot. And she moved with him then into the second room, which he had rented from her parents, to start married life.

So Leah knew, by every sound he made, what his needs were. He did not have to ask for anything. A good provider, Moishe was a just man if sometimes terribly ill-tempered. But rarely. Often it was her own fault. It annoyed him when she guessed disaster, foresaw it and made it happen. Her habit was to ask him, with the first dawn on the horizon, "Moishe, tell me about your dreams."

"What dreams?"

"I have to know. Your father may talk to you, or your mother, they would warn you if —"

"Leah, I do not dream."

But it was not true. He did. She heard him moan, say indistinguishable words, or just shout in pain. So they did come to him, parents or angels of the Lord. And she must know.

"You're a woman, you're not Joseph, Jacob's son, to know the will of the Lord and read it in man's dreams. Leah, people will point with fingers at you, call you names, or come and think you have 'magic ways.' Stop it! Enough."

Having sharpened her knife and heard Moishe move, she reentered the kitchen and said softly, "Moishe, my God-fearing husband, I have to talk to you." And she pulled that low stool from under the kitchen table to face him.

"Yes," he said with a covert voice that showed his controlled anger. "Yes?"

"I haven't told you that Naomi came over in the morning."

"And..." he said, remaining in his seat, holding on to the arms of the chair. "What for?"

"Give me a chance to tell you. Srul had not touched his bed the night before and she was worried."

"He is a young man of sixteen or so. They have a tendency to be up late —" he spoke a little faster now and so Leah knew to hurry up.

Time was of the essence, and she said, "Moishe, I do not know anything except that Sarah left early this morning, as you know. I heard her leave. I was in the kitchen, she knew it well, but left without a goodbye. I have to ask you, dearest husband, harness your horses, go and find her, before she is with child."

Moishe jumped to his feet, his eyes rimmed with red anger, his clenched fist pounding the table, sending the pretty sugar bowl flying and breaking on the slate floor near the oven, spilling the precious sugar.

"Leah!" he shouted. "Stop your crazy predictions. You open your mouth and disaster comes out. You dream things up at night. Every morning is black to you. I can't bear it any longer." And he shouted and paced the floor, stepped into the spilled sugar, heard the crystals crunch but did not register it. "Enough," he said. "Enough."

"Moishe, remember –"

"Stop it, Leah –"

"Dearest Moishe, go and harness the horses, call for help. Go and bring her home. Look, I was often right and you wished afterwards you had listened to my advice. Remember, when I told you, Moishe, do not send your sons through the Jew's Trap –"

"It's twenty miles shorter," he said, "Practical things or considerations seem of no concern to you. It's quite a shortcut, and there were years and years of peace. We traded and I went down that way several times myself. The peasants would greet me, hat in hand saying 'Good day Reb Moishe, may the Lord protect you, you're a good man.' Now you Leah, you better remember that this was so and don't accuse me of wanting to hurt my sons."

And Leah: "Sure, there was peace in years of good harvest, but Jews should never forget the past. If the place is called the Jew's Trap, our ancestors want to protect us, tell us that there is danger to go through a narrow furrowed path, where horses can't turn and woods are like walls on both sides. You have to listen to them and not be arrogant. We could have lost our sons, three of them."

"Well –" Moishe said. "They came back, didn't they?"

"Yes," she replied. "But how did they come back? How? What did they look like? Nathan's right eye is damaged forever and Israel has trouble breathing. His ribs were broken, remember – and Shimon... Besides, you lost your wagon."

"A wagon. What is this, I can replace it. It's money." he said.

And Leah: "Horses aren't money, you lost your horses. Those wonderful friends of yours, who neighed when they heard your step, obeyed your thought, let alone your reins, knew their way by the tone of your voice – how fast, how urgent – horses aren't money. Now you have these Pinces – idiot horses, good workers, but idiots –"

Moishe did not hear the rest of her lamentations. She had been right, he should never have allowed his inexperienced sons to go this way. It had given him the creeps, every time he went through that thicket, though he was an experienced old man. He should not have – and he went out there without another word to harness the horses.

The stables were a little way off. He did not own one for himself. A man does not need a stable for two horses. A few neighbours had built it, putting the money together and the labour; it had worked well between them. The stable, sturdy and aired, and kept clean by all of them, was another bond between the men. Something to do and talk about while grooming and oiling the leather. It wasn't a real stable as he had seen in Kiev or Krakov. Not a real riding stable, but for Jews, for their needs, it was good enough.

He should be faster, he knew that. But he was slow. Leah had heavied down his whole being with demons everywhere. Why should Sarah be with child, it was just a few hours that she had left, and perhaps her fears, connecting Srul, were also unfounded.

But he was heavy and slow. Every muscle hurt. Business was not great, and worrisome news about political agitation against Jews west of Poland and even south filtered through. Romanians, mostly peaceful, showed hostile faces. At yesterday's Synagogue prayers Suczorno citizens hurried through them like a wind to be able to hear what "the doctor" had heard from his Christian clients, who came to him if their own priests couldn't help.

Moishe was slow. Talked to his Pinzgauers: "Leah is stupid. She calls you 'Pinces.' You're dear and good German Pinzgauers. Hard workers, dear people. Just like me today. Doing one thing after another without knowing either goal or end."

And he put their bits in, which they did not like, and Moishe said again: "I know, neither you nor I like it. All my muscles hurt. When I'm angry, it seems they're wound around the nerves like a braided rope and I can't untangle it. Every stone stabs me through the sole and I'm sure it does the same to you. You're tired, poor things, you have not rested and here I am again" – and Moishe did not want to call anybody. To say what? To risk Sarah's reputation, when she was the dearest, sweetest, most intelligent girl in town. If stubborn – and Moishe smiled. "She is my child."

He had done it all meanwhile and drove into the direction of a sheltered ground on the lower side of the creek, where he himself as a young man had gone after an argument. But then, why would she be there – or they? His heart was heavy, and he took to the road, avoiding all thought.

LEAH FACED THE SILENT HOUSE. She did not expect the noises she heard to be anything else but wind shaking loose boards, rattling windowpanes. She always could tell dream from waking fears. But she had slept badly, had dreamt dark fugitive figures and they had remained with her. Persisted into the day. What message? Where from? Where do demons live? She tried to recall clothes they wore, objects in their hands, body movements or position to read their intentions somehow. But they eluded her. Yet she felt them moving the air around her, pushing her husband's chair, and when she suddenly heard the so familiar screech of slate she rushed to see if it had changed its place. She could not tell, but to make sure she took a piece of chalk and marked the floor in a square around the four legs. Or should she have made a circle? Demons hated circles, she had heard from her grandfather one day. Silly, she thought, and left it at that.

The wind had intensified and time did not move. Her sons were at work. She had made sure they learned a trade and they were willing to give up the "furman" occupation, fraught with the danger of Jews-on-the-road. "I won't have it," she had said to her husband. "Once near death is enough." And he agreed. The two elder ones complied, unwillingly though: "To end up with a crooked back for sitting and stitching, sixteen hours a day" – but Jews end up with a crooked back anyway if tailoring or praying. Shimon, the youngest, was in Synagogue. He was the scholar. A true interpreter of the law, and the singing voice he had could move a stone to tears. And she wiped one away, sitting low now on her kitchen stool, praying for Moishe's safe return and Sarah's rescue.

Why did she leave like a thief? She had heard her mother stirring the embers in the big oven to see if they were sufficient to get a fire started. She heard me distinctly; she left like a thief. Where to? And Leah jumped to her feet. She had heard the scratch of wood against slate. All blood left hands and feet. She trembled, had no strength to look at the chair. Had it moved? And she dared turn to have a look. Not a great deal, it seemed to her. But it definitely had. She remembered distinctly her chalk mark from the back of the chair and it looked different now. It was more on an angle now, and Leah froze onto the spot, supporting herself with her right hand on the table. Who were these figures in her dreams? They were around her. She knew they'd come to tell her that she'd never see her child again, her only daughter.

When she heard the door move, Leah rushed towards it and fell into the arms of Sarah. Leah, sobbing, was not to be consoled, and the daughter led her mother to the bench under the window, to hold her until she had quieted down, and then Sarah took her mother's tear-streaked face into her hands and said, "Mother, I'll marry Srul. I've been with him this morning."

And her mother kissed her hands, held them in hers and said, "Sarah, the Lord has spoken. You'll marry Srul in a beautiful wedding. As in times of old. When?"

And Sarah replied, "It must be soon."

"It will be," the mother said. "It will be."

And Leah rose to her feet. Laughing. As if there had been no dark figures pushing Father's chair about. "Sarinke," she said. "You'll be a bride with whomever you wish to be a bride to."

Leah busied herself, giggling, making plans, talking too fast as one who had just overcome mortal danger, had swum a treacherous river and was holding her rescued child in her arms, drenched and dripping.

"Mother," Sarah said, "one more thing. I know it is hard, but we'll have to cross the bridge over the creek, the two of us, and go to see Naomi. It's hard, I know. She has always been a thorn in your flesh, but never in mine. She is a friend to me. Mother —"

"Of course," Leah said. "Of course. Wait till I wash my face and put a scarf over my shoulders."

And Sarah led her mother over the bridge, so as not to tumble into the water, so unsteady she was.

MOISHE DROPPED THE REINS, jumped down from his wagon, calling his horses stupid and slow, as if they had caused all his anguish of coming home empty-handed. He dropped his reins, but sat a little longer on an old tree stump, polished with time, not wanting to face his wife. But not only her. Weary. Weary he was of life's burden. Of having to live his children's lives, without any control or dominion over them. Customs looked the same on the surface, but deep down in the heart of the families could be felt the torment, the breakdown of respect for what should be eternal. God and His laws. Work. Honour Father and Mother. The fifth of the Commandments, not the first – that belongs to Him – but not the fifth in importance. Without it, there were no bonds to hold the world together. A small community depended on that inner cohesion. Without the respect of the old, there would be no *Torah,* all would be splintered, broken apart, torn from the inside and flung into all corners of a hostile world.

"I'm weary," he said to himself, within clenched teeth. "I'm weary. Why should I run out when I have so much work to do, to make a living, provide for all of them. Why should I run through dusty roads all around Suczorno and further up where the road curls, and derelict barns, unused now, doors banging in the wind, looking like Sodom and Gomorrah, stare me in the face. The end of the world. That's what it will be, with no heeding of advice from your elders and all that new thought in the air.

From where does it sweep in? How do they pick it up? Or is this the promised payment for our own sins? I'm weary of all of it, and my heart breaks for my beautiful child."

He sat a little longer and took time to say a good word to his horses. Especially to the slimmer younger one, a brown-and-white mare, not fully a Pinzgauer, who learned a little better what Moishe wanted of her than the other one.

"Oh, you pretty thing, it's not your fault, these are the ways of the world..."

He stroked them both, taking their front pieces off and the bits and left them with a friendly pat on their behind to walk the hundred steps to the house. His legs did not obey. He was slow, muscles and nerves – as he put it – intertwined, did not obey his command from above and were live ropes binding him to the spot. Hurting. He stopped, looked at his shoes – perhaps he was hindered by the trailing shoelaces – saw his earth-dirt clinging, thickening them so they wouldn't fit into the hooks of the leather boot, and his tears ran into his beard. He let them flow, grateful for the release, and then with a fast wipe of his hand across his face, his back straightened, he walked faster towards the kitchen-entrance of his house. It was empty.

Moishe fell into his chair – as if thrown into it. Wondered for a second, looking down at the chalk marks on the slate underneath it, and lost consciousness as if murdered.

WHEN HE WOKE IN HIS CHAIR – after how many hours? – it was a voice from heaven that shook him. An angel's voice. Soft, harmonious, sweet. Sarah's. She sat on her mother's footstool, which had its place under the table. It was low enough, comfortable enough, when peeling potatoes or pitting prunes, or to talk to someone on Father's chair. Leah sat on that low stool when facing Moishe. And he dreaded it every time she said, "I have to talk to you —" pulling the low stool from under the table.

On that stool, his daughter sat, who had waited a considerable time before saying to her father, who had moved just a little, "Father, I have come for your blessing." Moishe heard the words of his true Jewish child and all his tears rose to his throat when she continued, "I am asking for your blessing, but also for forgiveness to have put you through such anguish. It was wrong. But I saw no other way." And she took both his hands from the arms of the chair, looked at them pensively for a moment, placed them on her own head, and said, "Speak the holy words, father."

And Moishe said, "Rise my child and come with me to the front room. We'll wait for your mother. But first, my Sarah, where were you from six o'clock in the morning? Whereto does a good Jewish child run from her father's house?"

There was no answer until Moishe heard a shy voice, "Father, I was with Srul. I had walked out of the house the moment I saw Srul under my window. It was still early, I saw no movement on either side of the creek, and we walked along its bank, downriver, not leaving it, holding its course until it turns south. We had walked in silence, when Srul took my hand and motioned me to sit down on a flat stone, high above the river, where you took us, when we were children."

"I know where it is," the father said.

"So we sat down, overcome by the beauty of the morning. The river bending, flowing down, shining with the gold of the sun. I thought of Ecclesiastes, 'All streams...' when Srul said: 'Sarah, we'll get married, as soon as the law allows it. I have my parent's permission. First, they said: "Wait, Srul, wait a year." To which I replied: "I can't." "So bring her home then, in the name of the Lord." "This is how it will be with or without your father's blessing." "Not without," I replied. "Not without."' And here I am now, asking you for it.'"

"Good," says the father, and seeing Leah approach the house with Naomi, Mordechai, and Srul, Moishe went to the front door, to open it wide, stepped out in front, extending both arms, and said with a certain gravity: "Welcome, my honoured *Machtunim,* welcome to Sarah's father's house."

And he led the company in and closed the door, knowing that every neck would strain to watch or listen in. For this was the life in the shtetl. Love, hate, and reconciliation. Every soul a witness. And what one did not know, one guessed or in the worst cases invented.

But this was good news. Too young of course, children will come, a living has to be made – but Suczorno guessed Moishe would build onto the back of his house a room for the newly-weds. There was enough room on the lot. He was not a poor man. So the folk speculated. Or they'd move into the spare room, where Moishe had stayed on his return from Odessa before marrying Leah. And so it went. They wouldn't be hungry. There might be strife, as the household got more crowded, but they couldn't move in to Naomi's. There was no room there at all, most of it was taken up by Mordechai's *atelier,* and the kitchen being so small, no piece of land behind, and a little one there still, a late-comer. "Who can tell the ways of the Lord —" and so forth. Suczorno knew everything.

It was Leah's father's old house. With no proper foundation, it was a solid house. Square wooden posts were at proper distances;

made of mortar and stucco, it had withstood the onslaught of marauding wanderers from the east, the pillaging, the occasional Mongol incursions, and the regular Easter visits. If not every Easter, so certainly when times were hard. The poor souls who worked the land with ancient tools, hoping for a harvest, depending on the benevolence of the heavens, descended when times were hard. They came before Easter, on the Friday of the Passion, led by their priests, with sticks to break the Jews' windows, to shout Christ-killers, and take what grain there was. But there was peace in between, not to call it harmony. Just friendly barter, and now and then deeds of compassion for one another: the Jewish doctor going to the peasants, helping with a difficult birth or with other inexplicable sicknesses befalling the poor, and the peasants always paid the Jew well. With eggs, or a hen, always with blessings, the sign of the cross the Jew could do without but accepted respectfully.

So Leah's father's house had seen it all, and the back room, which Moishe had rented at the time, was still good. With a little refurbishing, a new bed perhaps, a table and two new chairs, it might serve for the young couple.

Now all sat stiffly in the front room, which Leah remembered as *die geete Steeb,* the good room, which served as reception room in the daytime, a bedroom for eight children at night, and all purpose on any occasion. Here they sat now in the same "reception" room to talk to each other, where there never had been any talk before. Srul and Sarah, each with their own father and mother. The air thick with the unspoken word made breath short and glances turn shoe-ward.

Leah, mother of the bride, sitting erect in her own father's chair now, went to the rescue and said: *"Machtunim,* Srul, and my own dear family, welcome! It was in this very room, facing these windows that I sat a little older than our daughter Sarah, with my parents, to be engaged to my beloved Moishe. Right here." And she looked at him lovingly, turned then to Naomi and Mordechai. "Now we have Srul's parents with us, I welcome you with all my heart. As you know there were no *Machtunim* – no in-laws – as Moishe's parents had perished in the fire that nearly destroyed all of Suczorno. How much more reason we have to thank the Lord that you, Naomi, have been spared. And Mordechai also. You too, Naomi, had to suffer the loss of parents. Which I acknowledge for the first time. Dear Naomi, as I have said to you when coming over with Sarah, let mothers help to build the good life of our two children and forget all bitter worry and fear."

And Naomi rose, walked towards Leah, who had risen before to speak, embraced her, kissed her, and choking with tears, said, "We will, dearest *Machteineste,* we will."

The ice was broken. Tea was made, sugar came in a round lit-tle dish, as the bowl of porcelain, the famous "wedding gift," had jumped from the table; Leah smilingly started to explain its absence but swallowed the story. Not at a happy occasion, she thought. But who can forget lying on the floor to collect the sugar and having to wash all of the floor. In Suczorno if you do not keep clean, cockroaches will infest, ants will nest – Oh, life.

And Leah went over to talk to everyone. Her heart was light. Lifted from a premonition as dark as people pointing with fingers at her beautiful daughter, calling her a whore; and Suczorno could be a cruel place when it came to women's faults. It's always them: they have been tempting, they wear their hair over their shoul-ders, they sit outside, dangling their legs into the creek, showing

them. Suczorno watches its girls, from childhood on. Of men –
everything is expected. If not forgiven. It's our fault.

But Leah smiled, turned to Srul, urged him to partake in her
kuchlach, little oily corkscrew-looking bakery, with cinnamon on
top, which one made from the dough of the *Shabbat* bread. Srul
took one for his glass of tea, thanked his future mother-in-law,
and was silent. Did not look at Sarah, which would be unfitting,
and returned to sit next to his parents to finish his tea. The men
addressed each other, both relieved and worried. Where would all
the money come from?

"See you in *Shul,*" Moishe said, "when the happy news will be
announced. The children will stay in our back room until I'll have
enough money to build out into the yard. They can use our
kitchen. Of course, they'll eat with us. I'll provide the bedding
and everything else, naturally. Until –"

And Mordechai smiled back at Moishe saying, "I'll help out
with Srul's education. He is good at almost everything he wants
to do. Yes, he has to want it. I'm a father, I'll help too." And the
men shook hands: "See you in *Shul.*"

The women hugged, Sarah and Srul did not look at each
other, and the company left. "God bless and wishes for good
health."

In front of the door, they all stood until Srul and his parents
reached the bridge and then they turned in.

No word was spoken anymore about anything. The father at
the kitchen table, taking out his accounts from the table drawer,
immersed himself in numbers. Leah said only: "Come help me,
Sarah, to peel potatoes and get me the carrots and onions from
the north end of the shed. The boys will be here, supper has to be
ready in a couple of hours. First things first. And tomorrow,

Sarinka, we'll start thinking." And she turned to her daughter to take her around in a girlish whirl and said, "My daughter will be the most beautiful bride on earth."

Jubilation

JUBILATION. A bride. The town got busy to provide five kilograms of honey for the honey cake, twenty-five eggs, leavening, salt, raisins, a bag of the whitest flour! For everything. For the braided bread – the *Challah* – and spiced bread, cinnamon sweet pepper cookies, a small barrel of salted herring to be desalted. Twenty onions, coarsely cut, black kernels of pepper vinegar, sunflower seed oil, to marinate it all – the town was busy. Rich and poor crossed the bridge, carried dishes. Everybody was kosher. No problem. Some cleaner, some fussier than others. Everybody ate from everyone's dish – earthen or glass. *Kümmel* – caraway in Schnapps: "Not enough time to take the best out of it, but good enough for the herring."

And the Romanians from the south, with whom Moishe had always dealt in peace and honour, let him have their red wine for a song. "Because it's the first of your children, because you, Moishe, are an honest man, who has never cheated us like other Jews would – because we love a wedding." Good wine. He brought it home on his wagon in uncorked *damigianas,* these round-bellied, heavy, green ten litre glass bottles that look like pregnant ladies, and in fact, so his Romanians told Moishe, in fact – so the story goes – there was once a beautiful princess called Joana, the dame Joana, or the Dame-Jeanna, who was kissed – and so forth, got pregnant and that is why the bottle is so round-bellied.

"Oh, the Romanians with their tales – a really jolly people – not like ourselves, no kings, no queens, no beautiful princesses, just the Lord and life."

Moishe, taking his fat-bellied *damigianas* home full of a very good wine, tasted a little on the way and he hummed. Life was good and the Lord was great. *Hagofen,* the fruit from the vine, He had given us to praise Him. And Moishe thought of his good fortune, of all the miracles that had to happen to make life what it is. A celebration. There was no wine in the north, the Poles did not have any, and the Russians did not have any except in Odessa or near the Caspian Sea and the Crimea. It was hard to live without it and it made the poor wretches brew corn into hard liquor and it made them lift their fists against one another. But wine made a man soft, made you think good thoughts about your fellow man. One wanted to hug and kiss, sing and sing. So the Romanians had their wine and they came from where we came from, Rome, the Holy Land, Jerusalem. So Moishe mused. Things had worked out.

Jubilation indeed. No one celebrated as the citizens of Suczorno did. Everyone was there. To help, to give unasked advice, to lend a specific pot which holds the *kugel* better, the one made of noodles, with nuts and jam, sunflower seed oil, honey, or sugar. The jam could be any preserved fruit. But black cherries were best. They gave it the rich, dark, shiny crust that stuck to the pot. And if the pot was too small or inadequate, it stuck so badly that one lost half of the *kugel* or it burned and the whole thing was lost. The trouble was one had to control the fire, and Suczorno ovens – well! So one carried the *kugel* in the pot to the best oven in town. This time, it was a newly refurbished stove, where one could watch the fire through a grate, have the fire roaring in the beginning, and then feed it less and less until it burned gently. An art.

And there they sat watching it, at Selig's house, Selig, whose wife had died, whose children had left for the wilds of Canada, but who was a mason, a woodcarver-carpenter, and had finally finished his own house. Not really finished, whoever finished anything in Suczorno, what with the Synagogue, which needed repair work all the time, prayers, and making a living, somehow. To Selig they went with the *kugels*. Ten, at least.

So Selig prepared the fire, found kindling and big-cut wood, and the women took over his kitchen. Selig loved it. To relieve loneliness, feel part of the town, have gossip and laughter. Women. They were life itself, giving it to the world, feeding and sustaining it. What a gift of God. He missed it badly. He had no daughter, only three sons, and his wife died young. He loved the women. How they shouted, smacked their children, and held them close when they cried. But he did not remarry. He was too poor, a pious man, he kept to himself. All his longings he buried in his soul and in service to the Lord.

A storyteller too. Of all the little girls, he favoured Sarah, a thoughtful child, beautiful and tender, who listened to his wild tales, adventures in faraway places, where churches were tall and spires elongated; slim, strange figures of stone dancing on them. Sarah had seen only round ones, onion-domed ones. From the outside only, of course. Where should she have seen anything Selig described? He told of his father, who was an artist-wood-carver, though Jews did not need artists, it seemed. Because of the law. They could sin – God forgive – and might start making images of themselves or carving them out of wood or stone. All of that unimaginable. A sin of that magnitude! But Selig told stories his father had brought home from the great Polish city of Lvov, where people sat in church – pews of rosewood, carved with figures from the Scriptures, and he, Selig's father, had been employed for a season.

Sarah too longed to see this world. Artistic herself with pencil and chalk, she could make a man's likeness with two strokes, but was shouted at when discovered by her mother.

"Nonsense, Sarah, stop it! Learn your Hebrew letters. This is where God is. The Almighty does not like idols. Lvov is all right for the Poles. It's not for us. As soon as life gets hard – and God Himself knows it does – people start drawing pictures. Stop it. There is no God beside God."

But Sarah never saw harm in it. What had that got to do with God? Besides, He could see into her soul and know what she felt. And she always drew. It was strictly forbidden, but she sought and found a quiet moment, a corner of her own, to draw on slate and erase it. A flower, a demon with tail and many fiery tongues, or a pair of beautiful shoes with pearly buttons, which her father had brought as a gift to her when she was four. She was caught again and again.

"It is Selig with his terrible tales. You're not allowed to go there anymore. He fills your head with nonsense, imaginings, not right for a Jewish girl..." and so forth.

But Sarah had the nature of her father. Stubborn. She forced her family to give in to her because she could not or would not. She had a head of her own. It was hard to live in a group so tied in knots on all corners as Suczorno was, inspected, judgmental, and controlled, and remain Sarah.

"But she is stubborn like a mule who throws off the extra burden," her mother always said, sighed and gave in. Because the child was not unreasonable, one could follow that reasoning, and on its own, not find it wanting. For instance, why not draw God's world, which he had created in His wisdom? Was it not perfect? Seasons following one another, a bud flowering and bearing fruit, a yellow field of rape and a sky-blue one of the linen flower. Her mother found Sarah collecting ochre earth, black coal-rests from the fire, and old rusty paint pails with remnants of green or blue.

"What do you do with them?" her mother had asked her.

And Sarah had lied in reply, "Nothing, I just like old things."

But of course she lied. Her mother found her using sticks, finely sharpened pieces of wood, which Sarah dipped into these pails. Sometimes she thinned them with linseed oil she had pressed out of the seed, and sometimes she used rainwater.

"What do you do, Sarah, your hands are blue and green? Go wash your hands before dinner." Her mother knew, put her in her place, but let her be. If one couldn't win, what was a mother to do? Even her embroidery took on strange shapes. Designs on her blouse that came from nowhere – so Leah blamed it on Naomi. "Do not go there anymore. Who other than Naomi, with her strange ways, would want faces or animals on a blouse, instead of a cross-stitch?" But nothing worked; not if you were Moishe's daughter. One could only teach stubborn souls what they wanted to learn. So she gave up. And when Sarah wanted to marry Srul, forced the family by walking out one morning, throwing father and mother into despair, Leah knew there was no resistance possible.

"When you can't jump over it, you bend under it," as the saying was in Suczorno.

So one celebrated life with gusto, with wild joy, when all had been said and done. A wedding was a wedding. And one so desired by a young couple was – besides money and God knows what pitfalls – a heaven-sent thing, a cause to eat and drink and help them to their bed. A true wedding. The *Chuppah* dusted and re-embroidered in spots, seams and fringes re-sewn, the Synagogue back room swept, tables washed and dried, brilliant white sheets spread ready for the *Challah* and wine to be blessed. It was a morning God had created for a young couple to be united. Still separate, bride and groom sat with their families. Emotional little whispers at the appearance of the rabbi, all done up, with a sash around the middle to distinguish the holy from the unholy.

The little veil, taken out of her mother's trunk, covered Sarah's face fully, as if she had never laid eyes on her husband and master-to-be. Her mother tightening it a little closer to comply with the unwritten oral laws and be proper.

So all the Jewish world and Suczorno as well should remember Jacob's despair for having served seven years for the beautiful Rachel, when he had to discover that Laban had brought his older daughter Leah, fully veiled, to his tent at night. And then seven more years for the lovely younger Rachel, his love! But God's ways were inscrutable and full of purpose, pointing the way like an arrow flung from a bow. So Rachel, after fourteen years, became the fulfillment of Jacob's old days and her two sons closer to his being than the ten or so children born before them. Purpose in God's ways had to be read by the children of Israel, understood and lived accordingly.

So Leah, the mother, tightened the veil around Sarah's sweet face and waited for the bridegroom's party, all witnesses to the event, to lift the veil and make sure the face under the veil was the face of his beloved. The true Rachel-of-old. And with the bridegroom in the middle of the *Chuppah* and the bride's party moving seven times around him – memories, perhaps, of the seven years of labour or the seven of creation, who can tell? – the crushing sound of the broken glass under Srul's foot, and through the mouth of the rabbi the words: "May God bless and Keep you, may He turn His shining countenance upon you," and the ring on her finger, the company broke into sobs of joy; having crossed the Red Sea, they could watch the Egyptians drown in the returning waters. The little golden band on Sarah's finger did not fit well, but it had been the one Leah was wed with, having received it from her own mother on the morning of her wedding to Moishe.

And so it went in Suczorno. The days of old were today and would be tomorrow if God was willing. Jews remembered their ancestor Abraham sending out a servant to find a bride from his own tribe, a worthy bride for his son Isaac. And slipping two golden bands onto a beautiful kind maiden's fingers, a maiden who had quenched the servant's thirst and the thirst of his camels, he made Rebeccah Isaac's bride. Of course, after many delays because of her father, and with permission granted and the gift of a nose ring in gold, she followed, out of her own free will to become Rebeccah, the mother of them all. Just putting an old band onto a young finger today, all was renewed. From Abraham's time to tomorrow.

There was money of all sorts. A gold piece or two, to the jubilation of all of Suczorno – of course, mean tongues would record guilty feelings on account of the giver, the rich, spoiled Rachel and her horse-dealing father. The latter term amounted to as much as a cheat and a thief. But gold was pure as gold could be, and no money smelled of anything but the future. General jubilation in Suczorno for the generosity of the giver, guilt or no guilt. And there were many little things, used and new, a night table, a candle holder for that night table, and of course two beautiful brass, old *Shabbat* candle-holders for Sarah, a true Jewish Sarah, the wife of Abraham, to bless the seventh day.

When all had been eaten, drunk, and enjoyed, with *Mazel Tov,* the good luck wish, Suczorno quieted down. And Srul, that evening, took his few belongings in several trips across the bridge of the Suczorno Creek, to move into the back room of his parents-in-law – where they themselves had started married life – to be a husband to his beloved Sarah.

A Rapture of Love

THE CHILDREN CAME FAST AND FURIOUS. In a short few years, the house was full with little ones, one falling across the other, and Moishe found himself obliged to build on another room and another kitchen. Only God knew where the money came from. In Suczorno one did things and no one knew how. One dealt, one bargained, one bartered, one sold an old bed and bought a new one. As long as there was health, children grew. They started to go to *Cheder* by three or four. And no one knew who was chosen to live and prosper. If there was peace and bread, the priests were friendly. Pogroms were rare and one could lead one's children to the *Chuppah*. God willing.

But for Srul and Sarah, times were hard. Children, always a joy and benediction, but coming in so close to one another, were often ill and took all their strength. Money was short and tempers flared. Srul, a soft-spoken, learned young man, taught Hebrew to all the other children of three, four, and five, until *Bar Mitzvah* even, but was not well rewarded. There was no money for teachers in Suczorno – or so little. Sarah became impatient with her lot. And Srul knew: there was a limit to a woman's patience. An artistic, passionate spirit such as Sarah's bore all that strife with difficulty. She had never fully obeyed any law, neither did she bow to Suczorno's unwritten ones, nor to her father's. She wanted to draw and paint, and she drew and painted her pictures, albeit on the sly, the hidden, the unrepentant lying. And when it came to love, neither sticks nor stones got in her way, and no orders from above could hold her.

But now she had to deal with life itself. The little ones. Three boys and a girl so far, and no end in sight as her belly swelled very soon after weaning the last baby. The whole town chuckled. Did they – these two rebels – did they obey the law, did they stay within it – or? Guessing, but not judging them viciously. The young couple was cherished. For love would move Suczorno-ers to tears. The women would forgive, what there was to forgive, and the men did not care or looked away. Love.

For Sarah and Srul, when the day was over, the day started, neither thinking of a grueling tomorrow. He read to her, and she drew as he read. Kitchen table cleared, chalk, pen, and paper – expensive, expensive! – taken out of stashed-away places. It was never obvious or lying around. Simply to avoid argument with Moishe and Leah, who thought it extravagant and sinful. Upon the table at night, arrayed comfortably for her hand's reach, Sarah displayed her colours and papers.

"We'll do Ecclesiastes," Srul said one night. "I'll read it to you in Hebrew first, so you'll hear the sound of majesty. A language of inimitable power, a poetry subtle and thunderous, and then I'll translate it into Yiddish and Russian, so, though we'll lose a little of the presence of God, the meaning will replace it. The earth will replace heaven, or rather will complete heaven. And you'll see the waters flowing into the sea; never stopping to rise to heaven, in a circle of renewal, bringing forth a flower, a field of grain, and love of man for woman." And he smiled, "And woman for her man."

From that night on, they were a team. He read and she drew as he switched from Hebrew – the sound of awe – to Yiddish-Russian – the sound of earth. They fell into bed by midnight or past, in a rapture of love. Body and spirit. To rise with the first shout of hunger of their youngest, who slept beside them. Srul helped the little girl to Sarah's breast, whispering that one couldn't win in this household, as there was always someone for her breast. But there were two or three hours of rest to come before the day's onslaught.

And Sarah drew, painted, and illustrated. Jews obeyed and loved the law, but it was also the most demanding tyrant: an obsessive pursuer of a man or a woman's expression of anything other than the great books. It fettered, it shackled, it bound their feet with iron chains. And Jews lived within them, sheltered and certain of the love of God. But for those as Sarah was, and Srul, there was hardship. There was strife and combat and conflict. Not only with judgment or condemnation by the zealots, but conflict with duty, with life itself, which wanted or needed all of one's strength.

One night late, when they had read the Exodus together, and Sarah had done by the third candle a magnificent series of illustrations, Srul, looking at it, said, "I've heard of a Hebrew printer in Lemberg-Lvov of the Passover *Haggadah*. I do not know if he can sell an illustrated *Haggadah* to the rich Jews in Lemberg, but

Sarah, I cannot let your talent go to waste in our drawer. I'll go to Lemberg. With or without passport. Jews do not need one. Which country? Russian-Romanian-Polish – what for? I'll go to Lemberg. Everybody needs a Passover *Haggadah* – the Exodus storytelling book. And you, Sarah, told me that your old friend Selig said he had seen wonderfully printed illuminations of the Christian gospels."

"Right," she replied. "Selig said it would be permissable and beautiful to have the Exodus story illustrated. Maybe the Lemberg artist would print it. It does not matter, Christian or Jewish. Print is print."

And the next morning, to the amazement of Leah and Moishe, Srul announced his leaving. "I may be gone for a month. To Lemberg."

"To do what?"

"I've found business there."

"What business? Selling horses?"

"No, not selling horses. Not selling yet. I'll find a printer and buyers interested in beautiful things. Jews with money, who can afford to see the world beyond bread and prayer."

"May the Lord guide you, " Moishe said. And turning to Leah, who was holding a two-year-old, cradling him in her arms, said, not without resignation, "And we'll be left keeping his offspring."

"Sh-sh," Leah said, "Sh-sh, Moishe, these are your children."

It was a very long time to wait for Srul's return. For Sarah the hardest. Thoughts of all sorts; anger, alternating with "I have not been gentle enough – I have a terrible temper. Poor Srul." And so forth. "May God bring him home safely. I'll be better." And she prayed silently, not to be seen by her mother, not to give away her fears that murder on the road was possible and a life was so valuable.

"Such a precious life as Srul's." And she turned to her children with a story or a song. Work, work until Friday night's meal was assured, bread and wine for the blessing on the table and the *Cholent* in the oven.

Sarah had just spread the white linen, lit her candles for the *Shabbat* exactly before sundown, when Srul opened the kitchen door to see it. She stood silently before her candles, lifted her two hands above them, and spoke the blessing of a Jewish mother. Of gratitude. "That You have commanded us to keep holy the seventh day and helped us reach the *Shabbat.*" And then she turned to her husband, who stood at the door, parcels beside him on the floor, and fell into his arms dry-eyed.

It was a *Shabbat* like no other. That he had come back safely, that he brought a printed sample back of the *Haggadah* with Sarah's illustrations to Srul's text – Hebrew on the one side, Polish on the other – approved by the Lemberg, also by the Krakov, rabbis. Printing and bindings finished in time for next Passover. Money in advance and a gift edition for the rabbi in Suczorno. Srul was called to the *Bimah* that *Shabbat* and he did a beautiful *Alijah* – the reading of the portion of the week and the blessings. There was an *Oneg Shabbat* with *Challah* bread, wine, herring, and honey cake and all the children there, a Synagogue full of noisy, ill-behaved, running-around, undisciplined children of all ages. The women, of course, in the back were talking without regard for the proceedings, but knowing exactly where one was in the book. But when Srul went up there to read from the Scrolls, a respectful, loving hush went over the Synagogue. They honoured him for having gone out, without any help, courageously facing an enemy world, and coming back a conqueror.

"God bless the fruit of the earth and God bless the fruit of the vine." Spoken, enjoyed, lunch taken, Suczorno felt like one, undivided in its joy. As only men and women could, whose lives were so close, intertwined and dependent on one another.

"You're more beautiful than you ever were; undo your hair, let it down so I can see it," Srul said that night.

Sarah had not cut it according to custom when entering womanhood, to the despair of her mother: "It could have dire, unforeseen consequences."

"I won't cut my hair, it's disgusting; it's an hypocrisy to wear fake hair, a wig. What for? Either my husband will love me or he won't."

Her mother knew. One could not win against Sarah. She'd pray. She'd ask to make sure Sarah wore her kerchief when out there at the well or among other women whose hair was cut, and who could feel superior or see a demon's work in her lustrous hair.

"Let me take a comb to it," Srul said that night, when the two of them, after such a day of triumph, came to face each other. "Remember your brother, Nathan, was it he who said to you that Christian girls are prettier?"

"Yes, he did say that and I always wondered, why would they be and how –"

"Well, I've been in that big world. It is true, there are more beautiful women in Lemberg. Tall, blue-eyed, golden-haired, slim, dressed in dreamy clothes and moving as if they were not made of flesh. But not all. The poor peasant women in Poland get old sooner than our own, though they are pretty when they are young. They work too hard, bear children, and they are not more beautiful than our own. And thank you for defying Suczorno and giving me the pleasure to see your black hair falling down your shoulders."

Sarah smiled, it was good to hear him say it. But she replied,

"It was a long day. Come sit down by me. For a short while yet. My heart is so full of gratitude to God. That He has given you to me, that you love me for what I am or do. Srul," she said now timidly, "I am a grown woman, yet tonight – let me hold your hand –" And she reached across the kitchen table to hold it.

"Tonight I am that little girl on a Passover night, whose heart was full of wonder, who felt the presence of the unseen majesty with such intensity that when she ran to open the door, Elijah, the prophet, was there for her. A passing moment only, an air, a touch of his rough mantle against my cheek and His blessing fingers within my hair – I would never cut it. What do villagers know about the power of a godly hand upon your head? This is the hair He has touched. And His coming is always here –" and she pointed to her breast "a hope in dark moments.

"When our first child died right after birth, and I lay in childbed – fevered, delirious – remember, Srul, I said one morning, rising from it – that He had come, Elijah, a messenger of God. I felt it on my cheek, His cloak roughing it quietly, a calming air, a cooling of the feverish body. And I heard Him say, as distinctly as you hear me now: 'This is God's child, your own and Srul's, but there will be many to come and love.' And the fever left me.

"That night I took to my pencils and chalk and I drew His figure, in His cloak, His face hidden in His mantle, enveloping the body fully, flaring out a little while striding. Hidden, I haven't seen it, so I can't draw it. And maybe this is the essence of my faith. The inner awareness of God, the presence of the Eternal. And the hope. My fever left me. It was miraculous."

And Srul, holding Sarah's hands: "I remember the day you rose from that childbed and I heard you say: 'He has come to comfort me.' And thank you for recalling it tonight. When I stood up there on the *Bimah* in front of the whole congregation and read the portion of the week, I had such a feeling of promise fulfilled. And when I handed my gift over to the elders of the Synagogue, I felt as I had as a little boy. I felt the honour, the intense honour of the gift. To crown the *Torah* scrolls with silver or gold – as the rich do – would not have been what the gift of our work meant. Because your figure of Elijah, wrapped densely in His mantle – the little girl at the door, looking up to Him with a fervent face, and my text, both Hebrew and Polish on the opposite page, was our union.

"Remember, I too looked across the creek wondering, would He honour us first, because we're poor – it's childish. But I was yours, Sarah, from the moment I looked across the Suczorno River. And we both can give a gift that no one could buy for gold."

"And it is in blue velvet! Did you have this one especially bound?"

"Yes, I did," Srul replied. "Just for this one time. The rest is beautiful, too, in blue linen with a light-gold lettering. I was overjoyed when I first held them in my hands."

Slowly the day came to its close. Sarah and Srul shed their clothes, timidly, as if for the first night. And embraced.

Sarah's Elijah

SARAH'S ELIJAH – the Eli-yahu of her womanly years – took on a very different mantle. It changed as she did. His figure and suddenly his face also ripened under her hands. The Hebrew prophet who had the ear of God and, heard by Him, could speak for the little people walking His earth, she drew. The voice Sarah could not translate into pen and chalk, but an illuminated face she could. So she drew Elijah listening to His people. A face intense with compassion. For a birth-giving mother, for a child accused, or a man in toil, Sarah uncovered Elijah's face. In her first efforts, He was within his cloak, still a child's hero, enigmatic, wrapped to be wondered at and to reveal Himself only to the level of her feelings and wishes, yet unspoken. This was her Elijah for the first edition of their *Haggadah*. Srul's and hers.

Now it was different. She felt Elijah would reveal God to you in terms of your own as you reached for them. As all our concepts of the world, as all our hopes changed. As He uncovered His face to her or sometimes His eyes only, she drew Him. When Sarah, losing her first child, heard Him say: "This is God's – yours will come," she drew His face. It was a break of magnitude. Jews in Suczorno didn't draw faces. She liked to embroider flowers or animals on her blouse, and even that to the despair of her mother – but not faces yet. It was hard. The "Thou shall not" was her heartbeat. One couldn't live without it. Images – to worship, perhaps – God forbid!

But Sarah grew within – and with a leap of faith – out of the bind. The one bind that did not allow a new turn or a light coming from another source, revealing the Eternal; but as she grew, on Srul's side and with him, she had to face her children resisting her, as she had resisted her mother Leah and her father Moishe.

It was then that Elijah withdrew His mantle to first uncover a human face, yet she took time to show Him as a man. The face was of such otherness, when partly covered, shaded still with foreboding, but when fully uncovered was lit by a new inner hope. Sarah drew and painted now more by mixing subtle colour into her black and white, and she drew his head barely hooded, His face framed by a hint of early beard – as a man's face. She was jubilant. Did not sleep all night. Her youngest had just been weaned from her breast and she felt free to see the holy man, to not only have the ear of God but to be His mouthpiece. His voice.

The spoken word. The word. He still wore his mantle, one that was rugged, torn in tatters; He was crouching, with eyes blinded and palm open, at the south gate of Jerusalem, watching without seeing the giving or the denying. Often she drew His head showing this blinding band, but then one day she took it off and His eyes, full of knowing the beyond and the here, emerged.

Her older children had to help with the cleaning, the cooking, her mother Leah's needs. Moishe too was attended by all of them; a man being less able to live through the daily needs than a woman; impatient with God's design, he often did not fight for another day. He lived and died as he was. Srul, too, doing his best to attend to his father-in-law; but Moishe did not tolerate his body's misfunctions, his anger grew with the years. He raised, if not a stick, the voice unjustly against the huge roaming tribe of Sarah and Srul. The house was full with little ones. In two rooms, one big kitchen and a small one, it was always noisy, potties standing around and little children sitting on them.

Moishe disliked Sarah's forgiveness, easy-of-training behavior, and as he called it, "modern ways," un-Jewish and unbecoming. But mainly it was his own difficulty: the pain of not being able to urinate, the drop-by-drop-waiting, and Chaim Rosen, "the doctor," making him drink more, which made it worse. The "wise women," whom Moishe despised with words truly unworthy of a devout Jew, who brought the herb "that drives the water," the herb of the thousand ducats, or the root of ginger finely ground – and God knows what unholy whisperings to accompany their brewing the tea – he threw out of the house. Ignominious. Nothing worked, and to the despair of Sarah, Srul, and Leah and all the children, who had been fond of him in better days, he died. A huge funeral. All of Suczorno. *Shiva* – the seven days – with *Minion* and *Kaddish*. His sons coming from everywhere. Shimon and Ethel, married now, at his side also.

Then Leah declined more and more and there was little joy. The "green" or the "grey" covering both her eyes, she could not read anymore. The little ones had to do it for her. They read her beloved *Zena-U-Rhena* – the Zenerene – as she called it, a Yiddish beloved storybook, "for women," so to speak, about magic rabbis, local or German old tales, a book whose intelligence was of course belittled. They had to read. And the wonderful life story of Glickl of Hameln. Written by her own hand, her fortunes, business-deals, marriage-contracts of her children. Married first to a man from Hameln – the famous rat-catcher city of Hameln – and then to a man from Metz in the Lorraine, she was a clever, self-assured woman. Cunning, doing business, supporting her children by the side of her husband Chaim – Leah loved reading about her, but could not anymore. Neither could she the straight Hebrew portion of the week, which she had never missed, going to Synagogue or not. But she fought for life. For every hour, as a woman does, knowing its value better than man, and giving it up only when the hour strikes.

So Sarah laid her to rest also. Again, the seven days of mourning, all glass or shiny surfaces covered; if there was a mirror, then most certainly. The emptiness that followed Sarah had to endure: to see a pair of shoes with holes in the right sole – a pebble still lodging – the spot where Leah had trodden heavier, made Sarah sit down and cry. And so did her mother's daily apron, full of unbleachable grease stains and her hands' imprint, as she wiped them on it, still there. Sarah sat without moving, tears flowing, with those two unworthy objects pressed to her heart. And she rose to put these things, these witnesses above all others to their daily common living, and Leah's wedding ring, as well as a string of pearls – into her own secret drawer. There, where she had hidden pen, paper, and chalk to defy her mother's "it's forbidden." Now she was free of that parental constraint, but did not feel it, as if – more bound to it. Bound by larger bindings, holding life itself.

And Sarah drew Elijah now, day in, day out. Not a blind beggar only, but a seer, a stranger at the door, a child that feels injustice – an Elijah still young, but a very different one with his cloak lying on the ground. And so He emerged. Naked as at birth. Or almost. Not entirely revealing all human form, the mantle somewhere around Him, across His body, on His shoulders, back, or crouching on it.

He, Eli-Yahu, the Elijah of her childhood, who is what we all are: chosen to hear God. Why – Sarah asked – should we not be allowed to see Him – created? Well, she knew Suczorno, knew the danger, and kept her drawings to herself. But they became bigger and bolder; subdued in colour, yes, but daring, highlighted.

Her Elijah became what her mother's father and what Leah herself had always told her: a brother, a friend of the helpless, the very little children, the hungry and the poor. When she was eight or nine, Srul had told her: "He comes to us first, because we are poor, to honour us, because you on the high bank have the honours wealth can give!" Yes, he was right. Elijah went first to the poor on a Passover night. And she drew his face, in spite of the law, and hid it.

She was a mother of an enormous tribe now. Squeezed into two rooms, she did not mind the squirming life. Potties to be cleaned, the linen on the line across the rooms on winter days with the drying nappies never stopping, and going from one little one to the next, until threadbare fringes hung loose. Steaming buckwheat in the air, the cooking of the cereals always on the steady fire, summer or winter, tears, fights over torn rag dolls, punching little fists, bleeding noses and knees – and the five-year-old, now Moishe, named after her father when she gave birth soon after his death, clinging to her skirts!

This was the custom in Suczorno, never would the name be given after living family members, always after they've gone. To establish succession, to keep the line alive. Sarah knew there must be strains of Jews who named their children after their living parents, but not in Suczorno. Never. She liked it that way. It brought them back, and they were more in need of their return, their presence now.

So this Moishe – Ben Srul – wanted the kitchen table to be freed of all dirty plates, sticky with *mamaliga,* unwashed glasses of goat's milk, or the "unmentionables" littering – he wanted to study. Started to remove things with the swipe of an arm: glasses fell and broke, hitting Miriam, aged two sitting on her potty on the floor. A minor crisis. Mother as supreme judge – and so it went, to loose one's mind. But Sarah was happy. To be a centre, a heart, was good for her.

She was rooted like the oak tree, leaves sprouting from its branches, holding and feeding the trunk, empowered to gather the light and changing with it; and wind rushing through the noisy, waxy leaves was Sarah's favourite music. Her children and the oak tree, that was her life. It was a young one. She had planted it, watched it form a trunk, and protected it from her mother's dislike: "It will take the sun from the window, it will take it from the little space we have for beets and cabbage – Sarah!" She was adamant in her silent, self-possessed opposition, knowing what was absolutely necessary for herself: design, growth, the presence of miracle. In all things. Elijah's promise, prophecy, children.

The leaf of oak in its crenelations almost drew itself. From the young tender leaf to the now heavier one. Thicker, more demanding of ground and air, the oak tree did prevent the beets from flourishing, but she rescued them, placing them somewhere else. And as her children grew, Sarah saw them climb that tree, play in its branches, and she thought she had been right. But her mother Leah appeared night after night in her dreams, worried: "You won't have a beet to cook a *borsht* – with all your fancy ideas –" She simply replied, "Dear, dear mother, I love you so." Sarah's way, knowing where the miracle lies. Beets or no beets.

Life and the miracle of beauty. A battle. It did not come easy. Long stretches of winter days, alone to judge, weigh, make decisions, right from wrong, discipline or not – all these weeks that Srul was gone. He went to Czernowitz, Lemberg, and Krakov to print her work or have it done by the expert church shops. Sarah was known now across the Prut River, sold her work to Jews and Christians alike. But when Srul came home one winter day to tell her that a famous woodcarver had started to carve a huge Elijah-figure based on her work from a single trunk of walnut, instead of being thrilled, she was dismayed.

"Stop it, Srul – I do not want figures. It goes too far. Wooden sculpture, heavens, I can admire perhaps – but it is not for me to do. Moishe and Leah will assault me: 'Idols, idols, what have you done my child?'"

Srul went back to Lemberg, but it was too late. An enormous figure, his mantle spiritual, true to Sarah's wishes, was everyone's property now, Jew or Christian, no matter.

"And so it should be," Srul thought, "so it should be. Accessible. Not God but – of Him."

Srul told the carver of his wife's objections. But of course it was not just a piece of wood, but an object endowed with inner life, it was everyone's Elijah – and strange as it seemed for a Jewish man, Srul welcomed that unity. To learn from one another, to take freely what is beautiful in all heritage, change it, yet leave the essence. He rejoiced. Returning, Srul calmed Sarah's fears. He said it was entirely her own, one trunk – whole and deeply religious, and she had to accept it.

But Srul never went back on any other arduous journey. He had worked very hard, in all kinds of shops, printing, engraving in metal; had inhaled fumes of solvents, and a printer's tragic destiny came home to strike. He spat blood. It was an atrocious winter. Wood was dear, there was no coal, and Sarah fought hard to heat one room to keep the children from playing or coming near Srul. As Jews in Suczorno always knew: isolate the sick, wash absolutely everything! She washed as if *kashering* for Passover – putting linen with hot stones into the water to keep it boiling.

She helped Srul die. It was April by then. At least the frozen earth gave way and one could dig a hole for the coffin. It went so fast. Between *Chanukkah* and *Pesach;* and this last one had been a very special *Chanukkah.* All was well, at least it seemed so. Srul coughed a little, spotted red a handkerchief, but was in exuberant mood; an exaltation she had never seen before. She, Sarah, was the exalted one, looking for the spirit to move her, give her the delight of the unusual, a presence of the marvelous. Srul was the thinker, the prisoner of his own God within the ancient letter, but less given to wild joy.

This last *Chanukkah* was one of these rare events. Srul was so joyous, played with the little ones, sang the *Smir-ha-smirim,* helped light the candles until the eighth was lit. He had brought gifts from Lemberg. Polish delicacies, sugar-spun sticky things, and a basket of red apples. Money, too. These were Suczorno winter nights to remember. Eight of them. With the *Shames,* the unextinguished, watching light, kindling every night one more candle until all eight stood in a row, the miracle tale all told, the goodies all eaten from the potato patty, dripping chicken fat, to the baked apple – the feast was over.

The next day Srul took to his bed. The fever that had been with him for months now intensified, the cough shook him, and Sarah watched him bleed, helpless to stop it. Boiled the water to wash and clean his hands and face, changed his linen. An infusion of birch bark she had by the bedside, and fed it to him in small swallows.

He recovered a little, talked of the future, and of his love for her in such fervent, intense terms of intimacy that she blushed. Sarah had moved herself and the very youngest out of their bedroom to give Srul space and rest, had bedded herself down on the kitchen bench near the big corner mud oven. It was a coveted place, always cozy; her mother, Leah, had slept by it, near it, or on top of it; it was where the elderly parents rested in Suczorno. A few steps had been built of brick on the side by Leah's father.

Sarah did not go up the few brick steps to the top, but slept on the bench that circled it, to be in hearing distance for Srul's needs, to keep the children busy, away, and less unruly. And she heard Srul fantasize, moan, speak of his love.

Sarah had heard from other women that their men, once afflicted with this blood-spitting cough, got more insistent for love, less respectful of the strict law of observance on woman's unclean days. She could not believe it. It caused her pain, but she resisted his call; sat next to him. Very close. Attended to him. Rubbed his chest with pepper-in-goose-fat ointment, until it shone red hot and relieved the sting a little. Sat him up in cushions against the wall so he could swallow his birch-bark fever-reducing tea.

Four months. Four short and endless months between *Chanukkah* and Passover. The Christian year had turned; Suczorno counted the year in thousands. It meant little to Sarah. She had buried Srul. Menachem, the eldest, said *Kaddish.* Outside of town there was a small crowd on a blizzarding spring day.

She returned home to face her task, straightened her back, held her children close, smiled in their direction when they crowded around her. Life. The older two would take over, she hoped, they were apprenticing across the river – they'd earn their piece of bread.

For the first time, the oldest of the tribe, Sarah, seated herself in her father's chair. No one had ever sat in this oaken-heavy chair except the fathers – her own father Moishe, her grandfather before him. It had stood empty. "This is father's chair –" No one was allowed onto its broad seat, encircling arms, and carved head-rest. As a little five-year-old, Sarah had deciphered this carving as a *Chai,* intricately interwoven into what seemed to her to be olive branches. And sometimes they seemed oak, but always a *Chai* in between the branches. Life. This was what it meant. She knew.

Taking possession of the chair today – having been chased from it always – today she felt its burden. *Chai;* not life, it meant *passing.* She sat in her father's chair, head resting on its lettering; and held by its ancient comfort, she waited for the familiar brush of His coarse cloak against her cheek, for His hand upon hair. His mantle enfolding her, Sarah stretched into her father's chair, pulled Leah's little "woman's stool" from under the table to rest her feet.

Peace.

He had come.

SHIMON THE JOURNEYMAN

The Young Shimon

YES, A TIME CAME WHEN SHIMON REMEMBERED THE *Nigun*. It was a jubilant tune, a triumphant song of life. He sang it as if he had heard it yesterday, although it had been years. The melody surged fully intact from his heart; as if to address God the creator, the giver or the sustainer of life – he couldn't tell. Standing on the high bank of his hometown, Suczorno, he just looked at the slowly receding river and sang.

He had been away to apprentice as a printer. Shimon, like his brother-in-law, Srul, and his sister, Sarah, was a scholar, a poet, no good with his hands. To the despair of his father, Moishe, he would not go across the bridge to pick up a trade. He had started in the tailor's shop, but soon fell ill and gave it up. It happened right after his *Bar Mitzvah,* such a great event in Suczorno.

It was especially great for Shimon, because he could debate with the eldest, most learned men. "That we are chosen," he said after *Kiddush* – the blessing of the wine – sitting around the table with all the men, "that we are chosen puts a heavy burden on our shoulders and is no privilege." There was no argument to this, but there was wild disagreement when Shimon questioned God's intentions with: "Why?" or "Why us?" and "What makes us different in the eyes of the Lord to be given such a burden?"

Menachem ben Israel, the learned disciple of the Rabbi Shlomo ben Abraham and the one closest to him, replied with vehemence: "You, you young chicken, barely out of the egg, dare to contemplate God's creation! Are you with your feeble means going to penetrate the mind of the Eternal, His purpose in choosing us as His people, or as you like to put it 'to lay a heavy burden upon the chosen ones?' Answer!"

And Shimon felt assaulted when asked to defend himself so soon after his wonderful reading from the *Torah*. He was silent for another moment, but knew he couldn't escape, and replied: "It is for us, as you said, for the young, to quest, to query, it is for us to try and learn, so the law can be truly followed. So we can walk in its framework, in its limits, not with resentment but with a full heart."

"Is it not enough then for you wise guys to be elected to it, to be taught and shown the way? You have to take the Lord to task? Who do you think you are, Job?"

Tempers flared, but both camps soon settled to tea and honey cake, with the women shaking their heads.

Shimon was only good for books. And Srul, having made connections in Lemberg and Czernowitz with high-class printing shops, came home one day from a selling trip of his Passover *Haggadah* and told Shimon that he had recommended him to a printer in Czernowitz. Czernowitz was an Austrian city of great culture, where a gifted young scholar like Shimon could be properly trained in the art of printing. Shimon was at the right age to sever ties, to go away, as far as Czernowitz, even, six or seven hundred kilometres west.

He had had a happy childhood. He had been loved, cherished

beyond measure by his family. He had loved being a child. Peeing his pants for the longest time, he was chided and corrected and constantly told to grow up by both women in the household, his mother and his beloved sister Sarah.

Sarah, younger by a year and a half, was his conspirator, an accomplice in thinking wicked thoughts: those that led you away from *Torah* learning, those that doubted the eternity of things. Both of them picked up, as young minds do, the winds of change that were sweeping through ancient barriers of law and contrition. She wanted to draw, and was forbidden.

"Stupid," she said to Shimon one day, sitting on his bed without a candle, "how stupid they are. How could I destroy the Law by drawing your beautiful young face, Shimon?" And he agreed. With all their ancient wisdom, his people stuck to every irrational rule; as if, once they were removed, the whole structure of their lives would collapse, would bring Sodom and Gomorrah down and bury them under its ruins.

Shimon liked being a child, because he was free; free of owing anything to others, free to throw stones into the Suczorno Creek and watch the rings grow and diminish around them, free to watch Ethel from the other end of the row of houses do the same. Ethel, a wild, laughing child, would throw stones at him and wait for his. But he decided Ethel's stones did not travel far enough and would not hit him, and he would not play. That was Shimon. If he decided not to like something, it simply did not exist; that also was his inner freedom. It stayed with him into adulthood.

As he sat on the high bank of the receding river, on the very stone he had fled to as a child to escape admonitions to grow up, or to take over a daily task from his older brothers who had gone out of town, he was the same child within. He had always shirked encroachments on his thoughts and had fled, when shouted at, to this boulder promontory overlooking all of Suczorno and into the valley at the southern end. He was just a few steps around the corner from his house, but far enough away for a chuckling little refugee to gleefully sing, "Ha, ha, you can't see me." Though still the same Shimon, a freedom-seeker, an independent thinker, he had changed.

He had come back to a devastated world. Doors flapped in the summer wind, the river, now receding, had flooded the lower bank. The valley along the Suczorno Creek, recalling the unbearable beauty of his childhood mornings, was lush green after the torrential rains that had swept it. And all the other droughts and floods came back to him: wading through the muddy flats left behind when he was seven or eight, and his friendship – or his secret love – for the always barefoot Ethel. She said she had no shoes. And would not wear them if she had any.

So Shimon offered her his own shoes, taking them off with the easy gesture of the rich and generous. She slipped them on jubilantly. "Oh, it would be wonderful to be a boy, to go to *Cheder,* and to talk to Shimon!"

"Where are your shoes, Shimon?" his mother had asked on his return home.

"I don't know, I lost them."

"Where?"

"In the river, I think. Yes, the river took them."

"Shimon, we have no other shoes, all your brothers' shoes are much too big yet. You don't grow fast enough."

"I'll wear Sarah's," he said. But somehow there were shoes the next morning. Oh, to be so loved.

It was a summer of drought the next year and nothing could be stored for the winter. The peasants would not part with their rye and wheat, sold only a little of it, and the Jews lived on roots and the vegetables they could grow around their houses. But what saved them was the golden corn, or maize. It feeds the poor in hard times, and even the poorest harvest is good enough for a golden *mamaliga* or cornbread. And the children played with it, used its yellow-white silk-hair for the hair of their rag-paper dolls, built houses from its stalks.

But children liked best the round-faced flower-of-the-sun, for it turned its seed-bearing face to follow the sun across the sky. Shimon loved this pagan God's image. He spun forbidden stories and told them to Ethel. But not to Sarah, his sister, who would frown and say: "You're out of your mind. It's a sin. You're a Jew. Go study. You're going into your ninth year, and you think you're a baby – stop it." So there was no talking to Sarah. But with Ethel he conspired, "We'll get up early before sunrise, and meet in the fields behind the last house. We'll crawl on our stomachs, so no one sees us. And we'll pick the biggest sunflower and crack its brown seeds with our teeth. And we'll lie on our backs, and you will tell me what you see in the moving clouds and I will tell you what I see..."

He had loved Ethel always. She came from the poorest of their cousins. Her grandfather, the *Shoichet* – the ritual slaughterer of Suczorno – was a second cousin of Shimon's father, on the periphery of the inner family circle. Though unavoidably an important part of the town's ritual life, he was shunned by the townspeople. No one paid him well, and some didn't pay him at all. Yet Aaron, the *Schoichet,* would never refuse to provide his services. Aaron had married a simple, uneducated girl, a God-fearing child, called Shainah – the "bland one" – from Ehelm, where according to Suczorno lore all fools came from. While every other *shtetl* knew that all fools came from Suczorno.

THERE HAD BEEN PEACE in Suczorno for quite a long time: times were as good as times can be. But just one hundred kilometres to the north, the world might be at an end. Knives were loose, torches burned, packs of hungry or drunk peasants came for the blood, the bread, the beds, the pillows, the pots and pans. Noise filled the air, a roar of "Christ-killers, bleed!" rose to heaven.

So it happened that one day before Good Friday, those citizens of Shklov who were not murdered or burnt in their beds fled down the streets. A town could be made as silent as the earth in half an hour. Sometimes as few as ten or twenty souls might remain to rebuild the town, as was the case in Shklov. Young and old would run down the roads, no matter what direction. And so they went, singly and in groups, to other towns to be taken in. Marginal as the towns themselves were, a *shtetl* had a soul: there was no avoiding a stranger, the other Jew on the road. So Ethel's mother, Shoshannah, ran to Suczorno. A fifteen-year-old with all her folk – father, mother, siblings – murdered on that Thursday before Easter.

A very small fifteen-year-old, Shoshannah had crawled into a cubby-hole and lain flat on her stomach. Through the cracks in the boards she'd watched them murder her family with pitchforks and pillage the house. After they left, she, Shoshannah, the Lily, had covered her parents and sisters in linen sheets.

On that Thursday morning, she'd started walking in the opposite direction the mob had taken. Others crawled out to join her. Numbed, they walked across the fields, thinking to hide perhaps in straw stubble, but no, only walking thoughtlessly and without goal, to the limit of their strength. Then, at night, they threw themselves to the ground, and fell into an absence of self, into the benediction of sleep. There were around twenty of them, old and young, some babies in the arms of their mothers. None of the babies cried. What do the little ones know? But they do, it seems, having been born with some ancient wisdom in their blood; they know when not to cry. They perhaps have seen it before, in memories untold.

The refugees all slept the night, shared a piece of bread someone had grabbed before leaving, then rose to walk to where an old man knew a waterhole – or was it a well? – and a creek nearby. A motley lot, immodestly shedding their clothes, as if nothing mattered, neither custom nor law. "Thou shalt not...show your uncovered body" was forgotten. Everyone of them washed their feet, lay flat in the creek to cool their bodies, or drank, cupping their hands. As the sun rose, decisions were made wordlessly, and they all started to walk again.

And so Shoshannah of Shklov – and for the rest of her life she was either referred to as "that Shklover dumbbell" or simply "Shklovke," although to the family of Aaron the *Shoichet,* she was "Shoshannah the Lily" from the moment she reached the outer end of Suczorno, where the *Shoichets* had lived from time immemorial.

Scholarly, but not too Talmudically refined to hold arguments on subtler points with the "learned" of the town, the *Shoichet* is a divinely ordained institution. No *shtetl* can live without it. But unlike most hereditary kings, with their knights in armour, a *Shoichet* is often unprotected. He is reviled, gossiped about, denied payment, and outwardly paid only a grudging respect. He knows suffering: he watches all the chickens of Suczorno, running with their heads cut off; as if the body knows about pain, all by itself. The *Shoichet* washes the slaughter yard and his sharp knives from the spilled blood and teaches his son the art, to do it fast at the absolutely right spot by calling on the Eternal. So from father to son, it stays within the family.

The house of the *Shoichet* Aaron, on the outskirts of Suczorno, was ancestral, built over many generations. But of course Jews would not call it ancestral. Jews are often driven from their homesteads, their homes only lent to them by God, the earth underneath not theirs. So, how ancestral could it be? Yet it is. There is always one born before you, who carries the *Torah* in his hands on the *Shabbat*. If Jews return or not to the very physical place they were born in is of lesser consequence. The main thing is that the *Torah* be passed down to your son and daughter.

Aaron's great-great-grandfather had been a *Shoichet* at the time of Joseph II of Austria. Joseph gave family names and some citizens' rights to the Jews. But this did not much affect the small communities, which lived in an almost untouched and timeless world. Pogroms came as birth and death did and Jews dealt with it. Sometimes they ran from burning towns and sometimes with God's help they returned to their birthplaces to pick up the pieces. And so one day did the *Shoichet,* Aaron's great-great-grandfather. He returned and rebuilt. Well, this is how *ancestral* a home can be in Suczorno.

It was one of the less gruesome times and Suczorno could pick up its life, put new shingles on its Synagogue, and lay slate around its well. All the people worked together. Never was Suczorno so united as it was after a disaster. No matter whose money, whose labour, everyone pitched in. Gossip receded; no one seemed envious, thought ill of the other, or bothered denouncing the impious. These things are reserved for good times, when there is nothing to worry about.

When there was bread and peace Suczorno showed its underbelly, lifted every stone to see the insects crawl. Call it what you will – and who would know man's ways – but don't call it God's. Yet in times when peasants broke doors in with shovels and sticks, killed or smoked them out, Jews would see the hand of God. Of course only those who lived to see it would humbly love their neighbour. For a while. Good times would follow, prosperous merchants would build homes on the high bank of the Suczorno River, and the poor would eat also.

A *Shoichet* is never hungry, and this was especially true of Aaron, who had inherited the family dwelling with its inner courtyard, several henhouses, and wooden barrel wash basins, well fitted with rustproof iron rings. The old house, rebuilt every time its windows were broken, had served well for generations of *Shoichets*. But poor they were nonetheless, threshold-bound, pious, serving God and the people for little reward. Other men had horses, wagons, bought merchandise, bartered, were young and daring. *Shoichets,* it seems, were born old, their lives laid out for them at the age of four or five, and usually the eldest son deemed the one best suited to learn the trade, handle a knife and pray.

Shoichets did not get the respect they deserved from the town. Certainly not from the enterprising rich, who did not like to see their children consort with them too much. It was: "Shimon, you have better things to do than talk to Ethel. What can you learn from a woman from Shklov, a *Shoichet's* wife?!"

Shimon, though, liked the whole *Shoichet* family. He loved the mother, with her silent ways, the mystery of her past, her having come on foot from a mythic town faraway. There was an air of martyrdom about her. She accepted Suczorno's ways on the outside but kept house – as the women of Suczorno duly noted – differently from them. She braided her *Challah* – the *Shabbat* bread – in five or seven strands instead of three, and put sunflower seeds on top instead of poppy seed. Her kitchen sported an ancient mud stove, roomy and well built. On Fridays neighbours asked for permission to bake their own *Challah* in her oven, which she granted with the grace of a queen. But everyone saw her braiding of the *Challah* and how many eggs she used and they gossiped.

Perhaps because of the mystery of her past.

Shoshannah the Shklovke

WHEN SHOSHANNAH THE SHKLOVKE arrived at the edge of town, with feet bleeding, her hair wild in the wind, nearly grey with dust, she had sat down on Aaron the *Shoichet's* threshold and cried for the first time in weeks. She could not speak her name, nor tell how long she had been on the road, or when she had eaten last. She could not speak intelligently. Her words were Yiddish, but her sentences were broken, her words came slowly, unconnected to each other.

The old *Shoichet* and his wife Shainah lifted her from the threshold and bedded her down, to let her rest. It took days of sleep, bathing, and healing before she would take her first piece of bread. Shoshannah from Shklov never again left that household. She cleaned the courtyard daily, polished and sharpened the *Shoichet's* knives until they sounded like silver bells when plucked, washed and hung the linen, and kneaded the *Challah,* never uttering a sound. The *Shoichet's* eldest son watched her. More than ten years older than Shoshannah, he had not yet found a bride.

Suczorno was a funny place, when it came to the *Shoichet's* house. Everyone went there, for they absolutely could not do without following the laws of slaughter and the handling of meat. Immovable for millennia, those laws held Suczorno in their iron grip. But – with all due respect – even the poor from the other side of the creek avoided marrying into the *Shoichet's* family.

An old tale told of mayhem at a wedding in a *Shoichet's* home – no one remembers where or when – when the souls of all the slaughtered hens gathered to take revenge on the slaughterer and endanger a young couple. The hens' souls cried louder than the rabbi's benediction, and the bride's veil was lifted by invisible forces, turning bright red. Then the posts of the *Chuppah* suddenly started shaking and the wild crowing of roosters raised the roof. The people of Suczorno loved such stories, the more fearful, bizarre, and questioning the ways of the ancients, the better. Danger unseen and in the blood was ever present, even when it wasn't. Who wants savage roosters at a joyous occasion?

So the *Shoichet's* eldest son, Yankel, could not find a bride. It is true, he was not the most handsome of young men. Short-sighted, he had to hold books close, and bending over them from so early an age, as one does in Suczorno, his back was slightly bent. Sweet by nature, willing to work, and introspective, he spoke late and with a hesitating fine lisp on the letter *S* or *Sh*. But he was good and diligent, and wore clean clothes, which he mended himself, being expert with a needle.

Yankel had apprenticed with the tailor across the creek, and he loved the work; he could sit for hours on end quietly finishing a buttonhole by hand, reinforcing both corners with double thread. With a mouthful of pins, he would sit on the floor adjusting the length of a hem until it was absolutely straight all around.

But his father, Aaron the *Shoichet,* could not do without him. None of Aaron's other sons cared to learn the *Shoichet's* trade, and this role fell traditionally to the eldest in any case. But marrying? Making a life of his own? Well, Yankel was almost twenty-eight when Shoshannah from Shklov sat down on the *Shoichet's* threshold.

Yankel carried fresh water from the well, made kindling for the big mud stove to heat a cauldron of the well water, which – so the legend goes – could heal boils on boys' faces, wash away running pus, or cool a feverish body packed in soaked linen. Yankel carefully washed Shoshannah's wounds on her soles and heels with homemade kosher soap, letting both feet hang down from the rim of the bed and rest in a small basin of warm well water. His attentions brought comfort to her troubled spirit. So she sat with her washed feet in that healing bath for uncountable hours, Yankel coming and going to add hot water to keep it from cooling too much.

With hands idle in her lap, her eyes on them, Shoshannah sat fully still upon the very bedstead she had been laid on by Aaron when she arrived in Suczorno. And when she lifted her eyes, they looked straight into Yankel's. She saw his speechless love and she responded in kind. So they sat without words in an intimacy without equal. Her first piece of bread she accepted from his hand, a dry piece of *Challah* from the last *Shabbat*. She ate it slowly, savouring each crumb that fell and he collected. So they sat until she had finished. Then he rose again to bring a piece of clean white linen, and took her feet into his hands to dry them. He held her heels, which had suffered badly, in his warm palm, and covered them again with a clean sheet under a goat skin. Then he smiled a good night and left her.

Shoshannah did not rise from her bed until she could stand properly on her feet. And then, one day, she saw a pair of used boy's shoes in the corner of her room. Pointing to them, she asked for permission, and was handed shoes, knitted socks, a skirt, and blouse from Shainah. She dressed. A *Shoichet's* apron hanging from a nail in the courtyard she bound around her middle, and took over the cleaning of the yard after the *Shoichet* had killed his last chicken. She did it thoroughly every night.

Yankel watched her get up in the morning, run to the well to haul the water, fill the barrels for the evening wash; he watched her cut the potatoes for the *Cholent,* or take the cabbage leaves apart to rinse the insects out, or carry the discarded leaves to the compost heap behind the house. He loved her arms, the way she lifted the cauldron as if it were a feather, the way she sat down on Suczorno's low stools – those little *shtetl*-stools one can push under beds or tables – to think for a moment or find the next thing to do. Speechless, she moved about, and Yankel sensed her deep gratitude.

Yankel went first to his parents. He was alone now. His brothers had gone to find work in neighbouring towns, coming home only periodically, when life got too hard for them, looking for help or advice or simply a few weeks of rest. So he was alone now in the house. And after work one day, he sat down with his parents to ask in a very few words – and even these were full of stops and *s-s-s-sh-sh's* – if they would approve of Shoshannah. And Aaron the father responded, "She would be a fine daughter to us, but you have to ask her because – let there be no mistake – there can be no matchmaker, nor money changing hands. Ask her."

He could not ask her yet. Neither of them had uttered a word to each other. How to suddenly speak? How to speak of marriage, let alone what was in his heart? But in the end it was not necessary. One night at the evening meal – which all four took together – after prayers were said, Shoshannah turned to him in the presence of his parents and said in a clear, wonderful Yiddish: "I'll be your faithful wife, if you will have me." And Yankel replied, "With all my heart." It was Friday night. And the father rose, *Kiddush* cup in hand, and blessed his children: "May you be fruitful!"

After the announcement in the Synagogue, a proper time had to pass before the wedding day. Expectation and the permission to love heightened their days. Shoshannah and Yankel found themselves looking deeper into each other's eyes, trying to guess each others' hidden wishes. Not touching, not speaking, but guessing the next thing to do. Yankel would take the water pails out of her hands, grazing hers almost, a smile in the corner of her mouth acknowledging the touch. Or Shoshannah would steal his work clothes out of his room at daybreak to air them, brush them, and put them back before he rose. An intimacy of nearness, a lived, married love grew between them.

When Shoshannah regained her speech, she would tell her children of this time and of lands unknown in Suczorno, and always of love, work, and devotion. But she also invented tales of faraway cities, places where flowers bloomed in all colours of the rainbow, where all stones were gems, and rubies were thrown into the rivers just to watch the water rings widen around them, for the joy of it. But Suczorno had no heart for such outlandish behaviour.

All this came much later. Now was the time of unspoken love, though their glowing faces betrayed them. They worked harder to shorten the wait, and the father was gratified to see his son, twenty-nine now – almost an old man in Suczorno, regain his youth. Yankel took the work out of his father's hands, told him to go and rest, did the slaughtering for the *Shabbats* all on his own, while Shoshannah rushed around to keep the feathers from flying and laughed when she found them in the cooking pots.

Shoshannah learned how to make the soft green kosher soap from *Kali* and old chicken-skin fat. She cooked it until the mixture ran a clear green and thickened slowly into a paste. Shainah, her future mother-in-law, had taught her how, and now she did it by herself, letting Shainah sit on a chair and give advice. It was a complicated procedure – the fire had to be controlled and care had to be taken not get the corrosive *Kali* into eyes or onto hands. All of that filled their days, and the readiness to ease each other's burden was love itself.

The bride from Shklov, in one of Shainah's dresses under the *Chuppah,* was as glowing as any bride in silk or satin. To fulfill her obligations, she went down to the *Mikvah* for the ritual bath, in the presence of two witnesses. Suczorno had a wonderful *Mikvah,* an underground bath whose source must – according to the law — come out as a virgin spring directly from the ground, renewing itself constantly. A few steps, hewn from the same green-grey slate that surrounded the well, led to it. A healing natural spring from the bowels of the earth! Shoshannah had gone diligently and joyfully down these steps before the wedding. She knew it was the same water that had purified and healed her bleeding sores when she first came to sit on the *Shoichet's* threshold. And she went down these steps to her bath to cleanse and elevate her soul to be worthy of Yankel's love and to bear his children. She prayed, gave thanks, and was one with her God.

Since she was an orphan, she was led by her parents-in-law onto the *Chuppah.* The blessing was witnessed by a small crowd of townsfolk, who had brought gifts as well as honey cake and wine. No one had ever expected to see the stuttering, bent-over Yankel bring a bride home, and they came for the sake of Aaron, their hardworking, modest, and pious *Shoichet,* to wish him well. But the mystery surrounding Shoshannah brought them also: they wanted to take a good look at her from up close. What colour were her eyes, her hair? Would she cut it? Would she wear a kerchief or could she afford a wig? They were not malicious, just curious, and the women surrounding her showed friendly faces.

Shoshannah smiled and barely heard their chatter. Her heart was so full, for she had for the first time touched Yankel's hand with hers. It was when bride and groom were taking that drop of wine from the same cup that it happened. Furtively, unintention-ally she thought, but it had happened. She still felt it on the palm side of her fingers as a lingering, silky touch. As slight as it was, and perhaps forbidden no more, it went like lightning through her body and she trembled. The ancient blessing that had come down from Abraham and Sarah, and the drop of wine shared from a single cup, laid upon her shoulders the weight chosen chil-dren have to bear.

She had come out of her hiding place in Shklov alive. She had not asked any questions of God when she covered her dead parents and siblings with linen and took to the road. She had been chosen to live. God was with her in the same way as He had walked with the children of Israel through the Red Sea. She was one of the chosen. And Shoshannah smiled her mystery smile, and knew exactly who she was: a child of an ancient tribe, meant to carry the word of God. So she smiled and let the women talk while preparing herself for the days to come.

Yankel and Shoshannah moved first into the back room of the *Shoichet's* house. This was the very old part, where the wooden posts were so old that they looked and felt like stone. Shainah had prepared the room for them, had aired it and dressed the wide bunk bed – meant for many children to share – with linen she herself had not used for years. She provided them with feather pillows and feather beds – a *Shoichet* is never short of feathers.

With the first of their many children to come, they asked permission of the father to change the annexed shed into an extra room. The father was delighted to let them have it. He saw his son now as his true heir, a son to be proud of, one who carried on the ancient art with dignity and skill. Yankel became more active in Suczorno Synagogue affairs as Aaron himself grew older and less able to attend to it.

The *Shoichet's* house, the last of the houses on the upper bank of the river, a poor man's house among the richer ones, was open to the fields in the south and the east. It stood unprotected on Suczorno's outer end, open to the prairie winds, summer and winter, and also to the occasional fury of the peasant mob. But there were advantages to this: one could build on to the old house without angering any neighbour. One could let one's children run free and play, as Aaron's children had done. One could build on another room, and then a kitchen. And Yankel did all that for his

Shoshannah, who was never seen without a rich, swelling body.

He worked for his Shoshannah and for their children every moment of the long day. When he wasn't slaughtering the chickens, he improved their dwelling, cleared beeswax for candles, made kindling, fed the stove, and was willing to attend to things no other man would do in Suczorno. He had to – there were ten children granted to them by the Almighty, healthy, good children to be clad, fed, and taught. And one never heard a mean word or a curse coming from that household on the rim of the town.

But the children were a little wilder than the others. Neither Yankel nor Shoshannah were inclined to punish or scold them. Children had to learn through love, and they did. But the truth was, they were less inhibited, less held in, often seen barefoot in the fields or swimming in the Suczorno Creek, which widened more like a river at the bend as it descended into the valley.

And so Ethel, born somewhere in the middle of all of them, the playmate, the friend, of Shimon, was wilder, less obedient than children were allowed to be in Suczorno. She looked more like her mother than any of the others, and she was very close to Shoshannah's heart. Ethel listened entranced to her mother's stories, when Shoshannah had regained her speech. She told holy legends of love, of the great women: Ruth, Rebekkah, and Rachel. Ethel helped with the little ones lovingly, but she also ran away sometimes, and the whole house worried when the sun went down and Ethel was not to be found. But coming home, happy even with her toes bleeding, having swum all the way down the river, she would laugh, "Where would I go, where could I go? Don't worry. I just like to swim and talk to Shimon."

"What do you talk about?" her father Yankel asked her that night.

"You wouldn't understand," she said. "Not because you couldn't, but because it is gone with the wind and the river, carried away, and so it isn't mine any more to tell –"

"You're your mother's daughter; you don't speak, and when you do it is in riddles. Only a prophet could read your mind. Go to bed. Get up around five. Because my daughters will learn *Torah*, the same way the boys have to. This is how it is in this house."

Ethel rushed away, not afraid of him. It was a home without fear, except for the fear of God. The children were all used to hard work, taught to help by their mother, Shoshannah the silent. But Shoshannah changed when surrounded by her children on a *Shabbat* evening, when the spirit is free of duty to man and God and can roam into distant lands. "She comes from far," they would say in the village. "Does she really come from Shklov? We've met people from Shklov, none are so outlandish as she." "How true are her stories?" They felt true, but no one knew. Her children did not care. They sat around her, from the youngest of two to the fourteen-year-old.

The two oldest boys, twins of fifteen, were away. They looked so much alike that only their mother could tell them apart, and only by small signs, or sometimes by their gait. The one, older by half an hour than his twin, was more inward, his voice was more commanding, and he took the lead. The younger one was a little weaker, with slightly shorter arms, and slower to speak. Shoshannah had given them very ancient names: the names of Joseph's half-brothers in the Bible, which Suczorno thought strange. The two were inseparable.

The boys had been sent by their father to study at the *Yeshiva* in Lemberg-Lvov in spite of the enormous expense. The young men did not like their father's trade of killing chickens and praying while cutting their throats, or earning extra change for plucking the feathers and delivering them to the richer households. Sometimes Shoshannah cleaned out the insides of the chickens. She washed them, salted them with expensive sea salt, and laid them out until the blood-juices stopped running. So *koshered,* she delivered the chickens herself. These deliveries, and the *Shabbat* services on the high holidays, were Shoshannah's only contacts with the women of Suczorno. She smiled at them, gave them a *"Shalom"* or a *"Geet Shabbes"* as the case may be, but otherwise kept strictly to herself.

The village spun legends around her. She did not cut her hair, but wore a kerchief in public. It was a modern trend, others were doing it. It wasn't acceptable in Suczorno, but there it was. Shoshannah was not provocative like Naomi, who went out to the well with her hair not even properly covered. Never Shoshannah, she was modest. But according to Suczorno behind-the-back talk, the stories she told her children must come from strange forebears. Perhaps from the Chazars, perhaps from the converted Mongols or Tatars, who had accepted some strange form of Judaism out there in the vast regions of Asia.

And they wondered whether, perhaps, "the Shklovke" was not even Ashkenazi like the rest of Suczorno, German Jews who had lived for hundreds of years among the German tribes in the Middle Ages and who had invented the beautiful, cherished Yiddish. Perhaps her ancestors were the ancients, the Jews deported to Babylon, who did not return – when permitted – to Jerusalem, but wandered east, deep into Asia, keeping a forgotten form of the faith. Who could tell? And so it went.

But because of her modesty, her acceptance of hard work and

being satisfied with only a few *piasters,* Suczorno let her live in peace. Maybe she allowed her many children to run wild, but they were good in *Cheder* and did not do any harm.

Ethel

EXCEPT ETHEL – she was really wild, so Suczorno thought, and needed to be watched. One never knew with unruly girls what memories could be awakened of the serpent and the apple tree. One had to watch her. And when Ethel started talking to Shimon, everybody worried: "What was this going to be?" They had been swimming in the Suczorno River– not naked, God forbid – but how would a mother let her ten-year-old daughter swim in that dangerous river, and taking Shimon along. That Shimon may have taken her along no one considered.

In fact, Ethel and Shimon had just been talking. It was a hot June day, and Ethel, barefoot as usual, had run down from the high bank to sit by the water's edge and cool her feet in the river. Shimon took his shoes off to do the same. So they sat comfortably on a beautiful summer day, with breezes of the north-east blowing and a rich yellow sun above warming their faces.

It was one of those June days when a young man who is not hungry, has slept a full night and risen to a loving good morning, will step out into God's own world to walk down along a sparkling river and find a barefoot young girl to walk with. This was the day that Shimon talked for the first time to Ethel, sitting near the water, toes cooling.

The talk on the riverbank, in spite of Ethel's steady laughter or girlish giggles, was earnest. What to do with life? So many days to come. Shimon cherished her reply: "We'll see, let's just love God, enjoy His world, it's a gift." And she started to retell one of her mother's outlandish stories and Shimon listened, more with his heart than his mind. So he could not say what it was, when that night, he asked himself, "What was it she said?"

They had swum down the river, past the famous bend where the Suczorno Creek swells with underground springs and grows wider and more treacherous. They had heard all the stories about children who had been pulled down and never seen again. Every youngster in Suczorno had heard the threatening call: "Do not go down the bend of the creek!" And every child had disobeyed, at least once. So the two of them, Shimon and Ethel, were defying the order. They had learned the skill to swim in that river, they knew they could fight it, and it was a bond between them.

It was an unforgettable month of June. She was ten, he just a little older, perhaps a couple of years. And the bond lasted – one might call it in holier terms a covenant.

"We'll get married," he said to her one day. They were the age when children try to live by their own wilful laws and the fantasy of faraway days.

In Suczorno it was hard to be different, to be a child. Imagination was guided, hemmed in by daily observance, the word of God taught and work steadily corrected. But the spirit is indomitable; even if guided, supervised, and chained, it escapes between the links of its fetters. God is everywhere.

"A covenant can be made with the running river, which never fills the sea – as it says in Ecclesiastes," Ethel said on that June day to Shimon. "Why would God allow a rainbow for Noah and not allow a running river for Ethel and Shimon, when a river is so much more a sign of His eternity than a rainbow, which soon fades in the sky?"

For Ethel and Shimon, the river was their covenant. They returned every free summer day, and ran down past the bend, where no one could see them.

Since the *Shoichet's* was the last house on the high bank, the world seemed limitless on land and down the bank of the Suczorno River. Ethel and Shimon enjoyed a freedom none of the children of the inner town had. Controlled from the cradle, held to task and to study, they were forbidden the innocence of play, and if not forbidden, simply had no chance for it. The *Shoichet's* children, with open fields at their door, could collect stones, build castles, draw their mother's fables into the fine sand lining the creek, and were not chastised. They were free, which did not sit that well with the town, and they were judged for it. As was Ethel. "After all, she is one of the Shklovke's children, what can one expect of them? But Shimon, too?"

In Moishe and Leah's house there was order, Jewish order. Proper behaviour, good manners were expected of the children. But did Sarah not go across the bridge to visit with Naomi, who was another one of the strange women Suczorno had to accept? Well, the world was changing and Suczorno was not what it had been. So the women stopped whispering. On the way to the *Shoichet* or to the Synagogue, glimpsing Shimon and Ethel returning from their morning walks, they first shook their heads and finally let them be.

Shimon grew tall and straight. A light film of yellow hair played about his lips and down the sideburns; his leisurely gait was supported by tough tendons and muscles he had honed by running and swimming. He did not look like a Talmudic scholar. Only his eyes gave him away. Squinting slightly, they were always tired from reading at night and hand copying scrolls. At this task he earned money, good money. By sixteen or seventeen, when he decided to say goodbye to his own, he had a handsome pouch of savings.

And Shimon would soon set out to go west, walking, like any young journeyman, with letters of recommendation in his pocket to the printers in Lemberg and Czernowitz. Shimon decided first on the latter destination. "It is on a beautiful broad river, the Prut, coming down from the mountains," he told Ethel on their last walk together. "And it is our covenant, Ethel. I'll come back for you. Wait for me."

They had walked very far, silently that morning. What was there to say, when the heart was breaking? Ethel heard one word only: *Wait.* And she knew she would. *Wait.* They had not noticed how far they had walked. Suddenly Shimon called to Ethel, who had run ahead of him, to return and sit down. He had spotted the grove of trees that he knew so well, the one leading down to the "Jew's Trap." And he recalled lying on his back in his father's wagon watching the clouds fly overhead, then being robbed of the horses and wagon, his brothers hurt, he having to find his way back to get help.

Now it looked green, a dense poplar green, shiny on one side and olive-matte on the other when the leaves turned. The whole grove changed shiny-to-matte in the light breeze, as a moving mirage would. Shimon knew it well. He recognized the clearing, where the sun let wildflowers bloom on a patch of grass. Shimon called to Ethel, who had taken the wrong direction ahead of him, to return. Then he took her hand – a touch he had not dared yet – and pulled her a little towards himself. And then they walked in an even rhythmic step towards the clump of trees. The clearing opened in its unearthly beauty, a sheltered, round patch of high grass, sunlit and sun-spotted by the turning leaves. It was a sanctuary, a place to marry before God, with a *Chuppah* above of the bluest velvet. The two children sat down, leaning against an old poplar to cry. How many tears are there for such beauty? How many tears for parting? And they did not rise until the sun was past the zenith. Then they rose, brushed the grass and the yellow buttercups off their clothes, and their vows were made.

"I'll wait," Ethel said. "I'll wait for you, Shimon." And they started on their way home.

The family had all waited for him, Moishe and Leah, Sarah and Srul, all the children. They had waited for Shimon that day and guessed where he had been. No questions were asked. Leah had made the meal for her son, the things he loved. A noodle *Kugel* with mushrooms from the valley and fried onions, a chicken brown and crusty on top, and a small chicken liver were on her son's plate today.

Greti

HE REMEMBERED IT ALL, sitting on the high bank. The flavour of her cinnamon *kuchels,* the fatty fingers they left, her admonitions not to wipe his hands on his trousers. "My clever son has not learned the simplest thing." Of course he remembered, had learnt in the meantime, in the day-to-day course of life, and under less loving teachers, much more complicated things than not to wipe one's fingers on one's pants.

He had gone on foot first – at the age of sixteen or seventeen – towards the west. A journeyman, with one change of underwear, a starchy shirt, and woollen trousers, beautifully sewn by the tailor from across Suczorno Creek. Moishe, his father, would not let him go away like a beggar from his door. He was proud of Shimon, who had shown the courage of a seasoned man while still a boy, and was such a scholar. He wanted to take his son a good distance with the horses and wagon (two brown mares replaced the old trusted ones soon after the robbery), as far as the Djnester perhaps, advising Shimon to seek a railway station to take him at least part of the way after that.

Czernowitz was far and there were two rivers to cross, the Djnester and the Prut, and the father worried. He had been to Czernowitz, had also loved the city – where thousands of Jews lived, rich and poor. These Jews were not always kindly inclined to newcomers from the eastern *shtetls,* but they did not let anyone die of hunger or cold on the street. On the road, though, there was a great deal to worry about. One could be beaten and robbed of one's very shoes and clothing, Moishe knew, and left naked to breathe one's last breath.

Shimon's mother, Leah, had had the cobbler from across the creek sew a double pouch of leather with a snap-button and a string to hold Shimon's money, the coins she gave him and his own that he had earned as a copier of scrolls. There were five Napoleons, small gold coins, showing the French rooster. Leah's father had told her, and now she told her own children, that these coins were so trusted and popular because they had never lost their value since the invasion of Russian lands by the French Emperor Napoleon in 1812. True or not, this was good money, exchangeable everywhere in the east and as far west as Vienna.

The family stood around Shimon after dinner; everyone had an opinion how to hide the pouch best: in the trousers, in the lining of the cap, and so forth. Moishe decided that, according to his experience, it was best hung on a leather strip around Shimon's neck, directly under his shirt, close to the skin, where he could easily verify its presence.

And so it was.

Sitting on the promontory rock, overlooking the river, Shimon's skin remembered. And it was still there.

With the pouch on his breast, the *Tefillin,* the prayer book, and his writing materials – the copyist's trade – in a home-sewn rucksack on his back, along with a flask for water, some provisions, and the bag of clothes on his arm, Shimon had stepped out very early next morning. He told his father he wanted to walk. His swimming and the many kilometres he had walked as a boy now served him well, and he could make twenty kilometres a day.

But he made more: a kindly peasant he had known from his youthful forays had picked him up and took him almost halfway to the river, to a small Jewish settlement where he could rest the night. A strange friendship had sprung up between Shimon and the young Ukrainian, and Shimon was thrilled to see Vassily come his way again.

It had happened when Shimon, at thirteen or fourteen, had walked a fair distance and then lain down to rest in a peasant's field. He'd been awakened by a soft, kindly voice which said, "Jewish boy, let me take you out of here, my father will break your bones if he finds you." But then they sat down, the two of them, and Vassily said, "I have always wanted to talk to a Jew, and I never have. Here they say so many terrible things, how wicked you are with money, that it is your fault that we get drunk, because you push your liquor on us. But others say, 'Leave them be, they have written the holy books, they are the children of Abraham,' and so on. It can't all be true. Talk to me. I'm so glad I've met you. A young man can talk much better, much freer with another young man, no matter who his mother was. Talk to me. What is it like to be a Jew?"

Shimon smiled, offering his hand to the peasant, and in proper Ukrainian said, "First, give me your hand so we'll be brothers and neither will harm the other, so we can talk with honour."

"Yes, here it is," Vassily said, putting his big hand, that had collected many a harvest, into Shimon's silky palm. "But let's find a shady spot and crawl to it on all fours, not to be seen by anyone." They crawled to a small hill of hay with posts around it to hold the roof of pressed straw. And Vassily said, laughing, "This is where we go with our girls sometimes. But come, sit against this post. So, what is this creature? What is a Jew?"

Shimon sat still to find initial words. "It's a long, long story, and I have no time for it."

"Well, he is human," Vassily laughed, then continued, "but he is not allowed to have land, yet a Jew like any other man would want to till his garden."

"I will just say, " Shimon replied, "that the authorities, church and state, do not permit it, so the Jew does what he can to live. We study. Take up commerce. It is a long story of suffering, and so our people and your people do not know one another. There is suspicion, dislike of the unknown other. And the worst of all stories, violence. No one of your folk has ever asked what it is to be a Jew – to my knowledge – you're the first. Or perhaps there were others. But thank you, it is not answerable in one sentence, but were there one I would say: A Jew is a man who studies the Law given to him by God, tries to live by it, works for a living, and brings up his children, no matter where he is. God is his country, the soil he stands on."

NOW VASSILY, wanting to visit, said to Shimon, "Wait, have a little rest, sleep the night. I'll get you across the Djnester in the morning." He left, returning shortly with a full meal of *Kolbasa,* cabbage, a hunk of bread, and jug of buttermilk. The Jew, Shimon, ate the *Kolbasa,* well aware that it was pork. He was hungry. God allows it if life needs to be sustained, and he ate it knowingly.

It's a greater sin to refuse hospitality, Shimon thought, but when he came to drink the milk after eating the meat, his stomach turned. He couldn't go that far, whether God allowed or not, he couldn't. He felt vomit rising, and he said to Vassily, who carried sheepskins and a woollen carpet to bed Shimon comfortably for the night, "May I have water, please? I'll have the buttermilk in the morning. I'm full, and I thank you."

By daybreak, Vassily had a wonderful horse ready. Shimon knew the breed, his father had some. They were true, dear, hard-working, slow to grasp things, but sweet-natured horses. Vassily took him across the Bessarabian plain close to the river Prut and let him off near a Jewish settlement called Petruvkov, which Shimon's father had mentioned. Moishe had said people were friendly there, that they respected a stranger, according to the law, and that he could find shelter there for a time.

Vassily and Shimon had travelled two days with each other, had eaten and slept together in the wagon. The days were those eastern days when sun and shade alternate, winds are held by the wooded hills and come as light, sweet breezes through the trees to the wanderer, the man in the driver's seat, or the horse. No whip was necessary. Such peace in creation and the presence of God was felt with every breath! So Vassily and Shimon parted as brothers, kissing three times. They had learned more in two days than others do in a lifetime.

Shimon arrived at Czernowitz and crossed the northeast bridge on foot. The city, seen from afar, was bewildering to him, with its stone houses, its churches with spires or crenellated tops, and a few with onion domes. He walked on paved streets and under shady rows of poplar, tall, swaying, a kind he did not know. He asked a man in the street, "Good day, where do the Jews live?" He asked in Ukrainian, and the answer came in Romanian, "They live everywhere. But they have a quarter around the old synagogue, where there are more of them," and he showed Shimon the way to the *Synagoguengasse.*

This was a beginning. He found a room, set up shop, went Friday night to services, told the *Gabbai,* the man in charge of "everything," that he was a certified (by whom? and who cares?) scroll copier. This was the beginning.

Shimon was amazed. Czernowitz was a Tower of Babel. The Yiddish was Yiddish, yes, but not the Yiddish Shimon knew. The rhythm was softer, more Slavic, the tone lower. Babel, yet not Babel. The Ukrainians spoke a Yiddish of sorts, and they seemed to talk to the Jews, buying, selling, and as he found out a little later, even going to school together. This was still Austria, with the picture of the Emperor Franz-Joseph everywhere: benevolent, a father, elegantly bearded in a splendid red military jacket, his gold braids showing royalty. One hung in the printer's shop where

Shimon presented himself very soon after his arrival.

Srul's letter was a good introduction to the owner, a local German by the name of Baumgartner, whose family had come here two hundred years ago in an Austrian settlement drive conducted by the great Joseph II. Baumgartner was proud of his family history and started into his family tree at their first meeting, assuming Shimon understood High German. Well, Shimon understood a bit – with Yiddish one does get some of it – but heavens! Mr. Baumgartner switched from his High German to the German kind of Yiddish, and they finally understood one another. Shimon was thrilled to hear a Yiddish so exotic yet still truly Yiddish. Mr. Baumgartner told him, "We all dabble in it, it's a kind of *lingua franca* of the folk. But everyone speaks German, the Austrian kind. And is proud of it."

Mr. Baumgartner took Shimon on as an apprentice. His pay was low, but only in the beginning. In one year he had learned typesetting to such a perfection that he had been given a weekly column to set in German. With his self-teaching abilities, Shimon learned like no other and was now fluent in German. He was always studying written words, deducing their meanings, how they changed when embedded in sentences, revealing an unsuspected core.

He had moved up from the *Synagoguengasse* to more cosmopolitan quarters, now that he did not have to rely only on Yiddish. He shaved his young beard, cut his hair, and had a suit made to measure in the *Herrengasse* tailor shop. To his God he remained true: he attended services Friday night and *Shabbat* morning, wore the *Tefillin* on his arm at sunrise, and ate in *kosher* restaurants. It helped him feel secure, and he could meet other Jews. The cooking, *blintzes* or potato *kugel,* was familiar, yet strangely different.

And so were the people. They were Jews, but seemed to him not really Jews. Many spoke the high German of Mr. Baumgartner and the Ukrainian of the peasants from the outlying districts, colouring their own speech with a singsong cadence, a declamation unexpected and bewildering. But Shimon was happy to be in world so big, so varied! He let things happen, and smiled at his own new appearance.

He was not familiar with mirrors. Here they were everywhere. Every shop sported three-fold mirrors, two metres high, big enough to take a grown man in. Mirrors were frowned on in Suczorno. "They're for the ladies of easy virtue to view themselves in," Shimon had heard his mother say, and he smiled. She would not recognize me now, he thought, if I stood in front of her. Of course, nothing could change what I am, deep inside – nothing could take my soul, dress it up with German clothes, and think it another soul. It is not. But clothes – a high-collared shirt, a pin in the cravat, a watch in the vest-coat, and a cane at hand – do some strange things to you when you catch your fleeting image in one of these moving mirrors – what exactly, Shimon could not tell. But a slight change in his bonds, a loosening of the earth around his roots, and the palpable sensuality of the foreign...he looked at the girls now on the Sunday *corso;* flirtatiously, they looked back.

One, who Shimon saw surrounded by young men and women on the *Ringplatz* near the *Rathaus,* the City Hall, leaning against the corner wall, was tall, blonde, and supple, dressed in a flowery summer dress down to the ankles and up to the neck. She looked like a bound bouquet of daisies with blue ribbons tying her waist. He thought she was something unreal, and he smiled at this vision, who smiled back, shouting something in German, that sounded like, "Hello, come here handsome!" Or so it seemed to Shimon.

He had grown to be a very attractive man of twenty, with strong, athletic shoulders, a lithe waist, a chiselled profile, and lustrous olive-tinted skin. He walked fast past the group and did not react to her summons. Later, he could not sleep the night, not suffering, but longing for the unknown, the not-yet-experienced, the world-out-there. And he went back, a few Sundays in a row, and saw her smiling at him as if greeting a school friend.

One Sunday she was alone and did not let him pass. "Stranger," she called out to him. "Stranger, where are you from?" She spoke in High German, with a low, comfortable voice, strong, assured, free, different from the women of Suczorno. Perhaps as free as Ethel's voice. But no, more independent. A voice on its own, speaking for itself.

He stopped, greeted her with a light bow of his head – as he wore no hat – and said, "Good day, I'm Shimon." But thinking how to put his ben Moishe, he hesitated for a moment and said, with more conviction than necessary: "I'm Shimon Moisevitch," which was the truth but adjusted to this world. "I'm a Jew from a small town east of here – well, quite a distance east – I'm a printer. I do Yiddish, German, and have just accepted another post to learn Cyrillic printing. For Ukrainian and Russian, you know."

"I do," she said. "I am Greti, or Margarete Heller, a student at the university here. One of the very, very few women who have passed the entrance exams. There are not many of us, but I have – *de facto,* as they say – been accepted as a full-time student. We are desperately fighting to be allowed to study. It will be a bloody fight – but God knows if we'll succeed. I can't stay now, but come next Sunday and I'll take you to our *mensa."* He smiled. "It's a students' restaurant in the *Universitätsgasse,"* she added, seeing his incomprehension. "Bye." She smiled, gave a wave from a flowery sleeve, turned the corner, and was gone.

A world unimagined by a scholarly Jewish boy from the *shtetl,* a world without God, without His worship and man's search for the spiritual life, opened its doors to the unsuspecting Shimon. He had never before been exposed to secular ideas. The letter was Hebrew and the word was God's. Going with Greti to her *mensa* for next Sunday's lunch was as strange as if he had landed on another planet.

Young men, a few women were milling about, talking. There was beer, wine, bread and butter, a large bowl of soup. Laughter. Touching. Hugging. And earnest talk on subjects totally alien to Shimon. He sat silent and bewildered at Greti's side. He had bread and butter and tea, but did not look at the soup. His stomach shrank, his tongue went dry. Was it the smell of pork or the unintelligible subjects: revolution, women's rights, voting, divorce, university education for women, science, the *Wissenschaften,* the new search for knowledge. No God. Man thinking himself God, creating the world anew.

Greti was a leader, getting up and saying things, unbelievable words of incitement and excitement. Shimon's cheeks were burning and he asked her if he could leave. He did, and did not see her for a while. But his nights were troubled. In his dreams, he saw her pearl-buttoned blouse open, he felt his fingers undoing it. Holding the shimmery-cool button tightly, trying to push it through the buttonhole, he guessed the shape of a small breast, woke and trembled.

I will fall into sin, he thought. I'll leave the road of righteousness. I'll forget a Jew's direct link to God. I'll forget His word and I'll run after a man's lust.

But the new, the recognition of an age that demanded attention, forced reason to discern past from the present. Accustomed to thinking from age three or four, Shimon looked at the world around him and found it irresistible. His German he perfected daily. Cyrillic he printed now in his new position, and he invented a new typeface for it, being intimate with Ukrainian and Russian. He found himself reading, night after night, books of discovery he had never dreamt existed. Science. Shimon had no tools to handle it, but a sharp intelligence, a logic of accuracy that allowed him to see beauty in its laws, he slowly mastered.

And he could not resist Greti, her call was so powerful, a call to his body and his mind as well. And it was summer and it was Czernowitz, where Jews and Christians did not care who their parents were, but ate and drank together, wandered into the nearby mountains with rucksacks on their backs, and slept in the Carpathian herders' huts.

He was a different Shimon now, divested of Suczorno. A modern Jew, or not even a Jew. Human and universal, Shimon joined the world of his day. Greti called on him at the printing shop in the *Rathausgasse* one day, two weeks after he had left the *mensa,* and she said, "Join us, we science students, we have formed a debating club called *Modern Thought,* and we talk about truths discovered in the last twenty years that show the new paths we have to take. I like you – even more than that, but that is only a private matter. Come."

They went up into the mountains, the wild Carpathians. Shimon had been a runner and swimmer from very young, to the despair of Leah and Moishe, and he had a body that demanded training. When he first met Ethel on the high bank of Suczorno Creek and started to swim past the bend where the creek changed into a true river, it became a thing of absolute need to train his body. When he had walked twenty kilometres as a thirteen-year-old to seek help for his brothers, who were caught and beaten at the Jew's Trap, he did not tire.

Now he had grown tall, and his legs were muscular and athletic. There was a grace, a balance of harmony, in that moving body. "Why does a Jew need all that? What does Shimon do with his life? Why does he run and swim down that treacherous river, when he could study, perfect his Hebrew, and learn a trade?" He heard it still. It echoed in his ears, while sitting beside Greti, resting after the climb to the summit of the Cecina Mountain overlooking Czernowitz. He heard it and smiled. My poor mother, he thinks, what am I doing to her?

Greti was agnostic. She had rejected all supernatural forces, and believed all the animate and inanimate world ruled by causes discernible by men. In time, life would be explainable as seen through a microscope now.

Greti took Shimon to her laboratory one day. And he looked through the microscope with her help and was amazed at what he saw in a simple water drop. She showed him another slide with the feared bacillus Koch, which caused the poor to spit blood and die of a murderous lung disease. "It was discovered by Koch," she said, "so it bears his name."

It was a new awakening, but a rude one and painful one for Shimon, to find himself so utterly unschooled. He, who thought he was a scholar, to whom learning came as easily as breathing, an easy flow of logic and ancient memory. He was silent, and Greti wondered about him. Such an exotic, beautiful creature, an artist in printing, in all lettering, deeply ingrained with a wisdom that she had no use for and never suspected existed.

She saw his hurt and she said, "I know how you feel. You have studied, but if you have not gone through the Austrian Gymnasium you can't register for University classes, except as an extraordinary student, who is, in the end, not entitled to exams or a diploma. But it would help if you sat in to see if you could follow."

He was deeply disturbed. He had no Latin or Greek. He knew nothing about the microscope, the great Koch, the great Pasteur. He knew nothing. Again Shimon retreated into his shell and worked hard at his printing. He designed a new Cyrillic illustrated lettering of stunning beauty. He worked twelve hours a day, and after two years of staying in the city, he was wanted by every printer in town. The Romanians too came to him. He drew the Latin alphabet like no other, and knew enough to speak it from the peasants that came to Suczorno from the Transnistria region. They spoke a dialect, true, but a Latin tongue. And he liked the sound of it. Shimon earned well, saved his money, but he had a troubled soul. Which way now? Which way to go, where to, what for?

His nights brought dreams of all sorts: of Ethel, of his father and mother, of guilty and worrisome images. Of Greti's beauty, her arguments, reason versus God. And Greti's beauty again, with her blouse closed up to her neck, which he tore open now in his dreams, instead of undoing the pearl buttons. He now feared the night, kissing her breasts and waking, sweat streaming from every pore, and wet in forbidden places. Shimon felt that his God, the one and only ONE, did not exist. He went back every Friday to the Synagogue in the Jewish quarter, near the Turkish fountain, to pray, to call Him back, to make His presence real. But it was not what it had been, and he could not sleep.

He inquired at the University. Yes, he could register even if he had not gone through the school system. He could make an application, with a government-paid application-stamp, and ask for dispensation because of the locale he was from. If granted, he would have to pass the entrance examination in all subjects, which included Mathematics, Latin, Greek, German, etcetera. And if he passed, he could register.

It seemed too huge a hurdle to pass, but the world was not entirely closed to him. Though perhaps it was. He slept better, but decided to just work more assiduously at his job; he went out of guilt regularly to services, to make sure he had not forgotten God. He started at night, on his own, on Latin and Greek letters, was happier now. Letters he knew what to do with: draw them, turn them around, combine them.

He suddenly saw where the Cyrillic came from. It was Greek – Greek, Latin, and a little imagination of the priests who knew the thick Slavic consonant sound and had to find an expression for the time when Christianity expanded into Russia. Shimon bought history books. In Czernowitz, the past was intensely present. New research into archaeology, the digging for all that happened, made the past vividly manifest. Wherever man put a shovel, the Bible became alive. Names and events written into Shimon's blood from the age of three, mentioned by grandparents and his beloved teacher – the *Melamed* – were as if alive only yesterday, with no date in the past attached to them. The names of his Kings, of Saul, David, Solomon, of the great prophets, Jeremiah, Isaiah, and Job – all set into time now, referred back to Egypt's time, when hieroglyphics revealed historic coincidences – suddenly had precision. And not just man's history. Also the earth's. Where did it come from? What matter, force, or substance are we made of?

Shimon read day and night. He walked with Greti and talked:

in town, up the mountain, along the river Prut. They swam with other youths down that enormous, tumultuous river. Strong and competitive, he was as good as anyone. He dressed well and like everyone else, but there was something in his demeanour that set him apart, as if he came from or belonged to another world. He made other acquaintances, and some friendships with men. But he knew he was a stranger. His time was set. He had only a little longer perhaps, to study, to learn, to go through the bookstores on the Ringplatz, on the Herrengasse. Still, he was a stranger everywhere.

He was commissioned to set the type for a New Testament printing in the redesigned Ukrainian Cyrillic letters, which he had embellished elegantly. He started reading it carefully, for the first time.

So this is what it is, he thought. Here is the Jew reviled. He saw it clearly and without any doubt. First it was Judas who kissed Jesus, with betrayal in mind, then there were the thirty pieces of silver, then the wild condemnation of the Jewish folk and priests at the trial. Even Pilate looked better than them.

Unspeakably saddened, Shimon thought there would never be an end to it. And talking to Greti one day, sitting in the public gardens, a shady shelter only recently laid out with pebbles, walks and benches, he brought the subject up. And Greti, smilingly and sweetly, took his hand for the first time and said, "Shimon, this is all old, obsolete nonsense. The future is bright. Science will lift the veil. Prejudices must fall. The earth is round, not flat anymore. Ships do not fall off the edge into a void, they sail right around it and return where they started from. We're spinning around the sun, the moon spins around us, the law of gravity holds the world in balance. Everything is explainable, and will be clearer, and the old will make place for newer laws. Time moves faster. We're out of the thicket."

It was good of her to say it, but her touch had made him hot beneath his collar and sweaty in his palms. So he took his hand back gently and did what he saw other young men doing, he dared put his arm around her back, holding her close. And she turned to him, took his face into her hands, and kissed his mouth. So desired and so wonderful a kiss. Again and again.

Shimon's heart was full. All the angels sang. He thought he was floating and knew the intensity of the moment; its beauty, but also its brevity.

"Take courage," Greti said in parting. "Things will change. We are so lucky to live in this age, when every day brings new discoveries to us, brings us closer to brotherhood, perhaps Socialism, without churches and Synagogues. It's a new age. Come tomorrow, Shimon my love, come tomorrow, same time, same bench."

But he couldn't. The night was full of that kiss. He had never held a woman close. Even his arm around her shoulders was "a first time." One does not kiss in Suczorno on a park bench. There are no parks, for one thing, and no benches, but there is also a life to prepare for, prayer, work to do for a piece of bread. The women stay indoors.

Shimon thought of the one and only Ethel in Suczorno, who would run with him through poplar groves, rest in the shade, talk, swim down beyond the bend of the river. All under the rigorous inspection of the town. In Suczorno, no one was alone, no one did things apart from the others. If it was for mutual help and safety, maybe. But there were no private lives, except in the sense that all lives are private, lived within one's skin. And the awareness of "the other" was with you, as was the learning of God's will.

From birth to death, it was God's will. How else were you to take the "everyday"?

The night was Greti's, her first and her last, and he knew it. He marvelled at the courage of the new-world woman to have taken his head into her hands and kissed his mouth. Her wonderful, wonderful breasts against his chest, pearl buttons imprinting their patterns on his skin. He dreamt awake and asleep and went to work in the morning. "I'll think later," he said. "I'll think later. Perhaps one more time."

But when the hour came – he had worked intensely all day – he couldn't go, and he sat down to write a few words of parting, of love, of the unforgettable moment, but above all of thanks. Greti had given him a whole world to contemplate from a different angle. And he took his leave. Running to the park bench before she arrived, he pinned the letter where they had sat the night before, between two tight boards on the back of the bench. And he walked away fast, lest he see her and his heart sink.

Shimon paid his bills and took leave from his boss, saying he would be back, that he must go home to keep a promise to his parents and his fiancée. He packed his bags and bought a few modern kitchen things: remembering Leah's tired right arm, he got a whirling mixer with a lever on the side, and a few metres of white silk, he did not yet know for whom. Shimon had none of the grasp of the practical man of what makes life easier or more comfortable. So he did not know what to choose, neither could he carry a great deal.

He was still a stranger in Czernowitz. But what would he be in Suczorno after having seen a world unfold? A world where there were no limits to the mind, a world with changed relations between men and women, and particularly a world where God seemed almost obsolete. Would he not be a stranger at home? And then what? How could he stay and fit into an ancient stricture, where learning meant *Torah* and behaviour was God-ordained and immutable.

He left with a heavy heart, his rucksack on his back, his versatile, new leather suitcase at hand. It was a beautiful summer day with breezes from the north. He stopped at the Cecina mountain, and he looked up there, and knew he would be back.

But he had told Ethel, "Wait for me," as she sat against a birch trunk in the grove clearing. He had said that to Ethel, and he could not go back on his word. So his heart grew lighter, knowing that there was no other way than this true one. And he mounted the fire-spitting, rumbling train, not all that far from the bench in the park.

An Ancient Dress

ETHEL HAD WAITED TOO LONG. Something indefinable had crept into her dreams and she woke calling Shimon's name. Her love had drained her of fun, stalled her muscles, made her resist the coming dawn, and she was reluctant to rise. Almost two years had passed, and she had only twice received word from Shimon through occasional travellers passing through Suczorno: be patient, he'll keep his promise. But the days grew longer, the nights were harder to bear, and she took to her mother's habit of silence. What was there to say if every day felt like the one already lived? But she worked, took over the cleaning of the yard, the plucking of the chickens, the making of down. The fine down had to be stripped off the hard centre fibres, work her mother did when she first accepted shelter in the *Shoichet's* house.

Shoshannah, the Shlovke, let Ethel be but saw it all. It was ominous. And she sent her out with errands, or to the well for water. The mother of course knew Ethel's love of the river, of the untamed outdoors. "So," she would say, "go, cut the hedges around the house...go." It was to little avail: silent, head bent over her work, Ethel did not speak. She was her mother's daughter. Looked like her too, with her brown and velvet eyes, and a body curving in the waist. She read Hebrew like no one else and sought comfort in the psalm, but she had changed into someone unforeseen.

And her father the *Shoichet* said to Shoshannah his wife, "Let's go to the miracle-working Chasidic rabbis. They know how to talk to women in distress. Not our own rabbi, who is too entrenched in old ways, who is not a healer. *Chasidim* are the ones who look up and sing. They know the holy books just as well, but do not search for answers there if none are to be found. Take her there, Shoshannah."

"No," Shoshannah replied. "There are no miracles. Nothing can heal or change her mood, nothing except Shimon. We'll love her, we'll be good and patient with her, as you were to me when I came with bleeding feet and sat on your father's threshold. Ethel knows what to do, she works as hard as she can, and at night she reads and writes her Hebrew. Be patient and pray that the Almighty will guide Shimon's steps to her door."

So that was that. No rabbis of any sort were called upon. One woman knows the other; more so did Shoshannah know her own daughter, who was carved from the same trunk.

SHIMON INDEED STOOD ONE DAY in front of her door. He had hesitated, he had taken a little time to find his way through his maze of feelings, so he sat for a while on his beloved promontory overlooking the river and sang. The *Nigun* came back to him, and he wanted it back, so he would be able to enter his parents' home and to fulfill the promise to Ethel. But he did not feel her presence on the riverbank. What surfaced were the lovely childish games they played and his early teenage years; but he had become another person. The *Nigun* – the old Bible melodies – were there, but the singer had changed. And it was not the years that had changed him – one grows old anywhere – but his awareness of the world in transformation out west and of the rigid eternity of this closed, inward, Jewish universe.

Shimon had been a stranger out there. Czernowitz was moving fast into the new century. He had had to learn everything anew. The littlest thing, a birthright there, he had to acquire, make his own – such as learning to date history from the time of Christ; when Shimon counted, he counted in six millennia.

In Czernowitz he had mixed with non-Jews, learned their ways. They were different, yet the same, everyone born from a mother and going back to the earth...who was different? Even the concept of God, worship was different, yet not at its core. What drove him back, was not the shock, the collision of divergent cultures, but his having said "Wait" to Ethel.

Sitting on that beloved stone, with his mother's window just around the corner, he took his time. He took his time to recall his Ethel. They had not kissed, hardly touched, but he had held another woman in his arm, if even for so brief a moment. How could he marry Ethel? Had she changed in these few years? In Suczorno, nothing ever happened, except birth and death, prayers, and the year starting on *Rosh Hashanah* and finishing after harvest.

Having returned to the stones of his river, Shimon rose from the one he sat on to watch the muddy yellow river receding slowly from its flooded lower bank. Suczorno's high bank was never flooded by the raging river. It would beat and smash against the sandy rock, would take some of it along, but it never succeeded. It often ran over the lower left bank, its water entering the low-lying front kitchens of the houses of the poor, open and unprotected from all intrusions. And Shimon thought, How lucky am I to have been born the son of Moishe and to have grown up in the house built so solidly up high by Leah's father. And how lucky am I to have met Ethel so early in my life, when dreams are real.

He remembered Ethel's stories – or were they her mother's – that spun him into a web of the finest strands with shimmering water drops running along them, being torn apart by the more or less angry sounds of "Shimon! Ethel!" echoing from afar. How beautiful a childhood he had lived with her, and how immeasurably lucky he was to have known her as a young woman.

Shimon stopped there, turned away from the river, and walked to enter his father's house through the back door.

Sarah was there with two little ones, twins, at her breast. She told him that Moishe was on the road, gone as far as Odessa to purchase grain, as the year wasn't good around here. Srul, she said, was in Lemberg for a commission of his and Sarah's *Haggadah* Exodus story.

Leah, his mother, could not contain her sobs when she saw him, and Shimon and Sarah exchanged knowing looks of "What can one do?" and waited for their own embrace until their mother had released him, and, in good Jewish fashion, decided he must be hungry. "No," he replied. "I first have to go to the *Shoichet's* house before your dinner."

"You do?"

"Yes, I do."

"Did you come for them or for us?"

"Beloved mother, what kind of question is that? There is no one more precious than you and my family. But I did say, on my last day in Suczorno, I did say to Ethel, 'Wait for me.' I have to go there. I can't speak about it, please don't make me. Just let me go."

He kissed them both, saying he would soon be back to eat his mother's dinner. Shimon had dropped his rucksack and hard suitcase on the floor in the first excitement of greeting. Now he picked the small case up, opened the lovely metal locks, and put a few gifts on the table for the family – the piece of silk, an elegant package of Austrian tobacco, and a box of Turkish sweets for Ethel and the *Shoichet's* family.

He did not want to walk in front of the houses along the creek to get there, but went out the kitchen door to go slowly through the back lane, if one could call it that. How poor the houses all looked, hardly a shingle in place, those that had shingles and not just roofs of straw-filled mud. How crooked were the walls in the back. Hens ran across his path, cackling, a goat ba-a-a-ed, a curse floated through the air, either at children or the unwilling she-goat. He walked slowly, pushing pebbles with his city shoes. How could he live here, how? He knew all these houses of the so-called "rich" from the high bank, knew all their back doors in and out, as children remember thresholds they sat on, steps that led up or down. And there were not many stairs in Suczorno, where houses lay flat to the ground, huddling against each other for protection, whether from the winds from the north or the sudden hostility of other men.

So he walked along slowly. Glancing at a woman's face through a kitchen window, he recognized it and didn't. He saw no men, except the very old sitting at wooden tables, as they do in Suczorno – books open in front of them. It was the eternal world, no yesterday, no tomorrow, all was today. God has devised and man is to follow. And he does.

So Shimon reached the end of the village, saw the *Shoichet's* house and thought it looked respectable. It was certainly better, cleaner, in better repair than the others, including his father's. He entered the courtyard from the back. There was no activity, it looked washed clean, the barrel full with well or rain water. He took the last steps nervously to knock at Ethel's back door.

He tried the door and it gave way. At the table near the window sat Shoshannah the Shklovke, Ethel's mother. She had not seen him approach; though the courtyard was in her field of vision, she was bent intently over a book. The square, leather-bound volume was yellowed with age. She was reading the *Zenerene:* the life-stories, legends, fantasy, *Midrash-Talmud-*Psalms, fortune and misfortunes of Glickl of Hameln, written by her own hand. All grandmothers read it to the little ones. Nothing ever changed in Suczorno.

Shimon stood in the doorway wondering if Shoshannah was deaf, so still she sat, immersed in her story. And Shimon saw himself as a tiny boy on the knees of his grandmother, who read to him a Glickl story about a father bird who wondered how to save his three fledgling birds from a sudden storm. Taking the eldest in his mouth and starting over the wide water, he said to him: "Son, with all the trouble you have given me, will you look after me in my old age, if I bring you safely across?" The eldest fledgling replied, "Oh, I will do it all for you, all that you ask me to do." So the father bird dropped his eldest into the water, shouting, "Liar! Liar!" Then he flew back to fetch the second one, who assured the father that he would love and cherish and care for him. And the father called him a liar, dropped him into the water too, and flew back to fetch the third one. This time, halfway across the wide water, the father asked the same question, but this time he got a very different reply: "I'll try to be good to you. I'll do my best, but I can only promise that I'll be as good to my children as you have been to me." "This is my true son," the father bird said, and took him safely across the water.

Nothing changed in Suczorno. In their free hours, older women, slowing down, having given over the running of the households, read *Die Memoiren der Glickl von Hameln* and all the other Yiddish parables and moral tales. Nothing changed in Suczorno.

Shimon slowly approached Shoshannah. She looked up, then rose to her full height and with eyes in tears said, "I am a little more deaf now, so I did not hear you come in, Shimon, forgive me. The children will be back soon and so will Yankel. Ethel is at the well. Will you stay for a meal?"

"No," he replied, "I will have to return home. But I'll come back. Allow me to go to the well to see Ethel."

He had laid his few gifts upon the kitchen table and was walking out through the front door when he saw her. She was carrying two pails, one in each hand, a timeless figure, young yet ancient, a vision. He ran towards her, and without a greeting took the pails from her. Ethel, as if she had expected it, let it happen, her face earnest and unchanged. She had seen him also, and except for, "Did you have a good trip, Shimon?" and his reply, "Thank you Ethel, a little tiring, but I'm here," they did not speak as they walked around the back through the courtyard to fill the extra barrels. Her knitted brow, her slowed-down step, worried him. It was new, unforeseen, and Shimon, pouring the well water into the barrels she assigned, asked if he might come in for a very short while.

Ethel opened the kitchen door for him with an inviting gesture, seated herself next to her mother, who had risen and stood to welcome Shimon. Shoshannah was in tears, her face flushed with both hope and apprehension. She looked from one to the other without seeing any joy in either Shimon or Ethel, consoling herself with, "They're shy, they haven't seen one another for years."

Shimon sat a little longer. Tea was offered and refused. Shoshannah fingered the silk that he had unfolded on the table and said thank you for the Turkish sweets and tobacco. She filled the air with a little chatter, but was no good at it and stopped. Seeing the desperate efforts of her mother, Ethel smiled in her direction, avoiding Shimon's eyes. He rose, nearly extended his right hand, as was his custom in the last years in Czernowitz, but realized immediately he was in Suczorno, where men and women do not touch in the presence of others. Shimon bowed, promising to return the next day, and left through the courtyard.

He went in the direction opposite to his house, as if he were a stranger looking for shelter, or for sights to be explored, and through the fields still partly flooded but green and lush on both sides of the creek. He walked fast now. The day was like one from his childhood glory, clouds blowing across the sky and the creek a real river now. And Shimon knew there was no escape. He had said "Wait" and had to fulfill the promise.

I'll take her with me, he thought. If she'll go. I will hardly be tolerated in Suczorno, and worst of all I won't be able to face these men and women every Friday night in Synagogue. I'll marry quickly and we'll leave.

He saw no other way for the moment. He returned to his promontory, waited for the sun to sink in the west, and faced his father's house.

IT WAS A SMALL WEDDING, a true homegrown *Shoichet's* daughter's wedding. Ethel was dressed in Shainah's, her grandmother's, dress. The dress her mother, who had come from afar, hair grey with dust, feet bleeding, and had rested upon the *Shoichet's* threshold, had worn. The dress had made a long journey from Germany in unrecorded times. It had come into Polish hands and down through Krakov into Shainah's possession.

The ancient dress was taken out of a mothproof trunk to be aired for Ethel. It hung in the courtyard for days, and then was taken in by Shoshannah to see if there were seams to be rehemmed or any other repair to be made. It was perfect.

Of contrasting materials, it was coarse and delicate at the same time. The coarse-spun light wool fell from Ethel's narrow waist to her ankles, enveloping them in heavy folds. A yellowed, fishnet lace interwoven with silver thread, billowed over her breasts to a high stand-up collar. She was a vision of old, Shimon thought, seeing her approach. The intricately patterned silver thread shone golden in the lit candles. With her face covered and her head crowned in the piece of silk he had put upon the *Shoichet's* table when he had first entered the kitchen, she seemed to be from another age.

Shimon had not suspected such mystery. He knew the story of the gold and silver lace-making Jewish women of northern Germany. He had read about the fine metal-threaded material. Or perhaps Leah's grandmother, who had come from the great port city of Hamburg to Lemberg and married into a merchant's family in Suczorno, had worn that gold-threaded lace, had lamented its passing art, and had talked about it... Shimon could not tell. But here out of a fairyland from the past, embellished by the imagination of every storyteller before him, was his childhood, barefoot Ethel, a figure of that past, a Queen of Sheba come true.

He had feared this event, feeling he would be a stranger. He disliked the rule of the rabbis and chose a younger one, who only two years ago had been passing through from Khotyn on the way to Odessa, and had stayed. More *Chasidic,* less bookish, he was more open to joy than lament, Shimon thought. He could bear this man's sermon and ritual more easily than what he had known of Shlomo ben Avram, who was a rigid, absolutely unbending man.

But as his parents Moishe and Leah, his siblings Nathan and Israel, Sarah and her Srul surrounded him, straightening this or that, his shirt, the sash through the middle, which he had never worn before, he lost all his fear and submitted to the old customs with less heartache. He had come back to what he had known from childhood, and the Hebrew, its beauty and its majesty, he had always loved; it was the ancient law and he felt at home. He smiled bemusedly when his mother Leah laid her hands upon his yet uncovered head in benediction, before putting the *Yarmulke* and black hat on it. He grew earnest when on her silently moving lips he recognized the Aramaic words of his forebears. Then he let himself be led by his own, without any other thought than, "If it's God's will."

But when he caught sight of Ethel hidden within silver-threaded lace, her face only sequestered behind the marbled piece of silk he had brought from the west, it shook him. It came to him that almost unconsciously he had accepted a destiny ordained and ordered. In spite of questing and questioning, he had come back to take this bride, of whom he knew almost nothing. And more beyond that, he faced a man's ancient mystery: woman.

It shook him. He saw her face truly for the first time as her veil was slowly lifted. He was stunned by her eyes of burning amber, her soft, full upper lip. When he drank from the *Kiddush* cup, and she from the same spot right after him, he could not contain his joy, and came a little too close, as if in a kiss.

She was his.

A homecoming.

THE SAINTLY GUEST

A NEW MAN CAME TO TOWN. HE CAME FROM THE PIOUS mountain Jews in the Carpathian *Rus* – or so he intimated. Sidelocks hanging to his collar, silent as a stone on private matters, he rented a room on the lower bank of the creek, in a ramshackle house that had been built on the old tanner's homestead after the great fire. It was Moishe's father's home. The land wasn't his, as it was no one's in Suczorno, and out of the few charred posts, broken windows, and with a tanner's tools, a poor family had built two rooms, a kitchen for themselves, and a shed. To have a little extra cash, they rented a bed to a journeyman or anyone in need of it.

The new young man, a rabbi-to-be, stood one day in front of the home of Chaskel, who was trying with little success to glaze the windows in. One window, that is – into a slightly charred frame Selig's father had built, which still showed strength in the joined corners. No one had seen him enter town, but there he stood at Chaskel's door, looking cool on a hot summer day.

He stood there, a straggly red beard showing, black curls falling from under a round hat with a velvet rim, which had seen many a fingering, he stood there saying *Shalom*. He put his brief-case down on his right side and a brown calf leather, obviously hand-sewn bag, on the left, and with a *"Shalom aleichem"* – Peace be between us – and with an "Allow me," he took the piece of window glass out of Chaskel's hands and fitted it expertly and fast into the old frame. He accepted the thanks of the overwhelmed Chaskel with the modesty due to a religious man, and in a self-effacing voice asked Chaskel where he could find shelter for the night.

"We are poor people and have no spare beds, but let me talk to my wife to see if she would be willing to put you up for the night. I certainly would feel honoured to have you share our modest home."

"I am Samuel Ben Sharon, and I am on my way to Odessa to study with the revered Rabbi and teacher –"

Hannah, Chaskel's wife, young, jolly, round in the belly, wig-locks falling onto her forehead in disarray, appearing at the door, looked at the young man for a moment, and made signs of "That's fine with me." She had clearly heard it all, because in Suczorno nothing escapes anyone, and this time she felt justified at listening in.

He entered, was offered tea from a battered samovar of a pewtery-grey, punched-in look, obviously still working, at least where the embers were kept. It was a little unbalanced, so that the brown ceramic tea-betty sat crookedly on top. A touch of essence from it, and steaming water, filled his glass. Samuel was grateful for it.

"I thank you, may God bless this home. I am grateful that the Almighty has led me to an observant home, a home where Jewish law, written or handed down, is strictly followed. Let me not tell you what I've seen on my travels –" and he bit into a cinnamon *Kuchel,* yellow-rich and oily, offered on a glass saucer.

He had humbly asked if he might be permitted to have a drop of water to wet or wash his hands, and did so ceremoniously, wiping his hands on a blue-white piece of linen that hung on a nail by the entrance door. It was sparkling clean, and so was the small enamelled basin Hannah held out for him, and while he took his time, she took his measure and thought he would be a God-sent addition to their family life. And he judged them also, his eyes roaming fast from chair to table to his now displayed tea sitting on an embroidered tablecloth covering just half the table. But it was hard to tell from such a still, friendly face what his thoughts were.

He sat down with a relieved sound of "Ah" – and his lips moved silently before taking a sip from his tea. Hannah busied herself somehow, and Chaskel, slightly embarrassed at having stood there, excused himself, ran out, and returned to say that the pane sat inside the frame as if properly glazed in, but he'd have to finish it soon before it fell out.

"I will do it for you," the young man said, "if you have a little of that glazier's glue. Please, let me do it. I want to show my gratitude for having been so hospitably received in a truly Jewish manner."

And Chaskel seated himself on the bench under that window and watched this inscrutable face. Young lips as red as fruit, orange-yellow hair covering the upper one and the beard just coming – he had taken the ubiquitous velvet hat off, which shone green-blue-felty at the rim, and he sat now, head covered on the top with a *yarmulke* skullcap. Chaskel knew by the sharp creases in the black silk that the *yarmulke* could fold like a piece of flat paper, and wondered where could this Samuel be from, who sat now, having had several glasses of tea, and just as many *Kuchels*, elegantly leaning against the back of the only armchair by the table. Smiling, if not obtrusively, he showed brilliant teeth, had undone the one button on the outer coat, let it hang loose, and showed a many-buttoned, tight vest-coat, bordered by a little white on top.

How could a man come from so far and be so painstakingly clean, with hardly a speck of dust...? A slight terror of the unknown, a sudden fear of *God knows who he is,* Chaskel dismissed and started informally, "Have you been long on the road?" But received an answer that sounded like – Chaskel really could not tell exactly, what this answer was when he tried to recall it later. It was a friendly, noncommittal one that meant to say, Yes, he was tired and needed rest, could he please be shown to his bed? and No, it was not too terribly far. And so Chaskel, talking to Hannah in whispers late at night, could not truly tell what Samuel had said.

She had not come into the room, in a Jewish married woman's proper behaviour, except to remove the glass and saucer, remove the small half-tablecloth to shake the crumbs out through the open door and put it back – but in the middle of the table now – which seemed to satisfy her sense of beauty. He had smiled a timid *"Todah Rabah,"* a Hebrew thank you, and received a *"Bevakashah."* Hannah, running a little faster and addressing her husband – who still sat on the window-bench – in a subdued woman's fashion, said: "It is for you and not for me to show Reb-Samuel to his room and to mention the price for the night."

She moved her round body girlishly now, and Chaskel thought how young his Hannah still was. It seemed he had not noticed it since the first days of their marriage. Two years. How fast they had gone. She had grown rounder, from the good life perhaps, not yet bearing children. They were too poor, and he did not mind having her entirely to himself. Though without children there is no blessing. Hannah would go sullen for days, and a bitter tone would creep into the evening's spare talk, if there was any at all. They had lived in *Kest* – board and room – for too long, with her folk, which was better than being with his, where an older brother and his wife and three children were already filling the house. He was from the upper side of the creek, right at the beginning of Suczorno, on the western end, where the rich do not live yet but people are still better off than on the lower bank. She was from down here. There had not been an official matchmaker. It had just happened. If there was no money to go around – what was there to talk about?

He had loved her jolly ways, had seen her at the well, in the Synagogue with the women, and dreamed about her. He thought she held the jar of water – and not a pail – in the hollow of her right hip, the way Rebekkah had appeared to Abraham's servant at the well: graceful, jar within the hollow, a strong right arm holding it in there – a vision of the old and forever. But he couldn't ask her for a drink of water, as Abraham's servant had done. It was not customary, of course, so he stood among the young men in a group on the other side of the well. He could not just walk over and say, "I am thirsty, would you give me a drink? And would you draw water for my camels, ten in number, who are thirsty coming from Canaan?"

These were his fantasies, when alone. But no one in Suczorno could step out of a man's company to walk over to a girl and ask, "What's your name, pretty one?" It was a restricted, orderly world. One fitted in, as well as one could. Perhaps it was as natural as any other world. And Chaskel sent his mother over to the other side of the creek, to inquire if there was any dowry – there wasn't – and finally he asked her parents for the hand of their daughter Hannah. It was a happy time.

Well, in-laws, even as kind as her parents, were hard to bear, and Chaskel grew nervous. He was Yankel's friend, they had been in *Cheder* together from the age of four, and the tanner's house on the lower side of the creek was just straight across from Yankel's, the *Shoichet*. This end of Suczorno was a totally different world – this was the east end of town – and Chaskel had come from the west end on the upper bank. When they, Hannah and Chaskel, were about to move into the half-completed house, he said to her, "Look at this, I can talk to my friend Yankel across the creek. It will be a totally different life here." And he did go there, more and more. He liked the easy life over there, hard work but good humour, clean but not fussy.

Chaskel, in fact, was a *Luftmensch:* a Suczorno speciality. One that hadn't learned any trade to make a proper living. A piece of bread was occasional, and somehow no one died of real hunger. One starved at times, everyone did, trade or no trade. The *Luft* – the air – in Suczorno was rich in ideas. One woke up in the morning and said, "Ah, I know what I'll do." Sometimes one hauled junk – as Chaskel did for Moishe – and sometimes another Jew in Suczorno came up with the idea of helping the horse trader – who by the way, occupied a "mansion" in Suczorno with a "kind of upstairs" even – and who led the horses across a forbidden border, knew an officer or two and how to grease a palm. So Chaskel came home one day, after a dangerous *"Luft*-business" with enough money to start the house on the tanner's old ground.

Yankel was one of the reasons he moved there. They had met one day in the Synagogue, and Yankel had suggested to him that he go over to Moishe, who, nominally perhaps only, owned the charred leftovers of his father's house, and see if Chaskel could build on that ground for a small fee.

"Take it, build on it, in God's name," was Moishe's generous reply. Chaskel and Hannah then did. Overjoyed to get out of *Kest* from her parents.

It was a wonderful beginning: planning, the search for used and reshaped posts, old shingles, mortar, screws and nails. It was perfectly miraculous what a *Luftmensch* would find, when he put his mind to it. In one summer the house stood, if not ready, good enough to take the marriage-bed – the eternal wedding gift – a commode for bitter winter nights, and all the accumulated small items necessary to cook a *Cholent* and move into the new abode.

Hannah was thrilled to be her own mistress; not to hear her mother curse her *Luftmensch* husband for not earning a tarnished *Kreuzer* – using the German term. Her mother liked to show her daughter that they had come from Austria and were much more civilized than the Chaskel family with its Russian roots, definitely inferior in her reckoning. She cursed the "no-good" who ate other people's earned bread, had fancy ideas, and woke up every morning telling everyone of his dreamt-up grand plans, how to become rich by doing nothing!

Perhaps, Hannah thought, she would rent the other room or take a border in. It was an entirely different thing she felt – even if short of everything to make ends meet – to hang an embroidered curtain where a wall showed rifts, or starch and blue a piece of linen that she had picked up in her mother's house, which, bleached with vinegar and seamed with a few stitches, could make a fanciful tablecloth. Laying it on the table, half covering it only, would be lovely under a glass of tea, with a plate beside it. Civilized, answering Hannah's need for beauty. She was happy.

But the bitter feeling came because of Chaskel. He spent more and more of his free hours across the creek, up in the *Shoichet's* house. He loved them all, Yankel, his wife Shoshannah – the Shklovke, their wild children, barefoot as they were.

"Yes," he said to Hannah one day, "I intend to take up the trade of a *Mohel.* True, there were not that many male children born recently, but it is a respected thing to do for a Jew. A *Mitzvah.* And Yankel absolutely refused to do it. As he took over his father's work, he refused to learn the respected duty of *Mohel.*"

A pious duty more respected by the congregation than by the *Shoichet,* it was in some way a re-enacting of the covenant: the circumcision of seven-day-old Jewish males. Yankel simply did not want to learn it. "Let others do it, who are more religious, dedicated, handier with a scalpel. I'm not skillful enough."

Aaron, his father, the old *Shoichet,* who had done it to everyone's satisfaction, tried to convince Yankel to come, watch him do it, and, under his supervision, try. "It's a Mitzvah, a commandment, an obligation as a Jew. It is seen with joy and gladness, by both man and God, try!"

Yankel replied that he'd do other things, would fulfill other commandments to please God than handling a knife on a young life. It might go wrong, he couldn't stand babies crying, he wouldn't sleep at night. His father gave in, as Shainah his mother, having seen her son go through troubled times to learn even the less-demanding *Shoichet's* trade, said, "Leave him alone, Aaron, it is not for him. Besides, any Jew is allowed to do it, the father of the baby too. Anyone learned and willing. Aaron, leave Yankel alone!"

"Yes," Chaskel continued, "His father, Aaron, will let me assist."

But there was no money in it. It was a Mitzvah. Something one does for one another in a community of Jews, and Hannah thought that Chaskel would be away and have a thousand excuses, earning not another *Kreuzer*.

And this was how things stood when a mysterious, handsome stranger stood at their door one summer day.

"A breath of fresh air," Hannah thought, looking suddenly younger, stretching herself a little in height to serve him tea. "And his locks protruding out of the *yarmulke* at the back of his head are of a rustier red-black than the beard," she said to herself and rushed into the kitchen to seem modest, as a married woman ought to appear. "Wicked," she thought, "I'm perhaps wicked to even as much as look at the back of his head, let alone his eyes."

But she had seen them. As fast into and fast away as anyone could to have truly seen them. Black. Black against black. A pupil filling all of the centre, swimming within a soft milky white. A gentle touch of orange tainting the white, continuing in the wispy beard. Reds were not common in Suczorno, but they were there, and redheads were known for their violent outbursts, uncontrollable temper, banging tables with fists hard as nails. But Hannah smiled at the thought. "I'm not married to him, so he can be as red as he wants."

And she enjoyed the thought of an extra *Kreuzer* for the fresh linen she intended to cover his bedstead with. After all, this was their first customer. The second room was built for this purpose, and if this – her business – would prove to be lucrative enough, then Chaskel could go and learn to be a *Mohel,* which is an honour and the right thing for a good Jewish man in a community to do. Money or no money. There were always honey cakes, *Challah,* an extra litre of wine to go home with the *Mohel.* So there was something in it.

And Hannah, feeling virtuous now and useful, rushed in and out to see if she could get a glance at him from another angle. The young scholar had opened his coat and she, busying herself with the brown betty on top of the samovar to see if a few more tea leaves would make his tea richer, was so close that she could count the buttons on his vest-coat. Seven, she thought, seven buttons. A holy number.

"That's foolish," she chided herself, not for having looked, but for wanting to. "You're a married woman, behave yourself. He is a stranger, don't look." And she became as good as gold. Or so she thought.

After tea was finished, Hannah removed the glass and the glass plate. Samuel, nodding a sort of thanks, rose to give a hand to Chaskel, who had brought out the glazier's paste, and in no time, with the expertise of a master, he set the glass solidly within its frame, pasting it all around the edges or wherever glass and wood touched, to the *Ahs* and *Ohs* and thanks of Chaskel.

"Do not wash the window yet, let it dry," Samuel said, being already in command. "Is there any other one you would like done?"

"Yes," said Chaskel. "A small one above the kitchen bench, but don't bother, I'll do it."

"No," said the young scholar. "I'll do it tomorrow, right after prayer."

Samuel Ben Sharon, as he called himself, made himself useful, no, not useful, slowly made himself indispensable. Fixed the windows, knew how to open a rusty lock, glue a chamber pot invisibly, removing all cracks so it would shine as if whole, clean the wick of the Naphtha lamp of ancient soot, and even take a broom one day to sweep the front room, the threshold to the street, and in front of the house.

Of course, nothing escaped anyone in Suczorno. Across the creek, Yankel – Chaskel's friend – saw it but did not say anything, not even to his wife Shoshannah, the Shklovke. She had seen it also, but silent and discreet as she was by nature, she would not comment. All of the higher bank looked down upon the lower bank and knew: the new man was well entrenched in Chaskel's household.

Except Chaskel himself. He did not seem to notice that the young man ate at his table at every meal, had his shirts washed and pressed, *Shabbat* coat brushed, and the *Tefillin* bag – leather strap for the arm and law for the forehead – faithfully laid out. And that he started to go to services at Chaskel's side as if he were a brother.

With time, the town thought nothing of it and called him to the *Torah*, like all the other faithful. He read Hebrew well, but it did have a strange *Nigun*. Something foreign, not heard in Suczorno. But there were immediate explanations: Maybe he is a Litwak, from the Baltic region, from Riga or somewhere there, they do have a different sound, or – he may be even a *Sephardi*, from as far away as old Spain. He was here now, carried the duty of a *Gabbai* occasionally, when someone was sick or in need.

THE TOWN ONLY STARTED THINKING, when, to the joy of her husband Chaskel, after almost three years of barrenness, Hannah's womb was blessed by the Lord. The baby was the most beautiful boy the town had ever laid eyes upon. Chaskel by now had learned the art of *Mohel* from Aaron – and let it be said that it was particularly well seen when the boy's father was performing the ritual circumcision. There was, as was the custom, caraway Schnapps, honey cake, and tea at their home for the *Brith*.

Hannah of course not participating: it had to be the eighth day, and she still kept to her bed. She was not fearful. Chaskel had learnt it well; he was extremely adroit with his fingers and very gentle. He had consoled her the day before, telling her – what she knew, but it was nice to hear again – that a good swallow of red wine, poured over the baby's mouth, would make the baby so drowsy that he would not feel anything at all.

The *Brith* was a great party. Celebrating the Covenant of Abraham. Covenant as well as link to the long line of names before him. The NAME. Given and linked to all before you, to the father of us all. Chaskel's late grandfather Reuwen was the link – it could not be the living father – and so it was "Reuwen" to the tears, prayers, and good wishes of all of Suczorno.

The mother took him to her breast and he was beautiful. It filled her whole being. She could not stop beholding a miracle: elegant long fingers, every nail shining with mother of pearl, a bush of black hair, and the tenderest translucent skin hued in pink.

But soon Reuwen lost all his black hair and a fine reddish shimmer announced the coming of a new growth. Hannah, with Reuwen at her breast, saw it clearly: she had a red haired baby and her heart grew heavy. But she kept silent, did not divulge her fears to anyone. Both Yankel, the *Shoichet*, and his wife, the Shklovke, ran over the bridge daily, to cook, to wash, to comfort, to adore the child, to hand him to his mother, who kept – as was the custom in Suczorno – close to her bed for at least three weeks.

A new bridge spanned the two sides of the creek, stronger, anchored with heavy metal posts, driven deeply into the ground on both sides, held by turned-twisted metal ropes which Moishe had found derelict in Krakov somewhere and the young mysterious boarder, Samuel, knew how to fasten to the boards. The creek was not very wide at this point, and well-fitted and fastened boards could be made to reach both ends.

So here it was. Samuel Ben Sharon, scholar, glazier, and now bridge-builder, a hero of Suczorno! He was honourably mentioned at the *Shabbat* luncheon, after hours of prayers and more to come before the end of the day – What else could a Jew do on a *Shabbat* but stay in Synagogue to honour God and His creation? And above all a good man, a Jew, who had enhanced, furthered the lives of others by giving of himself.

So on the last *Shabbat* before he disappeared, Samuel Ben Sharon was *aufgerufen,* as they say in Suczorno, called to the *Torah,* to read, show his scholarship, and speak the *Baruch Atah:* "May You be praised and glorified, King of the Universe." He did it beautifully; nothing seemed different from any other *Shabbat.* On his person everything was in place; his *Tallith* lay elegantly around his shoulders, flowing in blue-white silky stripes down the middle of his back, and the gold braid with holy letters decorated his nape to the outset of his arms.

He did not speak much. He never did. To women one does not speak in Suczorno anyway, and men were accustomed to this young scholar's silence. It befitted a religious man and, being helpful and able too, they liked him and perhaps even loved him. A difficult theological question that arose and ended in a shouting match, he settled by giving a reasonable answer, satisfying both sides. And if he couldn't at the very moment come forth with it, he would return the next day or *Shabbat,* fully instructed, having read up on it and formulated it to the applause of all.

"Is there a female nature of God?" was a steady debate. Why was it that God created Adam – who was in the image of God – then took part of him to create the woman? Were they both imperfect and had to join to become one flesh, in search of completion? And was there, deep in the heart of God, a rib from which a woman could be built? Yet the deepest and central tenet of the faith was "God is ONE." This was what God had said, "Listen, oh Israel, the God of the Universe, God is ONE." And this was the faith. ONE. But every letter, every absent letter was debated. And the nature of God. Endlessly. Samuel Ben Sharon, answered, if not all questions, yet he answered some. To remain modest, and not show off his superiority. Or so they all thought in Suczorno. "But he must be a messenger of some sort, to have intimate close links to God."

A Messiah? Time would tell. Suczorno had had its fill of false Messiahs. Every time there was no wood for the winter, more cholera than usual, or no bread whatsoever, someone would come to town with hope, messages of *"Halleluja,* sing to the Lord, don't cry, the Lord will provide!" and more people would die of hunger that year than any other. So the people had had their fill. But Samuel was different. Certainly things were often strange. And on this *Shabbat,* he was a little more restrained than at other times, seemed to know the answer to things but was reluctant to speak when addressed.

He had appeared in Suczorno a little over two years ago and he was now a valued member. He did not throw any money or gold coins into the coffers, but had worked on repair. He had sat hours, during weekdays, to glue the old prayer books. Fingered through generations, the corners were ripped or illegible. He glued fine strips of paper to the ends of the pages and filled in, with his own beautiful handwriting, the missing and erased letters, and he cleaned the covers with a damp cloth. No work was too lowly. He washed the floor to the *Bimah,* dried and waxed it with beeswax someone had provided. When thanked, he would reply, "It is the highest honour to serve." They loved him.

On that *Shabbat,* after partaking of the *Oneg Shabbat,* a little richer one than usual because the *Bar Mitzvah* of one of Yankel's sons had taken place, he slipped out of the Synagogue unseen. Fiddlers played in the courtyard; the young man, younger than Ethel and looking like her, was the centre. He had read beautifully the portion of the day, and Shoshannah the Shklovke, a glowing mother among the women, and Yankel a proud father among the men, celebrated. No one had seen him go.

He had not returned to their home and had not left a note of any sort, but there was one thing Hannah found the next morning. Knocking on the door of Samuel's room and receiving no answer, she cautiously pushed it open to see the room empty, the bed carefully made – as she always did for him – and untouched. And, on his footstool, serving also as a night table, was a *Tallith* – if his own, Hannah could not tell – neatly folded along the gold braid and his, Samuel's, own silver *Kiddush* cup. She had admired it often, and the way he held it in his right hand, lifting it to his lips almost, to make the *Bruha* over the wine: "Blessed be and glorified, oh King of the Universe, who has commanded us to bless the fruit of the vine." She picked it up, held the cup close to her heart to quiet its beat, and sat down with her back against the wall to keep from falling.

For a little moment. Then she resolutely rose, straightened

with her right hand in a fast nervous movement the corner-bed she had sat on, and clutching *Tallith* and cup to her breast, she ran into the bedroom to hide them. From under the marriage bed she pulled her prize possession, a box of red mahogany, polished to a high shine to reveal the walnut-and-birch inlaid letter of *Chai.* Did not contemplate or stroke it as she usually did, but opened it nervously with the small key hanging on its side. Her great-grandmother's brooch of yellowed stones, a few rings, and a roll of Scripture she pushed aside, fitting the *Tallith* as a base and the cup tightly above it. She could barely close the lid and lock it. She hung the silver key onto it and, slowly only, succeeded in silencing her heart. Then she sat for a moment's rest, to hold her precious box. Strips of wood, handled as if they were silk, were molded into one another, from the southern violent red of the mahogany to the cool birch of the north over the local walnut brown.

The whole world in a box, held by silver corners on all ends to resist the wear of time, as living things could not. And a silver key. Made by Selig's famous father, Abraham, so far away and so close to her heart. Years that followed one another without trace did not mean anything, but a man's craft, his faith, remained. The faith in life, as the letter *Chai,* was life itself. And she touched the cleavage between her breasts to feel the letter *Chai* embedded, hanging on a thin golden chain. She could not recall from when. Perhaps from birth. It always had been there. She never took it off; it didn't rust, it was gold. And she touched it to console herself, and then lovingly traced the letter with her index finger across the inlaid box. Such a beautiful sign. *It's for Reuwen, my redhead golden boy; may he live and may he be as beautiful as –* and with a fast movement she shoved the box under the bed, and pushed it with a determined kick into the far corner. She heard it stop against the wall and was satisfied. She rose, shouted, "Reuwen, where are you, my blessed child?" and he came running, and so they sat, the two of them. She had opened her legs, her wide frock falling between them, and Reuwen settled into his own private cradle, her hands within his red locks.

THE TOWN STOPPED TALKING. The shock was too enormous; totally alien to people's memory, it numbed their voices. There had been Messiahs of all sorts, but never one so human, yet so inscrutable. Not God Himself. No Jew could think of God walking among them, but directly sent, a divine word through the mouth of man; yes, this a Jew in Suczorno could fathom. And Samuel seemed to be such a one. Pious, silent, charitable, anointed. A breath of the Eternal.

His being among them had become habit and it had seemed to make them better. Quarrels – ancient as the stones under the flowing water of their creek – abated, be they about ten centimetres of inhabitable ground between the houses, or a cheated inheritance. An atmosphere in the Synagogue of "We are brothers, each others' keepers," as the *Torah* commanded, "Let's live in its spirit," took hold. And – poor as they were, all of them were, the "rich" included – they gave a little more, money, labour, or study.

When Samuel ascended – just one year after his appearance in Suczorno – or had been invited to ascend to the *Bimah,* he said, "*Chaverim,* brothers, let me quote the text –" and by heart, out of his memory flowed eternal beauty. No one sat dry-eyed. The women in the back rows, always more sensitive to the spiritual, to what moved the heart, were silent with emotion, holding their little ones firmly so as not to have their glorious moment destroyed, and the men were overcome too. Because of the eloquence, because, for a Jew, learning was the "crown and sceptre" of life. They had no other.

His disappearance was not the loss of a member of the community only – many go away, die, move to other towns, or marry away – his disappearance was betrayal. Their trust in their own "feeling good," in their judgment, was shaken, and the shock perhaps – or God forbid! in the end the certainty – the shock of having been made fools of, made them pale with anger and incomprehension. They went about their business as if bereft of their tongues – cut out in the ancient way of having blasphemed. The women looked more into their own hearts and found the illicit love, the desire for love and acceptance – private matters no one acknowledged as existing in Suczorno. The men felt the cold anger of having been taken in by perhaps an ordinary clever swindler. And Chaskel and Hannah did not show their faces.

Chaskel had to, there was a *Brith* that month, and no Jew in Suczorno could – or was heard of – to miss Friday night prayers and the *Shabbat* day. As no one spoke, Chaskel did his mere duty, excused himself, and left for his silent *Cholent* with his wife and son. They had been four, with Samuel in the armchair, having taken over the Friday night blessing of bread and wine. Chaskel had not minded; he was not an ordinary father, master, household-head. A loving man, yes, a trusting man, not very able to make ends meet, but not seeing his inherited authority as binding. Tonight he did not look in Hannah's direction, he ate his *Cholent* – a beef-vegetable-potato stew in the oven since yesterday – silently. Looked smilingly at his beautiful son, who smiled back, playing with his food, smearing Hannah's starched tablecloth in the process, and he fed the boy a spoon of his own, a little mashed potato-gravy mixture. The mother did the same, and both, talking to the child, avoided each other.

And perhaps all the families suffered. There was a break between marriage-partners, children and parents, and friends stood against friends. The former love and co-operative spirit gave way to a tragic discord. *Yes – No. He was – he was not.* In the eye of the storm, Chaskel refused to accept that there was anything wrong. The man had come and gone. Though he hadn't paid him a broken *Kreuzer,* he had worked for food and shelter. Perhaps not adequately, but Chaskel carried no grudge. He had liked Samuel, his silent elegance, his occasional wisdom, his eloquence in fine points of *Torah* – he could not think of a better companion.

He thought that his beloved Hannah, who had done most of the work for Samuel, had not minded it. She had been cheerful, laughed more, brushed and aired her own skirts, these brown-black woollen things she had taken out of the dowry trunk. Hannah did keep a little more to herself, and he had wondered sometimes why she forgot to tell him which her "good days" were. He used to know. One day, returning from the ritual bath she'd said, "Well – Samuel," instead of "Well, Chaskel" – but he'd thought nothing of it. Women are sometimes moody, he'd thought, one can't blame them, what with all that work from dusk till dark – all they wanted was rest. He'd understood. She was his Hannah and he loved her. Every smile was a new day to him. That she was not with child for a few years had not bothered him because he'd had her to himself and he had not thought he was a good provider. But when she'd whispered into his ear the sweetest secret, he was overjoyed. Sang. Ran across the creek to his friend Yankel, kissed Hannah tenderly, called her "his dove," the blessed of God, the woman of his heart. And she had laughed, the silver laugh of Sarah who bore Isaac to an old Abraham.

And Samuel had been of great help. Why should he, Chaskel, have disliked him? Samuel had carried every drop of water they used in the house from the well. When Chaskel had gone to take occasional labour to earn a little more now that he would have to provide for a growing family, Samuel had made the kindling for the huge mud oven he had helped complete, had gone for wood, to see where he could find any extra, and had kept the fire going until the *Cholent* went in on Friday afternoon and was closed tightly with a well-fitted brick. He had done all that for them. And much more. Why should Chaskel hate him?

When Hannah was heavy with child, Samuel would not let her bend; he washed all the wooden floors and not just washed, but scrubbed and put beeswax on, which he himself had purchased from Chaim, paying a proper price. Chaim – whose wife Chaje had recently died – was a beekeeper. His honey was purple with *Klee,* as they called it, a kind of clover, but wildflowers of all sorts gave the Suczorno honey its heavenly aroma. And Samuel had bought it for Hannah's honeycake.

A true and brotherly co-operation had sprung up between the Jews and the peasants around them: caring for the wild bee families or having whole clusters of bee-homes installed, sharing the honey and the wax, keeping sufficient for the next season, and sometimes destroying them if they swarmed too badly. And when Chaim was in mourning, Samuel had gone to the *Shivah,* to be the tenth man. So many nice things Samuel had done.

Chaskel came home to his wife and child; it had changed him, though. He was less talkative, looked into his plate when he ate, and if he did not avoid Hannah's side of the marriage-bed – for it would be against the ordinances of God – he felt very tired and could not hold his head up after the evening meal. Hannah, more in her thoughts, moved silently about the house and left it rarely.

To go up, across the bridge, yes; the *Shoichets* were the same as ever. Perhaps a fine touch warmer even; calling both of them over, insisting on bringing Reuwen to play with the latest arrival, who was a little older than Reuwen. In the *Shoichet's* family, ten of them by now, the oldest was twenty, followed his father around to take over the business, as Yankel felt like sitting a little longer with Shoshannah after a meal, and though a relentless worker, he had become a little weary after the death of his father Aaron. Yankel had taken it hard.

Yes, the signs were all there: Aaron had been weak in the legs, held on to the walls and tables when walking or standing, and took minutes before taking another step. Yes, Yankel had seen it: the swelling of the ankles in the evening, when he helped with the undressing of Aaron's woollen socks; the loosing of the urine, into which one stepped unexpectedly; and Shoshannah putting pieces of soft linen, to catch it before it happened, into his trousers. They had both seen it, but none would dare think of the end to come. Life – the highest aim. Everyday – life. It was not the coming of death. Every breath was cherished; every breath was breath. Not a reduced breath, that would stop one day. No. One was not dying. One was living; but the omen was there, unspoken, when Aaron took to his bed and would not rise. Still, everything was normal, children running in and out to see *Zaida*, playing hide-

and-seek, and making noise. And in all that unregulated, tumultuous, breathing world, Aaron breathed his last. Shoshannah called her children to order, saw a smile around his lips, and did not have to close his eyes – there was peace in his countenance. The last prayer lay around his mouth and Shoshannah asked Herschale, her seven-year-old, to please bring Yankel to see his father's face and to cover it with a sheet. An ordinary event. But such inordinate mourning.

As simply as Aaron had died, as truly had he left a mark upon his own. The one mirror – it was not customary to have them – was covered. Yankel went to the Synagogue to announce his father's death, according to the law – and this was how one lived in Suczorno – the body had to be returned to earth within twenty- four hours. The *Chevra Kedisha* – the holy community – good women and men, washed the body, covered it in linen; and outside of Suczorno, where their ancestors lay, the crude wooden box was lowered. A few shovels of earth had to be heard. Perhaps seven, sounding when striking the box. All of Suczorno, the men in front, the women in the back with their children, some of Yankel's brothers had come, and Yankel at the open grave said the ancient *Kaddish:* "Praised be and glorified, King of the Universe" – only glory and praise. Old Aramaic words. A sound of comfort, familiar to every child in Suczorno, without any meaning other than the glory of His creation.

And all went back to the *Shoichet's* house for the barefoot sitting of the seven days, the *Shivah,* and the ten good men coming and going to say the morning and evening *Kaddish.* Food came from everywhere, no matter how bad a year, and this wasn't a particularly good one.

Chaskel came home only for the night. He stayed at the side

of his friend Yankel, at every *Kaddish,* until the *Shivah* was over. And in some ways it healed him also. Seven days of praying, mourning the loss, and thinking of the Eternal did change a man. He had cried with tears running into his beard and was not ashamed of it; he had mourned for Yankel's father and for himself also. About his doubts, about not having loved enough and not looking into his soul for what was true, for what lasted. But saying "Praised be and glorified —" from the bottom of his heart, with the other nine men, almost in unison, as every Jew said them all his life or heard them spoken and sung, these words had a healing power beyond comprehension.

Chaskel, Hannah, and Reuwen were at the *Shoichet's* from morning till night and came home the last day after seven days feeling fortified, a unit, a family loving and ready to face the world. And they would have to. The town had started murmuring: *Funny* that Hannah does not come more often to Shul. *Funny,* she never leaves Reuwen by himself for a moment. *Funny,* the boy should have bright red hair and dark eyes — well, both parents do have dark eyes — but no one has ever seen red in that family. *Funny,* that Chaskel is so demure, and has stopped talking, he who had the "gift of the gab" from whenever one remembers him. And *funny,* Chaskel kept Samuel in the house, feeding him *latkes* and delicacies — the best being just right for him.

The boy Reuwen grew. The best in *Cheder,* delicate looking, private. He came with his father and left with his father. And the town suddenly saw that Reuwen was special. Suczorno became aware of the godlike nature of the child. He was never looking for a quarrel, was ready to give in when he was wrong, gentle and very beautiful at thirteen. He had a *Bar Mitzvah* like no other, and everyone was making amends.

Gift giving was not customary, perhaps a coin, suit material, or a sweet, but for Reuwen the town went to town, gave more than they could spare. But he called all the children of the congregation to come up and choose what they liked because he had no use for so much. Godlike, they thought. Who wouldn't do it but a young *Zadik* – a just man. So the town stopped talking suspicion; their whispers took on a hue of awe, mingling with fear for having offended God.

Reuwen wore his gold-braided *Tallith* around his collar, enfolding his head as a mount of gold would hold a precious stone. And when he raised his *Kiddush* cup – his own – it shone with the light of reverence, blinding the worshippers. No one spoke, no child was heard, and the *Amen* came from every throat. The celebrations that followed were subdued but joyful, and questions unanswered or unanswerable were not uttered. The power of the moment overwhelmed them, and after helping with cleaning up, packing the rest of the uneaten herring or *Challah* away, the congregation – passing by the happy parents, grandparents, and the *Bar Mitzvah*-boy himself – left, with all their good wishes.

Now the six of them sat down: Yankel and Shoshannah, Chaskel and Hannah, the rabbi and Reuwen. They sat down on those long wooden Suczorno tables where children had sat for *Torah* study, and to argue, quarrel over money or, as today, for a celebration. They sat opposite each other, three and three, for a moment of intimacy. Ordinary parents and their friends. They were close, having grown up so near one another, so that when Yankel wanted to say something, stuttering and stumbling over all the *s-s-sh-sh's* which Yiddish is full of, he did not have to finish his sentence, as everyone knew what he had to say. They knew he wanted to come forth with an act of generosity, and indeed, he put his hand into his pocket and pulled out a Russian ruble of gold, coined at the time of Alexander the first – the Napoleon Czar, as he was called – and ceremoniously put it centre table.

"Yankel – what is this – no, do not give so much, keep it for your children –"

"No, this belongs to this young man." And sitting next to him, he said, "It was my grandparents'. I put it away on the morning of your birth, when I held you in my arms at the circumcision. The highest honour, and today, you have fulfilled my hopes. Keep it safely. Times are not always good. It can save a life."

He had stuttered through all these heartfelt words, and now Reuwen turned to Yankel and said, "You have held me in your hands – as a seven-day-old at the Covenant – and you were with me through these beautiful but also hard and troublesome years. I knew you both were there, Shoshannah and you, and I could run to you when my heart was heavy, as every boy struggles, day in, day out. I could always run across around the outside corner of your home, through the backyard, and into the arms of either of you. I had to. I had to spare my father Chaskel and my mother Hannah my incomprehensible moods, lest they worry too much. I flew into your arms. You made yesterday's *Zimmes* – oh, I love that sweet carrot dish, or Shainah's fat *Kugel* with the cherries burnt in chicken fat at the crust. Did you keep it for me?"

"No, no," Shoshannah said, "it was just there; who can keep anything in a *Shoichet's* house –"

"I loved your cooking. So much better than Mother's – no, no, not really. But it was comfort-soul *kugel* with burnt cherries – just different from *kasha* with milk."

Hannah sat, delirious with joy. He could say anything he wanted to, she thought; he had run over there, where so many children took the attention from him. With me and Chaskel he was the centre, everything turned around Reuwen, there was too much silence, no other little one came.

She remembered how Reuwen, one evening at the Passover table, the moment that he had to ask the four questions, had said unexpectedly, "I am the youngest forever, will you not give me a brother or sister so they'll be the youngest to ask the *Ma Nestanah* – why is this night different, and we replied that it is the will of the Lord. And perhaps –"

As if picking up his mother's musing, Reuwen turned to her and said: *"Mame,* no one can be blessed with a better mother or home, but over there – up the creek – there was noise and games. We could fight over the *dreidl,* the spinning top, and Grandmother Shainah, who cannot walk anymore and sits on the bench by the *Cholent* oven, always had something for me. 'Go find it,' she'd say, and I did. And the fun we had with little wicked things – no, I won't confess. It's to be ashamed of, and you won't like it –"

"We were young too, once," Shoshannah said. "Believe it or not."

It was all true: Reuwen, when seven, eight, or nine, ran away from a soundless home. Warm voices, hugs and love, food, and, yes, study, but Reuwen felt he was going deaf. His mother did not sing. Shoshannah did. Wonderful songs brought from her hometown – a myth, a legend – a place of the imagination for Reuwen. And the children sang, together and in parts. Eating corn porridge with goat's milk, they made up verses. Yiddish mostly, but interweaving sounds, syllables, no one knew what they meant, but they were so right for that rhythm.

One day, Reuwen had picked up a violin with three strings still there, lying in a corner next to a bass fiddle with all the strings on. The body had split somewhere, but sounded when plucked. It was taller and fatter than Reuwen, but he had tried to make it sound, and the bass had responded to his fingers. But Aaron, the old *Shoichet,* said, "Reuwen, you will be a fiddler. I predict. You seem to find your way through these strings as if you had heard the angels sing. Take the violin; the bass is too big for you yet."

Reuwen took the violin home, but it did not work there. He needed a chorus of wild kids and brought it back. "Make me a string," he said to Aaron. "I need a fourth string for the violin."

"I'll make one perhaps from a very young chicken gut – I'll have to clean it, dry it, watch that it stays pliable, and then beeswax it." Smiles all around. It took a while.

This fiddle Reuwen took home. It made awful noises, but he loved them. Every free moment Reuwen had, he spent in the company of his best friend now, the fiddle. He tapped his toe, remembered a *Nigun,* the *Kol Nidre* tune, the wild *Shofar* horn, the cries of Shoshannah's children.

When Reuwen was just four or five, he heard the Gypsies sing, just outside of Suczorno. They had set up camp down river, had appeared from nowhere. "From darkest India," his mother said. "They'll steal you, they like redhead boys, don't go near them." He could not go near them and they were too far away for a little boy to reach, but he heard them sing when they came closer to Suczorno. Making a huge fire in a cauldron, they heated metal of all sorts, came to the Jewish householders to ask for their broken enamelled jugs and leaking iron pots. Repaired them, mended the pots so finely that old, old pots would keep another hundred years – for a few *kopecks* or whatever. Reuwen did not dare speak to them, but he didn't think they'd take him. No one could be bad who sang like they did.

Their tunes came back to him out of his fiddle – to his amazement. Changed into Yiddish, with a Hebrew *Nigun* the fiddle sang on its own. He sometimes tried to recall the tune and couldn't, so he'd shouted and cried. Hannah would be astonished, not really worried, it was so different a cry. And she'd run to see – no, he wasn't hurt.

"I can't bring back yesterday's tune," he'd say.

"Oh my *yingale,*" she'd say, "my little one, it will come back, it will."

And it would come back, but changed again. Made new. He'd be overjoyed, and turn from tears to laughter because he had within yesterday's tune found Shoshannah's melody from Shklov, Russian-sounding suddenly. He'd tap his toe furiously, and then relenting, give it that slow Russian falling sound he had heard from Shoshannah. And then it stayed, became "One" like God Himself, Who is ONE. But not so totally unchanging. ONE, but changing.

So he tapped his toe differently, taking the first beat off, dislodged the weight, put it on another note – it was a different tune. The same, yet not. Sometimes the weary atonement of the Jew came out, his toe stopped tapping, the notes pulled out, *shlepped* themselves as Suczorno people would say. As long as the *Galuth* – the *Diasporah,* long crying notes, without knowing their end – or the fine gypsy notes in succession, would take over and it would sound as far away – as un-Yiddish – as any fairytale.

Reuwen played at home to delight Chaskel, who had an ear for all that was fanciful, uplifting, balanced, and comfortable to the soul. Reuwen's fiddle sounded like no other, and Chaskel attributed that to the fourth chicken-gut, or perhaps...he did not rest on the thought, being frightened of it suddenly. Pushed it away and listened to the scratching of the bow against this ancient body. Chaskel, who had played or had tried to as a child, had found the bow in some junky corner and had taught Reuwen to brush it with a piece of resin that he had loosened from a tree, when the resin had dried hanging in the shape of a tear from its trunk.

Reuwen was thrilled; it softened the sound, and the bow moved faster, binding the sounds together so they blended into one. And listening intently with his inner ear, Reuwen heard the calling for the new, the not-yet-heard sounds to come.

"It's in the bow. It sings almost of its own when barely touching the strings. It knows everything. It finds the unheard sounds, yet sends them into the old body of the fiddle. Yes, it is the bow, it grows into my arm, to become part of flesh and soul."

The father and the son had carefully nurtured their love for one another. It started early with singing or whistling, with comfortable harmonies of ancient intervals; repetitive, synagogue tunes. The father sang and the son pitched in. Walking Friday nights to services or *Shabbat* morning when Reuwen was four, five, or six – but then they parted. Neither Chaskel nor Reuwen understood what had happened to them.

Reuwen retreated into himself, studied for his *Bar Mitzvah,* and until his thirteenth year could not be reached. He would walk across the bridge to the *Shoichet's* to escape his own loneliness. But when Reuwen first plucked the few notes on Yankel's big bass fiddle and the violin with the chicken gut, he returned to his father, who found words of praise, and surprise, showing intense pleasure; the son looked up, and the love, the *Rachamim,* the compassion with the young in his father's eyes, brought him home. Now the door was open. Talk, all about the fiddle.

And returning one day from a junk deal, with a bow – hair trailing, but a perfectly workable bow – Chaskel, the father, knew he had given Reuwen his son the most cherished gift. Neither of them found words, but the bond had deepened, and they looked for each other every free moment as in the early days.

THE HINDSTREET BOY

Esther: Two Gold Bands

U P ON THE HIGHER BANK, JUST BEFORE THE END OF
town, almost attached to the *Shoichet's,* was the house of
Esther bas Yehuda and Meir ben Nahum. This was the wicked
Esther – of Sarah's pearly chicken. Esther, still young, was childless, and living so close to the *Shoichet's* – in fact, sharing a wall
between the houses – felt intruded on by the unruly, "wild, non-
Jewish" household, as she called it. "God knows if the *Shklovke*
did things when unclean or by magic, how else would she have a
swelling *Laib* – belly – all the time!" She refused to call it a blessing of the womb.

Meir, Esther's husband, had a tool shed, the best one in
Suczorno. The *Shoichet's* brood was in and out. "What is this for,
and what that?" A sharp awl, a serrated saw, and scissors hanging
in a row followed one another as ducklings would their parent.
There were iron clamps hugging the edge of the work table full of
cut-up wooden squares or rectangles to be used or discarded,
orderly, in heaps. But one day the diamond-tipped steel cutters
that Esther had brought from Lemberg were nowhere to be found.
Esther shouted, "It's that brood!" banging her wall adjoining the

Shoichet's with fists full of uncontrolled fury. Then she sat down and cried. She sat on her kitchen stool, the backless, low, under-the-table woman's work stool, and cried.

Meir had found the precious tool in a safe place, which was so easily forgotten. He came in from the shed to calm her down, wordlessly holding the tool up, saw her bloodied fists, her temples purple-blue veined, and could not bring her to her senses. She rose, and with a kick of her right foot pushed the woman's stool back under the kitchen table, and sobbed inconsolably. Meir stood by her and waited a little longer until the storm abated. There was nothing he could say. He knew – she was childless.

The *Shklovke's* children continued to visit whenever they liked. Esther, whose household was full of *yiddishkeit* and free of dirt, dust, noise, chased them with a broom, with a wooden spoon, and with the blackest tongue there was in Yiddish. "Louts, brood of an unclean mother!" and worse than that. "May the *Malechamoves* take you." But with the angel of death she finished, that was the limit even for her.

In Suczorno, life was simple, devout, and poor. Esther always felt superior, having come from the cultured city of Ismail on the upper delta of the Danube. She had been brought to Suczorno by matchmakers – merchants who travelled the borders, ignoring the Czar's police: *Their law is for the Goyim, Jews live by the Torah!* And paying them bribes, small and big, depending on the authority, they crossed these borders. They did it to connect families who could not find partners for their children, to do business, to set the price of gold, or of a karat of diamond. They changed currencies, such as the *dukat,* the *ruble,* the *zloty,* or any coin new or old, traded as securely and dependably as a banker would. They were a force, mostly men but sometimes women too on the road, knowing where to sleep and keeping ledgers in a subterranean yet perfectly orderly fashion. And they carried accurate descriptions of bridegrooms and brides. Well, as accurate as any merchandise could be, allowing a measure of exaggeration and self-interest to enhance it. But never total fraud.

With these merchants Esther had come to Suczorno, through tragic circumstances, at the age of fifteen or sixteen – a marriageable age, but young yet.

It was just before Easter, on a glorious April day, when a peasant boy of eight – not even missed for weeks – was suddenly fished out of the marshy Danube delta, and the mob, led by the priests carrying the dead body of the boy, entered the town ready for revenge, shouting, "Murder!" They entered the Jewish settlement clustered on the outskirts of Ismail with tarred torches burning. "Bastards, you slaughter our children; we find them in the rivers..." The irate mob burned and pillaged. Esther, who thought herself a princess in lace and velvet, born of cultured parents, fluent in Russian, Yiddish, and Romanian – not to speak of the sacred tongue – stood fatherless on the road at the age of fourteen, with a few books, holy and profane, and a wooden case beside her, in front of her house.

She had known the gold merchants – matchmakers – from very young, had seen them dealing with her father on several occasions, had often watched the weighing of the gold and had tried it herself. She knew the small weights, the ones that looked like tiny gold leaves, going from a hundredth of a gram up to the full gram, and had been permitted to handle the miniature scale, elegantly attached to her left index finger, in which, supported by thumb and third finger, she could weigh the precious stones.

Standing in front of the burning house, with the quick look of someone bewildered, she had seen the merchants instantly, decided not to wait for a second wave of terror but to join them, and behind a charred door – a businessman's daughter – she changed into a merchant's pants and gabardine. With locks falling over ears and forehead, and looking like a beautiful *Bar Mitzvah* boy, she had no difficulty traversing all of Bessarabia, many a time over the Djnester, over the Bug and back. The two men she travelled with honoured her womanhood, gave her privacy, taught her to deal, to be modest with profits in order to be trusted. But they grew tired of her company, and one day arriving at the small isolated settlement of Suczorno, they tried to convince her to find a husband.

Experienced matchmakers can find a bridegroom overnight, and a young furrier was willing to take her with the few gold coins she had, a *Hanukkahlicht* – a candelabra for Hanukkah – and a few ancient books in her coffer, as his bride. Meir was pious and good, a furrier-turned-businessman who was ready to settle down. From the moment Esther stepped into his house, she took over the reins. She knew gold. She sent to Lemberg to get a standard scale, and with the help of Moishe, got weights and measures from the official Austrian Mint.

The women too wanted to help. Esther knew little of a woman's life, of "unclean days," of the ritual bath – the *Mikvah* – at the end of them. The women of Suczorno came to teach or out of curiosity. But Esther paid them back with ingratitude, arrogance, and open disdain. "Medieval," she called them, "backwards, village idiots. Their Hebrew is so poor, they can barely read!" she shouted.

But she loved Meir, her husband, who was in awe of her intelligence. She loved him, he who had only eyes for her; yet she suspected every woman of evil intentions. She accused Leah, the good mother of Sarah, and played all sorts of tricks on her, like stealing the pearly chicken and slaughtering it without respecting the law. In later years her barrenness, her suffering, and her envy for other people's children she would see as deserved. "Suffering for sin, always linked." And "Because of my sins," she would say, "a kind of reckoning meant to humble my heart."

Almost equal in age, Esther and the *Shoichet's* wife never spoke to each other. Both in their marriage beds, so close, separated just by a wall, they could almost hear...and perhaps did. How could they not have heard the sudden moan, the jump from the bedstead, suspecting it to be inhabited by Evil? How could they not have heard or suspected it? But they never spoke. Not until late in life. They were too different. Shoshannah the *Shklovke* was simple, and grateful for abode and love; Esther, for her part, felt she had come down in station from the heights of Ismail, where Jews lived lives of the ancient law, yes, but were open to Russian thought and poetry. And having come from the Danube, with its Latin memories in song and wine, that cosmopolitan world took the harsh edges off Jewish life for her as well.

The Messiah had not come yet, but of course in Ismail as it was in Suczorno, He did not really have to, because He was there always, as hope or promise would be. And the Ismail Jews, with their deep inner knowledge of who they were, though conservative, did not break with tradition. They still sat *Shivah* for the loss of a son or daughter – to conversion or having married out of the faith – but less and less often. They felt progressive by eating bread baked by non-Jews in bakeries, and they were not asking if the pan had been larded – God forbid! Not all, of course, but Jewish homes were kept with less restraint and with more joy in the temporal world, with an allowance for the senses.

As a single child, Esther had been treated lavishly, and had always fancied herself better than her peers. Yiddish – though having risen to the status of literature with the greatest storytellers such as Sholem Aleichem – was less cultivated, and people preferred the classic Russian speech and upper-class behaviour.

Her father, a goldsmith, was an artist, a trader also; and from very early days, little Esther heard that she was not an Ashkenazi Jew – or so they reckoned – but had come from the Sephardic stock, over the Italy-Turkey-Constanza route after the forced exile from Spain. *Ferdinand* and *Isabella* were hated names in the family lore, but the pride of not giving in, of refusing conversion, was the banner held high by Esther's father, Yehuda Ben Ephraim, and Esther's pride as well.

Although not changing customs such as sitting with her mother separate from the men in the upper benches of the synagogue, she did not partake in women's or girls' chatter during services; but instructed by her father, she behaved "like a man." Well, not exactly; not called to the *Torah*, of course, but she was able to follow the readings, and keeping the women in order; as young as she was, Esther elevated the women's service to the level of the men's. But she was haughty in the eyes of the congregation. Studious and having had an adoring father, who had reminded her constantly of their ancient ancestry, she did not need anyone else.

Later, much later in life, with her sense of history slowly ripening, she could see the age-old Jewish interdependence of "To sin and to suffer" – or that to sin is to suffer. Sequence and consequence. Then she did penance, all the little daily things she had seen her grandmother do, taking a piece of *Challah* raw from the whole dough, she said her *Baruch Atah,* and threw it into the open fire, watching it go up in flames. It was a recreation of her own home burning to heaven, or the old ordinance of the paying of the tithe. Who is to tell? She did it to please God, *kashered* her Passover cutlery by removing stones from the Suczorno river, and heating them to a high point, brought the water to a boil. Little daily things she did, which she had ignored before, when she had felt superior, knowing everything better. This all was much, much later – years later, when she was able to approach the *Shklovke,* to talk about the *unspeakable.*

It was when Esther turned to God that she saw Reuwen for the first time. Living on the other side of the *Shoichet's* wall, she had watched him coming and going, growing up there. His striking beauty, his elegance, the smooth, lithe movements of body and limb, brought her longing back; a memory of "finer things" than the crude down-to-earth surviving Suczorno had to offer. She turned to God, when she sat in the women's benches at his *Bar Mitzvah,* hearing the voice of the Eternal flowing from Reuwen's lips. *Rachamim, not charity alone but the giving of oneself; it is the silencing of our wicked drives and dreams of revenge.* Reuwen hit straight into the heart of Esther. She fasted the next day, following the custom not to eat or drink *Muntig in Donerstig,* the old Monday and Thursday fast.

Compared to the Suczorno poor, she was a wealthy woman now. Having traded in gold and gems within a certain triangle of commerce and travel, she had added respect and honour – the *Koved* to the *Oysher* – to the wealthy woman she was now. The triangle she travelled – her beloved Meir at her side – was the one borderless Jewish trade triangle of Ismail-Lemberg-Odessa. The inns, where to stop and eat *kosher,* she knew, and Esther had learned to appraise partners or customers at a glance, by instinct, intelligence, and by the will of God. She often followed the route of the horse dealers, these sophisticated thieves – *Ganovim.* She learned the code of their jargon, which, spiked with Hebrew words, was understood across Europe as far as the Yiddish on the river Rhine, and used to cheat and sell a poor old painted-up horse for a higher price. It was not for Esther. But she learned their ways, their routes, and often had to consort with them. Once on the road, thieves were your enemies and your friends. They could save your life as well as threaten it. But she kept her dealings clean of deceit. "You cheat only once," she said, "and this is bad business."

She came home to rest, keep house and accounts, and continued to ignore the town. Her duty she did, honoured her in-laws, poor as they were, stood at the side of Meir – or behind him, when he said the *Kaddish* for them – lit the candles Friday night or on holidays when at home. But kept her private life private, which in Suczorno, where every childbearing woman knew the other and was bound to go to the *Mikvah* to take the ritual bath after her period of uncleanness was over, was almost impossible to do. The women knew one another, recorded all lives, even if care was taken not to spread open falsehoods. It was not for Esther. She despised that closeness, did not find the need to communicate with her kind, nor ask for advice.

Esther remained childless, and the women talked more openly, pointing accusing fingers. "She claims to be so high born, yet she curses like the most vulgar of men, shouts at other people's children in a Russian no one has ever heard before, and she locks all doors. What is she hiding? Her cradle will be empty."

But one day, Esther knocked at the door of Yankel and

Shoshannah and said, *"Shalom Chaverim,* may peace, my friends and neighbours, reign under your roof. I have come to invite the young lady Ethel to visit me."

That was new. All through the time that Ethel had waited for Shimon's return, Esther had never given any sign of compassion, but locked her door when at home and did not report when she left. But now she felt it was time, time to atone for her arrogance. Or perhaps a sudden desire to love, to give of herself, made her knock at her neighbor's door.

Ethel put the broom she held into its corner, did it as if Esther's visit was a daily routine, or expected, and smiled a welcome. "Dear Esther, I'll come right away, if you'd like me to. Just let me wash my hands." Ethel rushed out to fetch a little water from the rain barrel, taking a cracked earthen cup from the shelf. "I'll be right back," she said, hanging her apron onto the nail protruding between two posts next to the door. And leaving it slightly ajar, she called, "I'll be right back."

They're poor, very poor, Esther assessed, gauging the place with a glance. Need and necessity only. Oh dear, she thought. Esther did not expect luxury, but looked for a little beauty in a useless object: a vase perhaps, or a glass to catch a glint of light. There was none. The *Shoichet's* knives on the wall, arranged and sized, held in place by nails, reflected whatever light there was. There were pots and pans of iron, a copper kettle hung from the ceiling near the mud oven. As she heard the door move, Esther turned, ran towards Ethel, embraced her, and pulling her out of the kitchen door, said, "Come Ethel, my daughter, come to my house, we'll have tea."

They entered Esther's house; and the warmth of the wooden panelling Meir had installed on the wall adjoining the *Shoichet's,* the atmosphere of order, with things in rows, just being there for no detectable reason, made Ethel speechless for a moment. But she accepted a chair next to the centre table with a nod of her head.

"Dear Ethel," Esther started, "we have a little business before tea. I'm not a woman of many words, and I have to make good – please allow me." Esther turned to her armoire to remove a lacquered box with many drawers, brought it to the table, and opening one of them, where gold rings, sized and numbered, were lying in their purple velvet bed, said, "Ethel dear, show me your fourth finger and I'll mark the size of your wedding band."

Smiling at each other, they tried a few, until one flat gold band slipped gently on and off the finger. Esther removed two of these, rose to find a small black box for them, fitted them into it, and with the words, "May this be a blessed bond between you and Shimon," she handed the gift to Ethel and embraced her. Then they poured boiling water from the samovar into dainty cups, took a little colour from the brown betty, and a piece of crystal-sugar between their teeth. The women had found one another.

Meir: Two Gold Coins

THE LAST WEEKS HAD BEEN STRAINED. The days and the nights. She had not shown herself to her husband on her good days, dressed and undressed behind her Chinese screen. No one else had a lacquered screen in Suczorno. She had bought it in pieces in an Odessa junkyard. She, the merchant woman, knew value, and repainted the little Chinese figures having tea under blossoming branches, found the workman to do it, and all of that for a farthing. A merchant loves a bargain.

Now it was standing all joined in its corners, foldable, revealing in panels the successive scenes. A small fire she repainted herself with a glint of red-yellow, a perfect pot with handle sitting on top she redrew. Flowing garments on bald men, on the next unfolding panel, showed order and the hierarchy of their lives. Meir had admired and loved that screen, when it stood ready next to their bed.

"The things you can do, my Esther, to enrich my life. To have you at my side and to serve God – how lucky a man I am!"

That was years ago. Now Meir watched her retreat behind this screen and said, "Don't you show yourself to your husband? Aren't these your good days? Do I have to beg for my rights?"

And she had gone to bed with him, had done her duty, as a wedded wife ought to, but had not thrown a smile into his direction, not even a faked moan, as she had done at other times. She rose from their bed as soon as she could, pulling from under their bed a small bowl of rainwater to wash herself clean from the unloved smell. Returned to their bed with a fast goodnight, not to touch again.

Mornings were early those last weeks. Meir found his clothes properly laid out, seams mended, shoes cleaned and polished with beeswax by his dutiful wife, but Esther had risen before he woke to avoid his wakened desire. She called through the house, "Tea is on the samovar, I have to rush out." "Where to?" Meir asked, louder than necessary. "I've run out of –" Meir did not hear what she said. He heard the name Reuwen mentioned somehow and his eardrums started sounding, his legs gave in, and he sat on the rim of their bed, face awash in tears.

MEIR HAD BEEN A POOR BOY from the other side of the Suczorno creek. Not even on the creek, but born in the hovels, leaning one onto the other so as not to fall down like card houses would. Gales from the north sweeping through attacked the free-standing houses more readily, and so they huddled together. Not streets, but cobbled paths at best, if not wooden boards, separated the rows of houses made of mud and masts of timber in between. Thatched, the houses had no front, no back yard, only room for a goat or two, a shed of some sort. These abodes were poorer yet as they moved away from the river, and Meir had always loathed the specific smell of poverty hovering in the air, the loud voices of accusation, of neighbours against the neighbours, and the wait for the *Shabbat* meal, somehow put together, to sit around a table, with two candles lit to praise the Lord for having reached that moment.

But Meir was handy with tools. He worked as a twelve-year-old for the real tradesmen, the ones with their homes facing the river just a few rows of houses away from his, and life seemed orderly. There were carpenters, furriers, tanners with their little shops, if not at the front, so in their back rooms. Although it wasn't yet the high bank of the merchants, where houses had doors with thresholds, sometimes fenced front gardens and work tool sheds, or stables even, sharing horses between them. Rich.

Everyone knows where everyone is born, and takes advantage of it, Meir thought. And when, at the age of twelve, he entered the apprenticeship of the furrier, he knew they would make him work longer hours – sweeping, scrubbing the floor of the *atelier* and home – than any apprentice from the "riverside of the north bank," or differently yet, had he come from the high bank of the merchants. He knew. But he was prepared.

"I'll work from morning until night until I master the trade.

Then I'll build myself a proper house on the high-bank and marry into a rich family."

Some of it had come true. Diligent and very skillful, with delicate fingers which can hold a needle and thread it in no time, he was also of infinite patience. Chaim ben Nahum, who had recently lost his wife and owned a large bed, had let him sleep there, next to him, and had said, "I'll do you a favour, Meir, and you have to repay me by working hard." And Chaim put in front of him a mountain of pearly glass beads, to be sewn onto the Ukrainian short fur jackets the peasants so loved. In patterns of roses or garlands, green and red mainly. Ukrainian and Romanian peasants did it themselves, and the Jews had learned it from them. But they also came to the Jew to order them for their daughters' dowry trunks. In peacetime and in times of good harvest, there was something between them that felt like love!

Meir was not yet *Bar Mitzvah* and had little inclination for learning. He was twelve perhaps, when Chaim, his master, said to him, "I can't let you sleep with me the next seven days. I've rented my side of the bed to a journey-man on the way to Kiev and I need the money. But you'll be back with me after he leaves."

Meir had enjoyed the wide bed, the warmth of the feather-filled duvet, not heavy but hugging every part of his young body. He did not even mind Chaim's hand around his shoulder before saying goodnight and the unexpected nearness of the older man. It filled him with a strange excitement, a desire to stretch his limbs; he felt the muscles tightening, a faster beat of the heart, and a sweaty palm. He liked it. Moved closer to Chaim's backside and was not rebuffed. So he stayed, fell asleep, rose to wash hands and face. Near the small shed in the back of the house, stood the ever-present barrel with rainwater, a small pitcher hanging on the side.

Meir poured the night-cool water into an enamelled bowl from the shed, filled it to the brim, and washed face and hands first. But with a sudden movement pulled his day-night shirt over his head to wash underarm and touched a film of hair. The roughness of the sudden sensation shook him. "I'm a man," he thought. Dried himself on a used-abused towel hanging on a nail close to the door and went back to see if there were still embers in the big oven in the corner. There were some and he stirred them, put a few sticks of wood – prepared the night before – onto them, and went to the well for water, carrying a pail of sheet metal.

Meir walked along the river in the pre-dawn Suczorno air. He was bigger now, he felt, made longer strides than yesterday. He saw no movement, no flicker of a candle in the windows along his walk, so he sat on the rim of the fountain – a wide and comfortable rim encircling it – and smiled at the thought, a whole troupe of dwarfs performed on it last week, heavens! He followed the cracks between the slate pieces with his knowing fingers, and sat a little longer before lowering the pail. Returning home, he set water to boil in the good kettle and woke Chaim, his master. He loved him.

I'll work for him, he thought, I'll sew those millions of glass beads onto the inside-out sheepskins, I'll sweep the floor clean at night, I'll cook his meal, wash his linen and hang it on the back line. And I'll stretch and fold it into proper creases and if there are embers left, I'll fill one of his several irons until a little spit on the flat side of the iron becomes instant vapour, with the *z-s-sh-sh*-sound. I won't mind Chaim's curses, he does call me a no-good, slow, stupid eater-of-food and sometimes he hands me a smack across the ear and back of the head, and I do not know for what – perhaps to remind me in whose shop I am. But I smile back, letting him know that he can do with me what he likes as long as I can sit at his feet and learn.

Sometimes, Meir remembered, Chaim, sitting on the table, feet hanging, trying to stretch a piece of stubborn skin, and handing it to Meir, who sat on the small stool. Chaim said, "Meir, you have good, strong, young teeth, chew this skin a little, work it with your gums and spit, or else we'll never push a needle through, let alone make it look smooth." So Meir had chewed this stinky piece of leather for him until it became soft and pliable. And Chaim put his hand on Meir's head and said, "Good boy." That was the day I first loved him, Meir thought, much before the time that he let me share his big bed.

But today I won't be there, Meir thought. And I won't go to the back streets to sleep in my father's house, now that I'm accustomed to luxury.

He heard Chaim's voice, saw him taking a few tea leaves from the metal box his late wife had saved from God-knows-what, and felt a pang of regret to leave what he considered his own place to a stranger. For a week.

As he had to leave for the night, he thought to take off to a small Ukrainian farm a few kilometres from Suczorno, where he had to deliver one of the short inside-out jackets. He had finished it himself by turning the borders to show the fur, and had trimmed it with masses of red, green, and yellow beads. He carried it on a handmade wooden hanger that he was to reclaim for other deliveries; he knocked at the door but got no response. As he expected payment, he tried to locate the woman, and peered into one of the small peasant-windows, which, not bigger than half a metre square cut by a cross, allowed little vision. She was there, though he had caught her at a very private moment and felt he had to wait.

Not to be seen, he slid along to the back of the house, when he heard the creaking of the rough pine door and a young man appeared looking furtively around and hustled into the goats' shed. "I will wait," Meir said to himself. "I'll give her time." He decided to rest a little, as he still had a two-hour trek home. He found a shady spot behind a wooden wind-fence, and holding the fur jacket with both arms tight against his body, seated himself, with the fence post at his back, facing the prairies. The sun rose high and he fell asleep.

THERE WAS NO STILLNESS LIKE IT, no sweetness of rest as in the Ukrainian wheat field, nearly golden, stretching to the horizon. Meir, being born among the poorest of Suczorno's poor in the "hindstreets" of town, among many little children who followed one another with the certainty of the seasons, used to leave the encroaching presence of all that life to run out, into the open, to escape. He was brought in one winter day with the tips of nose, fingers, and toes frozen, by his older brother Jossel, who said to him, "No more, this is the last time, if you do this one more time, I'll let you die." Meir did not answer, but could not tell him how and what he felt indoors. Jossel, his favourite brother, was sixteen years his senior, and had taken Meir under his wing. But a wayward father and a mother with babies at her breast – all in one room – drove Meir out for a breath of fresh air.

It was the north end of town, away from the river, where all the one-room houses stood, and theirs was in the last row, unencumbered by neighbours, their back door facing empty, grassy lands to the north, so he could run out. In early mornings, when three or four, he would leave all the boys at their reading and writing, later at their *Torah* studies, and would slip out, to run into the fields. Summer and winter. Shoes or no shoes. To collect stones, to watch the sun rise, to build things. And when the *melamed* – the teacher – after years of neglect, noticed his absence, it was too late for Meir to catch up.

"I'll learn on my own," he'd said, and he had, but barely enough to read from the *Torah*. They were too poor, too many of them, so he did not have a *Bar Mitzvah* at the right time. Things just happened naturally with the poor in Suczorno. In the "hindtown," customs were strict, yet diminished by this absolute poverty, so a child could slip through the net of law, live a life of the wild, unrestricted by the stern discipline of the past.

Meir had one day, on his forays into the land, not far from where he sat now leaning against the fence, found a soul-play companion. Another seven- or eight-year-old from a world entirely different than his, a world of hard work, tilling the ancient soil with its implacable harvest-no-harvest destiny. They found one another under the roof of a sheltering windbreak. It had started to rain one early May morning when Meir had run out again. Barefoot. With the taste of raindrops on his tongue, he ran through the fields, when a sudden cloudburst frightened him and he looked for shelter. He knew the poplar row limiting a peasant's land and took aim. Ran. Landed next to a lad crouching on the ground.

Protective, thick poplar foliage had hidden the boy from Meir's view, and he had nearly landed in the boy's lap; they both laughed now with the thrill of the unexpected and the dangerous. Concerned only with keeping dry and warm, the boy, Ivan, moved a little to accommodate Meir, made room for him on his territory, his father's land, and said, "I know every hollow under every tree and I know where to come for shelter. How did you find it? You are from Suczorno, right?"

And Meir replied in a Yiddish-coloured Ukrainian, "Yes, I'm a Jew from Suczorno. I ran away from classes. I love to be outdoors." The rain had not subsided and the boys, with a dense roof overhead, their warm bodies close, releasing a light steam-smell, giggled.

"Come on a sunny day, next week perhaps, when the wheat is fully ripe, just before harvest, and we'll crawl together into my hideouts. All my brothers and sisters are older, much older. I'm alone. Come, we'll be twins!"

Meir loved Ivan with such immediacy that he took him around his shoulder to show it. *"Chodé, chodé,"* the Ukrainian said, and it sounded so gutturally wonderful and reminded Meir of the Hebrew sound with all its *H-ch* sound deep in the throat. "I will come," Meir replied in Yiddish. *"Eich wil kimmon,"* he said. They parted, exchanging a button from Meir's pants against stones from Ivan's field.

It was a summer like no other. Meir went again and again, until found out by Jossel, who said, "Let me not catch you again with the *Goyim;* they may be friendly but they can't be trusted."

Meir knew better. He had – as young as he was – bridged the gap.

"Ivan is good," he replied, "perhaps better than many of us from the high bank... No, not perhaps, better!"

"I do not care if one of them is good. When they come with their burning torches, watch out!"

But Meir did know better. Summers on end, they stretched into hollows with corn not yet ripe and then fully golden; boys know of love. Until he was twelve and had to go to apprentice with a master, this was his only love. Ivan. A Christian boy.

NOW HE SLEPT. Back against the fence. Some posts were missing, some, to be carried by the next storm or gale, were still hanging there, moving with the breezes, pendulum style. They had cradled Meir to sleep and now he woke startled. Voices and carriages were coming closer, he could not tell from which direction on the road. He flattened his back, stretched into the grasses, and heard wheels grinding to a halt, heavy boots pounding the earth: shouts, and what he thought were blows. These were not Ivan's people. He had known his mother, and some of his brothers, he knew their voices.

THE FIRST TIME Ivan had brought his little Jewish friend into the house was just before Ukrainian Christmas. And not into the house, but to the shed. The two of them had been caught by surprise. Ivan's older brother with their father had entered the shed, laughing, carrying slaughtered pigs, which they hung on hooks along the wall, letting the blood drip into a prepared trough.

"It's to make blood sausage," Ivan whispered into Meir's ear, "I'll save you some. It's freckled."

"Freckled?"

"Yes, pieces of pork-fat and cut-up pork tongue make it look – well, freckled, when sliced across. Smoked."

Meir moved closer to Ivan, looking for rescue, and felt Ivan's warm hand holding his.

"Don't worry. We have to get out of our corner, because when Gregory and my father come with the next load, they'll find us. Don't worry, they're all good people. Move."

Ivan pushed Meir out and onto his feet and was immediately spotted by his working folk and heard themselves addressed.

"What are you two no-goods doing here? Who is this kid? A runaway Jew-boy to tell by his clothes. Is he dumb? Speak! Are you a Jew or not?"

"Yes, my name is Meir ben –"

"Good enough. Get going or better hold on to this end of the ladder –"

So Meir learnt that these were good people. Rich people. With pigs and hens and geese and mountains of grain in season. White bread, black bread. Sundays in Sunday-dress. The young men in shiny black boots, white linen shirts hanging over the skin-tight trousers with a fancy fur jacket to finish, black hats with wild roses in hatbands, they seemed a different race to Meir. In a strange, envied world.

For a few wonderful years, Meir shared it. Did not touch the blood tongue-sausage when offered, but their *Paszka* – white, round, egg-bread at Easter – yes, they shared easily.

But forbidden by Jossel, his brother, slowly coming to terms with change, and going into his eleventh year, Meir's easy ways came to an end, and he had not taken that road again until today.

THE JACKET HAD BEEN ORDERED the year before and it had taken time to finish it properly. Now he held it in his arms. He was frightened: the people had gone, if only for the day, or moved or – the voices had been alien, unfamiliar, and if what he had heard were blows – he could not tell. As the house grew still as the fields, he realized that no dog barked, and no sounds came from the stables. He rose, hugging his jacket, and strode resolutely in the direction of Suczorno.

CHAIM, HIS MASTER, had rented his bedstead for a week, and Meir had to go home for that time. Unwillingly. And for the first time stepping over the threshold of the family one-room house, he felt a stranger. *"Meir, mein siss kind, kumin,"* the mother said. But it did not help. "Will you stay the night?" she asked.

"I'll stay seven nights," Meir said, hugged her, sat by her table. He picked up the peas she was shelling, broke them, threw some in the pot, and looked at her hands. She has aged, he thought, there are brown spots all over. And his own years felt heavier than ever before when he heard her say, "You'll be thirteen soon, not a *yingale* any more – and you have not studied."

"I'll do it still. By next year I'll be ready for the *Bar Mitzvah*. I'll talk to the rabbi. Don't worry."

"A year does not matter as long as you do it with all your heart," the mother said.

"I will," the son replied. "I will."

But it was not to be. He stayed a little longer, watched his mother rise more slowly than he remembered, suspected her to be with child. A sudden anger against his father made him push the chair with more strength than necessary, making the peas roll and his mother look at him.

"You're red all over, Meir, my son. What is it? Have I said anything?"

"It's nothing," he replied and bent to pick up the few peas to save her doing it as he knew she would. She had always borne everything without revolt. He loved her, but with a pity which slices the heart. Around her were two more little ones, of three and four years, clinging to her and now to him. He smiled but shook them off. Meir had always loved her. A silent mother, rarely did she lose her temper. So different from the shouting, cursing mothers on both sides of their huddle. From his youth, he'd plugged his ears to shut out the scolding, abusive shouting of desperate mothers which echoed through the makeshift walls.

These were the hindstreets of Suczorno, where everything was poor and loud. Poverty shouted, and smell of garlic and onions, the lack of soap and strength, all of these went into the hour-by-hour living. Meir watched the little ones and his mother, who was trying to make the fire go and couldn't. Pushing her gently to the side, he said, "I'll do it. Go look after Mariam, she is crying." And he knew he would have to get out of the hindstreets of Suczorno to survive.

Now, more than ever, Chaim seemed the way out. The lower bank first. Perhaps one day the higher bank. But this was too removed, and there were no trades to be learned on the high bank; they were all on this side. Besides, he did like the low-lying land where the power of the midday sun streamed onto the north bank. Windows gleamed in the houses with its reflection. Of course, not all had windows with proper glass set into a frame, but many did; and bulbs sprang up faster on the low bank, if anyone had time to notice.

Walking by Naomi and Moredchai's place on his way to Chaim the furrier, Meir saw Naomi putting a few bulbs into the ground by her front door; they had just put up a modest house. He watched her movements as she bent, and he blushed as he felt his young manhood rise, and thought, "I'll never have a wife as beautiful as Naomi – who would want me?" But a certain joy overcame him, and he smiled at his sudden awareness that he was a man.

And he hurried on to help Chaim, who as a widower had no

one to sweep the floor in his *atelier*, which was really a back-shed room with an earthen floor. Chaim was out, and Meir took the broom and wooden shovel from the corner to collect the bigger pieces of fur that had fallen from the table at yesterday's cutting. Then he stopped, sat down, and looked around. Chaim had hung a series of hides on wooden racks to be fashioned into *kuczmas* – fur hats with side flaps, Russian-style – which he could sell to Russians, Ukrainians, and Jews alike, to those that had the money. The peasants made their own of course. But Chaim's hats were truly crafted, hand and machine sewn on the foot-powered "big Singer," which Meir had not touched yet, except to oil it and watch the master take it apart to clean its intricate mechanism; this was something for Meir to aspire to. He had fine hands, almost girlish fingers, which learned fast and remembered sequence. That man could invent something so beautiful as a machine – something with an inner heart like one's own – thrilled him.

Chaje, the master's late wife, had been so orderly and thrifty that throw-away ancient cartons or crates had been repainted, holes filled with sawdust if the crate happened to be wood, or glued over with a carpskin and cooked-flour mixture if cardboard. Aleph, Beth, and so forth designated the contents – all clearly marked on top and arranged in order of size and shape, smaller containers in front, bigger ones in the back, and marked higher so the writing would show above the front row. Meir looked at this wonder-world. Coming from the hindstreets of Suczorno, with an overworked mother carrying her full womb forever in a one-room house – to Meir this was an undreamt-of heaven. Order. A household without children. Chaim, his master, the only object of care, accustomed to love.

A love that shook his own hand, now taking a few tea leaves from their designated box. He reached up for the earthen betty on top of the samovar and took a silent oath, this is what my house will be, as Chaim's is. He heard his voice and hurried, with a light stab in the soul, a regret at missing making Chaim's tea for seven days.

Meir had returned after a week. It had been a long one. Long in distress, for seeing himself so easily displaced, as it seemed to him, in the affection of Chaim. In truth, he had nothing to fear, because Chaim too had got used to the presence of Meir, who had assumed Chaje's ways to serve the master, who knew how many leaves made perfect tea, ground them a little between thumb and index finger to extract most of the flavour, and let them fall into the small brown earthen pot, pre-warmed on top of the samovar. Meir knew the orderly placing of used rags, the folding and heaping of washed-bleached-boiled-ironed ones. The beauty of the regular and the daily, and the setting aside of *Shabbat* things. A kind of harmony between the profane and the elevated.

And the one advantage Meir had over Chaje in the mind and feeling of Chaim, was that Meir did not ask any questions about his inner life, dreams, or visitations of any sort, as Chaje had done every morning when she woke. Pulling herself up against her pillow, it was, "Chaim, who came to see you in your dreams? I heard you moan." It was so different now. And though he missed her love, Chaim felt a sinful deliverance. Grateful for God's ways, as strange as they were, and accepting that a little boy of twelve or thirteen could replace his Chaje.

So one day Chaim felt he had to send Meir away. He was too dependent on him, he thought. "Sometimes Meir thinks he is Chaje," he thought and it made him blush. Meir had learnt her ways and did everything right.

But during Meir's week-long absence, loss persisted, a feeling of the irreversible. And Chaim, sitting on the edge of his bed, recalled another morning when he had woken early. It was five o'clock when he looked at the empty bed beside him. He had dreamed a strange feeling. That was all, a feeling.

Chaje had always said, "Chaim, the moment you wake – and you know you always dream in the morning – tell me the story." In the beginning of their married life, he did not care to tell her everything, the dreams disclosed too much of his inner life, and Chaje wanted to control him; to tell him what to do to improve his business, with whom to deal and whom to shun. He did not like her meddling in his affairs and mostly said, "It was just a feeling, Chaje, there was no story." But she was already sitting up straight in her bed, ready to participate. "Chaim! It may have been important, try to bring the people back. Who was it?"

"I can't remember, it's just a feeling. Go back to sleep, it's early; even the roosters don't crow yet. Why should I?"

But she did not let up. She sat, supported by her pillows, wide awake, arms raised behind her head, hair flowing down her shoulder. This was how she let it hang, down the right shoulder.

Oh, she was lovely when young. Just lovely. She refused to cut her hair, hid it under a kerchief or under a fancy *perruque,* to irritate her in-laws, anger them in the extreme. She would *not* cut that black thick hair; brilliantined it, washed it in camomile infusions – it had to be rainwater at that! – and rinsed it, with a drop of vinegar into the water, until it shone. "Yes," said her mother-in-law, "it shines black, like her sinful soul, and whatever will happen to her – barren as she is – will be because of her ways.

Imagine, to keep your own hair, a married woman!"

But he loved her: it was *all* for him, all that glory. She released it for the night and let it hang over her creamy white shoulders, a picture of beauty. These were often the days when she was lightly melancholy and he was not allowed to come near her. A partition – a small piece of wood, a roll of linen, or a little pillow was between them to remind him, these were her four or five days, and he had to wait for the partition to disappear and the ritual bath – the Mikvah – to be taken. But often by then his love was less acute. Still, she was beautiful.

He turned and looked at his empty bedside and only now, after a dream full of a certain feeling, did he come to realize that her voice had gone, yet he heard her within himself, "Chaim! Don't hide your stories, it's important, who came to you at night?"

"Chaje, my beloved, it's nothing, it's a feeling."

And she, "It is important to know who brought this feeling to you. It may have been a visitation!"

"What visitation are you talking about? It was a dream."

"No, no – this was how your father came to you last year. He came in your dream and told you to sell your business and buy –"

"Yes, you're right, he came and told me to sell and I lost it all; soon the money was gone – what with all the debts. Chaje, my father's advice I can do without. If you only consider his own successes – no, no more parental advice."

"But it could be an angel with a message from the Almighty," she continued. "It could be a warning how to avoid Bupbale's evil eye –"

And so it went on. And Chaim, looking back and into his soul, realized that it *was* a visitation indeed, and it was Bupbale.

She was a widow of means now, and they had known each other since childhood, and she remained a thorn in poor Chaje's life.

Yes, he thought, Bupbale looked at me again, after her husband had died, she looked at me with such loving eyes – and one day, Chaje doing business with the Russians in the next village and I being at my prayers, Bupbale had waited at the corner until the way was clear. Knocking gently at the door, she came in and brought a few sugar cubes for my tea and said, "Remember, Chaim, when we were children?" This was how she started, "Remember, Chaim." It made my heart pound. I forgot to say Amen at the end of the blessing, and I hushed her away, "What are you doing here, Bupbale, a married woman?"

"I am a widow, and I let my hair grow –" and she pulled the kerchief from her head and it fell to her shoulders, in brown curls with golden lights. She turned, as if she were still twenty, around on her heels to let him see all of the glory, laughed a flirtatious little giggle, then gathered her hair up with a comb and hid it in her kerchief, closing the door gently like a thief behind her. And a thief she was, coming to him at night, in his sleep, next to Chaje, as a visitation. What was he to tell his wife when she said that night, "It may have been a visitation, who was it? Try to remember." What was he to say? "A feeling," he would say. "A feeling." But a feeling it was, and there was no way he could tell his Chaje what an overwhelming feeling it was – shaming him into waking at five o'clock in the morning with something in the soul so unlawful, wrong, and despicable, not wanting, not desiring his own Chaje who had removed the partition between them the night before.

"Go back to sleep – it's nothing," he'd said. But it was difficult. Chaim looked at the empty side of his bed. He had only buried Chaje a short while ago. She had fallen ill with a mysterious disease; none of the wise women and rabbis could heal it or even say what it was. A mood of melancholy had taken hold of her, she had not talked or said her prayers, and she had lacked hunger – though Chaim borrowed money on interest from the *Gevirim,* the rich Jews in Suczorno, to feed her with the best. He had even gone as far as using the law of *Petuah* – the right to do unlawful things for the sake of saving a life – and had gone to the neighbouring village to buy "Christian butter" from the Ukrainian peasants. A good woman he had known as a child made the sign of the cross and said, "Do not give me any money, Chaim. If it is for the health of your wife, it will be counted for me in heaven as a good deed." And he'd thanked her, knowing full well that he held pork fat in his hands. But Chaje had refused all food, and it had frightened Chaim even more when she stopped washing her lustrous hair.

It seemed like yesterday. Coming home from the cemetery, washing his hands before stepping over his own threshold as is the law, saying the blessing, which is a *Mitzwah,* the commandment to do so, he sat down on the edge of their large bed. It had been the main part of her dowry. They were poor, the two of them, and some of their income – if all and everything failed except her stuffing geese with corn and selling them to the rich when the geese were fattened – came from renting a little space beside them both in that large bed. For a night or two. To Jews of course only, because one doesn't know what a Gentile would do when one is deep asleep and lying next to one.

Jews often travelled from *shtetl* to *shtetl* selling their wares – shoelaces, thread, ribbons of all colours; taking orders for another time. Or they had to go to Kiev to try to get their sons to school, or file an application with the authorities. Or maybe they just went to the neighbouring Ukrainian villages to help out in some way for small cash. Well, in such cases, a large bed could be rented out to a traveller and bring a little income.

And that day after the funeral, he had the sinful thought that Chaje – may she rest in peace – not being with him anymore, that he could rent the space next to him to a nice couple perhaps now and then, to make himself a neat little sum. He rejected the thought fast, though keeping it in the back of his mind for when the right moment would come – but he felt ashamed to think of money. How sinful I am when *Kaddish* has to be said and the holy seven days – the *Shivah,* with the *Minion,* the ten good men helping the bereaved to carry the burden of the loss by gathering daily for prayers, has to be lived through. How sinful of me! he thought.

And oh, how good she had been, his Chaje. How ready to earn an extra *piaster* to make his Chaim's *"Cholent* a little fatter," as she put it. How good she was at beekeeping. How she was able to talk to wild bees, tame them, taking some of their honey and never the wax. Unless the poor things had not survived the winter – like many of us as well – then of course she would collect the wild wax, melt, clear, and pour it into the prepared glass with a wick. It had to burn for twenty-four hours, to honour the dead on their *Jahrzeit* – the day each year on which our own have died. That was the custom, to feel our forebears around us. Protecting us. Or simply so we could shed a tear, reminded of the passing life and the eternity of it. Oh yes, my Chaje.

His fur trade hadn't started well. It had been a hard winter, and Chaje would help by selling a little honey, floor wax, or a *Jahrzeit* candle – as he could not always provide for the two of them. She'd done it all without a whimper, complaint, or reproach.

"I did love and honour her always," he said consolingly to himself. "I did love her."

He had said the *Kaddish* at the graveside, as they'd never had any sons who could do it. Well, she was barren, his Chaje, and no medicine, no prayers, no stroking in circular motion of the lower part of the body up to the navel, had borne any results.

"Poor sweet Chaje," he said to himself, sitting on the edge of their bed a little while longer, deadly afraid of his sinful thoughts and – God forbid – of Bupbale's visitation to his dreams before the year of mourning was over.

So he sat, until one after the other of his neighbours had drifted in, to put on their *Tallithim,* their prayer shawls, to start the *Shivah* prayers. He heard the women in the small kitchen adjoining their own room preparing the food for the day, talking in hushed voices. Then he slowly rose from the edge of his bed and said, "Blessed be the Lord King of the Universe, who has given us the strength to accept His ways."

And so he sat today also, the "Blessed be Thou" flowing from his lips. A covenant. A tie to the Eternal. To be able to look at daily objects without despair. And Chaim rose from his bedside to wash his hands, put on his *Tefillin,* and start his tea.

FOR MEIR TOO it had been a long week, but he had remembered the young man his own age who was not from Suczorno. And after a short visit to the hindstreets of Suczorno, to its muddied wooden boards over running refuse, to the air of drying diapers ripped from ancient sheets, to his mother, heavied in the middle with new birth – he fled. Out into the open. To his Christian friend, Ivan.

Neither cared who they were. All the long seven nights, Ivan hid Meir in a kind of a tack room – where leather gear and other horse paraphernalia was kept.

A look into a life, unexpected. So other. Huge pieces of land, open, owned and worked. A rhythm of work. With no books. Blankets of spun wool, meant for horses, heavy like a ton on the shoulders, smelling of manure, were a comfort, a protection Meir had not known in his early beds, crowded with siblings, who pulled the coverlet in all directions. The coverlet was feather-filled, which Meir loved, but feathers collect in corners, and the twins, just older than he was by a year or so and a little stronger, being a unit of two, fought for it successfully, leaving him exposed around the shoulders.

And he told Ivan, "My left arm was frozen stiff one morning. The embers had died in the mud oven, and Abe and Hake, my twin brothers, had collected all the feathers in their end of the blanket, and I found myself unable to lift my arm for a little."

Moving in closer to his friend Ivan, horse blanket up to their noses, Meir talked of Suczorno. In whispers, not to be heard or suspected. Giggling a little now, what with the horsehair strands intruding between his lips or up his nostrils, and the fear of sneezing! They dug themselves deeper into the heavy, smelly blanket roof, closer to one another, boys in comfort and love, with an added touch of danger.

Neither of them had words for "I love you," but the warmth streaming through their bodies as if they were one, the sudden heat in the crotch and the unexpected relief, made them shudder with joy. And they slept embraced. Night after night. They woke to talk, to look into each other's worlds, without much comprehension, except the wonder of having found one another, under a tree, in the storm.

Meir had taken the beaded fur jacket back to the shop and had hung it next to the door, calling into the kitchen to Chaim, who was at his tea, "The jacket is too tight under the arm."

"Yes," came the reply, "I thought it might be." It had been stretched in all directions, but was perhaps initially cut from too short a skin, and with seams upturned, the fur tightening it further, was more a young man's jacket now than a grown man's.

"I may find another customer. I know a young man who may be interested. May I please see if I can sell it to him?" Meir heard himself lie to Chaim.

"Take it, we would not know what to do with it. But it can't go under ten rubles."

"I'll try. It will have to be on credit for a while."

"Take it," Chaim said. "See what you can do."

He had lied for his love. "Tonight I'll take Ivan the jacket. I'll work it off to Chaim. I'll work a whole year for it —" Meir unhooked the crude hanger from its nail and left.

The fields were rich with golden corn. A harvest like no other. It would start in a day or two, Meir thought, and hurried through the waving, high-standing, swelling grasses. He had carved himself a path away from the road, where Suczorno-ers with their wagons, hauling things, iron junk or grain, could not detect him; had followed the river hidden from view on the lower bank, but had to cross it to reach the road leading to the fields. He was anxious. Hurried. Thought he was seen from above the stone promontory by figures lurking in the windows of the houses at the west end of town, and felt there were spies everywhere.

Accelerating his step, he stumbled on the so-called bridge,

boards over the creek really, which displaced themselves easily. Meir had never seen a real bridge, but had thought about it when working for Chaim and sitting once on a real threshold – which was so different from the ones in the hindstreets houses, where kitchens led onto the street without marking. He had thought he could lay an interwoven net of planed wood and support it on both banks, but could not yet imagine how and with what material. And he had smiled at himself at the time, at his wish for order and organization.

Like Chaje's kitchen, he thought, I want life to be in order, smaller things in front; to be seen, to gain space; to look and have an overview.

And he had sat, embroidering the short fur jacket, with space in mind between colours, between the patterned shapes, running and stopping to make room for a new road to lay out his beads. He loved the work.

It was a game to think about, he'd thought. So much better than the Aleph-Beth – Bible study – from dawn to dusk. But a stab of guilt reminded him, Oh, dear, it seems my thirteenth birthday will pass without a *Bar Mitzvah* – I haven't studied. Oh well, next year. And he'd gone on with the joy of stringing glass beads. A sudden field of poppies had looked back at him from the rim of the inside-out fur jacket, outlining the front. Meir had been thrilled. And so had Chaim, who had put his hand on Meir's head, saying, "You're an artist" – with the accent in Yiddish on the *-tist*, which had made Meir blush.

Now he hurried, holding on to that same jacket, tried to walk faster, and he hugged it, as one would a living thing. Over the wobbling boards he went, but he did not mind them on that August day, glad to be out of sight of the last windows. The road took his step all by itself, leading him into the gently moving sea of corn. A few steps only and he stretched into the benevolent bed of comfort with God above.

As long as there are no people – I fear nothing. God perhaps, who sees into my soul!

The thought of Ivan, the gift he held in his arms, and the heat of midday made him drowsy. A happiness. A dream. He felt Ivan near him. Saw him – strapping and young. Helped him into the new jacket and said, "Ivan, you're beautiful. It is from me. I will pay my master. Don't worry." And Ivan kissed him, the Ukrainian version on both cheeks and one more kiss to come – if it was for the Holy Ghost, Meir was too ignorant to tell. Ivan just stood there, beautiful and upright, watching Meir, holding his tears back.

And he woke, with a slight pressure in his head, holding the jacket to his heart. Then he walked through the corn, avoiding stepping on the poppies.

Harvest had started. The fields were suddenly full with people, carts, sickles, noise, shouts, elder men commanding younger men. Women and men. Ivan among them.

Meir had left Ivan at five o'clock or so at sunrise, after seven full nights. Ivan had accompanied him through a northern path that time, a more sheltered grove that partitioned property between the fields of corn and made it possible for Meir not to run into the peasants who swarmed the countryside.

In that grove they kissed, swore eternal love and brotherhood, and Ivan said, "I will never forget you. The jacket you gave me I'll show to my mother and she'll find a way that I can wear it on

Sundays, without the envy or questioning of my brothers!" Two kisses and the third for good measure and the Holy Trinity. Then the Jew and the Ukrainian walked into opposite directions, back to their lives.

Meir was to replay this scene over and over again, the night before parting. It had been as Meir, lying in the cornfields, had dreamt it would be, Ivan stood, leaning leisurely against the shed wall, wearing the jacket as if dressed for Sunday. Then he took it off, folding it carefully outside-in, hid it under kindling, and said, "I can never repay this." And they rolled themselves up into the horse-blanket "as if in a cabbage leaf for *holubtsi,*" Ivan said, tucked its ends in, and waited for the warmth to surge through their bodies. Giggling a little at the horsehair between their lips, which they could not easily remove, so tightly packed they were, they slept until sunrise. Out. Fast. A drink of milk and a hunk of bread Ivan had secured for them the night before. Fast. The boys almost ran to the sheltering grove, not to prolong the pain of parting. Kissed. Again and again.

Meir, on the way home to Suczorno and throughout his life, would recall this time, visualize a detail he might have neglected to think about before.

RETURNING AFTER THESE SEVEN DAYS to his daily tasks of sweeping the floor, collecting ends of fur and threads, saving pieces of lining that could be reused somewhere, and stacking and folding them on a so-called shelf that Chaje had devised, Meir encountered the grateful, loving eyes of Chaim.

"I have missed you. The other young man was not as orderly as you are, and though he paid for his bed – well, I am accustomed to you. Because – perhaps you do things the way my Chaje did them. I used to watch her move around, lift things to put in cupboards or hide them in boxes, saying God has given us eyes to see His creation. This is what she said while ordering, arranging, labelling jars with Aleph-Beth."

"I know," Meir said, "I'm learning her ways just by living here. Her spirit is everywhere. I have a good mother, but in one room on a hard-to-sweep, earth-pounded floor, and so many little children – well, there was no order. Clean, yes, she tried, but nothing extra."

"Did your father have a trade?" Chaim asked. Knowing the answer, he said, "I'm sorry I asked." Chaim sat at his tea. The samovar was boiling. All was in order. As if for ever, and he felt like talking. "Come sit by me, Meir, there is nothing more for you to do, you got up before me, you stacked the wood, the fire is roaring, and it is early yet. We'll make it a holiday. I missed you."

Meir too was glad. He had slept well next to Chaim. A son next to his father – warm, reassuring. But then Chaim started, assuming Meir had gone back to his parents house for the seven days, "How are the little ones and your wayward father?"

"Oh, they are fine," Meir said, glad to have escaped telling the truth. He felt Ivan was his. His secret, his love. And with a sudden fear of loss, intrusion into what could not be shared, his defences were up. He also thought, "Chaim is jealous, he'll kick me out if he knew. He wants me to be his Chaje, cook for him, put his *Tefillin* out in the morning, brush his clothes, and warm his back at night. He teaches me and he is good to me, but I won't let him – this is my secret. I won't let him force it out of me." And he smiled at Chaim with lying eyes, as if he were his only love.

And Chaim believed Meir, who continued to be diligent, ran

to him at the slightest raising of an eyebrow, and took a scolding as if from a father. But he was more silent now, less ready to giggle, and preoccupied.

"What are you thinking about, Meir?" Chaim asked him one Friday night.

"I haven't studied," he replied. "I'll be the only Jew in Suczorno who will not have had a *Bar Mitzvah,* and it worries me."

But it wasn't that alone. He had in fact started to prepare himself and had set a deadline for around his fourteenth birthday. He did not know the exact date, though he was sure his birth had been registered in the Synagogue registry. No it wasn't that alone. And again he had to lie to Chaim. "It is nothing else than my studies."

But there were many things. He felt his manhood ripening lying next to Chaim. Warm and tense around the middle, he moved closer to Chaim's back and felt invited to do so. It worried him and he fell asleep determined to leave Chaim tomorrow. But he couldn't. Where to?

This time Chaim rose before him and let him sleep, as if aware of danger. Split the kindling and brought fresh rainwater from the backdoor barrel. It had rained at night; the air, pure and perfumed, smelling like rose soaps one brought home from Poland, made Chaim light-headed and joyful. He hummed a benediction, washing his hands and face in the enamelled bowl. He had slipped into his cotton trousers and open-necked shirt, wound the *Tefillin* around the left arm and forehead. Hebrew sounds voicelessly sung, familiar reassurance of the Eternal, poured from his lips. A meaning of life, a daily return, a momentary devotion, it was as necessary as the piece of bread to come. A submission to the will of God, whose partner the Jew was. Chaim took the *Tefillin* off in the reverse, folded them in the pattern that almost folds itself, and stored it in its home, a velvety, shiny, daily handled pouch, with the shield of David embroidered on top. Chaje's handiwork. "Dear woman," he said, not giving it another thought. Then he hurried to put fresh water in the bowl after discarding his own, and called gently, *"Yingale* – my little boy – the beggar is already in the seventh village – this morning I've done all the work for you."

And Meir rose to the scent of tea, the air warmed by the humming samovar, saw his day clothes folded neatly, Chaje-style on the bed stool, and stripped the scratchy night-shirt. Naked for a little moment, he shivered, feeling Chaim's eyes between their lids furtively turned towards him. Meir grabbed his shirt from the stool, pulled it over his head, and noticed all the rips repaired. Yes, Chaim was a master with the needle. All that Meir knew, he had learned from him. Chaim should have been a tailor, not a furrier. But then a needle comes in handy in any trade, Meir thought. His shirt too was washed and ironed. Meir fought with choking tears, wanting to kiss Chaim to say thanks, and at the same time desiring to rush out of the door and run. Something he had felt, always, as a little boy in the poor huddle-house of his father, to run into the fields, for a breath of air on wintry days even, when ice-crystals inhaled pricked his lungs.

A humming samovar, a morning sun coming from the Southeast through the single window, all promised a fine summer day – yet he wanted to run. But he turned to Chaim and said, "You should not have done all that for me, but thank you anyway." Tried to avoid hearing the reply, "You are mine, *Yingale,* my child, my kid-brother." Tried to avoid sensing the tone of love, and did not totally succeed. He washed in the bowl prepared for him, finished dressing, and joined Chaim at the table for his tea. A sugar cone, broad at the base and moving up to a tall tip, that Meir had never seen in the house before, was proudly displayed on an earthen plate. Chaim, handing Meir a small spatula, said, "Scrape the cone and you can take all the sugar you want." And he showed Meir how to move the small spatula from the top down to get the fine crystal powder into the plate at the bottom.

So they sat, both unable to speak, scraping their sugar, filling their cups with hot water again and again, breaking bread together, prune butter on top from a small labelled pot, until Chaim said, "Today, I'll teach you how to sew by hand a piece of cut-out lining unto the fur with the special big-ear needles I have received from Lemberg."

"Yes," Meir said, "thank you." He got up, busied himself by cleaning the table. Where can I run? he thought. It's ungrateful to leave such a kind master.

And he stayed for a whole year, until he was fully fourteen.

IT HAD GONE FAST, and he passed his *Bar Mitzvah* in front of a small crowd from the hindstreets of Suczorno. His own. He was of course alone, being older than the others, and tables in the Synagogue were not heaped with anything other than the customary caraway Schnapps, and wine, of course, *Challah,* and herring. He passed the *Torah* reading with *oy* and *vey,* but it was over. Chaim was there, smiling and supportive. But Meir was bitter. No one from the upper bank was there. Yes Yankel, the *Shoichet,* was there. Came and left without *Kiddush.* And Yankel had no power. And Meir swore he would build his house wherever he found a lot on the higher bank, to spite them all.

It was just an ordinary *Shabbat* morning service, to praise the Eternal, to read the portion of the week, and Meir accomplished the task and said a few words to address his parents. And after *Kiddush* – the blessing over bread and wine – it was over. But when he looked into the prepared plate for voluntary gifts, Meir was stunned. Anonymously, as it has to be according to the law, the givers had been generous beyond imagination. There were *zloty, rubles,* and two other coins, still shiny though rubbed with time, heavy with gold, and he held them in his hand for a moment. Tried to read the letters under the wreath-crowned head but couldn't. He had not studied Latin letters, but he made out the numbers, which seemed to him to be 1810 or 1811. From whom? Hindstreet Suczorno relatives, who couldn't even repair their clapboard-houses, for lack of wood or paint? From such as these, gold coins?

And he looked at Chaim. It was you, he thought, it's Chaje's money. She had been of a wealthy family from the upper bank, old traders, who had gone across Russia on the Transiberian – these were the evening-tales, after work was done, prayer and Synagogue, and Chaim, ready to reminisce, would seat himself near the one window. He loved the last rays of sunshine, coming from the west-end corner, and, "Come, *Yingale,* we'll talk," he would call to Meir, who would busy himself unnecessarily, hoping to escape the endless tales. Nonetheless he would hurry to sit at his feet. Stories of hardship beyond belief and the triumph over it –

"God forbid," Chaim would start, "the Almighty should put upon your shoulders what you could endure, what you could bear." Always, the adventures of Chaje's father, travelling deep into

Russia, connecting on way stations, from Jew to Jew and dealing in absolutely everything. With Russian authorities even. If matches were needed, he found them; if leather gear for horses, he brought them from Poland; skins of lynx and beaver from Siberia – endless. But always, the great Transiberian and down the Volga on a boat. These stories, Friday night after Friday night, reinvented themselves with the sight of the coins. Images of the Governor of the island Sakhalin handing two gold coins to Chaje's father Nathan as a payment for a particular service, Chaim couldn't recall which – and the triumph of having stayed alive. How good it was to be born a Jew, with the law imbedded in one's heart and the necessity to worship God.

All Chaje's stories, embroidered still further, had come down to Chaim on their Friday nights before bedtime. Theirs being a childless home, there were not new histories to be spun, and Chaje, herself an only child, spoke of her father's adventures as if they had been her own. Livelier, they were as full of terror and delight as a second-hand life could imagine.

And then down to Meir. He stood with the two gold coins heavy in his hand, assailed by pictures of the prisoners for life walking at the break of dawn, clanging their heavy leg-irons, pulling them on their way to the mines. And the Governor of Sachalin, rewarding Nathan the Jew, for God knows what. Second-hand pictures, brighter than lived ones, burdened with the fate of others, had come down, pure, shiny, and unaltered as gold.

Going home that *Shabbat* afternoon, after herring and Schnapps, the blessing of his errant father was still with him. His father, who had appeared, thank God, somehow dressed for the occasion. Meir, a mother's son, did not expect him, had seen him rarely, except on some Friday nights. A *Luft*-existence, making a life out of air, Suczorno-style, with no skill whatsoever and only an occasional deal; yet his father spoke the ancient Aramaic words – "May He turn His shining countenance towards you, protect you, and give you peace" – with grave reverence. Meir was deeply touched. Looked at him, for the first time perhaps. To give him credit perhaps for having fed him and the many little ones that came – as God had prescribed – with his meager means. He saw his father's face, furrowed forehead, a worried line between the eyes, and he sensed in the words – learnt and repeated – the dignity which the covenant lent to a Jew. Even the poorest of them. No matter.

On that late *Shabbat* afternoon, Meir and Chaim sat themselves across from one another. Meir, in Chaje's chair, hands folded in his lap. As if all had been done, he said suddenly to Chaim, as if in continuation of something before, "I know, one does not talk about money on *Shabbat* and I will not go to collect it until tomorrow, but Chaim, these are Chaje's gold coins, are they not?"

And Chaim made a mysterious face and said with a hidden smile, "You're my heir. I do not have anyone else. I'm a poor man, you're my *Yingale,* and you cannot refuse it. Yes, they are. From perhaps Napoleonic times, more than one hundred years ago. Remember, lives are attached to these pieces of gold. Could they speak... Keep them in good health."

"Napoleon?" Meir asked.

And Chaim said, "Of course, Napoleon; Jews greeted him wherever he came. A crowned head. A promise of justice. We always bow to the crown. Jews prostrate themselves before the throne and often are heard. We all know of Napoleon. You're young yet. Listen to the tales of his advance into Russia, and how we ran towards him to serve. But of course the Russians turned on us after his bitter defeat, with a fury not to be forgotten. So my *Yingale,* may you prosper and guard the coins to save a life!"

There was nothing more to say. The evening fell, rest and oblivion freed the soul from all that living, movements slowed, things were lifted, stored away, or prepared for the next day, with the automatic know-how of the body. It almost moves by itself, makes a bed, stretches the linen, brings the water in for a sip at night, murmurs the holy words as if on its own. All declines, the sun and the warmth of the body, as it cools slowly, hoping to forget, all muscles extend. And both men, the older and the younger one, stretched alongside without touching, descending into their own stillness, and slept without a good night.

The Marriage

MEIR COULDN'T REMEMBER, after he married Esther, the succession of years that followed. They had gone so fast. The parting from Chaim, the packing of his bags, the goodbyes from Jossel, his brother, and the last kiss of his mother. Especially the parting from Chaim. He had carefully packed his small leather trunk the night before and stored it under their bed, had planned his elopement, but couldn't make himself do it the next day. That he remembered. And the tearful parting.

"Was I not good to you?" Chaim had asked. "Have I not treated you like my own flesh and blood?"

"Yes, and more than that. You taught me everything I know and my going has nothing to do with you – it is – just forgive me!"

Chaim had watched Meir secure the gold coins in a hand-sewn leather pouch, watched him pull it shut with a threaded string and hang it around his neck. Every skill he has, Chaim thought, I have taught him. I have cut these leather strips from the side of skins, have shown him how to join them without fraying, tucking the ends under, Chaim thought, feeling his tongue dry and gall rising. He had watched Meir intently to find fault with his sewing, and couldn't. The design of the seams, running parallel lines and sometimes obliquely crossing, were certainly Meir's. And Chaim couldn't help but smile between these unwept tears at his *Yingale;* and with a voice unsteady, coming closer to arrange the pouch a little better around Meir's neck, he said, "Go with God, may He protect you! Remember, you're my only heir. All I have is yours. Tomorrow I'll go to the Synagogue and have it witnessed and sealed that after I die Chaje's and my property is yours to use. Go, my son, go with God."

Meir still fingered that pouch from time to time. A piece of memory. It was always with him, on his journeys at the side of Esther, or when alone on business trips, always around his neck, under his shirt. No seam broke, ever: it was designed to hold coins, had inner pockets that sealed on their own, overlapped when turned so nothing could be lost. The beaver string, sheared of its fur, shinier with years, never showed any wear, warmed to his skin. So Chaim's presence persisted, but the years in between faded, rolled into one.

Upon leaving Chaim, Meir had first gone to see Ivan, had worked in the fields, was known as "the Jew for hire," for a few days of work and nights in the shed and meals with the men. He had no aversion to their food and grew strong on it; or perhaps on the true physical labour. Or both.

One long, full summer's work changed Meir. No thought

other than the morning before-sunrise prayer. His link and reassurance. Not for God to be on his side, and not for help, but to know who he was, the *Bar Mitzvah* lines sprang from his lips, a reconnection, a silent partnership reinforced with the rising sun.

"A Jew is never alone," Meir felt one morning when cutting his side-locks and looking like every other Gentile. "A Jew is never alone, as long as his covenant with the Eternal is not broken."

This summer had transformed a young Jew into a man. Brown hair and tanned skin, muscled arms from swinging the big hay forks, he lived his double life with defiance, and said to Ivan one night, sitting on a bale of hay, eyes towards the stars, "I love your people. Without you, Ivan, I would never have known the way you live. Outdoors. Not like us, who sit around tables, teachers pounding letters into our poor childish heads. I always ran away. Opened the doors and ran. Even on bitter winter days. But where can a Jew run? He'll always return to his letters. We're just so ancient. And I love your youth."

He drank his first vodka that night. Did not like the burning throat, but swallowed.

Encouraged by Ivan, his brothers accepted Meir good-naturedly and chuckled at this rarity, to see a Jew work in the fields and work harder, more silently, than most. The women liked him, but he kept apart. Finally on a Sunday's rest, singing and storytelling, the saga of Ivan's fur jacket broke.

"So you made it? Didn't you?"

"Not entirely. I just sewed the beads –"

The next night after work, he showed them the proper furrier way to use a needle.

All that he remembered. But the years across the river west and back to Suczorno blurred into one, with a sudden spark here and there of an image, an encounter, or a deal. He was good with money. Needed no writing down of accounts. He had a love of numbers, it was a game to practice during the hours on the road or at night at an inn many years later.

"WHAT ARE YOU MURMURING?" Esther would ask at night.

"I made our accounts; yours in fact," he would say and would come up with a number very close to what she had anticipated. "You see," he'd say, "I learned to be orderly when at Chaim's. I saw order for the first time. It is the most beautiful thing in a man's life, I thought then, living in Chaim's and Chaje's orderly world. I made patterns of beads, assembled them, crossed them, took some off, put them on the side, mixed numbers and colours, and sudden forms and shapes appeared on hats or coats that I worked on; patterns I had never suspected existed. It's a funny thing to look over one's shoulder, as if one were another: a stranger doing wonderful things. This is how I learn, watching myself solve a self-made puzzle, and as it creates itself, new doors open mysteriously, steps are taken without knowing where to, and you feel a guiding hand. All unexplainable. But you look at your handiwork with awe and a sense of wonder, as it lies before you formed and on its own. Is it God, order, and beauty intertwined? And so accounts do themselves in my head. I just watch as numbers become squares, triangles, rounds, and suddenly roses. Petals, as far as the core."

"My husband is a poet is all I can say. I love you for it, and certainly your skills come in handy. I'm good at money, too, counting comes easy, but not as good as you are. Never." And so they were a team.

All this was years beyond the day he returned, still a young man of twenty-one, to his hometown Suczorno. He had to, because there was only so much a poor Jew could do among the Gentiles. One remained what one was, with side-locks – *Peyoth* – on or off; in the clothes of a wandering journeyman even, one remained in contract, telling God who He is every morning of one's life. And calling Him the Master of the Universe, and that He is one and all is One, was enough to hold one bound to Him. His greatness, eternity, the even-handedness of His laws proclaimed every morning, and He stood in front of you created, resplendent in glory, crowned the only King imaginable. To serve. No matter if one's back was straight, upright as Meir's was now, and his legs carried him as if he were a feather or bent over one's studies.

It was night when he arrived in Suczorno, making the last kilometres on foot. Coming from the west and weary at this point, he had knocked at the last house on the upper bank. Jews do not open their doors to strangers. He heard a commotion, a creaking rising, the shuffling of feet, but saw no sign of a candle lit. So he tried again, and calling with his mouth very close into the lock, "I'm Meir ben –" he heard the opening scratches of the door and said whisperingly, *"Shalom Aleichem,* may peace be with you."

And they let him in, bedded him somehow, without any words exchanged or any recognition of each other.

Meir had looked back on those crucial days of his return to Suczorno many, many a time; when laying wooden boards into fine patterns for the foundation of his new house on the upper bank of the river, next to Yankel, the *Shoichet's,* and when he had brought his bride in to share it. There was always a return to these first days as a stranger in a known world. Being another *self,* he had to relearn all that he had known, the ways, the daily encounters with people's faces, their unchanged customs – a voice in Synagogue, raspier, older, but placeable somewhere into his childhood. These early, unconscious, lived days, where there was no reckoning or specific expectation, were deeply imbedded into grooves that had furrowed, and now sprang to recognition.

The smell came with it. Poverty. It smelled like itself; there was none like it.

When he heard, one *Shabbat* morning, the voice of the old *Gabbai,* all of the Suczorno hindstreets were back: gabardines brown with age, shining green at the edges, trailing in the wet – and the tobacco man-smell. Indefinable, recreating itself in Meir's memory. When only five, he'd first felt what he knew now to be his fear of growing old: the weakness in the knee, the shuffling, and the clothes without a name, smelling of garlic! It drove him out and into the fields at the edge of town. He had loved his mother's father, who grew weaker by the day; he had watched him. The old man's eyes red-rimmed and running over, his knees bent, pants slithering around them, and above all the tobacco smell, all were back – at the voice of the *Gabbai,* the all-round religious helper in the Synagogue. His love also. The piece of sugar on his tongue the old man had saved and rescued for him out of a torn pocket, mixed with the salt in his throat, and all were back as he prayed that morning in Suczorno.

But Meir had good reason to sing God's praises. He had been provided for. All that Chaim had ever owned, his house on the low north-end of the river, his bedstead, table, pots, pans and crockery, right down to Chaje's broom, had been properly recorded. All was his now. It was a modest property, if not poor, even by Suczorno standards, but it was a beginning.

Chaim had wasted away after Meir's leaving. Did not work, take a new apprentice or rent out Chaje's side of the bed. He had fallen ill with a high fever and the spitting of blood no one had a remedy for. But over the five years of Meir's absence, Chaim had marked every item. A letter within the *Tefillin* pouch was a revelation, when read at a *Shabbat* morning service the week after Chaim's death. A language of devotion, reserved for the Eternal, of course, and respect for Chaje, his wife. But unmistakable words of love for Meir, his apprentice and heir. Tender, simple words. "My *Yingale*, my little boy, my child. My only pleasure on earth. The apple of mine eye. My *Tallith* – embroidered and hand-stitched by my dear wife, Chaje – wear it in good health and pray with my own *Tefillin* on your arm and head – Then I can die in peace." Hearing these words addressed to the absent Meir, the congregation sobbed. They had kept everything religiously and waited for Meir's return.

He would not move into Chaim's house. Not only because of the invading daily memories, and not because of guilt of having neglected when still an apprentice to clean a fur with solvent, pretending he had done it. No. But he hated the sweet smell of this cleaning benzene Chaim had learnt to use. It made Meir sick. It spread through the air in fine invisible droplets, and his head spun. The worst of it was that he started to long for it. A feeling of drunkenness, of losing control took hold of him, almost with the first whiff of this fluid. And Meir decided, when he couldn't even pray or think of God – for the longing of it – that something eerily wrong inhabited the air. It wasn't for him. And he had lied about using it. It was not his habit to lie; it having been drilled into him that lies are seen and heard and there are no trenches to hide in, so lies did not come easily. But the swooning light-headedness, a nauseous desire for that loss of self or who one was, made Meir take this decision. He also recalled going one day to the well-corked bottle for an occasional breath; so he decided to break with it and not tell Chaim, and just brushed the skin of lamb with a special comb brush thoroughly.

Many other forbidden morning thoughts would tie him to the past. Emerge and trouble him. No, he would not want the house, with all the slow steps of early adolescence recalled. So Meir sold it to the first reasonable bidder, including that marked, last broom. What he kept was the *Kiddush* cup – copper showing by now through the silver on top – the *Siddur,* Chaim's private prayer book, the leather-strips for his arm and the law for his forehead, Chaim's *Tefillin.* That was enough for daily or hourly reminder. Perhaps it was not what Chaim had in mind.

But this was his life, he thought. Besides, he had sworn to himself as a young man that he'd live on the high bank; so he sold it all. There was plenty for a start on the other side of the creek. A small building he found next to Yankel's on the east end of the town, demolished it, retained all the sturdy posts, all the brick, left the old oven in place, and built around it. Suczorno helped. The old *Shoichet* in his last days, Yankel, and the *Shklovke.*

Meir had what few sported in Suczorno, a sense of beauty. For him it was a necessity, a daily need, a desire for delight. He wanted an airy house, without the accumulation of the poor and cheap crowding one another. Objects should breathe, he said, or they can't live and neither can I. A shed at the back of the house he wanted. Tools he acquired, polished until they shone, arranged according to size; and even after bringing his bride Esther into the house and going with her as far as Odessa to get all sizes of the sharp diamond-edged cutters she used in her trade, he continued to keep things sparse, orderly, visible, recognizable at first sight.

Esther had loved it when she first entered his house, a not shy but a silent sixteen-year-old with a cultured, learned eye for beauty. Esther assessed the young man fast as the only one she could have possibly considered.

Arriving in Suczorno, she and her travelling merchant companions had stayed at an inn, Suczorno-style, where an elderly couple, trying to make a living, rented two rooms "furnished." Not exactly deserving that title, the rooms had rough home-built bedsteads with clean linen, bed tables with candlesticks, and chamber pots for winter days. Tea was served in their kitchen, next to a blue-orange brick and tile oven. Mornings only. Esther would never forget these first days, and remained devoted to the couple all her life.

These were Chaskel's parents. Simple Suczorno folk. Devout, alert, a hand-to-mouth daily life, but living it with humour. And seeing an occasion to earn a little extra, they had gone out of their way to help the two merchant matchmakers. They brought pictures of young eligible bridegrooms – having done some matchmaking themselves from as far away as Kiev – but suggested a "fabulous" match, Meir, whom they recommended as skilled, hardworking, handsome, and above all, being the heir to Chaim and owning a house on the "famous" upper bank of Suczorno Creek.

The mother of Chaskel, Judith, the hostess of the so-called "inn," had appraised Esther with the experienced and shrewd look of the old, as beautiful, learned, and perhaps a troublemaker. But she thought it might be a good match for Meir, whom Suczornoers thought of as self-reliant and good-natured. Of course, there would be some money in it for Judith, if not a great deal, when eventually the *Ketubah* – the marriage contract – was written and sealed on her kitchen table. And so it was, with handshakes all around.

The scholar handwriting the *Ketubah,* specifying all the obligations of the future husband and all the conditions of a possible separation, decorated the borders of the document with birds, leaves, and stars, creating a true piece of art. He was young, and Esther could not remember which of Moishe's sons he was. A simple, beautiful wedding was to follow, and so Esther entered Meir's house.

It was not all roses. Fearful, having always kept to the company of men in his growing-up-years, Meir had avoided women's eyes. Shunned them. Unknown territory, they frightened him. I'll keep myself chaste until marriage, he'd said. But in these almost forgotten years he had worked in the fields, worn peasant garb, eaten whatever there was, and the peasant girls had teased him. He spoke Russian in Bessarabia, Romanian in the Moldava as if he were one of them, and Ukrainian from the day he slept in the shed with Ivan. But, "No, I cannot dance," he'd said to the girls. "I have no sense of rhythm – I have two wooden legs." And he'd sat with the men, drinking.

Meir was an easy target for the matchmakers. He looked like a virtuous man, went to regular Synagogue services after his return, built his house, set up an "accounting" business no one in Suczorno had ever heard of. But he called it that. Rented other people's horses and wagons, went into the Ukrainian villages east and west of Suczorno, the Romanian ones south, and the Russian ones north, to sell his expertise. Numbers he knew, and he calculated the amount of seed necessary for surface sowing. The peasants knew everything anyway, without numbers or surveying skills.

But in the first summer after his house stood, he rescued Ivan's family crop. Either Meir was lucky and the heavens sent all the rain needed by a very dry prairie land, or he did assess it correctly. Right after the last snow had gone he went out to Ivan, and using his "forgotten" years' experience – having gone as far as the Prut River – he said to his friend, "It's early, but I advise you to seed now and not wait. And use more rye this year, especially where the land is low and water accumulates." He spoke with such authority, yet prayed silently to have been right, lest disaster strike.

Ivan's crops stood in splendour and Meir's renown spread. But that year everyone else's crop was poor or failed altogether, and the peasants started to say, "It is the Jew's fault. He is in league with the devil. How did he know – why did Ivan trust the Jew?" However, the next year was good and peasants came to his house in Suczorno either for advice or with gifts of a jute-spun bag of rye or a basket of eggs.

Meir also kept a repair shop going. Furs, leathers, heavy woollen rugs, winter gabardine he knew how to repair with needles and threads, according to the weight and colour of the material. He mended or re-embroidered worn spots and made enough money now to lend on interest to Jew and non-Jew. It was dangerous business, but he thought nothing of it, relying on his memory number-games.

This was the time that Esther, a sixteen-year-old business-child-woman appeared in Suczorno. It was a natural match.

ESTHER WAS NOT GIVEN TO PREMONITION. "Nonsense," she always said, "utter *Narrishked* – a fancy sort of idiocy people are addicted to." A well exercised, cool reasoning forbade her the speculation of the yet unlived next day. But later in their married life, growing older, something unexpected happened to her: it seemed irrational, but it persisted.

One day she turned west to watch the sun sink into its night, when sitting on the promontory, that lofty stone above Suczorno river, and she felt the end of things. A premonition. A slowing down of the morrows. Or imagining none at all. They were all yesterdays.

The last year had not been that good. She had avoided Meir, for some inexplicable reason; had changed her bedtime hour, and dressed or undressed behind her Chinese screen, and lied when asked for an explanation.

Meir had never been a very passionate man. "Soft, thoughtful, and wonderfully tender," Esther smiled when images of their disparate attempts to love one another in the first months of marriage emerged. With their partnership, their curiosity about each other, something one could call "real love" took over.

But today. Why this feeling of loss? Esther wondered. Where did I fail? Accusations sprang from her lips with immediacy and fury. "You Meir – this – and you Meir – that!" Where from? Why the sudden gall on her tongue – then and now? Just fleeting questions, unutterable with a dry throat and a sudden "knowing" about the irretrievable.

Esther sat high above the river, felt the stone a flying ship suspended in mid-air, and she did not know how to hold her legs without dangling them above water. Here she wouldn't dare, so she supported her body resting on her right arm, legs inland. Covered them carefully with her black wool, ankle-length skirt, and let herself slip back to the time she dangled her legs fearlessly above the Danube, when only seven, perhaps eight – oh, she couldn't remember.

Peasants had brought her back when they had fished her out of the river. "It's the Jew's daughter," they'd said. "Look at her fancy dress."

The sun moved further down, caught the end of river, painted it a red and fiery yellow. She pulled her legs up, rolling them into her skirt, as if into a *Knäuel* – a spool of yarn – and then untangling herself, rose painfully.

No premonition, but a persistent slowness, retarded the next step. She had a pretty black shoe, showing from under the skirt; stared at it in the waning light and thought it had stalled on its own, as if not wanting to touch Suczorno earth. She stood rooted. A backward glance into the river, into the now darkening stillness, brought back her longing for it, for her jump into the Danube.

She shivered and turned fast.

Reuwen: The Longed-For Son

Suczorno, split straight through by the running river, never truly fell apart. The Synagogue held them in the middle and the well brought them together. *Briths,* marriages, and funerals. They talked, and reason prevailed, most of the time. But not always. Because of principles, which muddied the water between them. The creek darkened, and one could not see the stones or the living green in it. The well grew dry. Women were set against women, men against men. Only earthquakes could heal them, an Easter *pogrom,* an edict from Moscow, or news from Warsaw. None of this was good for Jews. The year was turning for the Christian world. It was an alien, incomprehensible world. Big, powerful, and inscrutable; except for the fear, this was understood, so then they stood together. Messiahs, true and false, new Western ideas, all were bewildering, disturbing the old ways, and Suczorno fell into camps. Not murderous ones, but not loving.

The year was old by Jewish reckoning, and Suczorno counted the years in thousands. A big number for a little people to live up to. A free people, though. Suczorno-ers were poor as the very ground they lived on – even the so-called rich on the upper bank – but they were free. Serfs they were not, like all those hard working, soil digging, and good people around them. Their allegiance was to God alone. Not to the Czar, not to the king. Of course, they had no shield from hunger or assault either. Exposed to the clubs, torches, and firearms of every invader, and with the strife within of course, with old ways and new ways crossing roads, Jews prayed for the Redeemer to come, to give a sign, to send the messenger Elijah, the precursor.

A stranger coming to town, a pious Jew even, setting up residence, a woman not cutting her hair, not going to the *Mikvah* – there was strife, judgment, and no one talked to her. The "righteous" ones moved a little away from her on the back benches of the Synagogue, as had happened to Naomi, the mother of Srul. It took a long time until acceptance came and the furore died down. As was the case with the arrival of the pious Samuel ben Sharon. Where from? Why here? In Chaskel's house? There was suspicion. Hannah was barren, now she had a redhead boy. There were no redheads in the family. Talk, talk. Everyone knew her great-great-grandparents. How did one suddenly have a red-haired baby? But then the boy grew, was very handsome, with strange orange hair against the matte side of olive-leaves skin: he looked exotic. And the boy was a scholar, fast to grasp, to interpret. No higher respect was given in Suczorno than to the learning of the law, *talmudic* thought; thought turned to all sides and inside out, to appraise and praise the nature of God.

Reuwen. The redheaded son of Hannah and Chaskel. A *Wunderkind.* Who read the *Torah* at the age of nine like a rabbi, and suddenly the town marvelled. He played every fiddle in Suczorno he could lay his hands on. Any fiddle of any size, with one string or four. Where did it come from? No one had taught him. On the evening of his *Bar Mitzvah,* after all had dispersed, the six true friends sat around the long, rectangular table across from each other to talk of love and the future, to recall the past, and to thank God for the guidance so far given. And having reached the threshold of manhood, Reuwen disclosed to all that he would be a fiddler. A musician. The elders were stunned. A what? You want to live by it? Fiddling you do after study, after work! What is this word "musician"? Who has ever heard of it?

The rabbi sitting across from Reuwen said, "My beloved son, I have reserved for you the next four years of study. You will be my successor, you'll sit on my side, you'll learn to be just, because in Suczorno and wherever Jews live, peace and justice has to reign between them. You'll sit on my right side next to Mordechai's son, whose *Bar Mitzvah* we all have witnessed a short while ago. Not as brilliant as yours, Reuwen, but a very fine effort. Reuwen! My son! Do not throw your life away! May the Eternal watch over you!"

Reuwen was silent. Then he thanked the rabbi. He realized, he said, that a rabbi had to be everything in a community. Often a judge, between man and woman, property against property, libel against truth. Yes, he would study the law. Yes, all his life, to his last breath, he promised. But, No, he did not see in himself the ability to judge without failing. And the rabbi intervened to say that Reuwen was young yet and he'd learn to weigh right from wrong. No, was the answer, he'd exalt in the beauty of the psalm, he'd set it to music in their ancient notes, but he would never learn to have dominion over the lives of others.

All were surprised and worried. How would he know who he was and what he'd be able to do as a grown man? But they did not insist. Not to spoil such a glorious day. With good wishes and the uttering of mutual respect, all hurried home.

The town grew still. After a day of celebration, food, and wine, a June day like no other, the town grew still. There had been rumours of holiness and certainties of demonic power, but the day of Reuwen's *Bar Mitzvah* put an end to all of it. A strangeness remained, there was no category that Reuwen fitted in. A scholar – a future rabbi – yes, his speech after the readings was full of quotes from the *Talmud,* reverence to Father and Mother, and the promise of fulfilling a Jew's obligation towards community and Synagogue, as every adult would assume. Yes, there was all of that, but the strangeness intensified when, after a day or two, the news spread that Reuwen had asked his parents permission to leave. Where to? A thirteen-year-old? What connections did he have? What money? Where would he go? It was puzzling and worrisome. But he continued to go with his father wherever prayer was necessary, be it as a minion to be the tenth man, for a burial, or at services, high holidays or minor ones – and the years passed.

Ruewen had one day crossed the bridge and knocked at Esther's door. She had seen him approach. She had always watched the lower bank, in some undefined hope – or one she would not consciously accept – that Reuwen would emerge. Her eyes had followed him, she had seen him grow, and had at times felt a frightening pang in her breast, loving him as she did.

He had knocked at the door with a crooked smile of shyness on his boyish face and said, *"Shalom,* dear Esther, I have come to ask you if you could be of help to me."

Esther pulled him in, sat him across from her on the window bench, and said, "Anything that is in my power, of course. I am here for you."

And Reuwen, reassured, said simply, "I have an old fiddle with three strings, the fourth Yankel has somewhat – well it's a chicken gut and I am afraid it sounds like it. I want to go abroad to find great teachers. I could go east or west, it does not matter. Let me work for you for two or three years to earn enough for a start. I cannot beg. But please, would you take me into your service?"

This was heaven-sent for Esther. She had longed for this moment, had played and replayed this conversation. He had come of his free will, she thought, and it made her unutterably happy. She, who had always said, No children, who needs them, they're noisy, interfere in married life, are ill, and often die. Heartache! Who needs it? Until she saw the boy on the hand of Chaskel, his father, on a *Shabbat* morning. They walked leisurely, books tucked on the inside of their right elbows. Passing them one morning, Esther had caught the hum of a *Shabbat* tune, familiar to her from her earliest days. Having been the only child, and reared almost as a son would have been, with knowledge of

Torah and its obligations, she knew it well. And both were humming, the father and the son, who was about four or five at the time.

She had stopped a step behind them so as not to overtake them, listening in to truly hear what she thought she heard. And it was harmony. Chaskel humming the tune or whistling it through his teeth and Reuwen, singing an absolutely correct third down. Down and not up. It was accurate but strange; the sound, unobtrusive as only humming could be, shook her. She continued to walk behind them, anonymous for a while, until she stepped forward with her *"Geet Shabbes."* And hurried on.

The tune pursued her. Esther hummed, then spoke the verse, to bring the other voice in. But couldn't. I'll call him, she thought. No, I won't. I will send him away to train his voice. One day, God willing!

Then she smiled derisively, thinking of Suczorno, What do they know of great cantors? What do they know of a great service? They have never seen the gates of heaven open, when a great voice chants in view of it and the congregation trembles. Esther had heard them in her childhood, once with her father in Lemberg and once in Czernowitz even – but at home also in Ismail. Great singing. True adoration and the call to repentance.

Looking at Reuwen now, almost fifteen, and seeing him in her house having come of his free will, she was overjoyed, but could not find the right words it seemed to her. But then she suddenly said, "Come tomorrow, right after prayers, I will take you as my apprentice, teach you to hold a scale, to weigh gold and precious stones. Then in two or three months, you have to learn the art of accounting. Strict reckoning. No cheating. Proper profits, but no cheating in numbers and none in quality of the merchandise –

well, of course not. But there must be a promise. A year's hard work for me. And then you will have earned enough for a new violin. Reuwen, I've heard you sing. You will be the greatest cantor a service has ever witnessed!"

Embarrassed at her exaggerations, he blushed, "Perhaps not the greatest, but perhaps one that truly renders homage to God and His word."

The pact was made. Reuwen stayed for a little while longer and was treated to gooey Turkish sweets. Esther still had *Rahat* reserved for special occasions. She had not been abroad for a time and her reserves grew thinner, but for Reuwen nothing was too precious.

"Take another little cube, the red one is raspberry, I think." Clad in a haze of white powder sugar, the cubes felt soft to touch, but were resistant to it. Reuwen took one, held it between thumb and index finger, and then lit into it. Esther watched him with joy she had never felt before. And she urged him to have one more.

"That was wonderful," he said. "But no more. It is so good – and hurts just a little at the gum." A glass of cool water, always served with *Rahat,* he drank eagerly now, smiled, and with a "Thank you, I'll come early tomorrow, as soon as prayers are over," he left.

Esther had found her purpose in life: Reuwen's schooling; to do something for the young. To see a young life unfold. It surprised her how fast Reuwen learned. But above all, she had not imagined the very life of the young so close to hers. The everyday. A turn of Reuwen's face towards her, inquiring, hoping for acceptance or praise perhaps, was the reward. The simple turning of this handsome oval face towards her with the quick eagerness of the young made her shiver. Her desire to nurture, to be important to this life, to play a role – all of that she had to discipline, not to do too much, not to lecture all the time. But she wanted to show him something Reuwen had not seen before, the categorizing of gems, the use of a magnifying glass of graded intensity, when observing a stone.

"Starting with an all-over look, Reuwen," she said, "please slowly reduce the surface and increase the strength of the ground glass."

He showed talent in organizing, arranging into patterns; he understood the emphasis on purity, design, colour, translucency; and he constructed a small device to hold the candle at a certain angle so the light would reflect differently from each side of the cut stone. And he sang while working.

Esther listened with her heart and feared its beat. She loved him. Too much perhaps. In a forbidden manner, perhaps, longing for him, watching his coming across the bridge, with his gentle swaggering now, the late-teenage lankier legs. "How grown-up in a year you have become," she said then.

Meir also loved him: there was just no resisting Reuwen's presence. But Meir often felt, if not anger, then a pang of jealousy, when watching the flushed face of his Esther instructing Reuwen. When it came to accounting, which was Meir's duty until now, he heard Esther say, from time to time, "Leave it, Meir, Reuwen can do it." It angered him to be replaced by this young man, whom even he had fallen for. "Not replaced," she said to Meir one day when she had clearly seen his displeasure, "and not displaced, no one can displace my husband, but let Reuwen learn the trade, and when we're old, since we're childless, he can be a support perhaps."

On Reuwen's fifteenth birthday, Esther crossed the bridge to the lower bank. It was a Friday night after supper and prayers when she knocked at the door of Chaskel and Hannah's house. She had waited, and looking diagonally across from the higher bank, had seen them returning from Synagogue. Entering the house, she bid them *"Geet Shabbes,"* and after a few minutes of sitting down, being offered a glass of wine or tea and refusing it with thanks, she said, "I will come straight to the point. Dear friends, the time has come to offer Reuwen the promised reward." Esther lowered her voice, took a breath to sound untroubled, but could not hide her emotion from Chaskel and Hannah, who both sat upright in their chairs, fearing her.

They knew what Esther had come for. A sense of loss, of abduction, this is what they felt. Reuwen had talked every day about Esther and Meir. Returning to share the family meal the night before, Reuwen had – almost at the door– said, "Esther –" and was not allowed to finish the sentence.

"Are we not enough for you anymore?" Hannah's voice, although not loud, was edged with pain. "Is our potato *kugel* and the filled *kishka* not good enough for you? Are the delicacies from the East more important to you than what we have to offer?"

"Mother, no, of course not, but there is a world out there..." and no more was said.

Now they sat stiffly, waiting for Esther to speak.

"I have business in Krakov," she said, "where the finest goldsmiths and silversmiths are. I will introduce Reuwen to them as my representative and heir." She paused to watch the faces of both Hannah and Chaskel. "And I will also look around to see if I can find an old, still worthy violin for Reuwen. A gift to Reuwen from Meir and myself."

The parents, stunned by Esther's generosity, could not find

words. But then Hannah broke into tears and said, "Dearest, most esteemed *Chavereth,* it is more for the recognition of our son's worth, his work, and his God-given gifts that I cry, than for the fortune that has come his way through your goodness." And both thanked Esther and let her go with blessings.

But Esther felt she could not go on any journey – which for a Jew in Christian lands always holds the fear of death – no, she could not go anywhere before settling her debts. A business-woman knows her accounts. She knows the wrongs she has done, the profits she has made illicitly or having indulgently given way to jealousy.

I'm too passionate, she thought, I have to come to terms with my sins. I have killed a chicken with my own hands and thrown it upon Moishe and Leah's table to be eaten by Jews. My ears are still ringing, I can never forget my wrong. And she recalled little Sarah's wild shout, "It is my Pearly, my sweet one-eyed Pearly!" And it was.

Sarah bas Moishe, the famous *Haggadah* artist and illumina-tor, had long forgiven Esther. A mother of a tribe of wild children now, she remembered of course. There is no childhood pain a child forgets. But seeing Esther in Synagogue or at family occa-sions, Sarah gave Esther the honours she truly deserved. Esther had contributed money and expertise to keep the Synagogue, she had brought an ancient, restored *Torah* scroll, and had presented it to the community at the *Bar Mitzvah* of Sarah's oldest son. It was a penance without words, and Sarah knew it was for her.

At Sarah's thirty-fifth birthday there was a knock at the front door. Esther had never come of her own volition, and Sarah was overjoyed to see her. She bade her come in. Offered tea and cin-namon bread, which was accepted. The women sat across each other at the kitchen table – Suczorno fashion – glasses of tea in front of them, sugar cubes on a round plate, and fresh ground bark of cinnamon in the air – a rare thing to have in Suczorno. They sat silently for a while, with a little "Thank you" and "Please take" here and there, when, with the first sip of tea Esther said, "It was I who grabbed the chicken you called Pearly; it was I who killed it by wringing its neck. It was I."

"I know," Sarah said. "It is long over. We all do things unpleasing to the Lord when we are angered."

"It was not ritually slaughtered and your family ate it – I want to atone."

"You have," Sarah said, "You have brought beautiful *Torah* scrolls to enrich us all, and I felt it was for me, just for me! Which is a selfish thought. But I knew it was for me from you. Dear Esther, let's hug."

It was a lovely afternoon in Suczorno. Late afternoons do not move, as if expecting peace to come before its time. Dust settles, the air does not stir, the last glint hovers on the western end of Suczorno creek as it quietens for the night.

Esther had never seen the inside of Sarah's home. She registered not much order, colours, pens, and brushes everywhere. Earthen pots filled with water and brushes sticking out, resting there to remove the sticking ochre-earth; containers with gasoline or some other smelly lighting oil holding much finer brushes, stacks of boxes. It was disorderly.

I could not live like that, Esther thought, smiling at Sarah as if she had thought, how beautiful your home is, just the way I like it. But it was penance day, and evening was approaching, with the longing for having done "all" or "all done well." And Sarah too felt this hour consoling. As if the end of the day were the end of a long life, with a short halt, a moment looking back to review the past. And it was morning, and it was evening, and God felt His work was good.

"So we all feel at night," Sarah said, leading her guest to the door, not wanting her to stumble over the threshold that needed repair. "My children rush in and rush out, and a threshold takes only that much banging," Sarah said, holding on to her guest.

"I wouldn't know," came the voiceless reply, "I do not have any." A little stab of pain was there at the end. It seems it cannot be done without. Esther smiled at Sarah and left her with a last hug.

She stepped over that overly-used threshold into an air of peace and benevolence. A lowered sun, hovering over Suczorno creek as if arrested, made the sky rose-pink. Esther had done her duty as she saw it, and she turned towards the promontory over the creek to wait for the sun to set. She had seen this primordial stone from her west window, had watched all the children sit on it, throw stones at each other and into the creek, hide behind it on *Shabbat's* frolics; had seen it at night when it glistened in the western full moon – an enormous, fearful, black diamond.

Is it truly as huge as it seems, she wondered, jutting out into the creek without foundation, as if hanging suspended and on its own? It is frightening, ominous, I should run, she felt. I should just turn and go home. But she could not any more.

The sun darkened fast, swallowed by the few bushes, and made the stone take its descending glow and hold it. She hastened her step, ran towards it with the sudden passion one feels for one's early love. Sat down, facing the flow.

"It is the same. It is the dark diamond I sat on overlooking the delta of the Danube. It is the same," she said to herself. "And how peaceful it would be –"

Sitting on that high placed diamond, she felt as she had done as a child. It had been hard to be an only child, loved and cherished, always watched by someone, taught from morning until night. So hard to please the world! So she had jumped into the cool Danube.

She had heard Russian voices, peasants putting her to bed on their hot mud oven. And had heard them say, "This is the Jewish merchant's child. Someone must have pushed her into the river." But no one had.

They gave me tea and spoke soothingly in that lovely Russian mellow sound, invoking God, they packed me then into their woollens and brought me to my father's house. So Esther recalls. Yes, it has never left me. I'll jump... And she closed her eyes as the sun sank. Such peace. She felt no guilt at the thought. She had done penance; God would be gracious. And slowly she rose to see if there was any movement in these houses above the river, if sitting there had been recorded by eyes and ears. Or not. The stone had felt warm, homey and receiving.

She knew she was allowed to return, and directed her steps back to the east end of the row, hastening them to give herself purpose and plan when entering her front door. But hesitated. Held still for a moment, as if whispered to. Turned towards the back door, passing the western window she had installed for the sake of her Ismail childhood, and peered in to find the room in total disarray. The centre-placed table legs were up in the air, Reuwen's invention lay broken in the corner, and gems were scattered on the floor next to the lacquered Chinese box.

She shouted, "*Shemah Israel!*" ran now to the back to enter the kitchen door. It was locked, so she ran towards the front, and it was locked. She had no key in her pocket. Shouting, *"Gewalt, Gewalt!"* – Help! I fear there's been violence – she banged at the *Shoichet's* door. Ethel appeared, stunned by the intensity of the *"Gewalt!"* With no man around, they tried a rusty key or two, but none worked, and Esther alone stormed the kitchen door, flinging her full body against it until it broke, splintered with a crash, to fall upon her husband's dead body sprawled on the kitchen floor.

Meir had fallen, it seemed to her, first against the table; had held on to it to steady himself, unbalancing it in the process and turning it upside down, sending the gems he had been working at flying. Marks of disorder led to the kitchen. Where he had fallen. Or – No, she saw no sign of an intruder, and the door was bolted.

For the moment, there was so much to do: the twenty-four hours of preparation, the washing of the body by the "holy-company," the wrapping of it into a piece of linen and the placing of it into an unlathed box. Rich or poor alike. A Jew remained a Jew, no matter how well or how poorly he had lived. The *Kaddish* was said by the congregation, as there were no sons to sing it.

A will they had written out together, making them each other's heirs, was read to the congregation. A *Zedakkah* – a gift – for the new roof of the Synagogue and a tenth of what they had was to be distributed among the poor in the hindstreets of Suczorno, to Meir's own people, among whom he had been born. That finished the small scroll. There was no mention of Reuwen. Esther, when they were composing it together, had asked him – she had a finer, more secure Hebrew hand then Meir – to include Reuwen's name. Not as an adoptive son, as Chaskel and Hannah would never permit it, but as a possible heir to the house or at least a small endowment for study.

"We'll see," he had said, and, "Later," and, "We're not that rich, you know." It had made him angry. As usual, without words to follow, but with lowered lids over flashing eyes, he hurried to collect pen and paper, clearing the table, storing them in assigned places. It was message enough, Esther knew. There was nothing more to be had. And that night also, she had refused herself to him. All the evening was laden with the unspoken; the will itself, holding the past, uttering its last word. There was no other. A meal at that very table of leftover fried potatoes and soured cabbage, eaten with little attention to it, was a poor harbinger of the night to come. "Why do you dress behind the screen? Am I not your husband?" And Esther couldn't recall what she had answered, but would not forget his repeated call to join him. And her refusal.

It would weigh on her in the years to come. But for the moment, after seven days of mourning, and daily existence with its healing oblivion, Esther felt something unexpected. Deliverance. A freedom of sorts, to be her own person; and passing her front window, she looked across the creek. Reuwen.

It had surprised her. Her own violence and the suddenness of her assault on the door. "Where did that passion come from? I never have had any physical strength or −" It had surprised her and it stayed on unanswerable. "That I was capable of the irrational and that there was no controlling it." But though the scene, the sound of the crashing-down door, would often emerge unforeseen to frighten her, she had dealt with it. Pull yourself together. Suczarno watches every move.

Looking across, she could not discern any movement on the low side of the creek. The air descended; a dusty yellow curtain did not allow clear outlines. Light but whirly winds lifted the sandy surface in front of Esther's window; it unsteadied her and she sat down to watch the other side and think. No, not think. Just fret. She had never liked this dry prairie air and longed for the marshy Danube delta of her youth. A longing, a loneliness overwhelmed her.

The utter quiet of her house multiplied the sound of the late afternoon wind, and she heard a repeated flapping of the shed door. Disturbed, she rose to check it, found it open, and a shocking thought arrested her in her footsteps. The door had been unlocked, all through the time of Meir's death. I broke the *kitchen* door down! There was no need, went through her head. The shed door had been open all through.

She never used that door. It was Meir's, and all the images of that day were back, her walking by the window, the upside-down table, the amethyst collection on the floor – heavens! She had left Reuwen sitting at that table, pen and paper at hand, scale and weights in place. And she smiled without wanting to. He'd spent hours weighing, classifying. She had let him do her amethyst collection that tragic afternoon.

Reuwen? An argument? A struggle? All feeling of freedom, of deliverance from bondage, left Esther suddenly. All questions were back, and the mystery of Meir's death. Only now his absence was real, and not at the time of turmoil, of immediate need of action. No, there was no awareness then. Only now, after days of silence, she felt it in the early hours of the morning: the change of ritual and that the voice had gone. Very soft, it had been an undemanding sound but an insistent emotional presence; it could not be side-stepped. It was gone. His morning voice was particularly low, "Do you think we could expect tea very soon?" And she had hastened to do it because of the way he stood before her washed, dressed, and after prayers. It frightened her sometimes. There was rigid order in that voice, it suffered no delay, and she ran to silence it. Now, it was silenced and there was no comfort.

She was alone. And not delivered, but bound to the question "How?" Not hoping for an immediate answer, but looking for work to fill her time, she directed her steps towards the Shanghai cabinet where she had stored the scattered amethysts. She pulled the drawer slowly open and there they were in their small silver pan, all in disarray, exactly as she had swept them up from the floor around the fallen table. Along with amethyst dust, an unexpected button, splinters of wood, and the hand scale, strings if not torn just barely holding the two tiny turtle-amber cups. Absentmindedly she looked for a clue, and closed the cabinet drawer fast. Let it be, she thought. *Shabbat* was approaching.

She would be alone for the first time to light her candles and to thank God for "having reached that day," and she felt nothing. There was nothing to be thankful for. But having to do it calmed her. She dusted the table of all debris and suddenly noticed, when spreading the white tablecloth, a diamond or a semi-precious stone stuck in a joined corner. She removed it, not without effort, as it clung to the wood, and wondered for a short moment how it got there. But then let it drop into a bowl holding odd things.

Evening was falling: candles were lit in all of Suczorno at absolutely the same time of the setting sun. Controlled by one another, the women knew the exact daily changes of the shifting sun. Rabbis on both sides of the creek calculated the time to the very second and posted it on the Synagogue door, so there would be no guessing the exact moment. She hurried to light them, not to be late.

Thank God for the *Shabbat*. Just not to have to think of anything but His greatness. Strange, she thought. That I so despised this half-understood murmuring, that familiar weekly worship that speaks almost on its own. Strange to find it now a comfort, a release. The words seem to rise by themselves, without my will. Strange. For me everything had to be understood always, and had to make sense beforehand. Yet words spring now from my lips without obligation or intent, as if they were melodies that sang themselves.

And Meir's absence seemed more tolerable, less in need of an explanation. This was the *Shabbat*. And Esther dressed carefully, but more slowly than usual, thinking of going across the creek to the Synagogue, but did not truly intend to. All those women, everyone prying.

Esther knew the town had talked, and questions remained. Meir, so young, had never done anyone any harm. Since his return from his journeyman's travels, the subsequent building of his house, and marriage, he had been entirely to himself, never raising his voice in dispute over Synagogue affairs and always at Esther's side.

Why so young? Why so sudden? The "holy company" laying out the clean sheet to wrap Meir's body in had looked it over – as is usually done, not as if they would assume foul play – but they looked for anything improper, since every death in Suczorno was the death of everyone. One looked for signs of illness, threats from unsuspected quarters. It was a group fear, where everyone was everyone's body, a blending of egos and a learning; something new to add to ancient wisdom.

"I'm not going to Synagogue today," Esther decided. "This is God's day, I don't have to see man." She wanted a good day, not to look back or ahead. But she sat near the window and watched the lower bank, its comings and goings, without thought, the mothers and the children, the men still in Synagogue. Perhaps at their *Kiddush*.

One o'clock, she thought. I like the *Shabbat* in Suczorno. Everyone prays at one's own speed. There are no great cantors to fall into communal ecstasy and the day is long and slow. God is all hours.

And she rose from her window seat to go to her kitchen, when her eyes fell upon a small bowl holding a diamond fragment. And all was back. Weighing the stone, by cradling it in her palm to assess its blueness or yellowness, and holding it a little further from her left eye – the right had become hopelessly dim – she detected and also sensed with the skin of her palm the sharp end of a silver wire. Yes, she said. Yes, this is the stone I wanted to mount into a design of silver wire, because the diamond was almost a light amber, spotted and not particularly well cut. Yes, and I had succeeded in partly mounting it.

And Esther turned around, facing the table on which she had been leaning, bent to find the tabletop joint, felt along it with her finely schooled fingers, and pulled the silver wire from its leg. Stuck in that joint was the diamond's frame – a delicately knit and knotted "modern" design her father had called the "new art" of mounting. It was more squarish, less oval or round, creating intricate petals and stems all of wire; and the cheaper, fragmented, or slightly impure diamonds with a distinct rainbow sparkle set randomly as raindrops in between. The stone she held in her palm fitted right into the heart of the rose.

She freed the jewelled wire from the joint with a slight pull, and it suddenly struck her that she had not seen her "jeweller's awl plate" for a while. To restore and mend the piece, she would need this intricate tool, which she had bought one day in Lemberg. Made of steel, with descending awl holes, from perhaps five millimetres down to a thousandth, they sat all in a row. She had taught Meir to pull silver wires through them, to thin and stretch the wire, from the first and down through the smaller holes, until it reached the thinness and length that were just right and pliable enough for the design.

Where was the plate and where had she seen it last? It was not to be found, not in the shed among his tools nor in hers. More raindrops and some of the wire lay around, but not the plate. And her heart stood still.

Is it possible? How? No stranger ever entered Suczorno without the women inside their windows recording it. There was peace with the neighbouring villages south and east of Suczorno. Who? Jews? No. Esther ascribed it all to her afflicted mind. You have suffered too much, she said to herself. You feel guilty, and fear to have caused Meir's death. And you have. You were untrue, lied, you have hidden behind the Chinese screen not to show yourself undressing, knowing his love of it. You stunted his desire, kept to yourself and – longed for Reuwen. The name alone made her shiver. Reuwen – she nearly fainted.

It can't be true. A child of sixteen – his arms embracing my neck. I dreamt of him saying, "Thank you, my teacher, my adored teacher." I kept my hands locked into one another, lest my fingers find their way into his red curls. And I watched him come towards the house, up from the lower bank. I stood at the window, hidden, to feel heat rising to my cheeks, then I ran to open the door for him and stumbled, "Good, you have come on time, I have to go out." But didn't. I stayed to repeat yesterday's lesson.

And there I was hovering over this youth, inhaling his breath, admiring him. How he was so much better than I! He pulled the wire through those holes, stretching them well, yet not any more than necessary to construct coils, serpentines, curves of perfection.

There they were and I said, "Reuwen, we'll use some of these silver shapes tomorrow, perhaps, when we'll mount the raindrops into these roses." Yes, this is how it was. And he replied, looking up to me, who stood behind him, "Thank you, Esther, there is no greater teacher." I dreamt of Reuwen that night and it killed Meir. May God help me. I'll talk to the Rabbi, the poor one from across the creek, Shlomo ben – no, I won't. No one understands, or could. They'll tar and feather me, they'll chase me out of Suczorno, and they'll call me "whore." Now, above all other times, because a widow has no protection, and perhaps she has caused his death, so they will do and say.

But then Esther resolutely recovered her habitual self, and said, "I'll have to find the awl plate first. Tomorrow." And setting the table for her *Shabbat* evening meal, she was glad of it. The day had grown old, had run its course, and a consoling, wordless benediction rose to her lips.

IN THE PAST, one glance at her burning home had been enough. She had not risked a second one. She had looked to the road and quickly took what hazard was offered. Or perhaps recognized whatever was meant to be. There was no next day there.

And there is no next-day-and-the-next here, she thought. I won't look back, I did not look twice at a home going up in flames, and I won't search for an awl plate. Meir has brought the house down, and it does not have to be arson for it to burn. I would stumble into a maze in looking into all these yesterdays, trying to find guilty parties in the cinders. I would be overtaken by despair, and that is not for me. I'll sell what I can, leave the rest to the community and go on the road.

Three letters sprang to her mind, but remained unpronounced. They were these three consonants, the backbone of everyone's Hebrew, a code, a deep knowledge, a pivot, *R W N*. Just consonants. In Hebrew, vowels do not matter, they are the breath, the living sound, but engraved are the *R W N*. One can't hear them on their own, but their presence is the more real, there is no exchange of air, no floating away on the sound. And for Esther every movement from the morning after the decisive *Shabbat* was directed by these three unspoken letters.

To make her decision known, Esther walked over the bridge the next morning, early on Sunday. Candles flickered in all the windows, spring was in the air, the creek was fuller than usual, just a dark velvet band. Esther walked over the bridging boards with a firm step, the three unspeakable letters steadying it. *R. W. N. – ReuWeN*. She did not knock at Chaskel's and Hannah's door, but hid behind a boulder on the lower bank, to rethink her strategy with them.

Suczorno, though awake, was soundless still, and she waited a little longer for the doors to open and close, for more early morning noises, before approaching the house. She had a good view of the morning shadows inside the house from where she stood, but could not distinguish whose forms they were. Shadows, bigger, in shades of grey, thrown from a candle or two, were hazy and indefinable. And it could be any of the three of them in there. But before the whole village rushed to the well, she gently knocked at

Chaskel's and Hannah's door. Chaskel and Reuwen had just sat down; the morning shadows were Hannah bringing corn porridge and a jug of milk to the table.

Esther had opened the door to no one's surprise. As if expected, she was given a *Shalom* and invitation to pull up a chair. Yes, she had eaten, but, thank you, yes, she'd accept a dish of *mamaliga* with hot milk. Hannah served her with a crooked smile and a fast wipe of the tabletop with her apron. Everything seemed clean and usual.

A widow so recently bereft of her husband could be expected to find her empty room alarming, invaded by ghosts or the soul of a reproachful husband, who only now, disembodied, dared to speak up. She could knock at doors, eat at tables, play with other people's children, be tolerated for a while, until accounts were settled. Until she had paid up, done silent penance for wrongs her troubled soul would conjure – his voice still in her ear – or debtors coming to claim her abode.

No one would be surprised in Suczorno to find Esther at anyone's table, sharing a *mamaliga*. It would also show a widow's humility, an awareness of forces spiritual in nature, outside of her control. And people walking by that window Sunday morning – going to the well to do business, or to the Synagogue as the day rose – would not find it extraordinary to find Esther eating at a neighbour's table. But they might silently, perhaps even vocally, have asked themselves or one another: Why not Yankel and Shoshannah's table, Esther's next-door neighbours? Why go still in the dark across the bridge to Chaskel and Hannah's? What could the reason be? Does she owe them something? Do they owe her money or respect? Has she not slept all night, with the thought of foul play, *dybbuks* whispering things into her ear? Or is her whole story of having found Meir sprawled dead on the kitchen floor, a fairytale, a cover-up story, perhaps, with Ethel in the middle as a paid witness. Everyone knew where Ethel's wedding rings came from – it was an open secret. There might be collusion, witnesses do not have to speak to be used. They may be *Kossov-er* witnesses, as they call them, those paid to have been there. All that was thinkable in Suczorno, its citizens seeing Esther at that table. They also would have seen Reuwen across from her, looking down into his bowl, wooden spoon in the milk and *mamaliga* mush. But no one would have dared speak the three letters *R W N* – yet.

So they sat, Hannah having joined them. The smile, wiped off her face, made room for tense alertness, one that seemingly watched to serve the table's needs, bring a little more from the scrapings of the pot, remove a dish or two, or look busy. But there was no fooling anyone. So few words were spoken that every clang of the wooden spoons against the enameled bowl was a wall of Jericho crumbling in Hannah's ears. Before all fell, she had to speak, if silently and above the turmoil in her soul.

"Shalom Aleichem, Chavereth," she said. "Have you slept well?"

And so it went with ordinary chatter between the two women, for a little. The two men finishing their meal faster, rose to leave the table, excusing themselves with a distinct bow towards the distinguished neighbour, and, avoiding Hannah's eyes, they left the room. Chaskel turned back once more to murmur something about piling up the wood or bringing it in or going for it with one of the *Shoichet's* children, Esther could not tell. None was of interest to her. She wanted the men away, to face Hannah, who rose to clear the table but felt Esther's hand firmly placed on hers, forcing Hannah to sit down.

"I have come to you humbly this morning, dearest Hannah," she stated, "with a plea, and I'll go straight to the heart of things. Give me your son Reuwen for two years. I will feed him, dress him, look after all his needs. I will take him to great teachers. West. Czernowitz first – it is a smaller centre – then to Lemberg to train his voice. He will be a cantor, sought after by all the important Synagogues. East and west.

"But this is not all. He'll learn to read music, without which one remains a country fiddler. As you know we sing from the soul, we Jews, and we have to go to the Christians to learn to write the tunes down to be able to read them."

There seemed disapproval in Hannah's stone face. A slight movement in the corners of the mouth, but detectable by the fine nervous tunings of her opponent. So Esther stopped, weighed her words, and stung by the fierce face from across, took on a fighting edge.

"Well," she said, "I am not talking about our ancient heritage, not about the thousand-years-old service, not about the sounds of glory we're almost born with. It is about being able to read anyone's music, and the Christians have in their monasteries found the way to put pitch and time to paper. This is what Reuwen has to learn."

"Enough," Hannah said. "I'm not in school here. It is enough."

"No, it is not," Esther replied, "I have more to say. If his violin can be restrung, we'll do it; if not I'll provide one from the Vienna workshops or their merchants. This is my offer. It entails no obligation on your side. Neither money nor work. It is all on me."

Hannah sat stone-faced. The walls had come down. Jericho had fallen, and though a Jew and a mother, she felt conquered, bereft, and plundered. She was not the one to triumphantly blow the trumpet, even if it were to the glory of the Eternal. She simply felt robbed and impoverished, and replied without a smile, "Reuwen has been *Bar Mitzvah;* he is now a man of conscience and has a will of his own. He will decide. Chaskel – I hope I can speak for him as well – and I will accept Reuwen's decision without question."

There was no need to say another word. The cool, simple reply spoke clearly of Hannah's despair, the "end of things," of the road closed in front of her, of no other day. They rose at once, the two women; as no offer to help with the table-clearing came forth, and would likely not have been accepted, Esther held her step back, as she did her tears. She felt the cradle robber she was made to feel, and in order not to storm out of the room she moved deliberately slower. Then she turned just as slowly to face Hannah in the hope of hugging her, but said instead, "We'll both be his mothers. If Reuwen accepts."

With no sound coming from Hannah's lips, Esther walked towards the door, which Hannah had opened before her.

SHE SOLD FAST. Sold the house for a pittance, almost for free to the adjoining *Shoichet's*. Calling in Ethel and Shimon, who still had the old back room of Yankel and Shoshannah's transformed shed, she made them sign an acceptance deed for a nominal sum. Shimon almost had to be coerced. Sitting stiffly with his Ethel on his side, at Esther's dining room table, he said, "No, I will not stay here. I do not need property. I'll go abroad; it ties me down to own bed and table –" Then taking a fast glance in the direction of his Ethel, body bulging under her woollen skirt, he took the pen and signed. The famous three Hebrew consonants, *Sh* – *M* – *N* ben Moishe with Esther bat underneath. It was signed and given.

A radiant Ethel, whose nest for her tribe came heaven-sent, gave effusive thanks, first to her Shimon, and then to Esther, who laughed, refusing any thanks, and said, "I thank you from the bottom of my heart for having made my life worthwhile." But she was in the strangest mood. And handing Shimon Meir's silver *Kiddush* cup and accompanying both through the kitchen door, she stood on the threshold, calling after them, "We'll be the god-parents of your first-born," only to realize that she had said *We.*

A sudden resurgence of the last days, a shock, intensified that strange mood, "I'll just give everything away," and with the memory of looking into the deep murky waters of the Danube when a child, she felt like jumping. As she had always felt, when sitting on the promontory overlooking Suczorno creek, that wonderful worthlessness of things and perhaps of life itself but never daring to think the latter, being a Jew. With laughter in the throat and the light-headedness of "Who needs this?" And "Who needs that?" A suicidal freedom from the obsessive Suczorno weekly succession of work and Friday nights to the crowning autumn atonement of New Year and *Yom Kippur,* took hold, and she decided not to write all the items down but to leave the house as it stood, handing the keys to Shimon and Ethel.

She packed a small movable trunk with the tools of her trade, weights, measures, scales, diamonds, the amethyst collection – no memories. Looked at the Chinese screen, No, it will stay, who needs it? She went through her house like a whirlwind, in the upbeat mood of destruction, yet cool and aware of the next day, she rescued her books, tools of trade and coins, not counting them, just made sure they were there. Laying the coins out in the order of their date, country, and value, she sewed them into small leather pouches.

Then digging into her cabinet, which she decided to leave – Who needs it? – she stabbed her finger on a sharp metal edge. Pulling the drawer out to see what it could be, she faced the jeweller's awl plate. And now she sat down upon the window bench to cry. Holding it in her hand, and having suspected the murder of her faithful Meir, she broke down.

"Too much," she said with words. "Too much to bear."

She sobbed, but wiped her face fast with the back of her hand because, looking through the window, she had detected Reuwen walking over the bridge with a determined step.

"Shemah Yisrael – oh, Glory be to God," she thought, rising from the bench.

SECTION TWO

THE SCARECROW DUO

S O WE WENT FROM VILLAGE TO VILLAGE, THE OLD
fiddler said.

In my young days, of course, I was ready to leave home. But
who can? And where to? Besides, I had my grandfather's fiddle to
make me happy; a richly low-sounding fiddle, not one of those
scratchy things that hurt your ears. My father, too, played it after
work or at any free moment with other villagers.

"Let Isaac play with it," he said to my mother. "Let him."

"No, he'll break it," she said. "He breaks everything, his back
is bent, everything is crooked, he sways like a windswept pole and
he stands on one leg, both arms don't match and –" On and on.

She loved me, though, and called me little sweet tender names
like "My only scarecrow – my only beloved scarecrow." This has
stayed with me as the dearest thing anyone could be called.

I did not exactly know what she meant, I was just three or four
then. But the sound of her love, of my being special, unique, of
there being no one else like me, closest to her heart of all her six
children, I will never forget. "Come have another piece of cornbread with prune jam thick on top, it will straighten you out.

Come." And I thought to be as crooked as I am couldn't be any finer quality.

My father was rarely home, but the few times he was he took me on his knees – I can still smell his chewing tobacco. And he said to me, "You know, Bubbale, a crooked child has to be cherished far more, because all the others can run, get what they want. But a Bubbale with one leg thinner than the other and even the straight one being a little awkward with toes walking inward – one has to really love, so he'll grow up and maybe with his good arm hold a bow."

He died young, my father, of a terrible epidemic, which killed half of Suczorno. My brothers and sisters also soon left for neighbouring towns, and my eldest brother went as far as Kiev. But I was left to look after my mother, and in spite of the fact that I was not as tall and upright as a fir tree, I was someone she could lean on, and the fiddle was given to me since no one else wanted it.

Strong, able bodies could go out, make a *ruble* or a *zloty* clearing rubbish or building other people's sheds, hiring themselves out for the potato harvest, or collecting the plums fallen on the ground. But me, a scarecrow, wagging in the wind – even if the air was as still as a summer day at noon – it would take me too long to do anything. The laughing stock of the village I was, and "strong boys" – not to call them "toughs" – would pelt me with stones, potatoes, or plums in season.

So my mother said, "Bubbale, you stay here by me, help me pit the prunes, read your portion of the week." And she had, after the death of my father, written out all the weekly portions for me. Oh, she wrote Hebrew like no one else in the village! I did my praying and the reading of the week's portion, so I was able to go through the whole Torah, the five books of Moses, and the rest, in a year.

And of course in my free time, which was considerable, I learned to play the violin so expertly that there was not a tune, sad or happy, fast or slow, up in the high register or deep in sound, that I could not play.

I had two useless legs that were so different from one another that my mother said she could never figure out how those two were fitted together by the Lord. That He – blessed be His name – had something to do with it, there was no doubt. If we were not to think that all the order of things came from Him, how could we live? Especially in the winter, when we were so short of everything. And peasants from the neighbouring villages would come to rob, steal, and threaten. Sometimes they would take the last carrots left over in the cellar or the last bag of flour and leave us hungry.

There must be order. How would we live if we did not think that there is order and that He holds his hand over His people? Well, He holds it – I'm afraid – in a very crooked or strange way over us – I must say that, may He forgive my trespassing – but it may be to teach us humility. Because – look at the rich on the high bank – one could become very "uppity" or "arrogant," if the larder were full. Well, "larder" is not the right word for a Jew in Suczorno to use, because it reminds you of pork. Oh well, maybe there is also "lard" from chickens.

But that is not what I wanted to tell you. I always get carried away with my stories and end up saying what I never had wanted to and it sometimes even astonishes me what daring and courage comes with old age.

Oh, yes, here it is: what I think of as my loveliest time in all those years is going from village to village, fiddle under arm! Sometimes alone and sometimes with two or more fiddlers.

I had one friend who owned a huge bass fiddle, and he was a small, fat, round-faced, ever-smiling Jew, who elicited sounds as tender as a lark in the spring from the enormous body of his bass fiddle. He taught me to hold it, and crooked as I am, we leaned on each other for support: the bass fiddle holding me up and I in turn, leaning over it, hugged it as one would – well, I took to it so fast that Jakob, the owner, my little fat friend, said I was extraordinary.

Sometimes we exchanged the fiddles, and he played mine and I thought that he played it much better than I did! With a swing of the bow and a run in the fingers so that you hear a brook running by. Such magic tricks. I hope the Almighty forgives us all such sinful thoughts as: the sound of our fiddles is greater than the sound of the *Shofar*. What a thing to even conjure up!

And it struck us both, when we looked into each other's eyes while going up or down our fiddles, or jumping in unison and in rhythm, or going apart and finding each other as if we were lost children in the woods, that there was no happiness like it. Just coming home together on one note or on two different notes that sounded like one; so unspeakably beautiful, such greatness in the soul we felt that we two would have tears in our throats, and hug and kiss.

So I said to him one day: What if it isn't the Almighty, what if some tempting *dybbuk*, ghost, or a real *Satan* – which is the Hebrew word for devil – what if all these dark forces are tempting us away from the service of the Lord? What if? That would be an unimaginable disaster!

But Jakob put my doubts to rest and said that couldn't be, nothing could be as noble as the feeling of love and embracing that we both had at the same time.

He was right I'm sure. My Jakob was right. And so we decided to go out as a team. Put an act together, with a 1-2 or a 1-2-3-4 and 1-2-3, sometimes counting till 6. For dances and weddings. We Jews do not have too many dances, there is not that much to dance about in Suczorno.

But we do have weddings, *Briths* – circumcision celebrations – but no funerals. Jews do not sing at funerals or dance or eat. They sit on the ground, take off their shoes, pray and cry for seven days: then they have a year long to think about their losses. When the year is over, they can remarry if they have anybody, and if they're young –

Oh well, I did not. No one wanted me, though I longed for love and a household of mine own, the respect it brings to one in Suczorno, and perhaps little ones if the Almighty is gracious. But it was not given to me.

My mother used to say, "You're precious to the Lord, more so than all these great citizens of Suczorno who know your sorrow and yet brag about their wonderful children to you and me. You can play the fiddle and God hears you; they cannot, and have to brag." That made me always happy.

And Jakob said, looking at me with tenderness, "You do not need a wife. You can have a fiddle, and especially a bass fiddle. I always call her 'Sweetheart.' One can hold her close, dance with her, feel her big belly, her warm brown wood, and she will coo-oo-oo to you like no real woman would."

We decided to make a *duo* – as I hear they call it. "They" who are "in the know." Christians mainly. Because they read music the way we read Hebrew. From the page. While we just have to play by ear. But I am not envious. Why should I be envious of other people's music? I have it all in me, it brims over with tunes and rhythms, new ones or combinations of old ones. And when we are together, Jakob and I, we laugh all the time because of the joy.

So there is no question that we sing to the Lord. We do. With every note we sing of His creation. I should not worry. But here and there the tears can't be held back. If a tune is too powerful it reminds one of everything, your loneliness, not having a wife, a beautiful gentle woman on your side, of having lost your father, so young and so beloved – and finally I think of my sad, enduring mother.

One day, when playing with Jakob a particularly heartbreaking melody, I said to him, "Jakob, could I ask you something personal?"

"Yes," he said, "you are all I've got, my friend and my brother."

"Call me," I said – since it was the *Yahrzeit* – a year to the day since my mother's death – "call me my sweet scarecrow, my darling little scarecrow. I do not hear it anymore, and I have even stopped dreaming about it, which is worse, because it robs you of your last memory."

"Oh," Jakob said, "I will, and not only that, I love the sound in that name, it has such wonderful rhythm within it, that I'll play you a tune on it." And he did.

It was as if heaven, the Lord, and all the angels – mentioned and not mentioned in the Bible, because there are lots of those flying-about ones and I always wondered why they were not written down – had come to fill our lives with music.

So we named ourselves "The Scarecrow Duo." Isn't that the funniest name anyone could think of? Well, we became famous. All the villages – our own celebrations, weddings or *Briths* – hired us to play, and our fame spread so far that the Poles, the

Ukrainians, and even the Russians wanted us to come to play for their dances, weddings, and other holidays.

We knew all their tunes; we knew the gypsy melodies, which are really strange but so wonderful — I must say exotic, as if from far, far away and yet so close to the heart; and of course we have our own sounds of joy, despair, and the hope of Jerusalem. The Christians loved us and paid us well. And we were both, Jakob and I, utterly surprised one day at a Polish wedding, when the hosts spoke kindly to us.

We had asked for a little boiling water – tea glasses we had brought along, though we would use theirs since glass is *kosher*, and a few cubes of sugar we had as well. But they said in reply, "No, no, you won't eat all by yourselves. Please, come and eat with us and drink at our wedding feast. You have played so beautifully and moved us all to tears you are the best *Klezmers* we have ever had."

We had brought our own food, of course, a piece of chicken, a potato patty with fried onion, and we needed just a little boiling water for our tea. But when we looked at their table, heaped with delicacies, and a roasted piglet in the centre table, we had to decline. Unfortunately.

I do not think God would have struck us down had we sat down with them. But it was against our custom. We thanked them from the bottom of our hearts and ate by ourselves, but accepted a glass of wine from their glasses. So friendly they were, so warm and dear to us, and we joked and laughed like neighbours would. The greatest surprise to us was not that they invited us to sit with them and share their food, but that Christians could be so kind. This was new to us, and a good lesson in humility.

So Jakob and I went from village to village, and played in front of their churches, in their fields, or in their houses with hearts full of love.

Yes, these were the best of all days, the old fiddler said. And he concluded thoughtfully: The best of the Scarecrow's good days, making people happy with music, no matter who they were.

THE OLD MAN AND HIS CIGARETTE

THE OLD MAN SAT BY THE SIDE OF HIS TABLE —
a rough-hewn, sturdy table, its rounded corners smoothed
with time, and spread a napkin under his glass of tea. He always
put a napkin underneath. A tablecloth, ironed and shining,
spread over the whole surface for all the twenty-four hours of the
Shabbat was just a memory. For a man alone, a small piece of
linen sufficed.

He had sold his samovar to the rich on the south side of the
creek. What did one man need boiling water for all day, for just
three glasses of tea? But he kept the stove going all day, except for
the *Shabbat,* when after six days of burning wood he blocked the
oven door with a brick, closely, so as not to let the heat escape.
And inside the big bowels of this mud hearth he cooked his
Cholent, the one real meal of the week.

He had watched the women do it. Everything was put in that
covered pot, an earthen pot round and womanly, like the bellies
of the women. He smiled at his own thoughts.

How foolish are the young! To think of those enormous round bellies, who let men in for their pleasure. And, I wonder, what do they take out of this banging, sweating, sucking of their throats, touching, holding, their flesh kneaded like a piece of dough? With words to match that no one is allowed to hear. What do these women take out of it? And then, in time, how these huge cauldrons swell with more flesh inside. I still wonder, no matter how old I am.

But it is cold without women, sitting alone. A sort of shivering to the heart. And all their chatter, their evil gossip about one another, their scolding with wicked tongues their men and children, slapping them with wooden long-handled spoons wherever they could hit – all that is better than loneliness.

I always felt that embracing presence, a life held and fed. "Come, Selig, come my light, my inner soul, the joy of my days, come!" my mother would say. And into the big lap, legs spread for the comfort of a little boy, into all those odours of unwashed skirts, underskirts, and aprons, I rushed. And I knew what God is like. Sustaining.

To feel so important, so central to a woman's life. Be it your mother's. And later – No, truly your mother's forever. In spite of all her chasing us, six boys, chastising us because of our dirty hands, because of lying, or not having split the kindling for the eternal oven – I loved her. The oven a voracious wild beast, insatiable in its desire to feed on wood, its open gullet spewing flames – and she chiding us for having left the cupboard empty.

In spite of all her noises and curses, there was this huge, embracing belly. I still feel it, when close to women. Not that close, not to touch, but just to breathe their presence in. A special odour of the body soap they use, or something more mysterious than that. Though in Suczorno, if you are alone, you are alone. Women, the warmth, the true life, are for others.

Still, I put a white, washed and starched napkin under my glass, a little dish for sugar beside, and sit by the oven; the *Cholent* is in there, with whatever I have, roots mainly, a piece of fat and ribs from the upper part of the beef. I truly can't understand. Why not the lower part? Does the blood not unify it all? Well, it is forbidden. Not by God, I'm sure. How would He command something unreasonable? Or could there be a hidden sense? Which is His habit of doing.

I have no time left now to ruminate on all of that. Thoughts of "Destroy the nonsense, think for yourself," are for the young. My time is short. There is a sweetness about it. I don't have to smash the old, the engrained customs, true or mindless. I just eat the upper part of the beef and do not care if it makes sense or not. And I particularly dislike the sound of destruction, the crashing, spilling, falling apart of what has been, until you watch it lying around you in shards. What's the use? Let them eat the upper part of the beef and let them think they're virtuous. I know better.

Oh, there is such sweetness in not fighting. Imagine, not having to! To sit by a hot, big mud oven, with a belly of a woman in mind, and the inner cauldron of the now sealed oven full with slowly steaming meat and whatever else, all mingling. Tastes, smells – call it aromas – textures, colours, suffusing one another within the brew, for twenty-four hours. Like a woman's belly. Mixing, holding, swelling to give birth.

I sip it slowly, it's more hot water than tea. Still, slightly golden from yesterday's leaves. Water gently simmering – to sit for hours – so sweet a life.

To think of all the stories! True – untrue. Bimbule's fools, wise men's histories of the past. Does he really hear them out in the fields, when the bees swarm? Does he? Oh, the lies. But then, who knows? He comes from a long line of *Kahanim*. We should trust them; they're priests. After all, everybody lies, why not they? The beauty of the mind, call it imagination or lies – it makes me smile.

Think of yesterday. Bimbule rushed in. It was late, I was sitting by my glass of tea, the sun had set, I'd said my prayers, smoked my last cigarette. The slowest, most restful moment of my day. Sweet. I had a piece of newsprint or – if lucky – a fine, silken little sheet of paper. And with three fingers of my right hand, I took a pinch of tobacco from a wooden box on the table and rolled it up, and wetting the edge by drawing it through my almost closed lips with a touch of spit, I got a perfect cigarette and lit it. I can do that all week, except on Friday night, of course, when just before sunset my need for tobacco just goes. It leaves me.

"Thou shalt not spit fire out of your mouth on *Shabbat,* or light a fire –" or something like that. When the Almighty speaks it seems that even my body responds. All yearning falls from me, there are holy things to do and think about, and I consider it a true miracle that one longs for that puff, that bit of comfort all week, but come *Shabbat* you're suddenly free. It's not there. As if you had never smoked before.

Then on the lovely *Shabbat* proper, just before sunset, the next evening, the craving returns again and I become impatient, my fingers tremble, I'm wet in the palm of my hand. I look at the time, which creeps like a snail, I hurry through the words of the prayers, as if this would make the time push forward. And oh, when all is done, God's work and man's work, and I'm holding a square little silk paper to roll my tobacco in – oh!

I like to stray. To amuse myself. Sometimes thinking about miracles or yesterday's visit.

Bimbule rushed in saying, "Everybody chases me from their doors – Go away, go away! – that is all I hear, and it's too cold to sleep in the field tonight. The peasants have brought their corn in, and the stubble pierces my rib cage –"

I love Bimbule. He may come whenever he likes, but he does not unless it is a winter night, or he at the end of his wits. Last night was cold; it is fall and I was glad to see him come. Yes. First we had tea, bread, honey, and an apple on a plate with a knife on the side. We sat awhile so he could get the shivers, the homelessness out of his body.

I smiled at him, asked him a few things, sat beside him, and he let me warm both his hands. He enfolded his long fingers around the hot glass and slowly his unearthly face returned with a foolish grin of wisdom and goodness all over. I love him, he is just young. He knows things, reads letters from all sides, sees meanings no one else does, so they fear him of course: who wants someone who looks at the bottom of your soul? God knows what's in there. So they feed him fast and chase him from their door, just not to see that grin.

I love the boy, he can look at my soul; not that it is as white as my mother's tablecloth, but he can look into it. I let him. If God has put it here – Well? Then I make his bed, our bed, and I let him sleep beside me. He took off his – whatever they are – one never can tell what Bimbule wears. He is so poor and things do not have to have a name like "trouser" or "shirt," and if they haven't got a name, considering the shape they're in, he calls them something fanciful, and we both feel good and giggle.

So he took it all off, except whatever I would call a shirt, perhaps, next to the body, washed his hands, said a few words in Hebrew that sounded like prayer but seemed more like hiero-glyphics come to life. He asked, "Selig, may I put the candle out? My story tonight does not like so much light. It's shy. It will get embarrassed and stop."

We needed a little time to get warm under my featherbed. So we rested. Bimbule has slept many a night in it and knows this bed can be his for the asking, because my heirs are far away and I have no one to leave it to. So I will let him have my house and all there is in it, pots, pans, glasses, crockery, my mother's linen – heavens, what man assembles, what man hoards in a lifetime! Of course, Bimbule may not want earthly possessions, may not be able to live in a house, with an outhouse and a shed, like other people. Old age perhaps may change his ways – bones do not carry you far out into the fields anymore and they shiver in cold nights. Maybe then.

So we got warm, and I was just about to commend my soul to the Almighty when he started, in a Bimbule-soft voice, a sing-song, a sweet and dear sound: "Selig, may I tell you a story? One that I would never want to know myself for fear not to disgrace it. But if I do not tell it to you, it will never be told, and I'll surely die or choke on it. For the beauty of the whole thing."

And he stopped suddenly, said he really could not speak, jumped from the bed to the table, taking a sugar cube to suck, came back, closed in on me a little more, and said, "It was just yesterday. Herschel had kept the head of the carp for me in the cellar, and he called me as I sat on the bridge – you know the one close to his house – washing my feet in the clear running creek. 'Come Bimbule, he called, if you do not come now I'll throw the head of the carp out, it's already a little' – and I said God forbid.

I was there in no time. I took it back to sit on the bridge – because he does not want me in there, thinking I may see things. He knows he is a thief, what with his horse tradings, painting the corners of the rubbed-off old flesh to cheat the customer, or binding the horse's legs a little so it walks better – for a day maybe. It was swarming time and bees can tell a cheat.

"Anyway, I'm sitting outside, dangling my toes in the cool water, picking the tasty morsels, when I distinctly hear myself addressed, 'Did you, Bimbule, see the eyes of Shulamith?' Oh yes, I did, I answered. 'It was for you. It was you, Bimbule, she fancies.'

"And sucking on the juices of the gills, I hear within me a joyful echo, 'It is for you Bimbule, for you.' I turn to look in the direction of her house, see her figure fleeting in and out, and suddenly am aware that her brother Mendel has taken his horse and wagon out. It was not there. He is another one of these thieves who sell old horses, painting them up to look young, though of course one can tell by their teeth – yes, he is one of these rich robbers."

Bimbule, sucking on his sugar cube, took breath and waited a little, then lowered his voice: "Selig, I heard it distinctly while slowly finishing the carp. It spoke to me; it always does. 'It is for you Bimbule, for you.' So I washed my hands in the creek, not to smell of fish, and sat a little longer, waiting for night to fall. And when all the rich had boarded up their windows, I noticed one of hers slightly open. I got up, walked towards it, looking around me a little.

"Suczorno lay in deep rest, and I rushed behind the shed into her back door without knocking. It had waited for me, it was open. And I heard her say, 'Bimbule, I am here in the kitchen, heating water for your foot bath.' And she took everything off me, whatever there was, and then she took her kerchief off, and I saw the colour of her hair. Of course, a boy's head looked at me, the hair cut short. Still, her own. Eyes underneath shining, laughing. A face full of eyes. We mingled our toes in the warm water, giggled like two boys behind their parents' back, thinking forbidden thoughts. There was no candle burning, just the oven. She only now removed slowly whatever you call it that she had on, and I saw her in the darkening light.

"Her bed, hard and narrow, made me turn to face her. Gently touching her boyish hair, I said, 'Shulamith, let me tell you a story.' And she replied, 'All your stories, Bimbule, all your stories.'

"When the roosters started their morning call, or just before, she said, 'Watch out, keep your body close to the shed in the back now, before the shadows return. Hurry and take these woolen socks I have knitted, waiting for you. Come, let me see if they fit –'

"And I, Selig, was young, truly *selig,* truly transported to heaven."

Selig, turning now a little towards Bimbule, felt with his naked feet Bimbule's woollen socks. He had not taken them off.

THAT WAS YESTERDAY. It was so good to think they were still young out there, still full of stories a burning candle could blow away. And it was so sweet to sit by a glass of hot tea, waiting for the *Cholent* to cook and night to fall.

THE OLD MAN'S
MOST BEAUTIFUL ENCOUNTER

OH, IT'S GOOD TO BE AN OLD MAN. ALL THE WICKED
thoughts – maybe not all, well, *all* is too big a word – but
many have gone. It's easier to live. One wants less. There is no
wild rushing about, what with making a living and looking into
other people's worlds. So strange they had seemed, so hard to be
part of, and what hurt most was the feeling of being left out. Of
not having received one's share. Feeling a bitterness; a quarrel
with the Lord. But as the years fall from you, peel away as the
skins of an onion do (leaving only a few at the inner core) one
smiles, as one sees them go.

Not always though. Today, for instance. You see, we live in a
little town, where everyone has been present for everyone's birth
and everyone's funeral, let alone weddings. Of course, one was
there too, but if you are poor and it is a rich man's daughter from
the south side of the creek – well, one has to excuse oneself. And
one is excused, of course, because the rich like to entertain each
other and are not anxious for your company.

So today I do not smile, though I did have cornbread and milk
and it is a warm winter day. I have eaten and have prayed, but I

am struck by a sudden awareness that were it not for me getting up in the morning would there be a world? Oh, sinful thoughts. So, there it is.

I'm a mason, and proud of my masonry. They all say I am the best. I helped with the fountain in the middle of town. It would not have today its artistic shapes were it not for me. For instance, the numbers four and seven are so intricately put into the stonework that only if you look very closely can you discern by colour, by angles, and by the inter-cut surfaces, a holy number built-in. Not so much to protect against evil thoughts or the poisoning of the well did I do it – one can never know who comes to the well, wayfarers, people from the vastness of the East, or peasants from nearby. And it was not to ward off supernatural powers of destruction that I put the holy numbers in.

I put them in for "God within things," for Him alone, for Him within the objects that surround us. As Jews, not having the right to anything, not to touch or hold anything except the fringes of our garments, the *Mezuzah* at the gate, or the scrolls of the *Torah*, for a man to be close to God is what remains.

Cutting the stones for the fountain, such overwhelming feelings of creation filled my heart, directed my fingers. My muscles moved expertly and quickly, and I watched myself with utter astonishment as, without any premeditation, I first carved the number four. Gently taking a fine brush to eliminate the stone dust that fell from the carving, I set the next stone fast, looking around me as if I were a thief.

Is it right, is it against the law to carve our meaningful numbers? Why not? These are not images or faces, they're just letters. There are four letters in the holy name. It stands for something. It's meaningful. There are the four brothers – the good, the bad, the stupid and I don't remember the last – on the Passover night. There is the fourth day of creation –

I looked around me. No one had noticed anything. They watched me work assiduously; but I always keep to my work and try not to look for temptation, which is around you everywhere.

Into the next row I built in the number seven, clearly, boldly, and without fear. Because nothing could be wrong with the seven. Not only because all of the Creation was finished in seven days, but because the Almighty has taken that last day to be the glory of the world. Not ours alone, though we are chosen to receive it from His mighty hands, but belonging to all of the universe.

Imagine lifting your eyes from the ground, which you scratch from morning till night for a piece of bread for yourself and all your masters; imagine being commanded to wash your hands, look up, think of Him, and rejoice. If this is not the greatest gift to the world, I cannot fathom another one. The *Shabbat,* when we become human, thinking beings, free of fetters. It is a day of freedom from the earth, freedom to soar; feeling and seeing His creation as if for the first time. He has commanded us to shed the shackles of work. Man and his animals, for a day to rejoice.

Everyone could see the magic number seven. Well, I do not mind a little protection. As I said, I'm not superstitious or blind, seeing occult forces where there is only God to worship. But I do not mind a little protection. Neither do I wish to pursue the thought and explain it to myself; it just feels good to have a little.

I built the seven into a stone a little different in colour and texture than the others, to give it prominence. But I did it with humility, staying within the design of the whole thing. A warmth went through my whole being at having served God in my own subtle, private way, seen by Him and those who have eyes to see. Which aren't that many.

"*Gut Shabbes,* Reb Selig," they would say after *Kiddush* on the *Shabbat* noon, "Thank God there is a day where you don't carve that stone."

But I just smiled because I worship in my own way. They have to go to the Synagogue and shake in fear of God. I don't have to. I have a contract, a relationship, He talks to me in numbers, in a language totally of our own. Of course, all the Jews of Suczorno could see it too, they just have to read their books right instead of mindlessly reciting the ancient words.

I looked at my fellow men that *Shabbat* noon with a little disdain, though it isn't a good, permissible feeling. Disdain is like murder. And if it is not like it – of course it isn't, nothing is like murder, which is the ultimate sin. But it does away with the other, excludes him. "Go away," I would say, "You blind, worthless –" and so forth.

One does this as if the other does not exist. Which isn't nice. It isn't, because he does exist and there is no one or no thing in God's creation without something special, redeemable, of worth, and it is forbidden to deny it. And how would the other – on the other hand – how would he not see the signs, where they speak so clearly of His greatness.

Take our most intimate true faith, with the number ONE imbedded into its heart. Who can show me a religion with a number in the middle? ONE. All inclusive. He being in everything there is. It explains itself. No words are necessary. That is what a number does. Even four and seven.

You do not have to look into the text, numbers explain themselves. I have asked the most famous rabbis, as far as Vijnitza, in my journeying days, to explain to me their nature. "Except for trust in God," they said, a number is a number. It can do things. It stands in a row; it is divisible; it can do away with itself and appear again. And it needs no words. It uses the letters, but there is the row again, and we can think about them in holy or more objective terms.

As we say on the first day of the year, which is also the first day of Creation: *Adonai Eloheinu, Adonai Echod,* Lord of the Universe, the Lord is ONE. So it remains in the heart of our faith, the most formidable fortress no one can take.

Even if the Christians split it in three, it still remains ONE for them. Or so they say. But this is not my concern.

Today I do not smile, and I wonder why. I should be happy. I am not hungry or cold, and I think back and wonder. It may be that the strength to carve the stone has been taken by old age, and I am left with a creaking in my bones, an ache from bending my knees and staying on them for hours. The finesse of my fingers in joining wood or stone, marrying the two, has gone.

I always thought they made a good marriage, the one supplying what the other lacks. Wood decays, and it is good to be reminded of it, and stone stays steadfast. Then man can redo, repair, replace, and participate in creation.

Well, maybe this is why I am sad; if not sad, just not praising God today. I cannot do His holy work. Not create, just read His letters. Not build. I feel like sitting down with a glass of tea in front of me and a cube of sugar between my teeth to sip it through.

One more thing. My journeying days are over. That also contributes to my melancholy. I can't walk from village to village, neither west to Lemberg nor east as far as Odessa. I used to walk and

sing, sit by a brook in Suczorno, with all its faces known to me –
or watch the blooms and grasses on new turns in the road, or at
the bank of far away rivers like the Prut or the Bug.

Finding strangers for a short span of time to walk with together,
listening to their misfortunes or happiness, and to hear what these
strangers thought about God. Of course, we are all His. So they –
even if not Jews, who are instructed in His letters – have some part
of Him inside themselves and must have some thought of His
majesty.

Once crossing the Djnester into the Ukraine, I met a young
man on his way to a far away monastery. This was the most beautiful encounter of my life. Young and handsome, he was straight
as a hazelnut rod. We met at the bridgehead of the Djnester
before crossing, still on the western side.

We stopped at once, having watched each other almost all
morning while walking. It was noon, and a hot late July day,
when I heard him sing with a voice like all the angels but with a
rhythm strange and accentuated by his step. We shook hands, and
he said, "My name is Vladimir, it's time for a rest, let's find a
shady grove."

We sat down. The sun was high, but we found a grassy spot
not far from the river so we could see it flow by, and with thick
bushes at our back, it felt cool and comfortable.

"I'll share my food with you," he said.

I was deeply touched by his offer, and did not know how to
refuse. But I had to because he pulled out a wonderful sausage,
fragrant with garlic, and took a folding knife from his bag and cut
a thick slice. God knows I had to decline. It was so hard, but I
accepted his cornbread and offered my potato kugel in exchange.

"You're a Jew," he said. "I can tell, but I have never met one –

person to person that is – and always wanted to. I thank God for giving me this chance. I'll be a priest," he said. "Christ came to me early. I was only four or five and I heard His calling. Distinctly. I felt His warmth, his love infusing my little body, and I grew up not playing with anyone, but learning the Cyrillic letters, to read the message. By myself, to know the truth, with no one else around me.

"Of course, I love the village church. Full of gold, and goodness in the eyes of our saints, but I do not want everyone else around me who is so different from me. Once at Easter time, just before the great day of Friday, the priests – there were two of them who made us go into Suczorno, a village, a shtetl, not far from ours, 'To take back,' they said, 'what the Jews had taken from us.' 'You're all poor,' they said. 'Just go in there and take what you can get. It's all yours. They've taken Christ's life. Go in there.'

"But I did not want to go. I did not think it was right. If God had sent His only son to be born among them, had chosen a mother – the mother of all of us – from among their women, they're a holy people, I thought.

"Well, I could not stay back home with all the old people, and not wanting to reveal my inner feelings, I went along. But I know I should not have gone. We did not murder, but we took everything there was left over from the winter, which was not that much. And if you say 'holy terror' that is what it was, especially in the eyes of the little children. It is not to be forgotten.

"I came home, went for the holy fire at the resurrection celebrations, and vowed deep in my own soul to atone. So now I will seek out the Siberian brotherhood. I have heard of this wonderful community. And devote my life to His work, the sharing of the bread and charity. I love to sing the liturgy. I know it well by now."

He was beautiful, Vladimir. He did not know much about how we lived, by what laws and customs. And I talked about many things to him, a stranger, that I would not have ever revealed to anyone, and likely will never do again. About God and our own ways to worship, but also about my private self, my loneliness as a young man, my shyness with women, and my decision to go on the road.

He understood me, felt my aloneness, my desire for love, and turned to me and said, "You are my brother, and as Christ atoned for all our sins, so I will walk in His footsteps, my path lit by His glory."

We did not fall into each other's arms, but felt like it. The sun was slowly moving west and we knew night was approaching. We still had to cross the river that day, and so we took our leave, hugging just for a breath of a moment. I did not tell him I was from Suczorno, born and raised. I could not.

THE OLD MAN FELL SILENT. To have lived such a beautiful moment.

THE DANCING DWARF

WELL, HE WAS CALLED THE DANCING DWARF, AROUND the time of Moses maybe. No, no, it was rather Abraham's. No matter, the old man thought, while boiling water for his evening tea.

The famous boy-Pharaoh reigned in Egypt just a few thousand years ago. What is a few thousand years to us Jews in Suczorno? We have come along a wide road of time, a journey on which one has picked up little objects, trifles, a glittering stone you pushed with your toe – a gift to give to your wife and child, or to keep hidden in a secret spot because it holds something powerful or forbidden.

Then one talked about it forever. As long as *Galut* – the dispersal – itself. Talk. Something encountered on the road, and it stayed with you as if it had occurred yesterday. So this is what we do, and because objects on a shelf decay, we store them in the mind, preserve them as stories in dark recesses. And they emerge then unexpectedly – fully restored, grown to unpredictable dimensions, enriched, the same yet different – from all the pieces of chanced memory.

So they are not in Exodus. And not in Genesis either, but you cannot deny them, because "It is told." Once the story is told, well! So it is with the "Dancing Dwarf" of the little Pharaoh, aged nine, who longed for the famous living toy. To see him juggle, stand on his head, roll up like a ball, and fly. Oh, the little Pharaoh so longed to play with him!

It is engraved on his tomb that no gold and no effort was spared to bring the dwarf from afar to delight a pharaoh, to make the boy's eyes sparkle, make him laugh and clap his hands.

ONE GOOD DAY Suczorno was in an uproar, a long time before life became so hard that one feared for one's wife and children. One day, in a whirl of dust and noise, the dwarfs appeared in town. From nowhere, from the east maybe, with cymbals and Indian sitars. They jumped from their wagons and started to perform. Flying from bridge to bridge across the creek, as if made of birds' wings. Magic. No good can come from such wonders.

But then, because Jews were always hopeful and believed the Messiah would come one day, they slowly emerged into the streets on both sides of the creek. Because this was a funny town, they were all curious, rich and poor, so they stood, men in front for the protection of women and children behind, and watched in amazement. Dwarfs. "God must have forgotten them," they said, "if we are all made in his image." It was hard for a Jew in Suczorno to comprehend. "But then, they are much like us. It's just strange what they can do!"

They flew from bridge to bridge, disappeared suddenly, made fire on a stick and swallowed it, threw little green balls at each other, catching ten at a time, and none ever fell into the creek.

The children ran after them, the mothers fetching them back. And there was a sudden silence when the whole dwarf company sat down around the fountain in centre of town. All of Suczorno followed them now – less afraid and a little amused.

Then one of them stepped forward.

The old man, recognizing him, said quietly to those around him, "It is the Dancing Dwarf. The ancient Dancing Dwarf of the boy-Pharaoh. It must be him. Who else would dance like that? Who would?"

Small as he was, all his limbs were doubly jointed; ankles and wrists could turn into all directions, and so could his head. Not quite as well, but he could see what was behind his back. He jumped onto the rim of the fountain and danced to his own singing on the smallest trim of slate, but then he twirled himself upside down onto his hands. A shiver went through all of Suczorno when they watched him dance on the fingers of one hand. He crawled backwards like a crab, folded in two on his belly, and on his back.

Now, everyone saw it. The ancient story became true. They knew the Dancing Dwarf does not die. He is made of spirits, and is divine. He just keeps coming back, all the six thousand years since Abraham's time. Did he wander with the Jews, forty years through the desert? Was he at the foot of the mountain? Did he dance around the Golden Calf? Was he exiled to Babylon? Did he come down the line past the destruction of the second Temple and all through the *Galut,* all the way to Suczorno? It was too much to contemplate.

So, while the Dancing Dwarf returned into his own body and the company slowly mounted their wagons, the Jews of both sides of the creek held council: Let's feed them first, collect some

287

children's clothing, and give them bread and wine for the road. What if they're Jews and *Shabbat* is approaching? Then we'll lead them out of town safely, watching the direction they're taking. The dwarfs, young and old – who could guess their ages? – all stood up in a row once more. Little dwarf children, and what Suczorno could identify as dwarf women, with the Pharaoh's, Pepi II's, Dancing Dwarf in the middle. He took a deep bow, accepted food, wine, and clothing, and all the Jews could see was the dust they whirled up from the road, so fast had they left, horses, wagons, and sounding cymbals.

Suczorno would never forget it, and no one knew whence they had come or guessed the direction they took. They left into the sunset, dust covering the road, filling the air.

BUT THE OLD MAN KNEW: old stories never died.

The water in his kettle on the eternal stove had boiled, and he prepared to set his table with a starched white napkin, to sip his tea in comfort. A name was suddenly on his lips, and he wondered from where in the recesses of ancient memory did Harkhuf appear? Harkhuf, a caravan leader of who knew when? Dates did not sit well with the old man.

The before and the after was not only vague but carried little meaning. Of course, all Christians went by this before and after, and perhaps he should also. But it was too late for changing one's view of time. Time had to do with the Almighty. To make a point in the past somewhere, and go on with "before" and "after" this point, seemed irrelevant for an old man.

He sat down beside his rough table with the rounded edges, on his straight-backed wooden chair his father had made. Objects that had escaped pillage and looting. And the old man smiled, thinking of his father and his preferred "Egyptian" stories. And that he always had said that "Time belongs to God. Man's is just a road set out for him to wander."

Even if a new Messiah appeared tomorrow – and there had been countless ones in hard times. "Beleaguered by hunger and the sword, any Messiah will do" – so his father said. And the Messiahs came. But the flow of God could not be interrupted only because a new promise had arisen in man's despair.

Now an old man himself, Selig, sitting in his father's chair, counted time by the Pharaohs. It was simpler; it was inscribed on the tombs. One had to trust – with reservation – what was inscribed, and then think about it.

He sat down after all the dust, noise, excitement, and wonder had passed. Sat down beside his glass of tea, and Harkhuf, Harkhuf sprang to his mind again and again. Slowly, step by step, he traced back the ringing of this name, and the story returned, the broken linkage clicked back unto the chain, and without warning the thread was repaired, whole and connected!

Yes. Harkhuf, the famous caravan leader, a traveller of old. With wondrous tales to tell, inscribed in the stones of Egypt and in our minds. A leader of caravans like his father before him, he went south to the land of Yam and Temeh, carrying ebony, incense, grain, carved ivory.

And Selig, the old man, smiled at the thought. All came back to him.

Yes, Harkhuf the caravan leader, carried with him real wild animals. Imagine! Panthers! To make peace in the south and south-west. And on his fourth journey he acquired for the boy-Pharaoh, Pepi II, the Dancing Dwarf of the divine spirits, a dwarf from the treasurer of the God – their God, what is his name?

And Harkhuf was warned by the boy-Pharaoh – in a letter preserved on the Pharaoh's tomb – to guard the Dancing Dwarf with his very life, to have someone trustworthy sleep on both sides of the divine dwarf, to inspect him ten times a night. And it was written that he, Pepi II, valued the dwarf more than any goods from Sinai or Punt, though they may have been of the greatest worth. And he promised rewards beyond measure for generations to come.

The old man sipped his tea and thought.

Was it before – after – ever? Well, we go by the record of the Pharaoh, Pepi II. And he reigned 90 years. So we Jews know when. Perhaps five or six thousand years ago – and here is the living proof! Did the Dancing Dwarf of the divine spirits not dance on the rim of the fountain in Suczorno? He did!

How good old stories are. They just rest a while and then spring to life.

As he drained the last drops of tea from his glass, the mixed fragrance of kale, carrots, and meat spiced with garlic rising from the stewing *Cholent* set his mind at rest; and blissful oblivion enveloped the old man's soul before nightfall.

Papirene Kinder

IT WAS THE DAY AFTER THE *Shabbat*. PEOPLE WERE DEALING, working again, harnessing their horses. The old man saw them doing things, living their lives, living their days as if they never ended. They'll notice, he said to himself, when these days get shorter, just curtailed by one's own strength and the lack of will to get up in the morning, being content with less of everything. Also love, less love. Neither to give nor to take. And words. To whom to speak? Even if you cursed your wife, cursed her reproachful eyes and tongue, and wished her dead, it is better than silence.

AND I THINK OF MY THREE SONS, when I chased them out, long before sunrise, to wash hands, drink a glass of milk with cornbread, to sit at the table for the two hours of *Torah*. But then, what would you be without it? So, we teach them. My heart breaks just to think how I woke them by the first crow of the rooster – by the second they rose – Avrum, Solomon, Chaim, up! I have no time for you! Up, my little ones. Up. All this is better than silence.

"The beggar is already in the third village," my own father – may his soul find pleasure in the eyes of the Eternal – yes, this is what he said to me, "Selig, my son, the beggar is already –" every morning. So long ago.

And my little ones. To get up for a long, long day with sleep in their eyes and in all their movements, not ready to face ancient letters and sublime thought. What do they have to do with all our past and wisdom?

Chaim, the eldest, quarrelling with me and God. "Let the little ones sleep – I'll get up."

"No," I said. "This is the lot of the Jew, he has to read the holy words; it's more than milk and bread, it's what sustains you all the days of your life."

There was no argument. It was I, the father. As my father Abraham before me, who made us face that grey morning – when all embers had gone down – in order to sit around the table to study, so I, Selig, had to do my duty.

I had to do it all, even cook their corn porridge in the milk. Later on they helped, when they were a little older, with all the chores and the milking of our only cow. She was beautiful, a lovely lady.

And Selig smiled at her memory.

The stable was right in front of the house; seemed more important than the house itself. One beautiful big lady in it. And sometimes a couple of goats. But they did not get along and I sent the boys out to pacify them, separate or take the goats for pasture. But in the winter –

I've taken down my father's house. It was well built, but I took it down to build anew. It is right on the corner lot, on the low bank, with a good piece of land in the back of the house. My wife was not much help, I must say – a willing worker, but not very strong; a fish from the market she couldn't carry. Slender in the midriff, I loved her. But work – it could not be expected of her.

She was a Meyer. All girls, embroidering tablecloths no one needed, talking city talk, they dreamt of the impossible, not of the real. But there was work to be done, a day to live through. Work.

I was not a rich man who lived off interest, usury, or theft, as some neighbours did. I am a craftsman from my youth. I work with my hands, on wood, on stone.

Of course, I read the *Torah*. What else is there in life? Were we not, Jews, chosen to hear the word of God? We are His people. He handed it to us. He chose us, gave us ears to hear Him, eyes to see His script, we have to be worthy. My sons sat evenings and argued with me. What this means or that. What a *Mitzvah* means. Is it just charity to give to the poor or is it commandment, law?

Not just charity, they said, which depended on your good will to give a crown to the poor on funerals and weddings; or the handing down of used clothing – true, still good to wear but cast off – once a year, or the sharing your Friday night carp with a stranger passing through town – all that will not do! This is not the *Mitzvah! Mitzvah* is commandment. The "must," the obligation to share.

As it is written – and they quote and search for the spot – and I am afraid I can't recall it correctly: "The last grape from the vine, the last olive from the tree, the last kernels of corn are not yours. They belong to those that have no land, the stranger, who passes through, the widow, the orphan. A share is to be left on the fruit tree. It is not your own to collect, to harvest. It is theirs. And you sin when you take it." So they spoke.

Such sons I have! Such scholars! All on their own they find a truth to teach me, their father. But then, we should learn from our children. I am a lucky man!

How the days dim. How little is left. Even yesterday's *Shabbat* meal. What was in that *Cholent?* I can't recall. But the plums at harvest time, the heaped wagons in the back of my father's house – yes, I can very well!

My father's piece of garden land, which wasn't really his, since none of the land can be ours, but was passed on to me, and I was allowed to rebuild on it and cultivate it.

Well, my father had customers as far as Poland. He once went to Krakow, the great Imperial Polish city, North of the Prut, to work on – may God forgive us! – church pews which had images engraved. He could carve images and angels flying, even the strangest, winged – I do not know what they are called. He told us children all about it. We were six – now they are all over the world.

My father told us the wildest stories and my mother was upset about all that useless talk. Well, he was such a special man! I learned the trade from him. I and my brothers. We loved his stories. The big world.

He drew with chalk on slate, paper being too expensive, the wonderful high steeples and inner architecture of those Roman churches, with archways, saints in their wings, and he said, "It is not for Jews, I just drew it for you so you would know it exists. It is interesting. But it's not for us."

Of course we children knew that this big world had amazed our father, sins or no sins. For us it's better to live with *Torah*. No architecture, no building, any humble abode where ten men can meet will do, a shed can house the *Torah*. And Selig thinks of his father's words: "Children, wherever you are and no matter how poor, buy or find the *Torah* scrolls and build a little home for them."

So I, Selig inherited my father's house, as most of my brothers left, and I, being the oldest, paid their share out with my modest means. No cheating. There is no use. I won't get rich on my brother's piece of bread. No cheating.

Arguments, we had plenty. Especially when it came to the tools. We had three carpenters – joiners – builders among us. Everyone wanted father's tools at his death. It was sinful. It stayed with me all my life. Especially now, that days are getting so short, the eyesight dims not just because of winter's darkness.

I can't use these fine things now. The finest awls, with pointed steely tops, reinforced with noble metals, father brought from Krakov. Drills, almost of silver, harder than silver, they could turn in all directions, having a special lever built in. So beautiful.

But with my three sons gone now – Chaim and Solomon to Canada, and Avrum a great doctor, who has machines of his own, the beauty of which I have never seen before, my father's tools have lost their importance. The modern world I can't comprehend. And I offered the tools to my Avrum when I visited in the big city of Czernowitz, but he said, "Keep them father, as a memory."

Yes, the garden in the back, the stable in the front. But on that angular wedge of land stands the house, where I, Selig, grew up, changed by my hands, of course, but designed and arranged by my good father. I still sit in that kitchen, watching the embers go down as I do tonight, a Friday night. My desire to smoke or take snuff goes down as soon as *Shabbat* approaches. What the law means to a Jew! I still smile to think that on Friday nights, my wish to smoke ceases, and only late *Shabbat* night – after dinner – it returns. A lifelong rest for body and soul for these holy twenty-four hours. The *Shabbat,* the greatest thing in the life of a man. To lift you from the ground. To think of His glory, His manifestation.

So much to remember: the kitchen was one very bright room, with a bench of golden oak joined at the corners, hugging the table, made by my father, and rubbed shiny by many a tiny scholar in the dark hours of the morning.

We had a big oven. Not an ordinary burnt mud oven as all the poor have. My father was a mason. There were tiles of green-blue hues and orange in between, a grate on top to see the fire, wood-fed. It had to be controlled not to burn the buckwheat or corn. Covered with a piece of flat iron, it served for the heating of the water cauldron – a huge iron thing that could hold the heat and was big enough to provide the *Shabbat* bath on Friday morning.

My strength is waning, and so is my desire to rise and start a new day. There is a gangrenous sore on my right toe spreading and I can't wear a proper shoe. Just a soft slipper; but to the Synagogue I can go as I am. The winters are hard on me, so I have missed the services last Friday night.

I've taken to sitting at the window, hoping to hear the gate open. Who should come to see an old man? But I am always looking forward to the summer when school holidays come and Miriam and Joseph will come running down past the stable to my door. Avrum's children, Miriam and Joseph. I love them. I start singing all the *Shir-Ha-Shirim* when I see them around my table.

My other little ones, Chaim and Sol, are *Papirene Kinder* – children of paper, as the play in the Yiddish theatre calls them.

Pictures. They are all above my bed on the wall, and I look at them. Yes. *Papirene Kinder* – will I ever?

AND SELIG rises to prepare for the night, to silence his thoughts.

THE VELVET CLOTH

S UCZORNO: A BLESSED PLACE TO LIVE. SYNAGOGUE IN
the middle, cobblestones around it. Slate of green and gold
around the fountain. A deep well with a rim of slate wide enough
to lean a pail on, lowered by a heavy chain from the centre – a
well at which to congregate, brag, and chat. Women from both
sides of the divided town are here for its heavenly water. The rich
from the high bank and the poor from the low bank. But no matter. So mortal, all of us! So depending on a drink that we are
steadily reminded that God must be here, around the fountain. A
Jew's most innermost desire being the search for his God.

It had rained the day before. The dividing creek was full of
water; the windows of the rich shone from the high bank. But no
one minded. Equality will be on the day of judgment, not before.
Well, if not equality, justice of a higher sort.

It had been a good summer. Rifka's husband, Herschel, had
returned from Poland. She brought along the velvet cloth he had
bought, spread it on the cobblestones around the well, to show
the glitter built into the purple-black. Still, no one minded. It was
a good summer, rain and sun alternating. The cabbages grew to

enormous sizes, pumpkins lay in the fields, and the Christians let the Jews have them. They washed and dried the seeds, salted them, and roasted them in huge pans on top of their ovens; the poor did it and the rich too.

The children loved it. The roasted seeds, thick, plump, and rich – the best God can provide – were almonds to the poor. Inhaled, the burnt aroma felt like the premonition of a good winter to come.

"Go," Sarah said to her children. "Go to Rifka and give her this bag full of pumpkin seeds. Her little son is crippled. He loves them, and she is too rich to stoop to pumpkin seeds. Go. It's a *Mitzvah!*"

Still, nobody minded Rifka, rich and a show-off; she was good-natured. And she brought odds and ends of her wardrobe to the well to give to her sisters from the North side, whose husbands never ventured farther than Vozhnov, a fifty miles or so, to make a living, so they stayed poor.

Rifka was spreading her cloth to the *Ah's* and *Oh's* of the women, when Shaina called out in fear. Grabbing her own head with both her hands she shouted, *"Shemah Israel!"* And the women asked, "What, what did you see, what did you hear? What? What?"

But Shaina, pointing wordlessly to the glittering spots on the luxurious material, just said, "There, there, can't you see it? Poor Rifka! Her new cloth!" She looked again, and all the women, jostling each other to get a glimpse of the spot, started seeing things.

Rachel saw a devil with three heads and each head sticking out three tongues.

"I can see it!" Yenta shouted. "I can see it."

"Look at their eyes!" they all shouted.

Where, where? Poor Rifka could not see the disaster. She did not see the twirling tail of the snake, slowly moving through the tissue, lighting up small diamonds, as it made its way.

"I can see it! I can see it!" they all shouted. "It's the ancient snake. Your cursed husband Nathan, who steals and robs and charges us rent, owning our very souls, has now brought total perdition to all of us. It's written into the cloth. If Shaina sees it, it is there. Plain as the words of the *Torah*."

And they bent over the dark purple velvet, with its gold and silver thread drawn through, and slowly settled down to council.

Rifka had fled in tears across the bridge near her house, and she nearly missed the swollen creek that had ripped the poor boards from their posts. She fled in despair. The women pursued her with shouts: "May your name, Rifka, not be heard for generations! Yours and Nathan's!"

Shouts and curses. Old Egyptian curses. Brought home to Suczorno by Moses or Jeremiah, who has a habit of being harsh.

"It's their fault that we are poor, that we have no light shine through a glass window. Nathan boards it up and he says, 'You do not need any glass window, open your door!' He needs windows for his Rifka and his deformed son. God has punished him anyway. But not enough."

And so, they held council. Looking at the piece of velvet. Just looking, not touching; for fear it might break out in flames, they push it with their feet – What to do?

Some men now, slowly approaching the few women that remained at the well, looked and tried to see. They called the Rabbi, called Bimbule – Eliezer the *narrisher* – who reads God's will better than wise men. Called on God to help them decipher

His will. They could not find what was in the cloth.

And Eliezer ben Kohanim spread his two beautiful hands over the cloth, fingers parting by themselves, leaving room, a space for God's light to shine through, and all men bowed their heads not to be blinded by the Glory. And in total silence, assured of the banishment of all evil forces, the men first straightened then gathered the piece of cloth.

And Eliezer said, "Let there be peace between rich and poor in Suczorno. *Shalom Aleichem.*"

They lifted the lovely velvet material, folded it, handed it to Eliezer, and said, "You be the messenger. Go over the other bridge, the one near Moishe's house, and turn back to Rifka's and Nathan's door, and say, handing it to her, 'Peace be with you, wear it in good health, it is clean. God's gracious light shone through a Kahane's hands!'

"But if there is a lesson to be learnt: Dear Nathan and Dear Rifka – send a glazier to set new windows into the poor people's houses."

THE LITTLE PALACE

"I HAVE BUILT THE MOST BEAUTIFUL PALACE FOR MY CHILDREN. A real palace," my father said. And it was true, made of the finest wood selected and planed to perfection, "So no splinter would be free to hurt your tender skin, it is joined in all the corners." And not just glued with flour and water or boiled fish skin discarded from the *Shabbat* meal. No! Wood joined close and filled with pressed sawdust; waiting until that settled, then filled again until it would not accept any more sawdust. For my father was a true joiner, not just one who nails two boards together and calls it a chair. His frames for windows and doors were a joy to behold!

A houseful of children! They needed a home, a roof. But the windows, for the moment, were for the rich. He was not a glazier himself, so the windows had to wait; he boarded up the future windows for winter that first year, saying, "We'll open the door instead of the windows; it will be warmer without them. We'll have the glass next year, when I'll be paid for my work in town."

But he decided to build his little palace in the back of the garden at the same time as the house, and said, "We have to have a spot for – contemplation." What a big word, contemplation! But we all, the six of the older children loved it.

It was special. Not everyone had a little palace at the back of the yard, just behind the potatoes. We were so lucky to have a patch of earth around the house, for the children to put in their potatoes.

And there stood the palace, ready. Painted in blue and white, with a door which did not swing in the storm, did not fly open or crash shut with every sudden wind. It closed with a swish of fine carpentry; and it had a doorknob of metal father found at the junk dealer – the main industry in Suczorno! – screwed in properly. And, of course, no nails! Not one, just screws of all sizes. This was my father. It had to be the best.

And, oh! the roof: shingles put into the most intriguing geometrical shapes to recall the sky in more ways than one; which means not only philosophically, but to let the sky in through designed crevices arranged in patterns. Well, one can't avoid the rain, sleet, and snow, which also came with sky and fresh air. But one can't have everything at once.

And the greatest of all things: my mother kept the palace in a state of utter cleanliness. It never smelled of anything but the purest nature mixed with lye or other clever things.

We were special and fortunate. Neighbours came to visit, inspect, and sometimes, with permission, go in to contemplate. They had to leave it in the same way of purity as they had found it, or it was the last time for them. But no one ever befouled anything, it was too beautiful to ruin. People said it had the spirit of my father and mother. Such deserving people!

It was a beautiful July day. Maybe the eighth or the tenth, when I took my time to spend a lovely moment. To meditate or contemplate. Two big words. But I think this is what I did.

Looking through the shingles put across and diagonally

again – well not real shingles, but pieces of wood dipped into tar, let to dry, and dipped again until my father thought it could hold off some of the seepage – looking through the spaces caught by the roof, I thought of God. His partnership with man. How we make designs and catch a space, an angular piece of the morning skies. That we would do this together, He, the Creator and we, the small and insignificant. Still we are His inventors. It occurs to us.

But then, what about the spider next to me? He or she lives here, and all of us love it. Just to look at an artefact of His hand-iwork. "It" also catches spaces, builds them into its yarn. Many-angled spaces in a wide net. So, this seems to occur to my spider as well, and I truly wonder: Would he or she or it think of God or just do it – catch the air, the space between its strands, a lace so fine that not even my learned father could achieve? Well, I will leave it for the clever people to answer. I just wonder.

It was a beautiful July day. Noon, a heavy sun; and our two cherry trees were just reddening their fruit when I passed them, praising God for all gifts heaped on us in abundance, and I entered our private world in the back of the garden. If the body has been fed, and functions well, we'll think of Him, as a Jew is meant to do. Contemplate, say thanks.

Startled by a wild sound of approaching noises that came from the west end of town, I froze on my little seat, not daring to pull up my pants. Splintering noises I could not tell apart. The end of time. And then a stopping. A harsh sound not identifiable, sounds I had never heard. I strained to listen, to undo the sounds, but I couldn't.

Yet I understood: my people were all lined up and killed. I heard the rifle shots reverberate through the air. I heard a thun-der, a breaking, a falling of beams – crushing noises, my father's house falling into itself. The air burnt, red and yellow shone through my geometrical ceiling, smoke made breathing heavier. I knew if they were not shot, my people would be charred within their houses. The fire would be wild, catching the huddling huts adjoining my father's good house.

A few more strange shouts, and then a silence of such contrast took hold that my body refused to exist. It began to empty itself, flowed out of itself, and would not stop. It seemed all my innards went down into the hole upon which I sat. And I did not see why I should rise from my seat. Even my spider was arrested, refusing to spin, and I said to him or her, "It's the two of us now. It's the two of us left to say *Kaddish*. But then what for? Even that?" And I slowly collected my strength, saw to it to be clean and leave it clean, rose to see if my legs would carry me after having shit out all my inner soul.

But then that is what legs do, they carry. I opened or tried to open the lovely door so quietly as not to hurt the dying or dead. Inhaled foul air as I stepped down from the properly engineered threshold, thinking my father's thoughts. Or thinking none. "Noah," I said. "This will be my name now. I can only think Noah."

In my mind my father had, with the will and divine inspiration, built me an ark. And this is what I am now, Noah. Just the spider and I. So we'll be two. Foolish thoughts.

What does one expect of a Suczorno fool, who thinks he is the centre of the universe?

A charred centre now. The few men and women emerging were heavy and slow to accept the price the Lord had made them pay for being Jews, true to Him.

And so I, Noah, gathered ten men to sing His praises, to bury our dead according to His law. And I glanced back for a breath of a moment at the only building that had withstood the onslaught, and said quietly, "May You be praised. But who knows Your ways?"

THE BEES ARE HOPEFUL

BIMBULE, RETURNING FROM THE FIELDS ON A BEAUTIFUL July morning, found half the village on the one side of the Synagogue, brook, and fountain charred, and on the other side all the houses standing untouched and people sitting on the ground in amazement, looking at the sky for answers, wringing their hands, or simply keeping them folded in their laps. No one was thinking of food except the children, though they had to be hushed away when they started playing in the ashes, looking for objects they recognized: a piece of children's toy they had played with or a rescued table that would not burn. Things like that. Their parents hushed them away – not because they did not eye things, mind you – but because it was too early, and their wonder at their own survival was so powerful.

Bimbule had got up that morning and thought the world was good. It was a wonderful, happy day, he thought. He wouldn't pray, he had decided. So, returning from the fields thinking – instead of praying – that His world was beautiful, he was a little stunned at the sight.

IT IS ENOUGH if I say the world is good, he thought. Why do I have to convince Him from morning till night that His world is good? He knows how good it is. And we won't talk about *how*. Because the moment we say "how," it becomes dangerous. It is definitely a disgraceful word, it could start a discourse with God, and He certainly does not like to be asked these kinds of questions.

For instance, the question: "How did You permit half of Suczorno to be burnt to the ground, and only Noah in his ark and the other side of town was saved by the wind turning? Did You send Your heavenly forces to turn the wind? And if You did, do You consider the other side of the little brook running through town – do You consider them more God-fearing, obedient to Your law, full of righteousness and charity, cooking for and feeding the poor on Friday night? Do You?"

I would wonder...if I started the question. But I won't, it's simple, because of the answer; one would not know where to look for it. Especially when one knows in advance that Moishe from the other side has used poor *shleppers* to build his shed, and Joseph – God rest his soul – Noah's father, Joseph, has built the wooden frames for doors and windows of Moishe's house, never getting paid a penny. Now, as all truly good men would know, not to pay within twenty-four hours for labour – and this is the law! – is a sin with a big S. It is written, and I could go on –

So I won't. It could lead again to asking all these questions that begin with "How," and the Almighty has made it a habit – since Job – not to answer. And when we look at them, answers come out too human, which may be – from God's point of view, being above it all – the wrong ones.

So it is a beautiful world, and that should be enough for praise.

Why do I have to mention this "How" with every breath? And if He does not speak or has totally given up and seems to be reckoning that He has it all written down, and doesn't have to bother any more to explain himself further, then it becomes what it has become: just men's answers.

Looking into His books for signs, for numbers, that would speak for Him, man searches for scratches on parchment: is this a scratch, a pen mark, or a fold in the scroll? And the world knows perfectly well, if there are ten Jews – not just for a funeral *Kaddish,* which here in Suczorno unfortunately occurs more often than in other places, and He can't explain that either – if there are ten Jews, there are ten opinions, fought over with conviction, and silently with hate, which should not be God's intent, the law being there to bind us together in adoration. And truly for good living, for living between friends; a community of brothers.

So if He does not speak, I will not say more today either. I will grant Him, though, that His world is beautiful. It is a high summer's day. Birds sing as if there had not been a fire yesterday, the clouds race across the sky. And last night, I had to seek shelter in the thick foliage of a beech tree because the clouds burst across the whole land. It has cooled and almost finished, thank God, the last embers.

Bimbule knows everything the moment things occur, because of his love of bees; sleeping in the fields and following them when they swarm. They know him and seem to have accepted him as one of theirs.

Who says, avoid the bees, they may sting you? They won't do it. Everyone likes to find fault with me, poor Bimbule. They all think I'm the greatest fool of all of them, and that I am a bee at night in the fields. No, no, the bees won't have me, except for a friend. But they do like me for conversation, jokes, and laughter. And they tell me things — but I won't start with this now, because what they tell me about our human world would not correspond with my feelings today that the world is beautiful.

Heavens, don't let me, absolutely don't let me tell you the conversation of last night from before the burst of clouds, which was God-sent, of course, to cool the tempers and the embers — No, I won't. But just maybe a hint, because it felt as if they were saying that in their, the bees', experience, men mend their ways after a real disaster.

So well, I think I can come out with it: yes, Suczorno fools will take their troubles, turn them inside out, and wear them as wise men would. And disaster will do that! They will look into their souls and realize their losses, and while the souls may be immortal, their bodies obviously aren't. A disaster like that brings it fully home to them, and the bees are hopeful: man will mend.

HE APPROACHED THE PEOPLE humbly, but was taken in as one of their own. There was no name calling. No *beggar, idiot, fool-of-fools, madman,* or "Here comes the bee, giving us advice and telling us over and over that his name is not really Bimbule but Eliezer ben Kohanim."

No one said anything other than *"Geeten tug,* Bimbule" — which just means good day. And then, "Have you eaten?"

As none of them had, the women started slowly to collect whatever was to be found in the still-standing houses and boil water for tea. A piece of cornbread, cooked millet perhaps, or buckwheat spread with plum jam, or anything else that could make a communal meal. Not that anyone could eat, except

Bimbule. But as it is a commandment to feed the body so the soul will be free for praise, Bimbule ate his fill, and the villagers let him.

And when Bimbule had finished and said, "Isn't God's world good?", they shook their heads.

It's a Singer

NOAH, A YOUNG MAN OF TWENTY, HAVING INHERITED the empty piece of ground where his father's house once stood before the murder and arson, felt good things were about to happen. His private little Ark had withstood winter gales and summer madness; he had sold anything saleable to the junk dealer from across the creek, a wealthy merchant called Geveer.

Well, Noah thought, on the other side of the creek everyone is called a *Geveer,* which means wealthy with a hint of power. But really, when you get to the bottom of things, what is the difference between us and them? None of us have kings, queens, and princesses with crowns of precious gems, and we have no generals, with golden braids and stars on epaulettes. Isn't it wonderful?

Noah felt truly self-congratulatory.

And to think, he considered, that we do not even have a church with a patriarch somewhere to come and ask for money and heat up the tempers at crucifixion time. And Suczorno is, with all its hateful arguments and pettiness, a blissful place to have and cherish.

Imagine, not even a pope from Rome to ask for – not just your money, but all your thoughts. Imagine uncovering yourself, all your wishes and desires, the beautiful and the terrible ones. Your most intimate soul, searched through and reported on.

Now this is perfectly unthinkable for a Jew in Suczorno. Granted, there is inequality. But, after all, how rich are the rich, considering we don't have kings, generals or popes? And some of us may have been lucky and our parents escaped many an Easter pogrom, so we have inherited a few things. Maybe all the beds, so every child can sleep in his own. So what if we sleep two or three together, or when young, between father and mother.

So maybe the rich have accumulated more junk or are clever at selling it and buying more junk, and selling it again with a profit so they could become rich, with a house, two cows, and linen to change for every Friday night. So what if we turn the tablecloth to the other side and treat it as if it were fresh? Maybe there was no soap that week!

It still looked good in my father's house, Noah thought, when it was just about completed and needed only one more year to be able to use a proper glazier to put the window panes in.

But today was a perfect day. No thinking back on losses – "Tate-Mame," the other kids, and the house. The piece of land – not a huge piece of land – but enough to put another house up, did not burn, so it was all there. And Noah offered all the partially burnt objects to the wealthy dealer: tables, beds, iron pieces rusty or not; having carefully noted them down on a piece of paper. It came to a goodly number. Maybe even the magic eighteen.

Or, if I am lucky, he thought, I'll get to thirty-six, which really means life.

The bridges had been rebuilt. He himself had gone to the

sawmill in the neighbouring Russian town to see what pieces would be for free; which, having fallen off the saw, had splintered a little and lost their value. He would not go at night, to be accused of stealing. But like a customer, in broad daylight, Noah would humbly go and ask for the price. He said, he was a citizen of Suczorno, and did not mention that the Jews of the town had stolen their own bridges to burn in the winter. No, no, a man had to have some pride and dignity.

And seeing him so well behaved, the owner of the mill let him have ten good boards for a price and the rest for free. But of course, having no rubles at all, Noah asked if he might work the money off and the owner – a good-natured, charitable man, a good Christian – said with a chuckle that it would be a week's carrying of lumber to the waiting wagons. "A deal," said Noah, and started his week's labour to rebuild his town.

It was not easy. But what is easy, if you want to help your home town and – must I disclose a secret – help yourself a little by getting a good name on the other side of the creek? Because the rich man to whom Noah had sold almost thirty-six pieces of junk, had a beautiful daughter. He had seen her from childhood. He had not really spoken to her, but she was lovely beyond words. When being on the other side of town for some duty, and it may have been that his mother had sent a *Challah* – the braided bread for the *Shabbat* – to be baked in the rich man's oven (of which the story went that all *Challahs* baked there came out more golden than from their own ovens), maybe on such a day, he would have glanced at this heavenly creature and thought, one day – perhaps?

And today was such a good day. Noah had brought all the wood in, bought with his own labour, and this time all Jews came out from both sides of the creek. What kind of disasters are necessary so people might find a way to work together? They all decided that this time they will be solid bridges, real bridges. Well, not with God-knows-what great foundations, but nailed with good nails.

But Noah remembered his father's teachings: "Son, good work can only be done with screws; they cost more but they do not split the wood and last forever." So he went for screws to his future father-in-law – or so he called him in his innermost soul – who gave the screws for free and came out to inspect the work.

Soon it was done, and Noah felt good. He had made a contribution to the town, to the good life of its citizens, who walked now across the boards that he had laid and had fastened to real posts. A new era, Noah felt, had come, and he thought: Tomorrow. Tomorrow I'll go over to my father-in-law to be and ask for her hand. Tomorrow. I'll go over the new bridge, the one closest to his house, because I paid particular attention to detail to that one. Well, it's not a sin for a man to pursue his self-interest. God likes that. He sees you want to live and better yourself. So He gives you a hand.

I used the most expensive boards on this bridge. It's not a large bridge, just three boards across, with solid posts underneath. And I'll say to him: "This is how I'll work for your daughter Rachel." And he'll laugh, thinking of the Bible and the famous son-in-law. Well, may God forgive me for comparing myself to such great men. But we all need to walk upright among men with a little pride in one's handiwork. These are my father's words: To walk upright among men.

I might plant potatoes next summer on the charred ground of my father's house. I understand ashes make potatoes grow better.

So we'll have enough for the whole winter, if my father-in-law lets me use his cellar. Oh, I'm sure he will, seeing how diligent a man I am. I'll need new clothes, or at least a jacket and a winter coat. Trousers do not matter. Who looks at them anyway? But a jacket, a good shirt, a man cannot do without if he goes courting. Isn't the word "courting" a funny word for a Jew to use? What courts? But it really means you have chosen the finest Jewish girl in all the world and now you have to earn her.

I am full of good ideas, and grateful to the Lord for having brains I can put to use. I know a widow on our side of town who is an artist, a magician — no other word for her than that — a true magician with clothes. A transformer, a changer. Riches out of rags. She would take an old cast-away coat, would cut all green patches, the ones where, when one puts a needle in it makes a new hole. She would cut all the green spots, especially at the hem and cuffs — those fraying so easily or with time at the elbows — and she would cut it short and sew good matching pieces over the holes. And heavens! What a jacket would emerge from her wonderful hands, cleaned and pressed with buttons, lovingly cut off from other derelict things.

And she would not charge much, not to us on our side of the creek. The others, from across, she would say: "Let them pay. Through the nose." The trouble is they did not need her services that much.

Take my father in-law, he would go one hundred kilometres with his wagon and two strong horses — he needed them, for junk iron is heavy. Well, he would ride to a city far away, once even as far as Odessa, to find a piece of cloth, wool and herringbone it had to be, and had it cut and sewn by a real tailor in a shop with a front door. Well, I'm not in that category yet. So, I will go to my Yenta up the road and say to her: "I want a jacket that fits. I'd like new trousers too, but they are not an absolute necessity. And a good shirt, if possible with a detachable collar, so it can be washed and changed by itself, without washing the whole shirt, which would be a waste."

And I started going to her. Talking to her about Rachel and all my private plans, that my little palace built by my father's expertise still stands – though it starts to leak and smell a little. My mother – may God be gracious to her soul and may she rest in peace – is no more with us to look after it and chase away all the strangers. But it is still there and I'll repair and paint it when I'm able to afford the paint. I told her I'll plant potatoes on the charred ground, that I have sold all the half-burnt furniture and garden tools to my father-in-law, but that I fear he has paid me too little.

"I do not want to think such sinful thoughts," he said to her, "as to say my future father-in-law has cheated me out of the little inheritance a burnt house can offer. God forbid, I'm not saying it out loud, but I fear it is really true: junk dealers make their riches from other people's despair. What an awful thing to say for a pious Jew like myself."

"Yes," said Yenta. "Don't say it, because the Almighty does not like to hear you say it, but I can say it, I'm a woman, a widow at that, and one can't fall lower than that, even among good men. I can say it: he is a cheat and a robber, feeding on other people's misery. And his daughter Rachel thinks she is – well, let me not sin. But I can say, she is stuck up, with her nose in the air, as if we weren't all made of mortal flesh.

"I can say it not having much to lose in the eyes of the world. An *almoone* – a widow, has no protection. I would even take a

man ten years younger than I am, to have someone close, someone to stand up for me when I go to collect the money for my
work. And you know the good work I do. But I am lucky. Thank
God for my sewing machine. It's a Singer." And she smiled at the
pun.

"Noah, do you get it? A singer she is, my sewing machine,
because she sings – get it? It's a funny thing to do, to play with
words, but she really sings, sad when I'm sad and everyone one
has chased me from their doorsteps when I come for my money.
Or she sings happily when I am well, the sun is shining, and my
door is open for customers! Well, then you, Noah, you should
hear her sing. I sit down at her, foot at the pedal, hands guiding
a piece of cloth along, and the two of us sing. Such joy, it's to
become truly pious!"

And Noah came the next day to try on his shirt. Yenta had
found a strong piece of material, a cover of some sort: "A little
bright," she said, "but we'll dye it black, no problem! You'll have
new trousers, you need them. What do you mean, trousers do not
matter? What do you mean? How can you look respectable in a
jacket, having holes in your pants?"

And she cut and dyed the piece of cloth and her sewing
machine sang as never before.

One day Noah looked into her mirror – a real mirror, a
seamstress-mirror, attached to the wall with a heavy nail – and
he did not recognize the person he saw. A gentleman looked
back at him with a detachable, white, shiny, stiff collar, a button in front which went both ways, through collar and shirt, a
jacket with bone buttons, big ones in front and small ones at the
cuffs. One was missing, but who counts? And trousers, with a
leather belt, a buckle to hold it, and to top it all off a pair of

Hosenträger – straps going across the shoulders in red and green stripes. To make sure the trousers don't fall down.

He wanted to kiss her, so grateful he was. But he was shy, said thank you, and sat down. She had cooked noodles for a noodle *kugel,* nice and fat. A few raisins she threw in, stirred the pot and said, turning, her face warm from the oven or from her love for him – who knows? – and said: "Sit comfortably on that chair over there, I have recovered it with all the extra pieces and it feels like new. Sit over there and wait until I have milked my she-goat-darling, then we'll eat and talk. Don't be in such a hurry to go over there on the other side of the creek. The rich have no pity for us, besides he is a pig, he has robbed you of your inheritance. Who wants to deal with such people, I'm asking you!!"

And she went out to milk the goat, and he sat, easing himself into the newly upholstered chair, and waited for her return.

RACHEL'S WEDDING DAY

Talk about the rich! About their homes, kitchens, and Friday night tables. They've built their houses, proper dwellings with shingles in patterns and shiny handles of brass or even copper on doors. Shiny handles, with locks and keys. Why do I need keys? On this side of the creek we just close our doors so the winter storms will not blow them in, yet on the south side of the creek they secure the doors with chains. Imagine! What would one Jew want to take from the other!

Why should I even talk about them? They do not believe in anything except selling for a profit and buying everything for a nothing. If someone on our side dies and the widow is in need they'll buy her husband's *Shabbat* gabardine, his bedstead, even if she is very poor. Which on our side is nothing exceptional.

I, Mendel Rosen – and I do not know how I got a surname, Rosen! Could it have been still from the Empress in Vienna, the famous Maria Teresa, or her Emperor son Joseph II? It's possible! Because we Jews do not go into the army. We would like to go to their schools though, Russian, Polish, or whatever, to have a better chance in life. And the rumour is that one could learn to read music from the page – while we just play by ear.

Mind you, we sing their tunes, too, mix them with our own heartbreak and a bit of the *Zigane* to tie it all up. They, readers of sheet music, Christians all, call us *Klezmers,* unlearned fiddlers, drummers and *zimbalists,* doing all the other instruments necessary to earn a *kopek.*

Why am I telling you all this? Oh yes, because I have a surname. Rosen. So I play for the rich. At weddings.

It was at Rachel's wedding that something fearful, unexpected, and bizarre happened, just before the wedding party were to assemble under the *Chuppah.* Imagine all the people on the south side of the creek, with all their doors open, strolling towards Herschel's house – was Herschel also a surname, heavens, where did he get it from? Or maybe, cheat and liar that he is, he just invented it to show – Well, it does not concern me.

Strolling towards Herschel's house, the women in new *sheitles* – perruques – not to show their seductive hair to any stranger – God forbid – looked at me askance, perhaps because I, a simple man from the north side of the creek, have permitted my wife Miriam to wear her hair openly and unafraid. Though she, my Miriam, has to endure many insults, angry looks, curses sometimes, a pan or a pot thrown after her, an incantation said, or something more horrid than all of that.

I don't think Miriam is going to upset other men's dreams if she dries her hair openly in the sunshine, after washing it in rainwater with a drop of sunflower seed oil. I have watched her do it, and have said, "Miriam, if you would cut your hair because you are afraid other men will fall in love and have the devil enter their dreams, it would be not right. But if I, your husband, blessed in union before the world and God himself, should not have the joy of seeing it, that would be truly wrong. This is my property. As you are. You belong to me."

And I sat down in front of her when she took a basin with yesterday's rainwater, heated it on the stove, then poured a few drops of oil and a teaspoon of vinegar into the water, released her chestnut hair, which was tied high up in a crown, and let it fall backwards into this warm bath. I sat in amazement, in wonder at her movements and elegance. She had taken off her dress – not the shirt underneath, God forbid! not to show me her bosom in the middle of the day – and I marvelled at her grace.

Her hair, all the streams of chestnut brown soaped and rinsed, shone. A king's daughter – royal purple and God-knows-what they have around their shoulders – would not have the power to evoke in me a feeling that sublime. That is what I feel, when I sit down to watch her.

Of course, I felt a pang of guilt, to give in to a woman, to permit her presence to fill my whole being with such lust and desire. But I kept it for the night. Such union is God ordained. And God could not have wanted to have her cut off these red-brown curls in order to wear an ugly, man-made contraption. And that was what they were going to do to Rachel, Herschel's daughter.

The whole south side knows how much Noah loved her, but after the great fire destroyed his father's house – which went up in flames like a box of matches – and all the huts around it, he could not have even thought of asking for her hand. An outhouse being his only property.

We were not invited. Though on the last *Shabbat* he, Herschel, extended his invitation to the whole congregation. At *Kiddush* – herring, *Challah,* and Schnapps, *Shabbat* chatter and comfort – he got up and said, "Please, all of you come to my daughter's wedding. You will hear it from the *Bimah,* you'll all be my guests."

But we did not feel invited. It's not enough to say these words "You're all invited," Miriam said that night, that unforgettable night, when the vinegar aroma filled every fold of my being, every part of body and soul, she suddenly very quietly whispered into my ear, "Mendel, beloved husband," she said, "let's stay away. Let's not go to Rachel's wedding."

I was taken aback. A little. It was of no interest to me if we went or not, and I wondered why Miriam chose this moment. But I have no inclination to look through all the forces between heaven and earth. Yet there must be some reason. And I answered, "No, my angel, we won't go if you don't want to."

"It's not that I don't want to," she whispered. "You have given me that new frock, black wool with black velvet stripes at the hem and sleeves, and a white bow around the neck for colour. You know, you brought it back from Lemberg last week when you had hoped for a deal which did not come through, but you bought me that dress. And it fits so beautifully."

"Of course I know," I said.

"Oh, I wish to show it off," she said, "but I think we should not go. It is not a whim! Something is going to happen. Something terrible. I feel it. A disaster of some sort. A punishment to come down on Herschel's house. Because of all the riches.

"Not because," she went on, "because he has robbed, pillaged, or burnt – he has not – but he has behaved like a robber. Imagine! Herschel came right after the houses, the whole row of them, five or six, had burnt to the ground, not waiting a second. Like a vulture he swooped down and started buying off the half-charred property. Well he has, with his keen vulture eye, not any different from the murderers, taken all their goods, burnt or not, for a farthing. And I feel," Miriam said, "retribution will come at Rachel's wedding. No, I don't feel. I know."

"Good," I said, "my turtledove, good. I won't go."

Because women know things. We do not. They have connections to the universe, they can see the forces of the dark, and where no man could look into, they discern shapes of fear. They can tell. And sometimes of hope. But we men with *Torah* in our heads, us *Klezmers* with ears to catch other messages, harmonies, and the rhythms of our fiddles and the tremblings of the strings, we do not have these feelers to look into the abysses of the soul to hear and see. They do. The women.

IT WAS ON THAT SUNDAY MORNING, when all doors were open on the rich side of town. And the ladies in perruques and freshly ironed or new dresses were walking out of their houses, and the men with the little boys around them, set for a wonderful day, were looking towards the tables, spread with white linen inside and outside of Herschel's house. It was on such a sunny July day that the sun darkened.

Suddenly howling winds lifted the tablecloths, damask flying through the air as if all *dybbuks* were brides dressed in white. The shapes they took, human almost, made people huddle together, rushing back into their own houses, seeing *dybbuks* dressed in the white of an underworld Jews in Suczorno only feared and suspected, but hoped never to see. Doors rattled, pots and pans clanged. *Klezmers* of the dark they were.

The bride's veil, the richest lace her father could afford, ripped from her crown, mingled with the *dybbuks,* and danced on the tables, adorning a famous She-Demon. It was not Jezebel, which would be nothing to fear. But it was Sharmeke herself. Taking the veil from the crown of the bride, sticking needles through it, and fastening it to her own head, she hid her face therein – a face no one has ever seen – and lifting her skirts high for all men to shiver, she showed her dark private hair between those mighty thighs as white as virgin snow.

Yes, Sharmeke herself. The women knew of her wickedness. They knew of men's longing. They knew of their pious husbands dreams. Not only because she materialized whenever she wished, in dreams asleep or awake, but because men called her. Wives would hear their loyal husbands, true and devoted in the daytime, moaning at night. They could discern her name clearly falling from men's lips. A yearning sound. A wild shout. A lust of the unusual, of the dangerous, of release from bondage. Or maybe a simple stomach ache, of having eaten something fat too fast, too greedily. But No! No! It was for longing of this –

The wedding party flew to the Synagogue, putting on their *Tallithim* – the prayer shawls – asking the Rabbi to dominate the She-demon Sharmeke. But the sun stayed dark for a little longer; the howling winds, the voices of all her She-demons surrounding her only slowly abating.

Miriam knew. She had asked me – inexplicably for me then – on that beautiful night, when all the angels had sung to me, she asked me not to go: there would be disaster. She knew. And we stayed away.

Rachel never married, and no one in Suczorno will ever forget her wedding day.

OCTOBER, 1941

I AM BIMBULE. I CAN UNDO ALL LETTERS; UPSIDE-DOWN
or backwards, I unravel them. Once marked, engraved by a
hand, they will address themselves to me. I do not only talk to the
living bee or the head of a cooked carp, which will tell me the
most intimate things no one even dares listen to. No, I hear men
in Babylon, watching the sun set over the Tigris, or a scribe by the
Dead Sea, recognizing within himself the voice of the Eternal and
marking the parchment. He will speak to me. To me, Bimbule,
the beggar, the singer, the unwanted, fatherless child. In Suczorno
I read letters, but I can also tell what is left out and then I would
put them in, where they belong.

This is what a story is, or a legend! You just fill in the missing
colours and shapes, the ones that are written in with an invisible
ink, for men to find. All the lives that I invent are true. They
come to me from a long line of lived days, encounters, and
thoughts. But when the markings on a page are erased it is frightening in the extreme. Life has been taken. Murdered. Was it a
sleepy dream, a half awake dream? Markings were once there, and
yet are not decipherable. The shadow of an Aleph or a Chet here

or there, but nothing could be read between the lines. It was as if a sponge had passed over a child's piece of slate. Smudged and gone. A foreboding. A disaster will befall my people. There will be no one left to sing: an empty page, not empty but erased, once engraved but razed. And I could not read it.

I jumped from her side. From Shulamith, whom I will never leave because she has given life to me, fed me, washed my feet, and knitted my socks. But I jumped from that bed and said, "Shulamith, wake, beloved, come and run, the village will burn, the pious will be destroyed. No one will remain to sing to the Lord. The stones will be silent, the ashes won't speak. Without Israel, the world is a desert. Wake, rise, come. I can never leave you."

And Shulamith turned to the other side and said, "Hush, my darling, put your head on my breast. Your dream will go, the letters will all reappear, and you will read them, as you will the unwritten ones between the letters and lines. Hush, come sleep on my breast. Do as your mother says, do. Rest. His people will not die. God will not allow it. Who will sing to Him, if not you? He will not allow it."

And she took my head, as had become her custom, into her two warm hands, and placed it between her breasts. And I believed her. Resting against her flesh, I said, "Yes, Shulamith. Yes, God will not allow it."

A COOL, FRAGRANT, October night. The odour of earth in the air. The ground slightly hard, but just right for a marriage bed. Why wait for spring, when the land is flowing with water and splitting at the seams?

Jessy had freed her window of curtains, had opened it gently, not more than the width of her thumb, to let the air stream in. It hit her face as if fate struck it. There would be no returning. Heavy, her legs gave up, and she sat on the edge of that bed to take her leave. But she couldn't rise. She looked around at the silent house, her brothers curled up, muddy shoes before their bed in disarray. Longingly, she rose to straighten these strange witnesses of their wildness.

"They're young, not yet melancholy, full of destiny like myself." She moved back to the edge of her bed, but sat on the other side, facing them. "They are so young, being loved and fed and made to study so early. Yet boys do not know life," she thought. "They live it but they do not know it. Girls are women. They know everything the moment they're born. Almost at that moment – a little while only on the breast, just living like them, but soon they know. They see their mothers bearing a next life. And a next."

Not fast as yesterday's, her movements were slowed. Not fast as today's, when she took Eli's hand to hold it against the wild blood rushing through her cheek. Not now. She was slow to leave, but did pull her curtain, watching the other bank, the low bank of the creek to get a glimpse of movement. Such a lovely sight.

A few bushes out there, lowly weedy things she had fed, to the despair of her mother. "I'll cut them down. Who needs them? They take the air and all your light." She had fought for them.

Oh Jews, she thought, they do not care for growing things. They may not have time to look at His manifestations. Men look into their books for them and women have no strength, no time with all their bellies swelling, giving birth. Oh, dear mother! All that love.

But she wouldn't go to the next room to see them both. No, it would break her heart, and she would draw the curtain back and close that window and never leave. The last embers were going, but still were visible. She looked for her things. What to wear? What to take?

She went into the cupboard on her naked feet to take the last end of the *Challah,* put it into the bag that she had sewn herself, her first try on the Singer sewing machine, the pride and joy of her mother. She straightened it out, and smiled at her childhood caught in those seams. Took a few apples, ran to the window, and looked across between her bushes to see a dark shadow moving. A jump in her heartbeat told her the hour had struck.

She dressed in whatever she could find around her. Now, she ripped the blanket from her bed, a light thing of linen, and folded it fast into the apples. She rushed about without noise while dressing, looking for her second woollen sock. Such good socks, wool and some cotton for strength.

Oh, my mother with her round needles, socks coming out at the other end. I never succeeded at anything as beautiful!

Shoes and laces. Looked around. Oh, the window. She shut it fast, bent down towards the drawers of her bed, pulled the handle on the small, precious one, the elegant small drawer with a handle for her left-handed awkwardness. It glided smoothly out, and she faced her wooden box inlaid with the symbol of *Torah* scrolls. With a last look at her gold, she took it, threw it into her bag, and closed the drawer with a pain in her heart she had no time for. A look through the window, and she leaned against the door, facing her world, turned again, feared the noise of the key, but it moved in its lock as if oiled the day before.

Jessy slid out and rested against the closed door, watching the lower bank. A clear night, a half-moon. And now she wanted to run across that bridge, to hide in Eli's arms, but waited to see him emerge clearly. He seemed taller at night. An enormous shadow following him, fusing with his steps; it made him a very dark, almost menacing figure. She brushed it away. It was her Eli. Different at night, never seen before in such light, and she followed the direction of his outstretched arm. It pointed east. Not inviting her to cross the bridge, it told her to walk east on her high bank, and watch his steps on the lower one.

Walking fast now, both separate on their sides of the creek; closer to it and closer yet, in the hope of bushes that will cover their shadows, they both reached the end of the village. Jessy crossed the last bridge, where the river bends. They clasped hands and walked on, east she thought. Too weary to kiss, they hastened their steps into a rhythm, with hands clasped in one another's just to have the blood rush through as if they were one.

With the river in sight, a moon in it without a ripple, they dropped their bags at once, fell upon the ground in total union.

And were awakened by echoing shots, a grey smoke-laden sky, and the vision of the village in flames against the horizon.

An Epilogue

O H, THE FOOLS, THE WISE MEN, THE MYSTICS WITH ancient memories, the storytellers of truth and invention, the wide-eyed visionaries who feel addressed, spoken to by God and entrusted to save the world – and the true believers, the practitioners of the hourly art of devotion. Oh, that intricate, deeply human world of the *"shtetl,"* the small Yiddish town of Eastern Europe I loved so! It is a canvas of characters virtuous and not so virtuous, cheating and atoning, ready for argument and fierce debate at any hour of the day.

An array of the subtle and the crude, the imaginative, the God-inspired, and the ordinary everyday, this canvas of colour and sound, "the live *shtetl,*" stretched from the Northern rim of the Baltic states all along to the Black Sea and Romania. It dotted the countryside.

It had lived for centuries by an inner cohesion of religious fervour, and by the centripetal force of the Law. The Mosaic law, ancient and proven, assured its denizens of justice. Justice they held Divine, a commandment, an absolute, a necessity for communal life, above charity even, though charity had to be daily practice. For they were poor, landless, and surrounded by "the others," the Gentiles who owned the land they lived on.

But not always was this so. Also very poor, the Gentiles did not always own it, but often leased the land from far-away landlords. Or simply bound to the soil as serfs, they were owned themselves, body and labour.

Not so the Jews in the small town, the *shtetl:* there they were free in a sublime sort of way. Living by the rules of the Ten Commandments, the *Shabbat,* their daily practice of cleanliness, prayer, and the thought of God as supreme master, they were free. Marginal, non-citizens, with no civic rights and insufficient sustenance, they were free within. They had no land to live on, but no kings, no dukes, no knights in armour. No one had a weapon, and if so, it was hidden.

A *shtetl* was an almost medieval world with rabbinical authority. The citizens themselves built in common the synagogue in the middle of town, where there was also a well, a spring underground for virgin water. Houses, huts, abodes of all sorts, minimal or a little more respectable, depended upon how well-to-do a man was or could afford for his family.

Intolerant of divergencies in the practice of devotion, but often challenged, it was a place of hot debate and pursuit of the permissible: "What is within the Law and what is not?" There was love and hate, and steady argument. Big egos were in conflict, Messiahs or would-be-so, who claimed to have read and interpreted every letter, every sign in the *Torah* from the age of four. Who, on occasion, when found to be correct, were honoured for the high distinction of having been right about the text, about "what-is-written."

On parchment, on copper, on sheepskin, the *Torah* scrolls

with the word and will of the Eternal was what mattered. All submitted if consensus had been reached. And when the day of atonement arrived in the fall, a week after New Year's prayers, there was a soul searching, a recalling of one's failings, an atonement – and then peace descended with the sound of the *Shofar*, the ramshorn.

They spoke Yiddish in these towns. A German medieval tongue that shines with the highlights of all their wanderings. In the nearly 2,000 years of *Diaspora* since the fall of Jerusalem and the Temple in 70 AD, Yiddish incorporated the Latin, through Rome, the German from Germanic tribes in the Rhine Valley, and the Slavic, through their being chased further East into Poland and Russia.

Yiddish is a gem, as a piece of amber would be, with an ancient insect's wing still visible. In Yiddish all the past is discernible. And that is what language does, it carries a people's past on its shoulders, sometimes obliterating it, and sometimes coming forth renewed from undetectable sources. So Yiddish is two-thirds German, with built-in memories from everywhere, and Hebrew of course, the sacred tongue, as well as Aramaic, the language of the time of Jesus.

Adjusted to the new sounds in Eastern Europe, Yiddish cries and laughs at itself with a self mockery and wit no other language can sport. From self-accusation and parody to self-protection and the presence of God, Yiddish written in Hebrew letters carries this multifold heritage with the assurance of that self which knows who and what it is.

With the destruction of the *shtetl* – itself a German word from the word *Stadt,* meaning town, in its diminutive form – by the advancing *Einsatzgruppen* in the beginning months of WWII, and in the Russian campaign in 1941, these small Yiddish towns were burnt to heaven, and their pious people assembled in front of pre-dug ditches were shot by *Genickschuss.*

Yiddish, that haunting, colourful, unique memory of an almost mythical past, with its inherent sound of liturgical *Nigun* and the folk-melodies they lived surrounded by and had absorbed, this love of ours, is gone. Because the spawning life has been extinguished, there is no reservoir for renewal or resurgent talent left to rekindle it. So Doctoral theses will be written in Academia, and old New Yorkers will hang on to the sound, but its life is silenced. I grieve for it.

It's my grandfather's tongue. My grandfather, Selig, who sang it and never spoke it without a tune to embellish it. Ancient *Smiroth* (melodies) from Solomonic times – I heard them one day exactly resung to my husband, Richard, and myself – when we entered a bus on the Road to Bethlehem. A tiny Yemenite boy sang it, with a high-pitched soprano that would be the envy of the *Wiener Sängerknaben.* A memory atavistic, and binding a world to its roots; an interval did it, a tune, and I promised myself to speak about my love one day. About this world, spiritual and deeply human, which was not allowed to live.

The *shtetl* is a tapestry, an intricate tissue interwoven with all strands of good and not-so-good; it is a colourful mosaic of humanity with a deep desire for God. In song not sung in the Western monastic style, because Jews of the *shtetl* could not read music. The *shtetl* had its own sound of biblical intervals, with cadences added of Russian-Ukrainian in the minor key, and the Gypsy sound coming from the most Southern India.

When a *Chasid* sang, he sang to ecstasy, to specific rhythms one would now recognize everywhere. In great Western composers as well. "I will write about these characters, who sang those melodies," I promised myself. "I'll return them to life."

I have lived in their midst, all through my teenage years. They were my companions on endless summer days until my grandfather's death. I knew the village idiots, tolerated as part of the panorama; I knew the dreamers consorting with the wild bees in the fields; I knew the rabbis and the prophets, who predicted doom and somehow managed to save their people; and I knew the young lovers, the Romeos and Juliets of their time.

I would like to dedicate this book to the people of the *shtetl*, to the ones possessed by God and the ones by *dybbuks*, to "Noah," who survived because his father had built the family an outhouse which did not burn when the town burnt, to the Scarecrow Duo, the fiddlers of the *shtetl*, the *Klezmers* who played wherever there was a Christian wedding or wake, and were loved and rewarded for it.

And last, but not least, to the *Torah* scroll writers – those artists of the hand-written, painfully accurate letter, as Shimon is in my story; and to the illustrators, the anonymous Chagalls, as Sarah is; and to Reuwen, the violin player in my tale, who will finally learn to read music.

To all these, my love.

ACKNOWLEDGEMENTS

I WISH TO THANK my friend and editor Geoffrey Ursell for his counsel, and particularly for his good advice regarding the whole concept of the book. And I thank him for suggesting the title *Children of Paper – Papirene Kinder* in Yiddish. As with my novel *The Walnut Tree,* it has been a great collaboration, and I hope we will work together in the near future.

Many thanks to Margaret Kyle. Again, as with *The Walnut Tree,* she read my European handwriting, keyboarded, printed, and corrected *Children of Paper.* I love her succinct remarks, which I find very useful.

To my friends, of course, who sustain me, read, judge, and support my work, go my heartfelt thanks: Susan and Henry Woolf, Ronald Mavor (Bingo), Don Kerr, Rosemary Hunt, Elizabeth Brewster, and Barbara Sapergia.

I would also like to thank Irene Watts for sharing her experience and erudition with me, whenever I needed it.

Last, but not least, I'd like to thank the Saskatchewan Arts Board for honouring me with a grant. It enabled me to devote myself fully to the writing of the book and helped with the expenses incurred. Many thanks.

I wish to acknowledge the inspiration I took from Natalie Zemon Davis's wonderful book on three seventeenth-century women, called *Women on the Margins.* One of them is Glickl of Hameln, whose autobiographical account was read to me by my grandmother Esther Glückstern, in *Vaiber Taitch,* the Yiddish of its time, which was fully understood by us in Eastern Europe. These were the evening tales of the *Shabbat* after dinner. Glickl of Hameln was in my ear when I started my fourth story, "The Hindstreet Boy," and I was delighted to find her so vividly portrayed in *Women on the Margins,* which I have consulted on occasion. Many thanks to my daughter, Irene Blum, who recommended this book to me.

MARTHA BLUM was born in 1913 in Czernowitz,
Austria (now Chernivtsi, Ukraine). With the defeat
of Germany and Austria in 1918, the city became part
of Romania, and remained so while she was growing
up. Her studies included pharmaceutical chemistry,
languages, and music at the universities of Bucharest,
Prague, Strasbourg, and Paris. World War II found
her family at the crossroads of warring and occupy-
ing forces, persecuted in turns by Soviet Russia and
Germany. She immigrated to Canada in 1951, by way
of Israel, and has lived in Saskatoon, Saskatchewan,
since 1954.